REBEL MAGE CHARLIE

THE DRAGON MAGE BOOK 7

SCOTT BARON

"Science is magic that works."
– *Kurt Vonnegut*

CHAPTER ONE

Charlie, Ara, and Bawb were fighting for their lives in the inky vacuum of space. Unfortunately, this was becoming far too regular an occurrence.

"Ara, there are three more on your left!" Charlie mentally warned his dragon friend, as she dodged the swarming Tslavar ships that were doing their best to knock him and his Wampeh friend from her back.

There was no sense using their comms system. Not in the heat of battle. Not when they were the only ones present, their friends nowhere to be seen. Not when the silent link that bound the three was so much easier than verbal communication when things got *really* crazy.

"Two on your tail," Bawb said, pivoting to aim his wand behind them and unleash a ferocious blast of magic at the craft that were launching deadly spells at them.

His wand had a bit of a tendency to cast stronger than he intended, and thus, required a lot of focus and control to properly wield. Being the first of its kind, a melding of several types of magic, all contained within a severed, yet living, piece of

Earth wood, it had a potency far beyond most magical devices of this galaxy.

Unfortunately, that also meant it could be unpredictable at times. However, on this occasion, the extra power the device's unusual heritage lent was a welcome addition to the spells the vampire assassin was casting.

It was the Earth wood, Ara had posited, that gave the wand such potency in this galaxy. Much as Rika's tattoo-bonded magical pigment seemed to allow her magic to cut through native defensive spells, so, too, did Bawb's unusual wand draw from its Earth heritage.

The tree it was fashioned from had been not only impregnated with a rod of pure, powerful konus inside its split branch, but he had wrapped that device in one of his lady love's incredibly potent Ootaki hair, which constantly drew more power from the planet's sun, feeding the device.

On top of that, the wood had also been magically healed, the split sealed tight with the golden strand and rendered whole by a steady, slow drip-feeding with the powerful healing waters of the Balamar Wastelands.

Handling the waters had been the most dangerous thing the seasoned assassin had ever done, for those waters would make his kind combust if it were to splash on his skin. Like holy water for vampires, so was Balamar water for Wampeh of his power-sucking variety.

But it was worth it, and the resulting device was a wand of exceptional power. And it was something none in this magical galaxy had ever seen.

"Nice shot!" Charlie exclaimed as one of the ships behind them tore to pieces, its counterpart spinning off into space from the force of the destruction.

"Thank you. But I was aiming for the other one," Bawb replied.

"Hold tight!" Ara warned them both, then spun fiercely into a

dive, avoiding even more converging vessels, all of which were bombarding them with a relentless stream of magical attacks.

The three of them shared their power, which was substantial, and if not for that combined strength, their magical defenses would certainly have fallen under the sheer force of the onslaught. Their attackers were not only many, they were also very, very powerful.

"I cannot jump," Ara said, the stress of her flight clear in her voice. *"They've cast containment spells that negate jump magic."*

"Yeah, I can feel it," Charlie said. *"And there are so damn many of them!"*

"Are you still feeling bad about all of the Tslavars you killed?" Bawb asked, firing off another salvo of deadly spells.

"Shut it, Bob," Charlie grumbled.

Prior to their being besieged by a few dozen Tslavar attack ships, Charlie actually *had* felt bad. Just a few days prior, in the heat of a very different fight for their lives, Charlie had merged his power with Rika's, the Earth woman's magic-imbued tattoos somehow cutting right through the enemy's seemingly unbreakable defenses.

They'd been outnumbered and fighting for their lives, and he had cast with all of his ever-growing power. Tapping into his bond with both an ancient Zomoki and the Ootaki hair wielded by his Wampeh friend, Charlie already had a very substantial amount of magic at his disposal.

Adding Rika's totally different power to the mix, however, had made his spells ever more potent, the deadly force of them cutting through not only the ships immediately in the fight, but all of the ships in the entire system.

He had only targeted the hostile Tslavar fighters, hoping to knock dead the men charging them on the field of battle and attacking in the sky above. What he'd accomplished was quite a bit more than that.

Every Tslavar in the entire solar system perished in an instant, Rika's magic adding far more potency to his casting than he'd expected.

It wasn't genocide. There weren't many Tslavars to be found in the system, as the lone planet they were fighting on was the only inhabitable one orbiting the twin suns. And that planet had become sparsely populated centuries before, when the Council of Twenty had unleashed a violent attack on Visla Balamar, rendering his realm a barren wasteland. After events like that, people tended to leave a place.

The result was, only the Tslavars charging them on the ground and crewing the attacking ships were stricken by his deadly spell, the craft and its slave crew left unharmed and drifting in an instant.

"If you can cast that spell again, it would be most appreciated," Ara said, snapping him from his memory.

"You know what? If I could, I would. But without Rika here, I can't."

"But you are still linked to her power, are you not?" Bawb asked.

"A little. But nothing like when I'm right next to her," Charlie lamented. "We should have stuck together."

"But at least the others are safe."

"You hope."

"Yes, I hope. But it seems likely, given what we know. And there was no way of knowing this would happen," Bawb said. "This was supposed to be a simple intelligence-gathering mission. We could not have anticipa—"

A strong magical blast rocked them, sending Ara tumbling to the side.

"Ara! Are you okay?" Charlie asked.

"Yes. But they are too many and too powerful to avoid for much longer. If we cannot get clear soon, I fear I will be too weakened to jump away."

This was bad. Ara was taking the brunt of the attack, and

despite their best efforts, the spell casters were unable to stop their assailants.

"Okay, I've got an idea," he said. *"On the count of three, bank hard to the clearest path you can see and jump us clear."*

"I told you, I cannot jump within these containment spells," the space dragon replied, grunting as yet another attack struck her defenses.

"You jump on three," Charlie repeated. *"Bob and I will cast directly in front of you on two. You got that, Bob? Use your wand. It draws from Earth magic. And I'll pull every last ounce I can from my link with Rika."*

"But what if it does not pierce their spells?" Ara asked.

"We don't have much of a choice," Charlie replied. *"There are too many of them for just us three to take on, so it's either that, or we keep draining our magic until they finally wear us down and take us."*

Bawb shifted in his seat, aiming his wand dead ahead, preparing to cast the strongest spellbreaker he could muster. Charlie, likewise, drew upon all of the strange shared magic with Rika, the traces of it mixing with his substantial power.

"Very well," Ara said. *"On three."*

Charlie felt his tenuous link with Rika across the systems flash with an electric surge as he tapped her power with all his might.

"One. Two."

Charlie and Bawb unleashed their full combined magic, not in a series of attacking spells, but in one enormous spellbreaker. Their magic flew hard and true, cracking through the dozens of overlapping containment spells blocking their Zomoki friend's escape.

"Three!"

A flash of Zomoki power surged all around them. A second later, the Tslavar ships found themselves attacking an empty space.

Their prey had escaped. But only just. The details would not be important, however. Visla Dominus would not be pleased.

CHAPTER TWO

Only a few days prior to the latest desperate fight for their lives, Charlie and his friends had just finished an entirely different fight for their lives. Only that one had resulted in them feeling far more positive about their whole situation.

Except for the whole mass killing thing, of course.

But aside from Charlie's utter shock at just how many he had slaughtered with a single spell as they fought for their lives on the Balamar Wastelands, the victory had been a resounding win for their team. Nineteen Tslavar ships had been in the skies and space above the battleground, and when the fighting had so abruptly ceased, fourteen of them were still intact, though some of the surviving craft were suffering from fairly significant damage.

Not as much damage as their Tslavar crews, of course. Death being the worst damage one could incur by far.

After the hostilities had ceased, Charlie's recently revived space pirate friends, freshly awakened from their stasis of hundreds of years beneath the sands of the wastelands, were shuttled up to the nearest of the ships aboard the *Fujin*, Rika taking them up in small groups to board the vessels and take control of them.

There were just barely enough of the rough and ready pirates to operate the assorted craft, but they had little doubt they could acquire a willing and eager crew in no time, given the nature of their prize.

The largest and least damaged of the ships was claimed by Charlie's old pirate friend, Marban. The man who had taught him the ropes during his sting aboard the *Rixana* all those years ago. And it was that ship that was brought down to the surface.

"It looks like you've got yourself an upgrade," Charlie said as his friend disembarked the captured warship.

Marban's smile was ear to ear. "Not bad, if I do say so myself, Little Brother. Once we jettisoned the trash, it cleaned up pretty nice."

Of course, by trash, he meant the bodies of their enemies. But Marban was a pirate, after all.

"You sure you're good with this?" Charlie asked his friend. "It's a pretty dangerous gig, and there are other ships big enough to carry Rika's mech."

"Dangerous? Charlie, are you forgetting who you're talking to?"

"Of course. My mistake. Sorry, *Captain* Marban," he replied with a grin. "I like the sound of that, by the way. Though we may need to come up with something to tack on at the end to give it a little more 'oomph,' like 'the Crusher of Skulls' or something.

"I'll settle for 'Captain Marban, Kicker of Tslavar Ass' at the moment," he replied with a laugh.

"Well, you most certainly are that," Rika said as she used her magic to float her transit-folded mech past them toward the storage hold on the ship. "And thanks for carrying my baby for me. It's just too big for the *Fujin* to carry and still have any hope of retaining maneuverability."

"And even if it could carry it, that would be mounted to the belly," Marban said. "Not a good way to fly. No, it's much better to just put it in the cargo hold, and we have plenty of room on this beauty," he said, admiring his new ship.

"So, *Captain*, have you thought of a name for her yet?" Charlie asked.

"I'll get around to it," Marban replied.

"Well, don't go flying off without one," Charlie joked. "Gotta christen her before your big mission."

"He's right, you know. Every ship needs a name," Rika added, as she floated her massive mech on a cushion of her strange magic.

It was quite a sight for the space pirate. The strong Earth woman with her faintly glowing tattoos peeking out from beneath her clothing. She was casting, and without using her konus, though she did possess a rather formidable one, he noted.

But this woman possessed a power never before seen in the galaxy, and he couldn't help but be fascinated by both her unusual magical nature, as well as her entirely natural one. Charlie noticed his friend's lingering, appreciative gaze but said nothing. Marban was a big boy, after all, and could more than take care of himself.

Following close behind, Jo and a few of Marban's crew were carrying tools borrowed from the *Fujin*'s supplies. If Rika was going to get the mech in tip-top shape, she'd need them.

"What exactly are you going to be doing to that marvelous moving statue of yours while aboard my ship?" Marban asked. "I see your friend is transferring a lot of what appear to be tools and supplies aboard along with it."

"I'm flying with you guys. Jo's gonna take the *Fujin* up and travel alongside for the moment, so I'll be riding on your nameless ship," Rika said with a wry little grin. "I want to see if I'll be able to get this baby purring like a kitten before our next encounter. Also see if I can give her a few upgrades while I'm at it."

"Upgrades?" Charlie asked.

A smile blossomed on Rika's face. She had her mech back after so many years thinking it was lost forever, and she was loving it.

"We've got some additional armaments in the cargo hold," she replied. "Stuff Cal pulled off the *Fujin* when his guys did the upgrades. He said it would be wise to hang on to the originals, just in case we had to reverse some of the modifications. The new weapons work fine, but we never got around to pulling the old ones out and dropping them at the depot."

"Probably a good thing," Jo said, catching up to her friend. "You never know when things will come in handy. Like now, for example."

"Precisely," Rika agreed. "So, she's gonna get a nice weapons upgrade, seeing as she wasn't actually designed for fighting."

"You could have fooled me, with the way you operated it, from what I hear," Marban said.

"Thanks. It's nice to know Malalia didn't take *that* from me, at least."

At the mention of the woman who had done such harm to her mind, a flash of pain crossed Rika's face for just an instant. Charlie and Marban saw it, but neither said anything. If she wanted to talk about it, they were there. Otherwise, they'd let her cope as she wished.

"So, anyway, I'm also thinking about seeing if I can make her space-worthy," Rika continued. "Attach some small thrusters, mag locks for her feet, that sort of thing."

"Space-worthy?" Charlie said, shaking his head at his friend's audacious plan.

"Hey, why not? I mean, it's not what it was designed for, but why not try, right? After all, giant robots in space? So cool. Who wouldn't want that?" she said with a laugh.

It was a bit out there, but Charlie had to admit it *did* sound pretty cool. "All right, you get yourselves situated, and let us know if you need anything," he said.

"Will do," Rika replied, then guided the huge mech into the massive ship's hold.

Jo would take the *Fujin* and fly alongside the commandeered ship until they'd flown clear of the planet and were certain there was no further danger. That way she could keep the craft's railguns and pulse cannons handy, just in case.

Once they were ready to begin their mission, she would then land atop Marban's ship and lock down to the hull, engaging her umbilical to seal with the ship and let her join her friend once they were underway.

Marban walked up to his new ship's hull and rested his hand on the gently hovering bulk, feeling the traces of Drook power keeping her aloft. They hadn't been able to remove the control collars the Drooks wore, but the power-generating aliens were nevertheless essentially free men and women now that the Tslavars were gone.

Fly the ship and be free while doing so, was the offer they'd been made. For a people who had spent their entire lives doing just that, being able to continue the one thing that gave them purpose was a relief, and to a one, they had requested they stay aboard the ship, even if their control collars were eventually removed.

Captain Marban readily agreed, and from that moment on, they were to be given free run of the ship as free crew. No longer a captive cog in the machine, but rather, willing participants in an adventure. It was exhilarating.

The man with the scar from his temple to his collarbone stood quietly with his ship, reflecting on how he himself had come to be a pirate so many years ago. It was a lifetime ago, and all he knew back then were long dead. Yet it was what made him who he was today.

"What are you thinking?" Charlie asked. "You okay?"

Marban collected himself. "Yes, Little Brother, I am okay. Just thinking."

"Oh? That's never good," Charlie said with a little smile. "Thinking about what, if you don't mind my asking?"

"About my ship," Marban replied. "And her new name."

"You have one?"

"Indeed I do," the pirate replied. "I shall call her the *Coratta*."

CHAPTER THREE

Possessing Drook navigators, inherited along with the captured Tslavar ships, meant something important had just occurred. Not the victory over the enemy forces, though that was a big deal. But, rather, their team now possessed the means to travel *accurately* in this galaxy.

Sure, Ara was a Zomoki from this realm, and as such she had no problem jumping from Point A to Point B. But for the rest of their friends, who were forced to rely on utterly unreliable warp technology from a distant galaxy, it meant that with just a modicum of spellcasting, they could now bind their warp systems to an accompanying magical ship.

And they had over a dozen of the captured craft. The tech ships crossing the portal could be split into squadrons, each of which would be assigned one of the vessels. The pirates now piloting them would simply lock magical handshakes with their designated Earth ships, and that should be that.

The captured craft would act as guides for the ships waiting to join them. That is, if they could tie them in and get that magic/tech system sorted in the madness that would undoubtedly ensue when their friends crossed over into the hostile galaxy.

Visla Dominus possessed an utterly massive fleet. Far larger than they'd ever anticipated. Unless things had changed drastically, it was still waiting just beyond the reach of the Earth's sun's flames spewing from the protected portal. The gateway was on a weekly schedule now, only slipping free of the sun's plasma for a few minutes each week before dropping back in and sealing the route.

Time was a funny thing, though. Every system had different lengths of the day due to orbital rates and mechanics of each particular world. But all of the Earth craft were operating on Earth chronos, dialed in and locked, telling them precisely when the portal would next clear.

This gave them an advantage, for they could now jump right to the portal the moment it was clear, while the enemy would have to close the gap from where they'd been lurking a safe distance away.

But to succeed in their plan, they'd first have to cross over and prepare the fleet waiting in the other galaxy.

"Don't worry about us, Little Brother," Marban said to his dear friend. "We'll have no problem jumping to the system at the correct time."

"You sure you've got it?" Charlie asked.

Marban let out his trademark good-natured chuckle. "Yes, Charlie, relax. Your Zomoki friend was very clear in the directions she gave to our Drook navigators. In fact, all fourteen of our ships now have the location locked away and ready to be used when called for. They're standing by in the system we agreed upon."

"Good. But first things first. You guys just get there, cross over, and then meet up with Leila and the others and let Rika and Jo brief the commanders of our fleet what's going on over here. No engagements. No skirmishes. Just get there, get across, and get the intel to our people," Charlie said, still not realizing Leila had not been with Eddie and Ripley when they crossed back to their home galaxy the prior week.

"Don't worry, Charlie. I've been at this sort of thing a long, long time," Marban said. "Well, except for the whole jumping between galaxies part. That, I must admit, is a new one."

The men shared a much-needed laugh, the stress of the pending mission silently hanging over both their heads. A lot was riding on them being successful. The portal was rapidly cycling through its weekly appearances, and if they didn't change that, and soon, they would be stuck on this side indefinitely. Trapped, with the bad guys on their backs and their reinforcements as good as non-existent.

"How about you, though?" Marban asked. "Your task seems a bit more dangerous than mine, after all."

"It's not so bad, really. We'll just be scouring the systems for any information we can find on this Visla Dominus," Charlie said. "We can't go into battle until we actually know who we're fighting, and exactly what resources they have on their side. I mean, we already got our asses handed to us once. I want to be damn sure our team is as ready and informed as can be for the next go around."

It was a good plan, and with the flight log intel they had been able to glean from the captured craft, there was at least a good road map of places to search. They'd be stealthy about it, just flying in, doing their recon, then flying out. If all went well, no one would be the wiser.

If all went well, that is.

"Hey, guys," Rika said, joining the two men outside for a last bit of fresh air as the *Coratta* prepared for departure. "I've got the mech stowed, and I have a fair amount of what I'll be needing to work on her. Once we get back home I'll be able to get the proper tools to really get her running perfectly."

"And you'll get better weapons," Charlie added.

"Well, yeah. That's a given," Rika replied. "Plus, I'll be able to source some power cells for her. Seeing as she was built hundreds of years ago, they've really come a long way with power tech. Why, I have to wonder if they might even be able to give her a little warp core."

"You want to warp in that thing?"

"No, of course not. But the tech is essentially endless power, which means I could focus my magic on things other than keeping her moving."

"Point taken," Charlie said.

"So, while I'm back with the fleet, what do you want me to bring back when we cross again?" Rika asked. "Supplies? Tech toys? You name it and I'll make sure Zed and Cal line it up for us."

"For now, I just want to get that portal secured and off that ticking time-bomb countdown it's on," Charlie said. "We had no idea we'd be stuck on the other side like this. I guess hindsight is twenty-twenty."

"I've gone over it with Ara, and we cast a tiny test of the tether spell on a small asteroid nearby. She said from what she could tell, when I try to manipulate the tether with my mixed magic, it was able to exert enough force for what we need. Not as strong as the three of you combined, obviously, but I should be able to adjust the portal's schedule on my own."

"Excellent news," Charlie said.

"Yeah. The only thing is, since my magic is going to have less force behind it than what you guys did, the portal may wind up on a shorter open and closed schedule. No way to know until I try it."

"We'll just have to cast and play it by ear," Charlie said. "As long as there's a way back, that's all that matters. That, and getting our fleet up to speed and casting a unique handshake spell on each squadron, as we agreed upon, so they and our jump vessels can lock on to one another and execute warp-jumps without going astray."

"And that's what it looks like we'll be able to do," she replied. "Okay, I'm gonna get cracking on the mech. I'll see you in a few days, Charlie."

"Catch ya on the flip side," he replied as his friend walked back into the waiting ship. "You take good care of her," he said, turning to Marban.

A little smile tickled the corners of the pirate's lips. "You have my word on it, Little Brother," he replied.

CHAPTER FOUR

One of Visla Palmarian's favorite ships was quietly orbiting a large planet in a system surrounded by a sizable asteroid belt. It had been a good try, given the similarities in look and feel to the system Leila was looking for, but she felt her spirits drop when, once again, there was no sign of either her friends, or the portal leading back to their galaxy they were searching for.

Despite all of their attempts to find them, Eddie and Ripley were simply nowhere to be found, and all her comms unit had registered at each location was static.

"Sandah?" Leila asked, absentmindedly scratching Baloo's ears.

"Yes, Leila?"

"Isn't it kind of strange that none of the other captains seem to know anything about this massive fleet of warcraft *someone* has been amassing? I mean, we've been to what, six nearby systems now, and still nothing."

Visla Palmarian's most trusted captain paused a moment, as if deep in thought, then turned to his guest. "True, we have not fared very well in either of your objectives, and I'm sorry we have been unable to find your friends. It is entirely possible they moved on to a different system far beyond where we've been inquiring. But as for this mystery fleet you mentioned, if what you say you saw is accurate, then it is quite likely that whoever might be in command would take precautions against discovery. Wouldn't you agree?"

"Well, I suppose. But it's just odd that no one would have seen or heard anything. And you're one of Palmarian's people. He's very powerful and very respected. You would think the others would give that some weight and be more forthcoming."

Sandah chuckled. "Oh, I may work for the most powerful visla in over a hundred systems, but that does not make me any more than a mere captain of one of his vessels," he replied. "And though I hate to place any constraints on your efforts, I really will have to return to Slafara soon. The visla often has tasks for me, and it would not be good if I were to request my services only to find I'm unable to assist him as required."

"Can't you just skree them?" Leila asked. "They could tell you when you need to come home that way, and we could continue our search."

"Unfortunately, we have already traveled well out of normal communication reach, and to source a long-range skree on short notice would be difficult."

"But you're with a wealthy visla," Leila said.

"Yes, but we are not on the visla's business, and as such, we do not have access to his resources. You must remember, magic is not cheap, and while Visla Palmarian has power to spare, when he is not present, we are forced to utilize conventional means of payment. Believe me when I say, you do not wish to return from what he will view as a minor errand with an enormous skree debt on the books."

"Then why are you even out here with me?" Leila asked.

"Because in the absence of the visla and his wife, young Karasalia is the head of the household, and I am bound to obey her commands," the captain replied.

He noted his passenger's flagging mood. She had begun their journey excited to find her friends and rejoin them on whatever adventure it was they had planned. But as days stretched on, her stress seemed to increase with each hour that ticked by.

Sandah sighed. The thing was, Leila was Karasalia Palmarian's friend, and as such, he was duty bound to look out for her. And if that meant a detour to raise her spirits, so be it.

"I believe it would do us good to make landfall this evening. There are some individuals on a planet in the next system who may have information of use to us in tracking down your friends."

"You think so?"

"Indeed. And in any case, I could really use a good home-cooked meal, couldn't you?" he asked, not hungry in the slightest, but Leila didn't need to know that.

"I suppose it would be nice to stretch my legs a bit. And I really should let Baloo burn off some of that energy. He's been a good boy, but being cooped up on a ship gets to him after a while."

The massive beast curled up against the wall raised his head at the sound of his name, but Mama didn't need him, it seemed, so he let his jaw rest on the deck again with a bored sigh.

Captain Sandah couldn't help but grin. "I can see that," he said. "So it is settled, then. We will land shortly, and then I shall take you to a wonderful little establishment I know that serves the best food in the entire system."

Leila smiled at the captain. Despite being a lifelong servant of a powerful visla, he really did seem like a decent fellow. And they'd had some interesting conversations over meals at the captain's table the past several days, which helped take her mind off of her missing friends and her absent king.

She wasn't worried about Charlie. He could more than take care of himself, that she knew for a fact. And with both Ara and

Bawb at his side, there was little anyone could do that those three couldn't handle. But lack of worry didn't mean she didn't miss him. Spending so much time apart since they'd crossed over, it was like a part of herself was absent, the itch of her missing piece nagging the back of her mind when she least expected it.

That was something she hoped to remedy shortly. But first things came first, and those were tracking down Eddie and Ripley and reconnecting with the others. *Then* she could worry about Charlie. And who knew? It was entirely possible he and their friends were already waiting for them at the portal, safely tucked out of sight of the hostile ships.

It was a lot to consider. But for now, Sandah was right. It was time to eat.

Baloo lay curled up at Leila's feet in the cozy little restaurant, happy to accept scraps, but really wanting to procure his own food. To hunt, as was in his nature. He had very nearly given in as they walked to the little restaurant Sandah knew on this world, a woman's pet providing a tempting target. But he was no mere pup anymore, and had behaved accordingly.

Of course, being a woman on a strange planet meant some idiot was bound to say something to the lithe newcomer. Yet another of a never-ending stream of unwanted attention Leila had become accustomed to as they traveled.

When the three ruffians lingering on the street started cat alling her as she walked with the prim and proper captain, she couldn't help but feel sorry for them. The poor lads hadn't noticed Baloo following a short distance behind, sniffing all the new things on this world with great interest. But as soon as he heard Leila clear her throat, his attention abruptly shifted.

"Come on, we'll show you a good time," the apparent leader of the trio said.

"I really must advise you to leave the lady alone and be on your way," Sandah said, speaking as a captain of a powerful visla must. Representing him with class and honor.

Leila, on the other hand, was under no such constraints. "I believe what the good captain is saying is, you had best run along while you are still able."

"What? Is that whore threatening me?" the man asked, incredulous. How could she not be the least bit intimidated by him?

The low, bowel-loosening growl behind the men answered that question.

"As I said, don't you have somewhere else you should be?" Leila asked.

The three nodded and quickly backed away, then took off running.

Captain Sandah had laughed nearly the entire rest of the way to the restaurant, and he even ordered a bloody cut of meat for Baloo. It was the least he could do for the poor animal. He obviously wanted to hunt, but for now he would be a good boy and sit quietly by his mama's feet, her fingers lazily caressing his ears as they awaited their repast.

A short while later, Leila was mopping up the last of her meal, having devoured every last morsel. Captain Sandah had been correct, it was startlingly good food.

"How ever did you come across such an unusual animal?" Sandah asked as he sipped his tea.

"It's a long story," Leila said, recalling her escape from Visla Maktan's estate and their flight across world after world while Ara was still in a weakened state. And then, the fateful day they discovered the tiny pup, taken from his mother far too young. Since the moment she first held him to her breast and told him everything would be okay, Leila had been as much a mother to him as anyone could be.

"And you don't need a control collar on him, despite his size and strength," Sandah commented. "Most impressive control you have over him."

"It's not so much control as he's my baby," Leila replied. "And all control collars do is force people into compliance. You get so much more from willing partnerships than slavery."

"I suppose there's an argument that could be made for both perspectives," Sandah said.

"Well, I see that you don't wear a collar," Leila noted. "And as a visla's servant, it would seem that even in this time of abolished slavery, if any might utilize them and be able to get away with it, someone of his power could."

"But I've been with the visla my whole life, essentially. If not for him, I'd never have become a captain."

"Which is my point. You're gladly serving him without the need for a collar."

Sandah flashed an amused grin. The woman was unusual, but she did have a valid point. "This has been most pleasant, but shall we head back and get underway? If any of the captains in town had any information, we'll know when we return to the ship."

Leila finished the last of her tea and wiped her mouth. "Yes, let's," she said, rising to her feet, Baloo likewise standing, right at her side, as always. "Good boy, Baloo. Good boy," she said as they walked to the door.

No one would dare harass them on their return to the ship.

CHAPTER FIVE

While one ancient Wampeh was flying across the systems with his Zomoki and human friends, searching for answers to who truly was behind the deadly mystery fleet, another far younger Wampeh––chronologically, at least––was taking a most unusual Ootaki woman and her odd, four-armed friend on a quest of a rather different variety. One that led them to a small, nondescript planet in a blue giant's solar system.

How the former Ootaki slave-turned magic user wound up there was an interesting twist in and of itself.

Having fought a battle to the death to a draw, using the ancient and secret combative and magical techniques of the Wampeh Ghalian order of assassins, Hunze and her new ally––a Wampeh Ghalian master named Kort––had come to an understanding.

The assassin would personally vouch for her safety, as best he could, and he would take her to speak to the rest of his order. But to receive the blanket protection of the rest of the secretive sect, she would have to face them individually, subjecting herself to the queries and tests of each of the other five masters.

"Bring it," Hunze had said, secretly reveling in using the

over-confident phrase she had learned from Rika several weeks prior.

Kort had cast a bonding spell between his craft and Kip, the quirky AI ship carrying Hunze and her Chithiid counterpart, Dukaan. With the connection in place, Kip's warp drive would latch on to the magic of Kort's vessel and follow it as it jumped—a merging of warp technology and space jump magic.

It was in this manner that the tech ship from another galaxy had finally completed his first *accurate* warp in this new galaxy. And he was thrilled.

"It worked!" Kip chirped, absolutely jazzed about the successful warp. "You guys see that? Right on target!"

"Yes, Kip, we are aware," Dukaan replied, stretching his four arms and cracking his neck.

It had been a rough time in this strange galaxy thus far, and he was feeling rather worse for wear for it. He hoped Hunze's lover's former sect would provide them a much-needed respite from those stresses, but first she would have to prove herself. And that was a source of a different kind of stress.

The blue sun cast a cool-appearing glow across the world, yet at roughly four times the temperature of Earth's sun, the color of the light was deceiving. Had the planet been closer to the burning orb, they'd have been roasted to a crisp upon exiting the ship.

Fortunately, the planet's orbit was quite far from the center of the system, and the resulting temperature was quite pleasant. The landscape was lush with vegetation bearing the signs of taking root in a system of this sort, the colorings tending toward the cooler hues of deep green and violet.

Kip followed Kort's little craft as the assassin casually dropped low over a large city on the edge of a vast ocean. The buildings were spread out and low, unlike some places they'd been, where the residents lived more like termites in towering nests.

Here, however, space was plentiful, and the result was an open skyline and wider roads and pathways. The architectural styles were rather unique as well, the builders opting for vast, wrapping porches with protective rooflines overhead, providing both shade and cross-ventilation without requiring magical expenditure to move the air.

"The construction reminds me a little of the handful of historical buildings we saw preserved back home," Hunze noted. "Do you see the similarities?"

"Akin to the Craftsman style in some ways," Dukaan agreed. "Fascinating. Apparently, some methods of natural climate control span galaxies."

Kort led them to a clear landing field not far from the city center. Space traffic appeared to be sparse here, and an open place for Kip to set down was easy to procure.

"I'll keep comms open, Kip, but please do not transmit unless absolutely necessary," Hunze said. "I have a feeling this will be a somewhat tense situation, and while I wish for you to be party to the conversation, I do not want to distract our potential hosts with a talking ship. Not until we've gained their trust."

"Don't worry about me," Kip said. "As long as we're finally somewhere I don't have to worry about being attacked at any second, I think we'll be fine."

"You would be wise to keep your weapons systems active regardless," Dukaan noted.

"Oh, I'll have 'em ready to rock, believe you me. But if Kort says we'll be safe here, I believe him. If he's anything like Bawb, his word means more to him than most."

Hunze smiled at that. Yes, she'd experienced this code of honor firsthand with her love, and it was an impressive thing to behold. Regardless, she slid the vorpal blade across her back just in case his associates were not so similarly inclined.

The airlock doors opened, and the two passengers stepped out onto the new world.

"Wampeh," Hunze said, scanning the planet's citizens. "So many Wampeh."

It was an unusual sight, this many Wampeh together. Of course, she knew there were worlds on which they were a majority of the population, but having spent her life in the possession of the Council of Twenty, they had never taken their valued slave to any such planet.

But here was a world full of the pale species. Of course, only the tiniest fraction of a fraction of Wampeh ever possessed the ability to steal the power from another by drinking their blood. And of those, an even smaller percent were able to do it with any real absorption of that power. It was from those the Wampeh Ghalian selected its potential new members and subjected them to training and tests. Tests the vast majority failed.

Then there were the precious few. The gleaming flecks of gold hidden on the sands of a vast beach. The Wampeh like Bawb, who could not only take another's power, but who excelled at it. The ones who would become not mere assassins of the order, but leaders of it, versed in the most secret of Ghalian ways.

"Welcome to Ashimaru," Kort said, walking up to his guests. "As you've no doubt noticed, this is a Wampeh world."

"Yes, there are so many of your kind," Hunze replied.

"All the better to blend in," the assassin said with a grin. "None know who we are. *What* we are. It is a secret you are being trusted with. For this reason, please understand the others will be rather judgmental and cautious of your motives when they first meet you."

"I can understand their reasoning," Hunze said. "Secrecy and invisibility are crucial to the Ghalian."

Kort smiled. "You understand, as a disciple of the Geist would."

"Not a disciple," Dukaan corrected. "She's his girlfriend."

The mirthful arching of the Wampeh's brow increased for an instant. "Yes, well, whatever the semantics may be, she possesses skills far greater than most Ghalian ever dream to achieve. And *that* will be of great interest to the other five masters. I had word sent to them to meet us here. I suspect all have arrived and are waiting for us at our local facility."

"You took the long way here, didn't you?" Hunze asked, already knowing the answer.

"Yes, I did," Kort replied. "Not an inordinately long route, but enough to afford them time to arrive before us, yes. You are most observant, Hunze."

"As Bawb taught me to be," she replied. "Well, come then. Let us go and meet these masters. I believe we will have much to discuss."

CHAPTER SIX

The secret training facility of the most deadly order of assassins the galaxy had ever known was rather unimpressive at first glance. And at second glance. In fact, any way you looked at it, the large building with its wide, sloped roof, and dirty, industrial feel was the last thing you'd think of if someone said, "Master assassin training grounds."

And that was just as intended.

There were several similar compounds scattered across the known systems, each housing a small cadre of hopefuls and their instructors. The masters, however, came and went, never lingering in one location too long. Whether that was out of necessity or merely habit for the men and women long-accustomed to the rigors of their trade was open for debate.

Hunze and Dukaan followed their Wampeh guide up the few steps to the front doors. For all intents and purposes, it seemed like any other building. The door was unlocked.

"I was expecting something a bit more *robust*," Dukaan noted as they stepped inside without effort.

Kort merely smiled and led them across the wide lobby area

to another unassuming door mounted in a wall adorned with decorative moldings and artwork.

"Wait just a moment," Kort said, holding up his hand and quietly casting a spell. A spell that Hunze found rising to her lips, joining his magic as the man cast.

The sudden addition of her power startled him, but only just. Hunze realized what she had subconsciously done and eased off. "I'm sorry," she said. "I didn't realize I was doing that."

"Doing what?" Dukaan asked, confused. "You weren't doing anything."

Kort grinned. "Oh, but she was. And something only a handful of the order can." He focused his attention back on the spell and completed the casting.

Dukaan, not being a magical being, felt and saw nothing. But Hunze, with her Ootaki magic and Bawb's knowledge, felt the shift in the building's power in her bones.

"So much magic," she marveled.

"Yes," Kort agreed, then tapped the wall a few feet to the left of the doorway.

The section of the wall he touched impossibly separated from the solid surface and slid to the side. A doorway where one could not exist, for on the other side of the wall was a courtyard. But that was not where this door led.

"But...how?" Dukaan wondered.

"Magic," was all Kort said. "Now, please, follow me."

Hunze and Dukaan did as he asked, stepping through the opening behind him, the wall sealing shut as soon as they passed into the long, magically illuminated corridor.

The Ootaki was a sensitive being by her very nature, and the sheer weight of the centuries upon centuries of magic layered upon itself, hiding this place, protecting it, keeping it safe, was almost overwhelming. Hunze herself could not make out every nuance of the magic, but she didn't have to.

Bawb had included that bit of information in the neuro-stim

transfer he'd gifted her, though she had to wonder if that had been intentional or merely a side effect of using the Earth tech on a vampire assassin from another galaxy.

In any case, she knew what this was, and just as their guide was quietly doing, she, too, cast a protective spell, adding it to the layers of spells every single Wampeh Ghalian cast when they passed into or out of the facility. It was a near-impenetrable jawbreaker-layered bubble of magic that almost none could breach.

This was not only a training ground, it was also a safe refuge for the deadliest of the deadly.

The corridor curved left, then right––which Hunze knew was to provide defending forces a blind spot from which to dispatch any would-be intruders––before opening onto a modest courtyard no greater than fifteen meters square. The faint shape of the building above them could still be made out through the magical transparency that allowed the space the illusion of open air, when ithe reality was the building's structure was actually just twenty feet above them.

Eighteen Wampeh stood stock-still at the far end. Male and female, each of them pale white with a hint of power in them that Hunze could actually sense at this proximity.

Most were teenagers, but several were younger, mere children, some who appeared to be as young as eight or nine. All were clad in the same plain trousers and tunics. All but one. A bruised and dirty boy standing naked among the others, bearing the same blank expression on his face, making no attempt to cover himself.

Bawb had never spoken explicitly of the difficulties he had endured becoming the man she knew, and he had not shared that part of his skillset in their neuro-stim transfer, but Hunze instinctively knew what the boy was facing. Training in the nude, forced to be unconcerned with one's outward appearance, and learning to ignore any thoughts of modesty in the face of your enemy, male or female.

It was a brutal lesson, but one that could be the difference between survival and failure in their chosen profession. For a Wampeh Ghalian, nude and unarmed and surrounded by soldiers, was still the deadliest thing in the room.

Three armed Wampeh stood by the aspiring students. Teachers, Hunze noted. Seated just beyond them on a slightly raised platform were five adults of varied age and gender. *These* had a different feel to them. A relaxed nature she knew all too well, for she'd seen it in her lover on countless occasions.

The appearance of tranquil relaxation, when in reality, each was alert to every single element in the area and ready to spring in an instant, unleashing their deadliest of skills if need be.

But for the moment, the five simply sat and stared, looking almost bored.

Kort walked to the others. He did not bow, nor did he show any sign of subservience. It was only then that Hunze knew for certain just how high his rank within the order truly was. For him to have been hired to capture her meant that Emmik Hunstra must have wanted her *really* badly, for Kort's services would not have come cheaply.

"This is the one you told us of, Kort?" asked a tall woman with her hair braided into several rows, securely fastened behind her ears.

"Indeed, she is," he replied.

"She claims to have been trained by the Geist?" the man seated beside her stated more than inquired. "Our brother passed to the other side centuries ago, at the fall of Tolemac, Kort. We all know this."

"Yes, and his passing was a great loss for the order. But this Ootaki knows things none but a master of our order could. And she knows things of the Geist never spoken of outside our circles."

"Might she have tortured this knowledge from one of our ranks? Ghalian do go missing from time to time, and while they're assumed lost to a failed assignment, it is always possible something more nefarious is afoot," the man replied.

"If I may," Hunze said, stepping forward, though slowly, and with her hands in plain sight. "Bawb, the one known as the Geist, did indeed go missing hundreds of years ago, thrown through a rift in space to another galaxy."

"All conjecture. This was long before any of us were born. There is no way you could know this," a wiry man seated at the end said.

"That is where you are mistaken," she replied. "I *do* know this, because I was with him."

"Impossible. You'd have to be hundreds of years old, and no Ootaki live that long."

"You are correct, we do not. However, when Malalia Maktan cast her spell and destroyed that world, we were not only thrown through space, but through time as well."

The master assassins looked at her impassively, but behind their blank expressions, Hunze knew they had been shocked by her words.

"Maktan's daughter," the woman finally said with obvious distaste. "The woman was a blight on the systems for years before she, too, disappeared."

"She came to us. Found a way to track us to where we'd been sent," Hunze explained. "A battle ensued, and at the end of it all, we were thrown back forward in time, but instead of returning to our own era, we arrived in the future. And the future of the planet we were on in that other galaxy, no less."

"A fantastical claim," the woman said. "And how is it you are now here, if you were in another galaxy, as you claim?"

"Someone was preparing to attack us. With a magical portal from this galaxy. But Bawb and our friends captured it and turned it against them, using the portal to cross over and bring the fight to this galaxy rather than the other."

She looked at their faces and saw the information quickly processing. The implications.

"So you see," she continued, "the Geist is still very much alive, and in his prime. And he's back. Somewhere in one of these systems, Bawb has returned."

"And you, an Ootaki, claim to possess his skills? You wish to be accepted and protected by the Wampeh Ghalian?"

"Yes," she replied, back straight and head held high, just as her love would have wanted.

The master assassins quietly talked among themselves a moment.

"Very well," the woman finally said. "You shall prove yourself. Prove yourself worthy."

"I am ready," Hunze said.

"I very much doubt that," the woman replied, smiling for the first time since they'd arrived, her pointed teeth showing through her parted lips. "For this shall be a trial by combat. And you will be tested by us all."

CHAPTER SEVEN

In some schools of combat, those about to do battle would be afforded a brief period to prepare themselves for the challenge, mentally and physically.

Wampeh Ghalian assassins offered no such luxury.

The largest of the five masters of the Order casually rose to his feet, gingerly stepping down from their raised platform and limping across the courtyard with the aid of his crutch. His physique was large and well-muscled, but it appeared to be so from years of forcing himself along, using his strength to keep his broken body upright.

He slowly dragged his lame left foot along, placing it in front of him and performing an almost grotesque act of physical contortion to lever the rest of himself ahead. It was uncomfortable to watch, and easy to see how most would avert their eyes from the crippled man.

Exactly as the master assassin intended.

His crutch flew through the air in a blur, whistling toward Hunze's head with blinding speed. But when it reached its intended target, the golden-haired woman's head was not there. Nor was the rest of her body, for that matter.

Already in motion the second the man had begun his attack, Hunze had launched herself through the air, executing a precise diving roll while simultaneously casting a pair of powerful, but non-lethal counterattacks, one of which nearly passed the man's defensive spells.

That got his attention. A thin smile creased his lips as he unfolded from his crippled form to his full height. He was far larger, and far stronger than his act let on. Decades of infiltration had honed his favorite disguise, and much as Binsala the Trader was second nature for Bawb, so it seemed the cripple was for this man.

But now, here, in this place, it was time for a proper, unconstrained fight.

Using his crutch for its true purpose, he cast a trio of spells, while also hectoring his opponent with the length of wood. Hunze could feel it, though. The crutch was far more than just that. It housed an enchanted rod––much as Bawb's wand held a konus and a strand of her hair––and seemed quite capable of smashing through most defenses, as well as those casting them.

Kort watched impassively, but a slight hint of mirth tickled the corners of his eyes when his Ghalian comrade and the Ootaki woman expertly countered one another, sending each of them flying backward, only to land at the ready. He had already fought this woman, and knew full well what she was capable of. But seeing others of his Order have the same difficulty he did make him all the more certain that bringing her here was the right thing to do.

The two fought for just two minutes, then the attacker ceased his efforts, all hostility gone in an instant. With a respectful nod of his head, he walked back to his seat.

"Why have they stopped?" Dukaan asked in a hushed voice.

"This is not a fight to the death," Kort informed him. "And a true Ghalian attack would end nearly all fights in seconds.

Minutes, tops. So, you see, there is simply no need for a prolonged trial if she survives that long."

Hunze was not remotely out of breath. In fact, she'd not even broken a sweat from the brief sparring session. The lean and wiry old woman who strode to face her next intended to change that.

While the first combatant had used his skills of deception to mask his size and strength, this woman appeared unconcerned with misdirection, simply walking to face her opponent. She was old, but not ancient. However, Hunze knew full well that to be one of the masters of the Wampeh Ghalian, the woman's appearance meant nothing.

"Shall we begin?" the woman asked with a little smile, her pointed teeth extended for effect.

"Whenever you wish," Hunze replied, utterly unfazed.

The magic she unleashed was ferocious and instantaneous, and Hunze found herself sliding backward despite the defenses she'd been quietly casting. The woman, it seemed, had no intention of a physical altercation, though Hunze was certain she could more than do so if she wished. It was a magical barrage, honed by a lifetime of use, that was hammering down upon the Ootaki like crashing waves.

Hunze's link to Bawb's knowledge was stronger with every use, and her own magic responded without having to search her memory for the right spells. She cast and countered and cast again, layering her magic in small bursts rather than large ones against the sheer strength of the small woman.

She had feasted on a powerful spellcaster recently, Hunze realized. It was that additional power that was being brought to bear in the display of raw strength.

But soft counters rigid, and Hunze followed her instincts, continuing to pick away at the magic with flurries of small spells, eschewing the use of any large ones. Those would just meet stronger resistance, but by dispersing her magic to dozens of smaller spells, the end result was the same, but also forced her opponent to divert energy to counter the ones that slipped through.

As abruptly as she had begun, the older woman ceased her attack, nodded respectfully, and returned to her seat. The whole exchange had lasted no more than thirty seconds, but it was more than enough for the woman to have gauged her enemy. And she had deemed her a worthy opponent.

Next, the young, androgynous master casually strolled out to face their opponent. This master was different from the others, not only in their youthful appearance, but also their undefined gender. They had fine features that could easily be considered attractive on both sides of the spectrum, and a style of dress that was likewise neutral.

Hunze saw immediately how useful this appearance would be for a master assassin plying their trade. To shift from one persona to another, changing genders in the process, would make tracking the expert in deception and disguise near impossible.

The attack began with the slightest tickle of a spell. Just a feather's touch, reaching out and testing Hunze's defenses. When her spells reacted, however, the nature of her barriers were made clear, and in that instant, unusual spells of the most arcane variety began flying her way, along with several enchanted blades concealed on the Wampeh's person.

The magic had done its job, slipping past her defenses more than once, forcing the Ootaki to shift her casting to compensate. As she did, however, one of the blades found a gap and pierced her tunic. Dukaan was alarmed and almost moved to help her, but Kort held him back.

"She is fine," he said to the Chithiid.

And indeed she was, for the little weapon fell from her body with not a drop of blood on what was left of its blade. Hunze's hair, wrapped around her body, had reduced it to rubbish.

The attack stopped at once. As casually as they had begun the attack, the young Wampeh strolled to where Hunze was standing, then bent and retrieved the melted weapon.

"Impressive," they said, examining what was left of the blade, then returned to their seat with the others.

The dapper man who was obviously next in line was already up and moving before his predecessor had even taken a seat. The cut of his clothing was impeccable, and even for a Wampeh, his angular cheekbones and perfectly groomed hair gave him the appearance of a model more than an assassin.

Unlike the others, he walked right up to Hunze, fixing a warm smile upon her. "My name is Pimbrak," he said. "A pleasure to meet you."

Hunze reached out to shake his offered hand, an instinctive reaction to most. Only as their flesh touched did Bawb's training override her error, but Pimbrak had already begun his attack.

The magic flowing through his hands drew from Hunze's power. Not much. Not like drinking her blood would, but she nevertheless felt the visceral tug deep within.

She shifted, pulling back as he pushed closer, slipping into a magical dance of proximity, attack, and defense. This one was different, she realized, for he could steal power by touch as well.

Hunze's power surged, forming a thin shell over her exposed skin, invisible to the eye, but effective against unwanted touch. Pimbrak's hand snaked around her wrist for a moment, but he felt the change immediately. He could no longer tap her power.

The Wampeh smiled. This was a fun surprise, and he hadn't been surprised in a very long time. That meant he would need his other tricks.

Having seen what Hunze had done to the prior assassin's blade, he attacked with his weapon held backwards, the blunt pommel of the knife striking rather than the point. Hunze absorbed the impacts, but her hair did not destroy the weapon like the other, as it did not penetrate her clothing.

A clever adaptation by a skilled assassin, but Hunze quickly adapted as well, her combatives flowing into a push/pull dance between the two. Less than a minute had passed when Pimbrak stepped back and pocketed his blade.

"Thank you. That was most enjoyable," he said, returning to his seat.

The tall woman with braided hair picked up a sheathed weapon that had been sitting beside her and strode down from the platform. Hunze felt the weapon's magic before it was even pulled free of its scabbard.

"A vespus blade," she noted, drawing her own as the Wampeh pulled hers free from its home.

"I see you possess one as well," the woman said. "But you are not Wampeh Ghalian. Let us see how you handle it."

With that she launched into an attack, her blue blade beginning to glow faintly at the promise of blood and battle. Hunze's, however, stayed the same, its metal unilluminated as it parried and blocked the deadly blows. Her opponent smiled at this and pressed harder, forcing the fight into a shifting duel all across the chamber.

Metal rang out as they fought, and the combat ranged all over. If any had later examined the traces of footwork left on the floor, the stride length, the quickness of the foot feints, they'd have clearly seen both combatants were at least masters. Probably better.

The glowing blade was unrelenting in its attacks, the enchanted weapon forcing Hunze to defensive posturing repeatedly with its strength. The woman smiled as she pressed her advantage.

"Unable to call upon the blade's power, I see," the woman teased.

Her opponent merely smiled tranquilly despite the rigors of combat.

"No," Hunze replied. "I choose not to." She winked, then let a pulse of her Ootaki magic flow into the weapon, which flashed blindingly bright for a moment before returning to its normal state.

Her attacker ceased her aggression at once, fixing her with a curious look. "You wield a blade of the Wampeh Ghalian. An exceedingly rare item."

"That I do."

"It has happened from time to time when a master falls," the woman said. "Most have been lost to time, yet two of us possess such a weapon." She sheathed her sword and looked at Hunze's prize. "May I?"

Without fear or hesitation, Hunze handed her the vespus blade. The woman turned it over in her hands, admiring it with a sharp eye, then handed it back. "You have restored it recently, I see."

"Yes, it was in quite a state of disrepair when I acquired it."

"You have done good work. It is nearly as good as new. We know this sword well. It originally belonged to Master Hozark, then later passed through the hands of many of our order, until it was finally lost hundreds of years ago when its master fell."

"Soon it will be Bawb's," Hunze said.

"You are not keeping this?" the woman asked, a note of shock in her normally controlled voice.

"It should be in Wampeh hands," Hunze said. "He is my love, and I can think of none more deserving of it."

A murmur passed through the room. Talk of love and a Wampeh Ghalian simply did not happen. The two were doomed to be strangers forever. But Bawb had been wrenched from that world, thrust into a galaxy where his rules no longer applied. And as a result, a Wampeh Ghalian had done what none before them had.

He had taken a lover, and not of the mere physical variety.

"You were obviously trained by one of the Geist's skill level," the woman said. "And you have proven yourself to the masters of

SCOTT BARON

the Order. I am Zilara," she said, effecting a slight bow. "You are accepted and protected by the Wampeh Ghalian as one of our own."

The other masters' postures relaxed from false casual to the real variety. Hunze had passed their test. She was part of the family now.

"Come, you must be hungry from your journey, and we have much to discuss. You are the first Ootaki caster ever seen, and the first non-Wampeh accepted to the Order in thousands of years. Today is a day that will be recorded in history, so let us dine and celebrate. And then you must tell us your tale."

CHAPTER EIGHT

Karasalia Palmarian and her best friend, Visanya, had only recently taken refuge in her mysterious and reclusive uncle's manor far on the other side of the planet. How they arrived at his distant location was something of a mystery in its own right.

In fact, it could be the greatest puzzle ever seen on her world, and possibly in her entire galaxy. For Kara and Vee had flown to her uncle's land in a pod. A ship the likes of which none had ever seen. The likes of which defied the laws of magic. Simply put, the impossible craft couldn't exist.

But it did.

The teens had discovered the vessel hidden in the floating gardens atop Kara's father's towering abode. But it wasn't parked and plain for any to see. No, it had been camouflaged in a most novel manner. What the pod had called 'active camouflage,' whereby its outside shifted to project the appearance of whatever was on the other side of it, giving the illusion of invisibility.

It wasn't a shimmer spell. In fact, it wasn't magic at all, but rather, something the odd craft had called 'technology.' And without the mysterious prophesy of the heretic assassin locked in her father's tower, Kara might never have stumbled upon the hidden craft, so tantalizingly close, yet unseen by all.

But with the help of the woman she now knew was named Daisy, she and Vee had come to meet the pod––whose name was actually Pod.

And that was the even more disturbing part of the whole thing. The flying tech-magic craft *spoke*. It spoke, but not with a recorded voice. It possessed what it called an artificial intelligence. It had a mind, albeit a basic one, and it could think, and talk, and reason like a person might.

When Pod offered to take them on a flight, the opportunity to escape her father's tower was too tempting for Kara to pass up. Ever since she had stumbled upon his hidden records detailing a horrific, destructive fleet of ships destroying and enslaving all in their path, Kara had realized, to her horror, that her father was not what he said he was.

Her stepmother, while like a sister to her, wouldn't be able to help. For all she knew, her father was keeping his wife in the dark as well. And besides, she was off-planet anyway. No, she needed to find out what was really going on from someone outside their household. Someone whose power, while not as strong as her father's, was exceptional just the same. Someone she could trust implicitly.

Uncle Korbin was the obvious choice.

He wasn't her father's actual blood brother by birth. He was, rather, the only boy to possess anywhere near his power growing up, and the only one not afraid of him. The two had been friends their whole lives, and Uncle Korbin had been there for both of the visla's weddings, as well as the birth of his daughter and death of his first wife.

He was as close to family as one could get without the same blood flowing through their veins. And as her father once said following one of Korbin's rare visits, there is more to family than blood.

And so she and her best friend found themselves headed to the distant village in which her uncle had lived the better part of the last twenty years.

It was a rural land he had chosen. Rugged hills surrounded the lush plains and forests, bordered on one side by a fast-moving river, the tributaries of which ensured an abundant flow of nourishing water for the crops grown by the local inhabitants.

Korbin was a wealthy man, as well as a powerful visla in his own right. But to see him in this setting, none would be the wiser. He possessed what could be considered a somewhat lavish home, given the humble residences of the area, but compared to even the least of power users elsewhere on the planet, he seemed to almost be living in poverty.

As a result, he went unnoticed. Just another man living his days in the quiet little hamlet. Never using his powers, anonymous to visitors, and accepted by neighbors. It was perfect for him. A tranquil existence where none took note of him.

That is, until a strange semi-invisible craft came hurtling through the sky, landing in the field just behind his home, the flickering image smoothing to invisible once on solid ground.

Uncle Korbin came rushing out of his house, his appearance calm, but the deadly magic within him ready to strike if need be, a small slaap casually riding on his hand, ready to focus and add to his considerable power.

He didn't know what to make of the strange illusion before him when, out of thin air, a hatch appeared, sliding open and revealing a pair of teenage girls sitting inside what appeared to be a command module of a design he had never before seen.

"Kara?" he said, quickly powering down his magic. "Kara, what in the worlds are you doing here? And what is this thing you arrived in?"

Kara climbed out of the pod and rushed to her uncle, wrapping him up in a fierce hug. "Uncle Korbin, I'm so glad to see you!"

"Hello, sir," Vee said, exiting the pod and joining them.

"Visanya, it's been a long time," Korbin said. "You've gained a foot since last I saw you. And how your hair has grown," he said, noting the long, woven braids of brown locks hanging down her back.

Vee felt her cheeks warm at his comment, but the man had already shifted his gaze, his attention now firmly focused on the little pod, unlike any he had ever seen. Korbin found himself utterly fascinated by the invisible craft.

"This is not shimmer magic," he said, reaching out with his own power, probing the vehicle.

"No, I don't use magic," Pod said. "This is adaptive camouflage, as I told Kara and Visanya."

The powerful man paused, unsure what had just happened.

"The craft. It talks," Korbin said, hiding just how startled he actually was. "And yet I sense no enchantment. What manner of thing is this, Kara? And how did you come to possess such a vessel?"

"It's a long story, Uncle Korbin. And his name is Pod. But I really think it would be better if we talked inside," Kara said, looking around for any prying eyes.

Korbin was about to say that they were perfectly secure discussing whatever they wanted right there on his lands, but the look on his niece's face told him something was off. Something far more worrisome than the usual trials and tribulations of a teenage girl.

"Very well," he said. "Let us step inside. I will prepare us some tea, and then you can tell me all about your little adventure. Something tells me you have quite a story to tell."

CHAPTER NINE

Korbin, after hearing just the most primary of Karasalia's recent experiences and concerns, realized his niece was likely justified in her paranoia. Not only was her father behaving strangely, but to be attacked and kidnapped in Palmar itself was unheard of for a visla's daughter.

He felt it only logical to keep her presence, and that of the unusual craft the girls had arrived in, secret, moving the once-again-invisible pod inside a large animal enclosure that just so happened to have relatively high walls around it, sheltering them from any prying eyes as he attempted to learn more from the strange vessel.

It was odd, speaking to an inanimate object. Even enchanted weapons, while possessing a 'feel' of their essence, were unable to think, let alone speak. But this thing, this vessel, was a conscious entity. And from what it revealed, it wasn't from this realm.

"You say your name is Pod, and you were created by someone named Daisy on a planet called Earth, is that right?"

"Yes, it is," Pod replied. "Though, technically, I was created aboard Freya, and some of the time I was under construction was during space travel."

"So you said. But tell me more of this magic that drives your intellect."

"It's just a basic fusion reactor, not magic," Pod replied. "A modestly powered unit that is sufficient to power my operating system as well as all flight and navigational componentry. Magic, however, does not exist."

"In your world, apparently not," Korbin noted. "And this 'fusion' is a common means of producing power?"

"Yes, though larger ships will typically utilize warp core technology. It has near limitless power potential, and can transport a ship across great distances in the blink of an eye," Pod said. "Freya possesses one such system, though hers is a rather specialized unit."

"Oh?"

"She was the first, you see."

"First what, exactly?"

"The first AI ship to integrate warp technology to her drive systems. She is one of the greatest artificial minds ever created, though her birth was an accident. But that is what made her unique, even among AIs."

"So this Freya, she is like you?"

"Oh, no. She is much larger, and much more powerful. My knowledge stores are limited due to my size. I also possess no armaments to speak of, and my nanotech components are minimal. I am only intended for short flights, and only limited autonomous travel. My function is as more of an onboard assistant to the non-AI pilot."

Korbin spoke with the unusual consciousness a bit longer while the girls snacked in his kitchen. Then, once he felt he had gleaned all of the useful information the odd craft could give him, he joined them inside.

"What do you think, Uncle Korbin?" Karasalia asked.

"A most interesting thing you have brought to my doorstep, Kara. And you say this was hidden on one of your father's gardens? And unnoticed?"

"Yes. It was hidden, as one does with a shimmer."

"Yes, I've seen how it does that. And with no discernible magic, no less. It is rather disconcerting, to be honest."

"I know. Me and Vee were freaked out when we found it."

"Vee and I," he corrected, but without the tone of tired judgment her father always used. "And this prisoner you mentioned, she was the one who landed it there? Landed it and then made it across the gardens, nearly all the way to your father's chambers unnoticed? And armed, no less?"

"Yeah, pretty much," Kara replied. "And you should see her sword. No one can feel any enchantment on it, but when Father hit her with a stun spell, as she fell she somehow managed to drive it all the way into the tower wall. All the way to the hilt! And no one has been able to pull it free since."

"It's still there, just sticking out of the wall, then?"

"Yeah. But Pod doesn't seem to know anything about that. Me and Vee––I mean, Vee and I, kept asking about this Daisy person and her attack on Father, but Pod really isn't terribly helpful."

"No, he wouldn't be," Korbin replied. "He is much like a foot soldier in that regard. Useful to a point, but not informed of any more than is needed for his limited role. And this AI, as he calls himself? He is powered by some strange force called 'fusion.' There is no magic anywhere within his craft. And believe me, I checked."

He took a piece of thick bread and spread some of his homemade fruit preserves on it, pondering the situation as he chewed.

"I have to say, girls, I've never seen anything like it, and to be honest, I'm more than a little disconcerted by this turn of events. It looks like times may be changing in ways none of us could ever have predicted. And I think we had all best be prepared for it. And I do mean all of us."

Evening had come, and with it the reclusive visla had taken his niece and her friend to his private workspace in the outer building. It was a nondescript place in a village full of unnotable buildings and huts, yet inside were countless layers of protective spells and wards, all of them keeping the goings-on inside that building secret, the carefully placed magic woven into a dense shell over his many years living there.

Korbin tossed a wooden ball to each of the girls.

"Uncle Korbin? Really?" Kara whined.

It was part of the Hakanan Test her father relentlessly had her practice. Practice and fail.

"Humor me," Korbin said, holding his hands out and reading his niece's power as she reluctantly began casting the spell her father had drilled into her head.

The ball, to her surprise, levitated far easier than usual, hovering in the air in front of her with just the slightest of wavers.

"Visanya?" he said.

"I can't," she replied. "I've already taken and failed the Hakanan Test more than once, including the official Trials. I'm afraid I'm destined to be non-powered."

Korbin flashed her a wry little grin. "Oh, I don't know about that," he said. "But if you've already faced the Trials, then your role in our society is fixed." He turned his attention back to his niece. "And what of you, Kara? You've always had such great potential within you. Both of your parents possessed great abilities, you know."

"Yes, I do. And that's what makes my continued failure all the more frustrating," she replied, the ball wavering but not falling, for a change.

"You look surprised," Korbin said.

"Oh, it's just I usually drop it when I get flustered, is all."

"As is the point of the test. To apply more and more pressure. Ever-increasing distractions and surprises, until you finally lose control of your magical grip."

"Yeah, Uncle Korbin, we all know what the Hakanan Test is."

"And do you know why you all take it?"

"Originally? Sure. It was so the Council of Twenty could identify potential recruits."

"And potential threats," the man added.

"I suppose," Kara said. "But nowadays it's just a way to maintain a classist society, even though the Council is long gone."

"Not gone," Korbin said. "Never assume them gone. Merely dispersed and weakened. But we must remain vigilant, lest they attempt to make a return." He crossed over to a small basket containing some local fruits. "You know, your father, even as a teenager, could not be made to falter. Three vislas were casting at him, yet his ball stayed aloft."

"I've heard," Kara said.

"Have you heard that one of them, in frustration, cast a violent spell, not allowed in the Trials?"

"I hadn't heard that," Kara admitted.

"She was censured for the act afterward," Korbin said. "But your father's reaction was far more damaging to her reputation than that."

"Oh?"

A little smile formed on Korbin's lips. "Your father batted the spell aside and, also against Trial rules, cast a counterstrike, knocking her to the ground. A visla, stunned by a teenager. And one only just undergoing the Trials. She was humiliated. Your father was acting in self-defense, however, and no penalty was assessed."

Kara was shocked. She knew he was powerful even as a youth, but this came as something of a surprise.

"You always did like Orvan fruit," Korbin said, picking up a burgundy, apple-sized fruit from the basket. "I remember when you were just a little girl, you couldn't get enough of them. Your mother was worried you'd upset your stomach with the quantity you ate," he said, gently tossing her the fruit.

Kara fumbled it, but then caught the fruit with her magic, pulling it level with the ball still floating in the air.

"Kara, did you see what you just did?" Vee exclaimed. "She always drops it. Like, every time. That's why her father hasn't let her stand for the Trials yet."

Kara's focus shifted as she realized what she'd done, sending both the ball and the fruit falling to the ground. But she'd done it. Vee was right. She'd just made a huge leap forward in her magic, and of course she'd done it when her father wasn't there to see.

"It was just lucky," Kara finally said, bending to pick up both orbs.

"Your power is growing," Korbin said.

"No, I'm weak," she replied.

"No, Kara, you are not. I can feel it building within you."

"Well, I suppose it is a little stronger this week, but nothing special has happened. I mean, Father and Mareh left me locked in the tower by myself while they each flew off on yet another outing."

"Hey!" Vee said.

"Sorry, Vee. I mean, left me in the tower with my best friend for company," Kara amended.

"And where did your father go?" Korbin asked.

"He never says. Probably off to quell another uprising, I suppose. It seems he spends as much time away from home as with us these days. And, of course, Mareh makes up for it by constantly flying off to socialize with her friends."

"Ah, yes. Mareh, the social butterfly. But Nikora does love her so, and she's been a good stepmother to you, though none can hold a candle to Azaraella, of course. Your mother was one of a kind, Kara, that much is for certain."

"She was," the teen quietly replied. "I miss her."

"As do we all," Korbin said.

He studied her a moment as she lost herself in the memory of her mother.

"Kara, would you please send me that little box over there?" he said, pointing to a small metal box no larger than a loaf of bread sitting on a shelf across the room. "I wish to get something out of it."

"What? Oh, sure," she replied, effortlessly sending the box across the room with a simple variant of her levitation spell.

"Thank you," Korbin replied, opening the box and removing a single coin, then placing the box on a nearby table.

He hoped the wood was sturdy enough to hold it, for the box contained a huge weight in coins, amassed over the years one by one. More importantly, though, was that Kara had just sent it with no trouble whatsoever, unaware of the weight she was lifting.

She had the power, of that he was certain. What was holding her back, however, remained a curiosity. One he hoped to unravel if at all possible. There were many new mysteries that had arrived on his doorstep this day, and it looked like he was going to have his hands full unraveling them.

CHAPTER TEN

Despite being clad in a tank top, the pale, white ink of Rika's swirling tattoos was largely obscured, thanks to the layer of grease, red sand, and traces of green Tslavar blood that had somehow mixed with the other two as she helped clean up after the battle with the alien combatants.

Her mech was now unfolded from its storage and transport configuration, courtesy of the large cargo bay aboard Marban's newly named ship. The *Coratta* was a sizable craft, and with a little careful maneuvering, Rika had been able to lay out her mech full length, allowing her access to pretty much all of the areas she needed to reach to give it a proper overhaul.

The fight in the Balamar Wastelands had forced her to push the machine harder than she'd have liked to without first triple-checking every connector and joint. But shit happens in wartime, and she had made do. Unfortunately, that also meant that a few of the bits in need of attention at that time were now desperately crying out for repairs. Repairs that she'd be hard-pressed to carry out, as she was lacking the correct parts.

Jo had been exceptionally helpful at sourcing acceptable bits and bobs from aboard the ship that they might use to jury rig the repairs until they could get proper pieces. And with Rika's magic also helping hold the craft together when it operated, she felt pretty confident it would function just fine if they needed it.

As for making it space-worthy? Well, that was another story.

"Are you having any success?" Marban asked the pair of legs sticking out from an access hatch leading deep into the mech's leg just above the knee joint.

He had come bearing a tray of not only cold beverages, but also an assortment of little snacks he had thought his guest might like. Had Charlie been aboard, the poor man would have faced a relentless ribbing. But as he was off with Ara and Bawb on a far different mission, Marban escaped the good-natured mirth of his friend.

"Hey, whatcha got there?" Jo asked, entering the cargo bay from the other side, dragging a ridiculously heavy bag of components salvaged from his ship.

"Food and drink," he replied. "Would you like some?"

"Nah, I'm good," Jo said. "Busy day, today."

"I can see that," Marban said. "I hope you're not gutting anything important from my ship."

"Don't worry," Rika said as she crawled out of the narrow space, grease smeared on her cheek. "Jo's a top-notch mechanic. She'd sooner cut her own hand off than strip out something a ship relied on to function. Isn't that right, Jo?"

"Well, I'd rather not lose an appendage, if I'm given the choice," she joked. "Anyway, I need to go grab the next batch. Oh, and Marban here brought you some treats," she added with a wink.

Rika's blush was hidden by the grime on her face, but only just. She'd have been fine on her own, but with Jo pushing her buttons––and enjoying every second of it––she found herself more self-conscious than she'd otherwise be.

"Oh, you didn't have to do that," she said, eyeing the cold drinks on the tray.

"Nonsense. You are not only Charlie's dear friend, but you are a guest on my ship. I am honor bound to take as good care of you as I'm able."

Jo's chuckle could be heard faintly as she walked out the far end of the cargo bay. Rika did her best to ignore it.

"Well, I suppose a little something to drink would be nice," she said, accepting a glass of violet juice. "Thanks, Marban."

"It is my pleasure, Rika," he said, his eyes slowly peeling away from the Earth woman to the amazing machine she was working on. "You know, while it has been hundreds of years since Charlie first took this walking statue––"

"It's a mech."

"This *mech* into battle, it was only mere minutes from my perspective. And imagine my surprise when this amazing creation suddenly appeared somewhere it hadn't been just moments before, and operating far more quickly and capably than I'd thought possible."

"Yeah, I can see how that could be a bit of a head spinner," Rika laughed. "And when we dug you guys up, we moved you from the original burial site too."

"And found me new clothing, for which I thank you," Marban added.

Rika felt a flush fight for a hold on her cheeks, but she once more forced it down.

"It seemed the least I could do," she said, turning her attention back to the mech.

"You are a skilled pilot," Marban said. "Don't tell Charlie I said this, but the way I saw you operate this mech once you'd roused me and my men, I can safely say you are far better than he is."

Rika couldn't help but laugh. She'd spent so much time trying to get Charlie up to basic proficiency with the training simulator, it was no wonder her effortless piloting of the huge machine would seem almost magical by comparison.

Of course, it actually *was* magical, her own powers driving the mech and tying it in to its pilot's will.

"Thank you, Marban. I appreciate that you noticed."

"You're hard to miss."

"Did Charlie tell you we trained together on Earth for almost a year?"

"That he did," Marban said. From the look on his face, she felt pretty sure he'd said more than that.

"So, I assume you also know about the crash. That, and what the Tslavars did to me."

"I've heard the stories," Marban said, a pained, sympathetic look in his eye. "Charlie was quite broken up over what was done to you, you should know. Many times he lamented not being able to keep you from harm. I feel it is one of his deepest regrets."

Rika actually knew that. But then, she and Charlie had hashed everything out in the months since she'd been freed from her servitude and had her mind and free will restored to her.

"You know, more happened after you were frozen, Marban," she said. "Things you simply couldn't know."

"Such as?" the pirate asked.

"Such as, Malalia Maktan," Rika replied.

The look of distaste on Marban's face told her all she needed to know about his feelings about that woman.

"Malalia was an evil woman," Marban said. "And as powerful as her father."

"Whom she took over for when he perished," Rika said. "But it gets more fucked up."

"Do tell," Marban said, curiosity piqued.

Rika took a deep breath. It was old news, but bringing it up again like this, nevertheless, hurt a bit.

"After he destroyed her forces and escaped, Malalia wanted to hurt Charlie," she said.

"That sounds like her," Marban noted.

"Yeah. Well, she found a really messed up way to do it."

"Oh?"

"She spent almost a year, but finally tracked me down where I was living as a brainwashed servant."

Marban kept a blank face, but she could see him tense.

"She acquired me from that household. I was important to Charlie, you see. And then she set to work, doing a number on my head. She took her time, and did it right, using all the tools at her disposal."

"What did she do to you?" Marban asked, horrified.

"She turned me into a weapon. A weapon she then turned against Charlie."

Marban looked at her a long moment, then let out the breath he hadn't realized he'd been holding. "And yet you are whole again. Restored to your former self and back where you belong."

"Not entirely," Rika said. "I've lost so much of who I was forever. Parts are still there, like how to operate the mech and pilot a ship, but other parts? Gone. I don't remember much of the friendship I used to have with Charlie, Marban. I lost that, and then I tried to kill him. He may have found a way to break me from Malalia's spell and heal my brain injuries, but to be honest, it's amazing he trusts me."

Marban placed his meaty hand on her shoulder and looked her square in the eye. "He is a very good judge of character, Rika. And I like to think that I am too. Whatever that bitch made you, you are your own woman once again. And a powerful one at that."

Something in his gaze and touch made her squirm a little, consciously suppressing a blush.

"Well, uh, thanks, I guess," she said, then quickly changed the subject. "So, how about you? I mean, you were in stasis for centuries. That's gotta be a trip. How are you handling waking up in the future?"

Marban's warm smile faltered. The smile remained, but the joy pulling at the corners of his eyes and mouth had evaporated. Rika couldn't help but notice, and she felt like an ass for it.

"I'm sorry. I shouldn't have--"

"No, that's all right," he said. "It's not so bad, really. I lost everything long before being frozen. So now I'm back, living as before. Existing day by day." He paused, gathering his thoughts. "I'll leave you to your work, then," he said, quietly excusing himself and heading out of the cargo bay.

"Stupid, Rika. Stupid, stupid, stupid," she grumbled to herself.

At the far end of the chamber, Jo, with her cybernetic hearing, stood quietly observing, refraining from agreeing with her friend that yes, that was indeed tactless and stupid. Instead, she watched the shape of their ship's captain recede down the far corridor.

He was a good man. And, despite her gruffness and shortcomings, he seemed to have taken a shine to her friend. And, while not possessing actual clockwork machinery in her body, that observation got the proverbial gears in her head turning a little faster as she pondered her dear friend and the stoic space pirate they'd only just met.

"Hmm," she quietly said to herself, then dragged her load of parts to her waiting friend.

CHAPTER ELEVEN

Ara had no trouble navigating the vast distances between systems in this galaxy. Being a native of it, her jump magic was easily able to steer her to her intended destination with pinpoint accuracy, as only a powerful Zomoki could.

Naturally, a ship powered by a talented complement of Drooks could do the same, but Ara's species was unique in their ability to jump completely unaided. And more than that, she could do so with even greater precision than a Drook.

Charlie had asked about that early on in their flight from Visla Maktan's estate, when he'd first freed his dragon friend. It was all so new to him back then, the very concept of an animal being able to not only talk and use magic, but also fly in the vacuum of space, and then flash out of existence in one part, popping back into existence in another? Well, it was enough to make his head spin.

Or it would have been, had he not just spent several years as a gladiator slave fighting alien combatants in arenas across a strange galaxy.

Ara had explained that it was the Zomoki's keen sense of smell for all things, magic and otherwise, that allowed them such accuracy as they flew. The skill translated into an ability to almost subconsciously home in on the location they had selected. And Ara, being as old and experienced as she was, had a long memory of places she'd been and the unique smells of those systems.

So when the time came to jump back to where the portal to the other galaxy was hidden, she had no trouble jumping to the periphery of that system, rather than into the thick of the hostile alien ships they'd encountered on their first arrival.

The plan was a simple one. Place the bulk of the magical Balamar waters they had collected in a safe hiding place on a particularly dense moon they had scouted out on their last visit.

The waters, priceless as they were, would be protected by layers upon layers of wards and booby trap spells, in addition to being buried beneath a carefully layered, then sealed, pile of rocks, magically marked so only those with the correct spell could locate it.

If this Visla Dominus truly was a Wampeh of the same type as Bawb, then those waters could very well be their best weapon against him. Of course, that would mean they'd need to get close enough to splash it upon his skin if they ever hoped to weaken him, if not make him combust outright.

In any case, it was a cache of something that was both a weapon, but also a panacea for their forces. For the Balamar waters would not only harm the Wampeh visla, but would conversely heal all others they touched. And if their recipient happened to be from the other galaxy? They could actually drink the water, taking the healing properties within their bodies to increase the potency.

It was the one thing that those from Charlie's realm could do that would kill those from this galaxy outright, with the exception of Ara, and that was only because of her exceptional age and strength.

For his part, Bawb had been calm and professional while

handling the sealed containers as they stashed them on the little moon. Yes, he had been wearing his spacesuit, which should protect him quite well from any spillage should one of the magically sealed vessels rupture.

But for the man to help carry gallons upon gallons of a liquid of which but a few drops would mean his end spoke volumes to the Wampeh's commitment to their mission.

"Okay, that's all of it," Charlie said when they placed the last of the containers in their hiding spot. "I'm keeping just the one smaller container with us, but I'm double-bagging it for safety."

"Double-bagging?" Bawb asked.

"Earth slang. It means I'm putting one container inside another so that even if one breaks, the second will still be intact. Wouldn't want you accidentally blowing up on us, after all."

"Your consideration is greatly appreciated, Charlie," Bawb said with a chuckle as he laid a deadly series of booby trap spells around the now-innocuous pile of rocks.

That they were sitting on a moon so close to the enemy fleet waiting to pass through the portal and conquer Earth and its surrounding worlds was more than a little disconcerting, though with Ara's stealthy approach from the far end of the system they had been able to arrive entirely undetected.

Still, the proximity of so great a number of deadly vessels had them all a little on edge. It would take just one scout ship spotting them to set the whole lot of hostile craft upon them. And without Rika's strange magic on hand and ready to help negate the enemy's containment spells, Ara could very well be overwhelmed by sheer numbers, boxed in and unable to break free of their spells to jump.

But Marban had his own mission, and that was keeping Rika clear of the system until their chrono aboard the *Fujin* told them the portal was about to open. The *Coratta* did not possess a shimmer, so they had to stay away until just before the designated time. Only then would they risk jumping into the area near the portal, for they, too, were carrying a priceless cargo.

Charlie and Bawb had unloaded half of their stash of Balamar waters into the *Coratta*'s hold, ensuring Rika would be able to distribute the magical solution to the key members of their own fleet, standing by on the other side of the portal. Of course, Rika was also crucial in that plan, in that they'd be flying a Tslavar warship into the midst of a deadly group of Earth's defenses, all of their weapons pointed at the portal, ready to fire.

Rika would be squawking out their identity on open comms the second they passed through, the *Fujin* flying directly beside the alien ship as an escort. Only in that manner could they ensure they wouldn't be blown out of the sky by their own forces. 'Friendly fire,' as it was called, though there was nothing friendly about it.

Once they'd rejoined the fleet, Rika would then distribute the waters, as they'd discussed, helping Zed and the rest of his AI fighting force figure a delivery method to use some of the liquid in an offensive manner, while spreading the rest to key members of the fleet, helping bolster them from magical attacks, as the waters would do, for a short while.

"What about an explosive sabot from a railgun?" Jo had suggested as they brainstormed ideas on how to turn a simple water supply into a weapon.

"But how would it reach the target?" Rika wondered. "They'll have magical shielding to deflect projectiles, I'm assuming."

"Perhaps. But if we coat the tip with the waters, as well a bit of your other galaxy magic, that should help it pass through, right? Wouldn't that possibly pierce the shielding?"

"I don't know, Jo. And the water would just peel away at those speeds."

"Not in space. No friction," her cyborg friend replied. "And if you magic it on there real good, I'm sure you could find a way to make it stick, while also letting whatever it is about your magic that conflicts with theirs do its thing."

Rika pondered the idea. It *could* work. Her power definitely did not play nice with the enemy's magic, but she wasn't sure if it would when the time came, and stakes were the highest they'd be. But given the circumstances, she supposed anything was worth a try.

"All right, I guess we can rig something up. And yeah, if the sabot is designed to vaporize once inside the target's hull, you'd be looking at a fine mist of water that would be deadly to this visla Charlie was talking about. But I'm just worried what it might do to any of the rest of the crew it comes in contact with. We know what these waters do, and we don't want to be healing our enemies in the process."

"I would normally agree," Jo said. "But if we help a few of their foot soldiers while taking out their leader, I think it's well worth the trade-off."

"Valid point," Rika said. "Well, we've got a few days until the portal opens, so I guess we have time to rig something up. I still need to finish mounting the weapons systems on my mech, though. Can you start fiddling with a few railgun sabots to see if they can be converted to hold fluid without losing structural integrity?"

"Sure thing," Jo replied.

"Good. I'll finish up the mech, then we can test a couple of rounds with regular old tap water to see if they'll hold up."

"Sweet. I'm on it," Jo said, heading off to work on her new project.

Rika felt a small flush of hope spreading in her chest. She knew it was a dangerous thing to harbor, but the feeling remained. They were fighting an uphill battle, but it really did seem the tides *could* turn, if their luck held out.

But that was a big *if*.

CHAPTER TWELVE

"Do you smell it?" Ara asked as they drifted in space after jumping to the next system.

"Yeah, there's something familiar about this," Charlie replied. *"It's kind of like that strange magic when we first crossed through the portal, you know?"*

"Yes, I do," Ara replied. *"Though the magic is only residual at this point, it would seem this Visla Dominus we are seeking was here not too long ago."*

"So what do we do? Can you zero in on which of these worlds they landed on?"

Ara chuckled softly. *"Oh, I can do better than that. I have secured a trace that should take us to the very city they were visiting. I believe it is there that you will be most likely to source the information we are seeking."*

"I agree," Bawb said. *"This is recent, and the odds are in our favor. We should land at once and make our way into the city the Wise One has determined was their destination. Rika and the others will be crossing back over very shortly, and I think we all would like to be able to join up with them if possible, to bring this information back to the fleet."*

"*Yeah, and it'd be good to join up with Leila,*" Charlie said. "*But are you sure about heading back with Hunze still out here somewhere?*"

Bawb's brow furrowed slightly. "*She is more than capable of taking care of herself now. And while I would naturally prefer locating her as soon as possible, the threat is too great. This information must be brought to the fleet the moment we acquire it. And once we are safely on the other side, we can modify the portal tether to allow a return flight whenever we desire.*"

"*Which would be pretty much immediately, I assume,*" Charlie said.

"*You would be correct,*" Bawb said.

"*You know I'm coming with you when you hop back, right?*"

"*I do. And I know better than to try to talk you out of it,*" Bawb replied. "*But we are getting ahead of ourselves. First, we must source our intel. Then we can think about these other options.*"

Ara took the two of them on a direct path to the mid-sized world orbiting the red dwarf sun. Their intended destination was the middle of the three planets residing within the Goldilocks Zone.

Charlie was glad for it, as while the other two would be either too warm or too cold, this planet would be just right.

They landed just as night fell in a small wooded area quite a distance outside of the bustling city, the darkness hiding their winged friend. Ara would have liked to have been able to deposit her friends closer, but even at night there would simply be too much of a risk of them being observed landing while atop a giant, red Zomoki. Not exactly what you wanted to do when stealth was the order of the day.

The dragon was rather hungry after their flight, but, annoyingly, there was simply no way she could safely hunt in the area without being spotted. Ara would have to wait to feast until later.

Charlie stowed his space suit and slid on a konus, though he didn't really need it at this point, his own powers having grown so substantially in recent weeks. But the device would allow him to cast without obviously tapping into that internal magic, and that was key when it came to remaining anonymous.

Bawb, likewise, stowed his suit and put on his most ornate konuses, leaving his customary armlets in his storage bin mounted to Ara's harness.

Also left behind was his Ootaki hair from Hunze. While useful in battle, it would merely draw attention if worn while gathering information. He stowed it along with his other possessions, safe under the protection of their dragon friend.

"Are you ready?" Bawb asked.

"As ready as I'm going to be," Charlie replied.

The two then began the long trek to the commerce route they had noted on their initial approach. Within just a few hours, they had secured a ride aboard one of the floating conveyances and reached the city. Now they could begin their work in earnest.

Bawb was in character, Binsala the trader already in attendance as they set off to gather all the intel they could manage. Charlie was always amazed at the assassin's ability to shift into such a polar opposite persona like flipping a switch. But with that many years of practice––and with your life on the line if you failed––he supposed it was only natural he'd be so proficient.

One of the benefits of Binsala's profession was that it was never thought unusual when a trader offered up some strange item in exchange for goods and services. And having effectively wiped out a dozen ships worth of Tslavar mercenaries, they had acquired quite a collection of items they might use in trade, as well as coin pillaged from the dead.

It was distasteful, but in war, anything goes.

The city itself was a bit like a crocodile in a calm pond. Everything appeared tranquil and serene on the surface, but there was unseen danger lurking just beneath, ready to take advantage of any misstep.

Bawb was very familiar with this sort of place, as was Charlie at this point. It was dangerous, but also the exact sort of city where the right amount of payment might be able to overcome people's reluctance and actually acquire them the information they sought.

The men two sidled up to a cantina and stepped out of the night, into the artificial light and music. An odor of sweat and pungent-sweet smoke greeted them, along with the stares of a good many of the establishment's patrons.

"Come, Binsala! Let me buy you a drink!" Charlie said, slapping his friend on the back and ushering him to the bar.

It was the third such establishment they'd been to, each of the prior having been situated likewise in close proximity to where they'd learned the mysterious ship had landed just the day before. Someone had to know something. The only question was, who would that someone be, and how much would it take to buy that information?

"I tell you, Binsala, I hear it was a magnificent vessel. And parked so close by. It pains me we missed it by only a day. Oh, the wonderful trade we could have made with men of that type of power and wealth," Charlie said, loud enough for a few around them to hear.

"Yes, my friend, it seems we will have to take our goods elsewhere. It is such a shame, though. And we were prepared to offer such a sizable commission to whoever arranged a meeting with their captain," Bawb said, slightly slurring his words as he downed another drink, completely sober as his fluid displacement spell yet again deposited the beverage twenty meters away as soon as it passed his lips.

"Did I hear you mention missing a ship?" one of the scantily clad women working the bar asked. Her skin was a lighter shade of green, but Charlie had learned to tell the difference between

Alatsavs and Tslavars some time ago. This woman, while quite pleasing to the eye, was of the latter, not the former.

"The ship?" Bawb asked.

"I'm sorry," the woman said. "I don't mean to pry, but I couldn't help but overhear you just now."

"Nothing to be worried about," Bawb said, drunkenly putting his arm around the woman in a manner Hunze would not have been pleased about were he not merely playing a role. "But do you mean to tell me that such a divine creature as yourself is caught up in the unsavory business of men of trade like my friend and I?"

"Oh, I'm not involved in that sort of trade," she said, her eyes saying more than her lips. "But I have a cousin who is, and perhaps he could help get you in touch with the ones you so narrowly missed doing trade with. I know he had dealings with them while they were here."

"Really?" Bawb asked, his blurry eyes locking on her with greedy interest. "That would be amazing! And there would be a commission for you. Oh, yes! For you and your cousin. Did you hear that? She says she can help us get in touch with them."

"I heard," Charlie said. "That's fantastic. It looks like this may be a profitable stop after all!"

"Shall I skree my cousin and arrange a meeting?" the woman asked.

"At once!" Bawb replied. "But tell me, what is your name, my most delightful of new friends?"

"I am Calimana," she replied.

"Calimana, it is a pleasure. I am Binsala. And this is my dear friend Charlie."

"Like the rebel? I haven't heard that name in a while. Is it back in fashion?"

"When my parents had me it was," Charlie replied. "But that was a long, long time ago."

"You don't seem so old."

"You'd be surprised," the human replied.

"I like surprises," Calimana said as she grinned at Charlie with a look that made him blush. She was game for whatever the night might bring, it seemed. "I'll be back in a little bit," she said, then sashayed away, a little extra sway in her hips for the admiring men's benefit.

Charlie leaned on his friend drunkenly. "You think she'll come through?" he asked.

Bawb watched her with practiced eyes. "Oh, yes. This is going to go just as we hoped."

CHAPTER THIRTEEN

Calimana had contacted her cousin shortly after making the offer to the two men at the bar, but it had been nearly two hours until her break finally gave her the freedom, to take them to meet him.

To their surprise, the cafe they arrived at was just a few minutes' walk from Calimana's place of employment. And more than that, it was a well-lit establishment of a respectable nature. The contrast to where they'd just spent far more time and coin than they'd have liked was striking.

"That's my cousin," the woman said, leading them to a deep brown-skinned, wiry man with black hair and bright yellow eyes.

"Your cousin?" Charlie asked.

"By marriage," Calimana replied, giving the man a kiss on the cheek. "Oxhan, these are the ones I told you about."

Oxhan was lean, but he had that coiled whip feel to him, as if his body was under constant tension and ready to spring. Both Charlie and Bawb recognized it as the posturing of a man who had learned enough about combat to know what dangers might befall him, but not enough to be more of a threat to others than himself.

"So, you're the man we need to see," Bawb's drunken trader persona began. "Your *lovely* cousin tells us you have engaged in trade with the owners of that magnificent vessel that was so recently docked here. You know, we've traveled a long way in search of just such a trading partner, and if you could tell us where they've gone to, and perhaps arrange a meeting with them via skree, we would be glad to pay you a commission on any trade we might make."

Charlie drunkenly shouldered past his friend. "And we have amazing things of great value, for the *discerning* buyer," he said, dropping a valuable, yet blank, vid disc on the table. It was just one of many things taken from the captured Tslavar ships after their battle at the Balamar Wastelands, and Bawb had told Charlie that vid discs of this particular quality were exceedingly rare to come by in all but the most moneyed hands.

Therefore, the plan was to allow a glimpse of it as a sample of their wares to help pique the interest of their contacts when the discussion warranted it. And that time was now.

Oxhan's eyes flashed to the device, but his poker face was good, and he didn't show his interest. At least, not too overtly.

"Now, when can you get us in touch with these men you traded with?" Bawb continued.

The lean man shifted in his seat. "*Well...* I didn't exactly *trade* with these particular men. Not the vessel's port contacts, who happen to still be in the city, that is. We didn't exactly get along."

Charlie and Bawb shared a concerned look.

"I'm sorry to hear that. But thank you for your time. I guess we'll just––" Charlie said.

"Oh, but I can still help you in your trade," Oxhan said. "They may not like *me*, but I'm sure when they see what you have to offer, they'll be interested in discussing trade. And I know exactly where they will be."

"You do?"

"Indeed. And I'll tell you where they are. For a price, of course," the lean man said. "I'm sure we can come to an arrangement."

He nodded to Calimana, and the woman slid behind Bawb and began massaging his shoulders.

Bawb smiled with drunken delight. "You know? I think we can work something out," he replied.

A commission was agreed upon, and a few pieces of decent worth were left with Oxhan as an initial good faith deposit, with the remainder to be paid once successful trade had occurred.

Calimana left them to it, apologizing that she needed to finish her shift before she could join back up with them later. She then left them to it, but not without giving both Charlie and Bawb a smoldering look before leaving them to their business.

Oxhan guided the two men across town to a quiet area frequented by the hardier of the working class. It was a place where laborers unwound after a long day of work, and was precisely the sort of area a local trade contact would spend their downtime in.

"Three Tslavars," the wiry man said, pointing to a dimly lit bar. "The heavy one is Jorkan. He's the boss. The two with him are his assistants."

"Muscle, you mean," Charlie said with a laugh. "We are not concerned about such things. We merely wish to establish a profitable trade for all involved."

"Then I wish you the best of luck," Oxhan said. "I will meet you tomorrow morning at the little cafe where we first met. We can then discuss further trades I may be able to help you with."

"Excellent," Bawb said. "Binsala the trader is ever in your debt for this service. And if it proves a profitable exchange, you can be assured that word of Oxhan's value will be well-known in my circles."

"It is appreciated, Binsala. Now, I'll leave you to it. Best if I don't show my face in there if you wish to get off on the right foot," Oxhan said, then turned and headed off into the night.

Charlie looked at his friend. "You ready?"

"Always."

They casually entered the establishment and made their way to the bar, where they took seats to observe the other patrons. It was a busy evening, the workers recently off shift letting off steam with drink and laughter.

"*There they are. Far end of the room at the low table,*" Charlie silently noted, spying the men they were looking for.

"*I see them,*" Bawb replied.

The duo actually had no intention of engaging in trade negotiations with the men. Far from it, in fact. Their intentions were of a different bent. One might even be to watch the men and follow them, separating them from the rest of the bar patrons so they could get information out of them in a more old-fashioned way.

Not more than a half hour had passed when Jorkan, the Tslavar boss, and his lackeys rose from their seats and headed out into the night. After waiting a minute, Charlie and Bawb followed, walking with the weaving gait of drunkards as they blended in with the crowd on the streets.

The foot traffic was rapidly thinning when their quarry turned down an alleyway up ahead. Charlie and Bawb hurried along to ensure they wouldn't lose the men, but only a dozen steps into the alley, they noted they were not alone.

Tslavars were coming out of the shadows, and not just the three they'd been tailing.

"You've been following me," Jorkan said, walking toward them as more and more of his comrades crowded in around the hapless traders. "I don't like when people follow me."

"There's been a terrible misunderstanding," Bawb slurred. "We are merely seeking trade with––"

"Shut it, Wampeh. If you wanted trade, you'd have spoken with me the moment you entered the bar. Isn't that right, Oxhan?"

The wiry man stepped into the light. "It is, Jorkan. I told you there was something odd about them. Nosing around. Asking about the visla's ship."

"You did good," the Tslavar said.

"Oxhan? You double-crossed us?" Charlie said, shocked. "But we gave you a good faith deposit."

"Which I will be keeping, by the way, thank you very much. Along with whatever goods you may be carrying," Oxhan said. "Ooh, and I get dibs on that one's konuses," he added.

Jorkan shrugged and turned to his men. "Take their weapons and bind their hands."

Charlie and Bawb looked at one another. There were over a dozen well-armed Tslavar mercenaries crowding around them in the tight alley. If there was a fight, it would be bloody.

Bawb nodded to Charlie once, and they both stood down, allowing the back-stabber and his friend's men to take their konuses, and even the blade hanging at Bawb's hip.

Disarmed, they were then ushered farther down the alleyway, until they reached a squat, wide two-story building. Jorkan's men shoved them inside and took them up to the top floor, where they found themselves in a room full of men of action. *Unsavory* men of action. Tslavars.

Another person was waiting for them as well. A person Oxhan bent down and kissed warmly on the lips when he entered the room.

"Why am I not surprised?" Charlie said, taking a seat.

"Because maybe you're not quite as stupid as you look?" Calimana replied, her feet propped up on the same table her drink was resting on.

"So this whole thing was a setup?" he asked.

"'Fraid so," she replied.

Bawb took a seat beside his friend as he counted the number of enemies present in the room, taking stock of their weapons and locations, all while maintaining his drunken outward appearance. To any observing, he was a defeated man. But Charlie knew far better.

"But if you knew we were looking for information, why go to all this trouble? Why not just steer us the wrong way, or say you didn't know where to find Visla Dominus's ship?" Charlie asked.

That got Jorkan's attention. "You know the visla's name?"

"Obviously," he replied. "But you didn't know that when you set all this up."

"No, we didn't," Calimana replied. "We just wanted to take you for all you were worth."

"A simple shakedown?"

"Yes. Though now it looks like we'll need to skree to the ship on Rupsaval and inform them you were looking for them, nosing into things you shouldn't be."

A little smile teased the corner of Bawb's mouth, but he stayed silent.

"So, the visla is on Rupsaval?" Charlie asked.

"Oh, they're figuring it out, Calimana," Oxhan said with a sneer. "Yes, that's where the ship you so foolishly seek is. Not that it will do you any good. Not now that you're our prisoners. You fell right into our trap, you fools."

Bawb's smile grew, his pointed fangs peeking out slightly.

"And you fell into ours," the Wampeh said.

The way he said it unnerved Oxhan, despite their numeric superiority and the captives being unarmed. "What do you mean by that?" he asked.

"*Well...*" Charlie said, "the thing is, that's really all we needed from you idiots. And, if you don't mind, we'll be going now." He rose to his feet, Bawb casually joining him.

"What are you talking about? You're surrounded. And we have your konuses," Jorkan said.

"Yeah, but I don't need one," Charlie replied, casting a little spell. His and Bawb's restraints dropped to the floor.

"He's a caster!" Jorkan managed to cry out before things got *really* interesting when the roof of the building abruptly tore free, and a hungry Zomoki stuck her head in and swallowed him whole.

Charlie and Bawb climbed up onto Ara's back as she merrily devoured everyone in the room. The scattering Tslavars who had been stationed outside weren't privy to the conversation that had taken place inside. They didn't know what the two prisoners had been after. All they did know was a giant Zomoki had swooped down from the sky and eaten their comrades. It was fortunate, for Ara and her friends really didn't want to go hunting down the survivors.

Ara flapped her wings hard and carried them aloft, making quick time for their wooded hiding spot so her friends could don their space suits before they made for the void of space.

"You think maybe that was a bit of overkill?" Charlie asked with a laugh.

"Perhaps," Ara replied. *"But I was rather peckish. And though I'm not normally a fan of Tslavar, that really hit the spot."*

The three shared a good laugh, quickly suited up, then continued their quest, flying up into the night sky.

"Are you two secured?" Ara asked.

"We are," Bawb replied.

"Very well. To Rupsaval we go."

Then, in a flash of magic, the space dragon and her passengers were gone.

CHAPTER FOURTEEN

"Again, Karasalia," Korbin commanded, though in a far gentler tone than her father ever used.

Kara nodded and focused, sending a series of small force spells forward, making a wooden dummy in her path wobble ever so slightly.

"Better," Korbin said, watching his niece practicing her spells under his knowing eye.

"It was still pathetic," Kara griped.

"Nonsense. Even the greatest vislas had to start somewhere. Now, I want you to focus on calming your mind. You're too caught up in your own thoughts to cast effortlessly. Just relax for a count of thirty backwards, then cast once again. Okay?"

"Okay."

Kara closed her eyes and took a deep breath, then did as her uncle asked, slowly counting backwards as she tried to clear her mind of all extraneous thoughts.

Unlike her father, Uncle Korbin's methods were a bit unconventional, to say the least. Where Nikora would badger, Korbin would soothe. Where Kara's father would demand perfection, her uncle cheered her results, even when less than optimal, which was pretty much every time.

Korbin stepped aside and gestured for Visanya to join him.

"Tell me, Visanya. You and Kara have been friends pretty much your whole lives. I've not seen my niece in a great many years, which is entirely my own fault for living the lifestyle I do. But tell me, how long has she been so weak?"

"I don't know, really. I mean, she's stronger than I am, that's for sure."

"You just cannot cast," Korbin said. "It's not your fault, though I would assume having powerful adoptive parents such as yours could make a girl feel pressured at times."

"Yeah," Vee replied. "Wait, you knew I was adopted?"

"Of course," he replied with a warm smile.

"I thought they kept it a secret," Vee said. "But as for Kara, she's been this way pretty much since her mom died when we were little. She never really grew into her power after that point. Why do you ask?"

Korbin looked at his niece as she opened her eyes and cast the spell, this time with a clearer mind. The wooden dummy rocked in place, far more than before.

"Better still," Korbin said, turning his attention back to Vee. "Because, Visanya, she is growing stronger, and rapidly at that. In just the day you've been with me her power has come more sharply into focus."

"Well, she usually does seem stronger when we go on little trips. I think getting away from home does her good. Lets her mind relax a bit."

"Yes, perhaps. But this seems rapid. More than normal for someone her age. Most growth spurts happen several years younger," Korbin said.

Vee didn't know how to respond to that observation. Kara had always been Kara, and assessing her power was not something she'd ever really paid attention to.

"You know, I really should get back home. My parents are going to be worried by now. I mean, normally I'll stay with Kara for a day, maybe two, but beyond that and my parents will be concerned."

"I understand," Korbin replied. "I will have one of my trusted associates send word to your parents. He will deliver the message personally to either your father or mother, and no other."

"Why would you need to do that?"

"Because it seems something strange is going on with Kara," he said. "First, she is kidnapped, and in Nikora's own city, no less––a wildly brash move for even the most brazen of criminals. Visla Palmarian's power is known throughout the galaxy, so for Kara to have been targeted tells me something big is going down. And you are her best friend."

"Yeah, but what does that have to do with anything? I was there when they took her, but they didn't look at me twice, so what does that matter?"

"Because, Visanya, whoever is up to this mischief would know you are special to Kara, and they would likely use you to try and find her. For that reason, it is too risky for you to go home just yet, and also too risky for you to call your parents yourself. Should the communication be intercepted, then whoever is doing this would know where you are, and thus where Karasalia is."

Vee's pale-yellow skin turned a bit paler at the man's words. "Do you really think we're in danger?"

"I can't say for certain, but I do know that it is always preferable to be overly cautious rather than under. Especially given what we're seeing from my niece."

"What do you mean?"

"I'll show you," he said, walking to where Kara was again attempting to center herself and control her power. "Karasalia, your father has trained you in the use of a konus, I see, from the small one you were wearing earlier."

"Yes. He's actually having a new one made for me. Says I need something powerful and befitting the daughter of a visla. Something that will give me the appearance of a talented and formidable user to help deter people from any foolish ideas like trying to kidnap me again."

"A logical proposition," Korbin said. "And you've trained with more powerful konuses?"

"Not really. I mean, I've worn one a few times, but never for long. Father always said a visla's daughter must learn to draw from her own internal power. I guess I've been failing him pretty miserably in that regard," she said, a slight shadow falling over her demeanor.

"Well, I would like you to try this spell again, only this time wearing something special," her uncle said, pulling a heavy, ornate konus from his wrist.

"But that's yours," Kara protested.

"And you're family, so it's only fitting you should learn to cast with it. Now, please, try it on."

Kara hesitated. Her uncle was a powerful man, and to wear his konus would be to step into some *very* large shoes.

"Go on, Kara," Vee urged.

The peer pressure worked, and she timidly accepted the device, sliding the still-warm metal onto her wrist. It felt no different than any other konus she'd ever worn, but that was sort of the point. Until you started casting, it was just resting potential. Stored magic waiting to be unleashed.

"Go on," Korbin said. "Try the spell again, and this time, give it everything you've got. Let's see what you can do with that on your wrist."

Kara had to admit, the thrill of using so powerful a device with permission was an exciting prospect. Her father never let her use anything of real power, and even when training in his presence, she was always required to maintain complete control.

But her uncle was a bit of a rebel in that regard, and with her father nowhere to be seen, she had carte blanche to really use the device.

"Come, Visanya, let's step back and give Karasalia some room," Korbin suggested, ushering the teen away from the wooden dummy. "Don't forget to calm your mind and center yourself," he called out. "Even with a konus, your power still must be directed from within. The *intent* of the spell comes from you."

The teen and her best friend's uncle stood by, watching as Kara prepared to try yet again to knock the target over. Thus far she'd only managed to wobble it at best. But if she really tried, with the help of her uncle's powerful konus, she felt maybe this once she could actually succeed.

With the utmost focus and concentration, Kara summoned the spell from within, just as her uncle had instructed her. She let her mind relax, the words of it effortlessly sliding across her lips as she channeled the intent from within, her mind making the invisible connection to draw power from the konus.

Kara was nearly knocked from her feet as the wooden dummy burst into hundreds of tiny pieces, shattered by the sheer force of her spell. She stared at the aftermath, her eyes wide with shock.

"I-I'm sorry, Uncle Korbin. It was an accident. I didn't know it would do that. I told you I shouldn't use your konus," she blurted, quickly sliding the band from her wrist and pressing it back into his hands, then running from the training chamber.

Vee flashed an angry look at her friend's uncle, powerful visla be damned. "Why did you do that to her? That's really messed up, tricking Kara like that. She's insecure enough as it is without people like you playing games with her."

Visanya was about to storm out when Korbin gently grasped

her shoulder. "A moment, Visanya," he said quietly. "There's something you should know."

"What?" she hissed, her anger palpable.

"You must keep this between you and me," he said. "Swear it." The look in his eye said he was dead serious.

"Ugh. Fine, I swear," she said. "Now, what's so important?"

A smile crept onto the man's face as he tossed the konus from hand to hand. "This is not my konus," he said. "I mean, not the one I use. In fact, if you'll try it on, I'm sure you'll notice there is no magical charge stored in it at all. Kara was simply too flustered to notice."

Visanya took the band and slid it on, reaching for any sense of power. But Korbin was telling the truth. It was bone-dry, with not a drop of magic within.

"But if this isn't powered..."

"Yes," he said, watching the realization dawn on her. "Karasalia did that entirely on her own. All she needed was a push to get her over her own mental blocks."

"But-but she's not that powerful. She's never been."

"I know," he replied. "And that is why we must keep you both secret and safe until we can figure out what is really going on. Now, go check on your friend. I will be along shortly. And remember, you mustn't say a word of this to her."

Vee looked at him differently than before. There was more to her friend's uncle than met the eye, that much was certain. With a slight nod, she turned and went in search of her friend, leaving him to ponder just what this all might mean.

Whatever it was, things within the Palmarian household were definitely not what they appeared.

CHAPTER FIFTEEN

Vee and Kara were out back of Korbin's main house, sitting on the long porch, looking out at the rolling hills of the unusual, rustic town a man of such power would choose as his home, fleeing the pressures of civilization.

They were both notably calmer, sipping from mugs of frothy Trokkan nibs, ground to a powder, heated, and mixed with diluted Boramus milk. The resulting beverage had a calming, restorative effect. That the taste was pretty amazing was a fortunate side benefit.

Uncle Korbin casually strolled over to join them, taking his time as he examined the tall, violet flowers just coming into bloom along the pathway. He'd planted them from seed a few years prior, and with a bit of nurturing, they'd grown tall and strong.

He had made several skree calls after Karasalia's impressive display in the training space. First was to one of his associates who had done business with Visanya's family.

While he was certain they were good people, strange things were afoot, and confirmation, even of what were expected to be facts, was an extra step he deemed reasonable for all of their safety.

He'd also reached out to one of his most trusted couriers to take a message to them in person. No skree calls for the girl's parents. Not with his niece in whatever trouble this might be. The message would be presented with a personal affirmation from the girl herself that she was fine and merely away on an impromptu trip with Kara but would be back soon.

It wasn't a lie, exactly. More of a stretching of the truth. And it would hopefully afford them a little breathing room before the girl's parents tracked down the visla to inquire of their daughter.

Other resources had been activated as well, following Kara's display. Not just on Slafara, but across the systems. Korbin may have presented as a laid-back country gentleman, but he still possessed a robust network of eyes and ears, put in place over the decades.

"What are you up to, Nikora?" he wondered, after he had finished tasking the last of them to *quietly and carefully* dig into the visla's affairs. They'd known one another since they were children, and even though they'd grown apart over the years, that was more due to distance and the pressures of work life for one, and the desire to avoid precisely that sort of thing by the other.

Secrets were normal for a man of his friend's power. Normal, for any visla, really, and Korbin certainly had his fair share of them as well. But this? This was looking like something different. Bigger. And he was honestly surprised at what he'd seen so far, and that was with just the slightest of probing.

"How are you feeling, Kara?" he asked, taking a seat with the girls on the porch. "I hope you aren't concerned about the damage. These things happen when we train, after all."

Kara took a deep sip from her mug, composing her thoughts before replying. "Better," she finally said. "I guess I'm just so used to my father's reactions when I mess up."

"You didn't mess up, Kara," Vee said. "You're learning. Everyone has things go weird when they're learning."

"Visanya is right," Korbin said. "And believe me, Ser Braxxim put up with a *lot* of mistakes from his pupils."

"Ser Braxxim?" Kara asked.

"Ah, your father never mentioned him, I see," Korbin said. "He was our teacher when we were just boys. An amazing caster and wonderful instructor."

"How is it I never heard of him? It seems Father has talked about pretty much every power user in the system at one time or another," Kara said.

"Oh, he's not a power user," Korbin said, the warm smile of memory creeping onto his face. "The man possessed hardly a drop of power of his own. But, oh my, could that man wield the konus and slaap like no other. In fact, despite his lack of natural magic, he could even use a claithe better than most vislas."

"I thought that was impossible," Vee said. "Only the most powerful of vislas have the ability to wield a claithe. That's why they're so exceptionally rare."

"Normally, yes. And you'll be hard-pressed to find a claithe anywhere these days."

"I think Father has one," Kara noted.

"And he's strong enough to use one. But for most, the use of them became simply too difficult to predict, and too many underpowered casters were attempting to use them after the Council fell and their assets were pillaged. Several of their strongest weapons made their way into hands that had no business possessing them, and great tragedy befell those poor souls every time."

"But this Ser Braxxim could use one?" Vee asked.

"Yes. An amazing man, and a most patient teacher. I pale at the thought of what might have happened if your father and I had been under the care of any other, in fact."

"Why is that?" Kara asked.

"Because, while I always possessed a sizable amount of power, your father was simply on an entirely other level, even as a young boy. Why, once, when we were out playing in the woods near Ser Braxxim's training facility, we were practicing spells on local wildlife, seeing who could stun a running Drozan as it ran from burrow to burrow."

"That's not very nice," Kara said.

"Not particularly, in the hindsight of maturity. But we were boys, and boys do things to test themselves. It is a part of the male growth process. Part of our typically more aggressive natures. But this was all in fun, and no harm was meant by it."

"Tell that to the poor Drozan," Kara replied.

"Comparatively, they got off quite easy," Korbin replied. "You see, that day was when I saw your father's *true* potential. And to be honest, it frightened away most of his other friends."

"What did he do?"

"We were just leaving to return from the woods when a Bundabist crashed out of the bushes and startled him, nearly knocking him down. You know how large Bundabist can get, and this was a full grown one that very nearly trampled him."

"What happened?" Vee asked.

"He was scared, and he cast purely on instinct. We were so young, we'd only learned the most basic of spells at that point, you see. But what came out of him was pure, unfocused power, and rather than stunning the beast or pushing it back, the poor animal was torn to pieces and scattered into the trees. We were all covered in bits of gore, so I think you can understand why the others were hesitant to be friends with him after that. They were afraid, and rightly so, I guess."

"But you stayed," Kara said. "Because you knew you'd be safe. Father always said you're almost as powerful as he is."

Korbin laughed. "Oh, my dear. That's very kind of him, but your father only says that to make me feel like an equal. But truth be told, I'm nowhere near his strength. No one is."

"But you're a visla," Vee interjected. "And a strong one. So why live all alone out in the middle of nowhere when you could live in a city and be running things?"

"Why do people always want to run things?" Korbin joked with a chuckle. "Visanya, your father is an emmik, is he not?"

"Yeah."

"And is he regularly stressed by his duties? Taken from his personal matters at inopportune times?"

"Well..."

"So, you've seen what that life can do to you. I must say, I admire your parents for what they did. Despite the strains of their positions, they adopted you and raised you into quite a well-adjusted young woman."

"I guess I never really thought about how they're bound by their power," Vee said.

"But now you see," Korbin said. "And for Kara's father it is so very much worse. Always being called upon, always forced to do for others when sometimes he'd rather do anything else. No, I like my life being precisely that. *My* life."

He rose to his feet again and looked out across the hills of his quiet little homestead. "What do you say we train a bit more?" he asked. "You too, Visanya. I have a smaller konus I'd like you to try out for size. And who knows, maybe you'll learn to cast yet."

The girls, relaxed and in good spirits, finished their mugs and joined him walking back to the little outer building to train a bit more. Though he didn't say so, Korbin was very interested to see what else Kara could do. She was improving rapidly, though whether it was her innate skills or his talents as a teacher, he was unsure.

CHAPTER SIXTEEN

Cleaned up and free of grease and red soil, the swirling ink within Rika's skin was visible where her tank top wasn't covering. Though the white pigment possessed incredibly strong magical properties, it was not glowing or otherwise standing out as she relaxed with the pirate captain of her current ride.

As the two shared a drink in the commandeered ship's galley while the rest of the crew entertained themselves, Marban couldn't help but be interested in the intriguing map of interwoven lines faintly decorating the strong-willed woman. And when he was told of their properties, his interest only increased.

"You *absorbed* power from a black sun?" the pirate marveled. "Actually took the magic and stored it within yourself? That's amazing!"

Rika felt slightly uncomfortable in the face of all the attention. "Well, yeah. But it wasn't an intentional thing. It just sort of happened, and now it's bonded to me for whatever reason. I just have to wonder what might have happened if we didn't get out of that system sooner."

"You might have become the greatest caster ever to live!" Marban exclaimed with a jolly laugh.

"Yeah, or I might have accidentally killed myself along with everyone in the city," Rika replied. "No, I think we got out of there at just the right time. At least until I learned to better control that weird magic."

"And that's how you powered the metal—I mean, the *mech* in the cargo bay? With this absorbed magic?"

"A combination, really. The magic from my galaxy is what I truly control. The new magic I absorbed is like adding a power booster to it, only it's hard to direct. Or it was. I'm getting the hang of it, finally."

"Being forced to use it in battle didn't hurt," Marban noted. "One tends to act and not overthink when fighting for one's life, I've found."

Rika chuckled. "True, that. And jumping into a mech and making it function after, well, *everything*, was interesting, I'll say that."

"I can imagine," he replied. "And thank you for allowing me to assist you in upgrading your mech. It is such a drastically different type of thing from any we possess in this realm. I am greatly enjoying learning more about this thing you call tech."

"You're a quick study," Rika replied. "And I'm glad for the extra set of hands. I just hope Jo doesn't lose one of hers," she added with a laugh, looking across the galley at where her mechanic/co-pilot was entertaining several of the pirate crew.

They were quite fond of their Earth visitors, and so was their captain, though he was certainly more taken by one than the other. Across the room, her associate was bonding with his crew, and that made Marban glad. It was a strange situation they'd all been thrust into, and this novelty was helping ease them into it. The liberal rations of alcohol he allowed his men at the moment didn't hurt either.

"Hold him," Jo said with a laugh as she accepted a long knife from the lean, rather inebriated pirate at her side, gripping it pointy bit down.

Several sets of strong arms were pulling one of their crewmates to the table, forcing his arms from his side and spreading his splayed hand onto the table. Jo placed her hand on top of his, lining her fingers precisely with the unwilling pirate's.

She placed the knife's tip between their shared thumb and index finger.

"Hold still," she said, flashing him an amused grin.

Then she began moving, raising and lowering the knife, the tip gently tapping the space between their shared fingers one by one, the metal ringing off the table with each impact. The poor pirate didn't want to look, but one of his "buddies" was holding his head as well, forcing him to observe.

The knife started to move faster, Jo picking up the pace with the precision only a cyborg could manage, until it became a blur of motion, the knife flying across their hands, the tip rapping out a staccato on the table as it moved.

Jo drove the knife into the table hard enough to actually pierce the material, leaving the blade standing at attention.

"Thanks, buddy. That was fun," she said with a laugh, then got up to get another round of drinks for her friends.

The poor pirate was even paler than his usual shade of gray, a fine sheen of sweat on his brow. He gingerly lifted his hand and examined his flesh. There was no blood on the table, and his fingers, to his delight, remained attached.

"She loves that one," Rika said with a chuckle as she took a sip from her cup.

"An interesting woman, your friend," Marban replied.

"Oh, you have no idea."

Marban took a swig. "This waiting is horrible, you know. How much longer?"

"Jeez, why don't you ask 'are we there yet?'" Rika snarked back at him.

"I'm sorry. You're right. It's just, I'm a man of action. I guess I've forgotten how to simply sit and be for such long periods of time."

"Did you actually call yourself a 'man of action'?" Rika chided. "Wow."

Marban, space pirate captain and man of action, blushed a little.

"Anyway, the chrono says we've got to wait, so we wait. We can't jump there until the moment the portal pulls free. Any sooner and we'll risk a run-in with the bad guys, and trust me, we don't want that. We're seriously outnumbered."

"But Charlie said your magic could pierce their defenses. Something about it being from a different galaxy making it able to do what magic from this one simply cannot."

Rika focused her power a moment, causing her tattoos to glow slightly. She wasn't going to cast, and it was really nothing more than a party trick the way she was using it, but the reaction on Marban's face was worth the effort.

The glowing of the lines slowly faded back within her, but Marban's eyes remained glued to her skin. From across the room, Jo couldn't help but notice the man's interested gaze.

"The lines," he said. "They seem to converge, in a way."

"Oh, that," Rika said. "I'm still learning exactly how it works, but, essentially, they all draw power from my wellspring. That's why all of the lines trace back to the central power source."

"The wellspring?"

"It's the prime symbol. A dense pattern of arcane runes and designs that form the base of all my power. It's what connects me to my magic. I was almost dead when I received it, but the magic healed me. Healed me, while giving me power no one ever expected. I think it has something to do with what they did to me on this side of the portal, and the magic I had implanted in my head while I was here."

"A tattoo that serves as the core of all your power? Fascinating," Marban said. "I would very much like to see this design. It sounds most intriguing. You must show me one day."

Rika laughed and tapped her tank top. The spot right between her breasts. "Well, it's right here," she said, one eyebrow flicking briefly upward.

For the second time that day, Marban felt his face redden. Flustered, he abruptly rose to his feet. "Oh. Well, then. Uh, I really need to go check on the, uh, um––I should go see that we're on course," he said, excusing himself from the table just as Jo walked over, a thoroughly amused grin on her face.

The cyborg leaned in and gave Rika a big hug. "You're torturing the poor man," she whispered in her ear.

Rika and Jo laughed, both of their gazes flashing to the pirate making his way out of the galley. Marban couldn't help but note the closeness of the two women, and for just a moment, he wondered if perhaps they were more than just friends.

Confused, flustered, and desperately in need of being anywhere but there at that moment, Marban hurried out the door, leaving the confusing and surprisingly unsettling woman behind. Why she affected him like that was a mystery. But one he nevertheless hoped to solve one day.

But not today.

CHAPTER SEVENTEEN

Kara and Vee had slept well in the spare room Uncle Korbin had set them up in. Whether it was the exhaustion from their flight, the mental strain of their uncertain situation, or the physical result of their training sessions didn't really matter. What did, was that they greeted the new day rested, refreshed, and revitalized.

The reclusive visla was sipping a cup of tea in the kitchen when the teens came in for a late breakfast.

"Good morning," he said. "Though I should almost say good afternoon," he added with a grin. "I take it you both slept well?"

"Yes. Thank you, Uncle Korbin," Kara replied.

"Yeah, thank you," Vee said.

"I have some fresh Yortron jam and baked flat cakes prepared just this morning if you are in the mood for something sweet. Or if you prefer, I'd be glad to whip you up something savory instead. I have a full larder, so please, help yourselves to whatever you like."

The famished teens accepted his offers and tucked into warm stacks of the baked delight, while Korbin quickly prepared a savory hash with fresh vegetables from his garden and some smoky cheese made by one of his neighbors. It was quite a feast, but then, it wasn't every day he had visitors. At least, not those he invited to stay.

After the girls had slowed down their hunger-fueled food inhalation, he felt it was a good time to address the issue at hand.

"So, I've had word back from my people," he said. "Strange things they've heard rumor of. Unusual goings-on in multiple systems, not just our own. It correlates somewhat with what that odd little vessel parked out back says, but it's just *off* somehow, though I can't quite put my finger on how. It's disconcerting. Usually my sources provide rock-solid intelligence."

"You know you still talk like a visla, even though you live on a farm," Visanya said.

Korbin flashed an amused grin. "Just because I live on a farm does not mean I am a farmer," he said. "You'd do well to remember that not everyone is as they appear. You'll find this holds true more often than not as you get older."

"So, my father? He's not what he seems?" Kara asked.

"I really cannot say," Korbin replied. "Nikora was always a powerful man, but a good one. But something has changed, and I intend to get to the bottom of it."

"So you'll help us?" Kara asked.

"In the process of clearing this all up, yes, Karasalia, I will help you."

The girls both felt their spirits buoyed by his words. Having someone of his power helping, even if he chose to keep it hidden, was a huge boon to their cause. And he was a lifelong friend of Kara's father. If there did wind up being a price to pay when their parents found out what they'd been up to, having someone of Korbin's stature on their side would weigh greatly in their favor.

"You said you checked out what Pod was saying. Is there anything to all of that rambling?" Kara asked.

Korbin mulled over what he'd heard yet again. The reports were odd. Cryptic. But some bits did seem to hold a nugget of truth, and in his experience, that often meant there was likely more to the story than readily apparent.

"We spoke at length," he finally said. "Pod is a most unusual little vessel, but he does truly seem to be alive, though how, exactly, is still a mystery to me. But he kept speaking of a more powerful intelligence than he. A female called Freya."

"Yeah, we heard," Kara said. "But he said they split up while the heretic called Daisy was pursuing some sort of enemy ship. Apparently, at that time he lost the, what did he call it? A 'Navs tether signal' I think."

"Yes, he mentioned that. Akin to a skree, I believe. Something that allowed him to remain in constant contact with this Freya person. But he's lost that signal, and without it, I'm afraid he's somewhat useless to us."

"Useless? What are you talking about? It's a *talking* craft from who knows where," Kara replied.

"Yes, but he possesses a limited intellect, per his own admission. If we really want to know what's going on, we need to find Freya."

"Well, he's lost the signal, and he's too small to carry us all, so I guess there's no chance of that," Kara grumbled.

"Oh, but there is," her uncle replied. "He is a small one, that's for sure, but I've already loaded him into my personal craft. Also, my craft can fly much farther and faster than Pod is capable. And without drawing unwanted attention from onlookers."

"Yeah, he does kind of stand out," Vee said. "Even with his camouflage on, he makes a kind of blurry image when he flies."

"Precisely why we are taking him riding within my ship," Korbin said. "And as for finding his missing friend, my sources have sent me rough coordinates and information on several unusual disturbances in the system that occurred right around the time this assassin you speak of made her attempt on your father's life. With that to work with, I have my hopes that we might yet track down this Freya person and find out what's really going on."

"But what if the location is not in this system?" Kara asked. "What do we do then?"

"Pod himself said he separated from Freya when a craft they were tracking split off from a larger ship and headed to Slafara, docking at your father's tower. If that's the case, then it is highly likely Pod's counterpart could still be in the system."

Vee wolfed down the rest of her food and rose to her feet. "Come on, Kara. This could be it. We might actually get some answers."

"No need to rush your meals, girls. We can leave when you've fini—"

"No, Vee's right," Kara said, scarfing down her last few bites as well. "This is important, and the sooner we figure out what my father is up to, the better."

Korbin nodded and cleared their plates from the table, leaving the cleanup for later. "Then let's get to it, shall we?" he said. "My ship is out back and ready to go."

The teens followed him out to the sleek vessel and loaded aboard. Within moments they were airborne. There were Drooks at his disposal if he needed, but for this occasion, he preferred to use his powerful Drookonus to drive the ship, the device easily launching it up into the skies with the stored Drook magic it held. Though he didn't use it often, Korbin could power his ship for months with the amount of magic he'd placed in it.

He hoped their search went smoothly and would not require even a fraction of that power. But only time would tell.

CHAPTER EIGHTEEN

Korbin's ship was much like the man himself. Namely, incredibly powerful, yet with a deceptively normal appearance. As such, none took note as the trio—plus one rather unusual talking pod—flew high into the atmosphere, following the directions Korbin's stealthy eyes and ears had acquired for him.

The first location was startlingly close to Slafara. One of its three moons had apparently been the site of some sort of disturbance right around the time frame he had told his agents. What exactly had taken place there, they were unsure, but something had definitely happened that was out of the ordinary enough to hit the rumor mill.

Unfortunately, with his visla-level magic, Korbin was easily able to discern the actual culprit in that case.

"Joyriding," he said distastefully. "Someone was joyriding with on overpowered ship. Can you sense the magic, Karasalia?"

Kara reached out with her power, trying to feel the traces that lingered around the small moon as her uncle did. Much to her surprise, she actually did feel something. It was like an itch in the back of her mind. One she couldn't scratch, but was aware of nonetheless.

Following the sensation with her mind, she unraveled the path, feeling the strength of the magic lessen as it neared the moon, then increase as it nearly crashed into its surface. Only at the last second did the trace veer and skim the lunar landscape.

"It was so close," Kara said.

Korbin smiled. "So, you *do* sense it, then?"

"Yes. I mean, I sense *something.*"

"You said it was close. What else to you feel?" he pushed.

"I feel its power waning as it got really close, then surging, just in time to avoid crashing into the moon."

"Precisely," her uncle said, beaming with pride. "Well done, Karasalia. Few would have been able to make out that magic as you've just done. It seems your skills are greater than you realized."

Kara blushed slightly at the flattery. "But what does it mean? It makes no sense."

"Yeah, and what did you mean, 'joyriding?'" Vee added.

"What Kara sensed was the power signature of a dual-powered vessel being pushed well beyond what it was intended for. The main source of power was a small complement of Drooks, though not particularly strong ones from what I can tell. But the pilot also layered their own Drookonus power on top of that, pushing the craft even faster than it should have been able to travel."

"So they almost crashed because of it," Vee noted. "Idiots."

"Not exactly," Korbin said. "They did come very close to the moon, that much is true, but it was intentional. A calculated risk to get even more speed from their ship by utilizing a slingshot maneuver, allowing the moon's limited gravity to pull them in and spit them out the other side even faster than they'd arrived."

"That's impressive," Vee said.

"Yes, I suppose. And it's an incredibly irresponsible thing to do anywhere, but especially so close to a populated world such as Slafara. Things could have gone horribly awry, and then poor

Nikora would have been called upon yet again to put a stop to some poor fool."

"In any case, not what we're looking for," Kara grumbled.

"No. I'm sorry, Kara. On to the next coordinates my friends gave us," Uncle Korbin said, plotting a course for their next stop.

"Friends? You mean informants, don't you?" she asked.

Korbin grinned. "My dearest niece, that doesn't mean they aren't friendly," he replied, then keyed the Drookonus and jumped to the next destination.

"Wait, I think I hear something," Pod said.

"You said that the last four locations," Vee griped. "Are you sure this time?"

"I'm not *sure*, exactly. But I do have readings that match Freya's emergency transponder coming through. At least, I think they are. There's so much interference in this region, it's hard to tell."

The reason for the interference was pretty obvious. They'd been working their way outward in the system, passing through asteroid fields and orbiting gas giants as they narrowed down the list from Korbin's agents. When they were nearing the far edge of the solar system, a dense patch of floating rocks greeted them where their next recorded incident had occurred.

It was the location of a collision between a speeding asteroid and one of the outermost moons orbiting a freezing planet far from Slafara's warmth. The incident had been thousands of years in the past, but the remains of the shattered moon and the space rock that had hit it had coalesced into a rather dense asteroid field.

Only it wasn't just an asteroid field. It was also the burial ground of countless vessels, small and large, that had fallen victim to the shifting debris. A craft with enough power and an alert captain could either avoid or disperse the hazards around them, but the promise of salvage had sent a good many smaller ships and less-skilled captains to their doom.

The very makeup of the area made all signals, magical or otherwise, difficult to send. It was a vortex of negative power, and this was where the strange little pod thought his friend had gone.

"You're sure?" Korbin asked again. "*Inside* the debris field?"

"I have an eighty-six-percent certainty rate that the signal is from Freya," Pod replied. "Only Daisy, Joshua, Marty, and myself are in possession of this particular encrypted transponder frequency ident code."

"Wait, Joshua and Marty? Who are they?" Vee asked.

"The others," Pod replied. "Perhaps they've come to help us."

"Focus, Pod," Korbin said. "I cannot sense anything. Can you, Karasalia?"

"No, Uncle Korbin. I don't sense anything either."

"There is a mélange of magic churning in this mess, but no signal I can discern," the man grumbled.

"Oh, it is not a magical signal," Pod said. "As I have explained, magic does not exist. We utilize technology for all communications."

"But magic *does* exist, Pod," Kara said. "It's what's flying this ship right now."

"I do not know about this craft's propulsion systems," Pod replied.

"Look, we can argue semantics later. Just focus, Pod," Korbin said. "I can't direct us without a trace, so you have to guide us in."

Pod was a limited intellect, but once he locked onto that thin signal, his AI mind focused solely on that one task, showing the true power of an AI processor, even one as limited as his.

In a short time, they'd managed to weave through miles and miles of rock and debris, pushing smaller chunks aside, while carefully circumventing the larger ones. As they neared a huge piece of the shattered moon, Pod's instruments began flashing with activity.

"This is the signal!" Pod exclaimed. "I am now at ninety-nine-percent certainty that Freya is on the surface below."

"Not one hundred percent sure?" Korbin asked.

"She is not responding to my attempts to hail her on comms," the little pod replied. "Otherwise there can be no doubt. Freya is down below."

Korbin rolled his neck and prepared himself for whatever craziness might follow. "Okay, Pod. Guide us in."

The little pod directed Korbin, following the signal as it strengthened, until he said they were right on top of it. But as he looked outside, he saw nothing but darkness and rocks. But there was *something* there. He could feel it. Traces tickling the periphery of his magic. The powerful visla set his ship down just a short distance back from the area Pod had guided them to, then cast a strong atmospheric bubble spell to provide himself and the girls safe passage as they looked around for signs of this alleged ship.

He could have just gone himself, using far less magic to create a simple bubble that moved as he did. But Korbin knew one thing about his stubborn niece. Having come this far, there was no way she'd stay in the ship.

"Well, then, let's go," he said, unsealing the outer door magic and stepping onto the fractured surface of the lunar remnant.

Korbin cast several floating illumination spells as they walked, the glow making the piles of rocks throw strange, angular shadows every which way.

"Where is it, Pod?" he called into his ship over an open skree. "I don't see anything."

"Directly ahead of you," Pod replied. "You should be upon her now."

"All I see is a big pile of destruction-scorched rocks. There's nothing else––" His voice faded off as he noticed something else within the black shards. Something equally dark, but smooth, and not of lunar origin.

Quickly, he summoned a lifting spell, moving thousands of tons of stone from where they'd come to rest. And apparently recently at that, likely sent tumbling down when a massive impact shook the crag above. The impact caused by the sleek black vessel he now saw lying before him. At least, the portions of it he could see. Adaptive camouflage covered much of it, but not all, apparently frozen halfway in place.

The ship itself, however, was undamaged, her powerful shields having protected her even as she crashed.

"Oh my gods!" Kara exclaimed, rushing up to the craft. "It's enormous! And look at its surface!"

"Don't touch it," Korbin warned. "Now that it is uncovered, I can feel the magic that binds this ship. Can you sense it, Kara?"

"Not exactly. There's something, but I don't know what it is," she replied.

"It is a powerful spell. One meant to incapacitate entire crews and disable their Drooks, rendering their craft vulnerable for salvage," Korbin said.

"But from what we know of these strange vessels, they don't operate by Drooks," Vee said. "So why did it crash?"

Korbin held out his hand, feeling where the spell encasing the ship and its own shielding were fighting to this very minute. It seemed that whoever had cast that spell had done quite a number on the ship, knocking its drive systems offline somehow, and immobilizing everything within, even though there was no living crew aboard. A misfire of a spell that got lucky, for, so far as he could tell, the craft was far, far more powerful than the little pod riding aboard his own ship.

"Freya, why won't you respond?" Pod called out both over comms, as well as the open skree Korbin was carrying.

"It is a magical binding," he informed Pod. "It appears your friend was hit by the spell while evading pursuers within the debris field. The ship became disabled and crashed here on this lunar remnant. When it did, the tumbling rocks must have hidden it from its pursuers."

"Wouldn't they have seen the dust trail?" Kara asked.

"Not if it hit multiple fragments on the way in," Korbin replied. "The makeup of these rocks interferes with magic. Something from within the moon or asteroid's core."

"So they'd have been looking at a big, dusty mess and not know where it went?"

"Precisely. Remember, Pod said this ship was following a large craft. Something that size would have had a very hard time pursuing this vessel as it wove through the hazards. And from what I can tell, the ship is intact and undamaged. Whatever strange magic protects it is still active, but a strong spell is fighting with it, immobilizing it. But I sense some sort of activity within."

He reached out with his power, and for just an instant, a flash of a brilliant intellect slammed into his probing spell. The ship, whatever it was, possessed a mind the likes of which he'd never encountered. And it was trapped. Trapped within its own body, unable to move or speak. And it was, impossibly, magically bound to the rock around it.

It would take all of the magic and skill he possessed, but Korbin hoped he could find a way to break through the ridiculously powerful spells holding it. But he'd need time.

"Looks like we'll be up here for a little bit, girls," he told Kara and Vee. "This isn't going to be easy."

CHAPTER NINETEEN

After all those days of waiting, the time had finally arrived. At long last, there was something to do. And that something would be action. There would be marvelous, exciting action, and Marban and his pirate crew were almost giddy with anticipation.

The chrono aboard Rika's ship had ticked down at what seemed a snail's pace, but finally, they were within minutes of the portal making its next scheduled weekly appearance.

The plan was for Rika and Jo to detach from the much-larger pirate vessel a few moments after it used its magic to jump to the correct location, and then fly the *Fujin* through the portal ahead of the *Coratta*, blasting out their ident codes as soon as they reached the other side.

It would be crucial to confirm who they were as soon as possible, so they could then relay the really important bit of information. Namely, please don't shoot the giant-ass stolen alien pirate ship coming through hot right behind us.

Not only did Rika not want her new friends to be shot down, she also had her newly restored mech stowed in that ship's cargo bay. It would be a terrible shame if anything were to happen to it, especially under friendly fire.

"You take good care of my baby," Rika joked as she and Jo donned their gear and headed for the soft-seal boarding tube leading to the *Fujin*. Her ship had been riding secured atop the *Coratta* ever since the battle at the Balamar Wastelands, and it was going to feel good to be in the pilot's seat flying free once again.

"No one's going to lay a finger on your mech," Marban replied. "You have my word. They'll have to get through me and my men first, and that's just not going to happen."

"Glad to hear that," Rika said with a grin. "Okay, you guys have one of our comms units aboard, so make sure you keep it open at all times once we make it through the portal. You're flying an enemy ship, so there's a good chance you may get a little incoming fire until we can get word out that you're one of ours."

"I'd appreciate it if you could have your friends keep the shooting at us to a minimum," Marban said with his signature laugh in the face of danger.

"Speaking of shooting," Rika said. "As soon as we jump into position, I'm gonna go weapons hot with everything the *Fujin*'s got. I'm hoping we won't need to engage with the enemy at all if we time it right, but you never know when some idiot will decide to throw a monkey wrench into your plans. Fuckin' Murphy, am I right, Jo?"

"You said it," her friend replied.

"I may not always understand what you're talking about, but I get the gist," Marban said. "It was pretty much the same way when I first met Charlie. Though I have a leg up this time, having picked up at least a little of your Earth slang along the way."

"Just wait till you see the planet itself," Rika said. "It's a gorgeous blue-green marble of a world."

"First things first, right?" Jo butted in. "Gotta focus on the task at hand, after all. Like kicking names and taking ass."

"Such a dork," Rika chuckled. "Okay, we're gonna be buttoned up and ready to go. The chrono has us at thirteen minutes, so just to be safe, let's give it an extra twenty seconds or so before jumping in. Wouldn't want to catch the tail end of the sun's full force, after all."

"A wise choice," Marban replied. "I'll be ready with the communications device active and all of my men arming the casting stations. They're not the most gifted of spell casters, but the equipment our dead Tslavar friends left behind should more than make up for any shortcomings."

"Excellent. Then let's get to it. We'll see you on the other side," Rika said, then climbed the tube into her ship, the pirate watching appreciatively as she went.

The chrono aboard the *Fujin* read ten seconds. With their self-determined delay, the *Coratta* would be jumping in thirty.

"You ready?" Rika asked over comms.

"We're the men of the *Rixana*. Well, *formerly* of the *Rixana*. In any case, we're *always* ready," Marban replied.

"Good, 'cause we jump in twenty seconds. Jo and I will disengage our mag-clamps and pull away from you once we've oriented with the portal and have a clear shot at it."

"All as planned," Marban said. "Ready on our end. Just hang tight. Our Drooks are about to jump us. If your mapping was correct, it should take us just beyond the reach of any residual flames from the sun."

"Great. Then let's do this."

Marban's inherited Drooks––now serving aboard the ship as free crew––were highly skilled, and at precisely the twenty seconds after the chrono beeped its alarm, marking the portal's shift.

The commandeered pirate ship flashed into existence a little bit farther from the portal than they'd have liked. The coordinates given to the Drooks having been inexact at best, but now that they were dialed in, future jumps would be spot-on.

The enemy fleet was already moving toward the now-clear portal at great speed. It would require some pretty fine flying for Marban to reach it before them. But for some reason, Rika had a calm confidence in the man. He had just begun his run for the portal, and Rika was about to disengage her mag clamps to separate from the *Coratta* when the unexpected happened.

"What the hell is that?" Jo blurted as a tiny, yet fast gunship, bristling with weapons ablaze, burst from the portal, opening up with a massive barrage of railgun, pulse, and plasma fire.

The comms overloaded with incoming encoded signals of incredible power. Obviously, whoever was in that ship hadn't expected there to be anyone capable of hearing them so close. And the aliens didn't have Earth comms tech.

But hear it or not, the enemy had certainly taken note and immediately swarmed the lone craft.

"Sonofa––they're blocking the portal now," Rika growled. "Dammit, there's not a clean path through, and they're all in pursuit of that idiot."

"But how could one ship come through? Zed and Cal would have known about it," Jo wondered.

"I don't know, but something's up. Look at its shields. The Tslavars are landing direct hits, but it's somehow deflecting the power. At least most of it. They must've figured out a way to change the phasing of their defenses."

"You think this is a test ship to see if it works?" Jo asked.

"I doubt it. They wouldn't have armed it to the teeth if that was all it was."

"Ladies, I'm sorry to interrupt, but my Drooks say the ship is attempting to perform what you call a warp, but apparently, the spells it's enduring have damaged that system. The Drooks can feel the power leaking all over the place but not engaging."

"Fucking great," Rika lamented, flipping a switch on the *Fujin*'s console. "Hey! Who the hell is that out there?" she blasted over open comms. "You've just flown right into a goddamn hornet's nest of bad guys."

"No shit," a man's voice replied, cool and calm despite the harrowing circumstances. In fact, he almost sounded amused. "We were sent through with a message for the survivors," he replied. "Judging by your voice, I'd wager you're Rika Gaspari, is that correct?"

"Congratulations, you win a prize," she replied. "Look, you've gotta get out of there. The Tslavars are going to pick you apart."

"I've been trying. Damn warp drive system is having problems. Stupid magic, always messing with things, am I right?"

"Who the hell is this guy?" Jo asked. "He's got balls of steel. I like him."

"Well, if we don't do something you'll never get to say hello face-to-face." Rika replied. "Marban, can you get us close enough for me to grab him?"

"Can do. I'll drop us right on him and flip a one-eighty, then have the casters divert all of their efforts to the rear shielding as we make a run for it. Should work, I hope."

"You hope?"

"Even one hundred percent certainty has room for failure," the pirate replied. "I'll need you to grab him, though. Can you do that? My guys will be too busy to pull that little ship in."

"Leave it to me," Rika said, her tattoos already glowing purple. "Okay, listen," she called over comms. "We're coming to get you. Just don't shoot us––we're in a Tslavar ship."

"Joyriding a stolen car? I like your style," the man replied.

"We're focusing all of our firepower on our six, so if you drop in front, we should be able to rendezvous."

"That was our plan."

"Figured as much. Makes tactical sense," the man said. "Just hurry, if you can," he said as his little ship was buffeted by another salvo of magical attacks. "I don't know how much more of this we can withstand."

Judging by the battering she could see the craft somehow enduring, she was wont to agree with that assessment.

"Jo, fire up everything we've got as soon as Marban pulls us close. I'll layer my magic on top of your railgun sabots. That should poke a nice hole in those fuckers' defenses and buy us a few seconds to scoop this guy up. You ready?"

"Finger on the trigger," Jo replied.

"Let's do this, Marban," Rika called out over comms.

The pirate expertly spun the ship into a roll at high speed, coming out of it directly below the little Earth ship. Jo opened up with a blistering salvo, the magically enhanced railgun sabots doing precisely what they had hoped they would. Namely, causing the enemy to pull away and regroup. It was just enough time for Rika to reach out with her magic and latch onto the little ship, pulling it tight against the *Coratta*'s hull.

"I've got him, Marban. Jump us the hell out of here!"

The enemy regrouped quickly and unleashed a brutal wave of spells at the commandeered ship, but all they found was empty space. The *Coratta* was already gone.

CHAPTER TWENTY

The *Coratta*'s Drooks were good. Really good. So much so, in fact, that they had executed a perfect emergency jump to a distant and unknown world, the location of which was conveniently tucked away in their memories.

They'd never have dreamed of taking their Tslavar owners to this place, but Marban and his crew? Why, they'd set them free and treated them as equals. They were all in this together, and thus, the pirates were taken to the secret world, known only to a few groups of Drooks.

The *Fujin* had not once unclamped from the ship's hull, the audacious plan scrapped the moment the strange little ship came blundering into their carefully plotted out attempt. The damaged craft, however, was released from Rika's magical grip and swung around into the decompressed and waiting cargo hold.

By the time Rika and Jo came storming down the corridor, the two burly men piloting the craft had already stepped out and were talking with Captain Marban. They seemed to be getting on all right with the space pirate, but Rika was *not* amused.

"Okay, fucko. Now that you've shit all over our plans to cross the portal, would you please tell me who in the ever-loving hell you are? You just ruined everything," Rika growled, striding right up to the pair of square-jawed men with close-cropped hair, her tattoos faintly glowing in anger.

"Hey, I'm really sorry about that," the dark-haired one said. "We honestly didn't think there'd be anyone near that portal, based on what Rip and Eddie told us."

"And Leila," Jo said.

"What?"

"She said, 'and Leila,'" Rika snapped. "She was aboard Eddie, too."

"Nope. No Leila. From what Rip said, she was dropped off when they first arrived, before they realized they couldn't warp properly. My guess is she's still on that world, waiting for them to come pick her up."

"Oh, shit," Rika said.

"Yeah. Thing is, we were hoping to go find her while sending out our encoded message for the rest of you survivors, but it looks like the bad guys were a little more prepared than we'd expected. Our ship took quite a beating on the way through. Seems our warp drive got knocked offline in the mix."

"Lucky for you," Jo said. "Warp doesn't work on this side of the portal."

"Well, yes and no," the man said. "Thanks to the data Eddie had gathered from their experience, we were able to modify our warp drives to be about fifty percent more accurate in this galaxy. It's an estimate, obviously, but we figured with their data points, we had a decent shot at finding her."

"And what about this signal you were sending?" Jo asked. "I don't have the decryption code for it, so it's just a jumble of noise at the moment."

Marban stepped into the conversation, doing his best to

defuse the tension that was building. "Oh, before you joined us, Sergeant Franklin was just telling me about that. It seems the AI ships possess the key and would have been able to understand it. But your ship is not an AI, hence the problem."

"Hang on a second," Jo said. "Sergeant Franklin? *The* Sergeant Franklin. George Franklin, from the Great War?"

"Pleased to meet you," George said. "And this is Corporal Hicks."

"Not my real name," the corporal noted. "It's actually Thompson, but Ripley kept calling me Hicks when she was little, and after a while it just kinda stuck."

"You know these guys, Jo?" Rika asked.

"Know of them? Sure. Everyone does. They were a big part of the battle to reclaim Earth. These guys are legends."

"Stop fangirling out on them. You'll blow a gasket," Rika said with a chuckle as she walked over to examine their damaged ship.

It was one thing to be partnered up with a chatty cyborg, but it was quite another to see her actually fawning over anyone like that. It was a side of Jo she didn't know existed, and Rika found herself wondering just how anatomically correct her cybernetic partner actually was. And if she would ever––well, the thought kind of freaked her out.

"So, this thing is pretty much a testosterone express," the pilot from Earth noted. "All engines and guns, no style or subtlety."

"No time for either, I'm afraid. We were in quite a hurry to get something fast enough and deadly enough to stand a chance of punching through the enemy defenses without requiring a full military engagement to help it break free. The idea was to cross over and run, blasting the ever-loving shit out of those bastards on the way. But that plan was obviously a clusterfuck the moment we hit this side."

"Yeah, we noticed," Rika said. "Though, to be fair, at least the modifications to your shields seemed to be working."

"Good thing, that. Otherwise we'd be little pieces floating back through the portal, and that would most certainly be frowned upon by the higher-ups," George said with a grin. "Anyway, the first part of our mission is to do what we can to rally the troops, as it were. To track all of the missing ships down and see if we could get you all back across to the other side."

"Where we'd much rather be," Jo noted.

"With good reason. But we're on a ticking clock here, and there was always the possibility that we wouldn't be able to find the dragon out here. It doesn't operate with the same systems our AIs do, so there was a good chance we simply wouldn't have any luck."

"Her name is Ara," Rika said. "She's a she, not an it."

"Sorry, no offense intended," George replied. "Anyway, Zed tasked us with doing whatever was necessary to get a hold of whichever caster we could to get someone back through the portal to do their magic thing and keep it from sealing up permanently into the sun."

Rika and Jo and Marban all sighed at once.

"What?" George asked.

"George, old buddy, *that's* precisely what we were attempting to do when you came crashing into our party and threw a monkey wrench into our plan. We had one shot, but before we could take it, you pulled the Tslavars onto your trail, effectively blocking the way."

Sergeant Franklin stroked the stubble on his chin with a quizzical look on his face. "Well, shit," he finally said. "We went and screwed the pooch royally, didn't we, Hicks?"

"You said it, Sarge," his sandy-haired comrade agreed.

"But I don't get it," Marban said. "You knew there was a good likelihood you would have a faulty transportation system, and even if it functioned, the odds of you finding your intended targets would be incredibly small."

"Needle-in-a-haystack small," Jo added.

"What's a haystack?"

"Never mind, Marban. It's an Earth thing. I'll explain later," she said.

Rika ran her hand over the battle-scarred metal of the over-confident pair's ship. It really was impressive what they'd attempted to do. Impressive, and downright foolish. But still, she had to respect the effort, even if they had unwittingly stymied her own plans and likely jeopardized their hopes of ever regaining control of the portal before it, and their homeworld, became lost to them forever.

"You knew this was basically a suicide run, right?" Rika asked, turning to the two men. "I mean, odds like these? You're either incredibly brave, incredibly stupid, or incredibly deluded. That, or some cruel bastard sent you off without ever telling you it was a one-way trip."

Franklin and Hicks laughed hard at that, their mirth spreading quickly to Marban, who, despite being from another galaxy, found he had much in common with these most unusual men.

"Oh, thank you. That's priceless," Sergeant Franklin said.

"I fail to see what's so funny," Rika replied.

"It's just that we're professionals. This is what we do. And let me tell you, we didn't spend hundreds of years standing down deep beneath a mountain, armed to the teeth with fuck all to do, only to let someone else have all the fun now that there's actually some real fighting to do."

Jo and Marban both seemed pleased by the stoic man's reply. He was a ballsy sonofabitch, and that was precisely their kind of guy.

"Oh yeah, we're going to get along just fine," Jo said. "Come on, let me show you around the *Coratta*. With your permission, of course, *Captain* Marban."

The pirate flipped a little salute her way. "Permission granted, Jo. You all have a nice time taking in the sights. And now, I believe Rika and I have some drastically revised planning to do."

CHAPTER TWENTY-ONE

Baloo was sitting straight, ears up, his eyes locked on his mama. Something was up, and he could sense it.

Leila was in a state of agitation and elevated concern when she left her quarters, her furry companion glued to her side, and made her way to the command center of Captain Sandah's ship. She'd stayed sequestered on her own for several hours, trying to figure out what the dark green stone hanging around her neck was trying to tell her.

It hadn't *done* anything––that she could tell, at least. But it had unexpectedly glowed for a brief moment before going dim once more. But there was no new threat around her. Not that she could sense. The stone, however, had never been wrong since she'd had it.

There was no way, of course, that she could have possibly known that a massive use of deadly power had been brought to bear on a tiny ship from her adoptive home galaxy, nor could she have known she was presently only a fairly short jump from the very system she sought.

Unfortunately, in the vast expanse of space, close was

relative. In this case, it meant the system in question was still thousands of light years away.

But something in this system was different. Something had made the stone react. And it was her intention to figure out what it was.

"Captain, is everything normal?" she asked as she walked onto the bridge.

"Normal? What do you mean? Why wouldn't things be normal? Has something happened?" Captain Sandah asked, curious, but not alarmed. Not yet, at least.

"I can't really say. It's just a feeling, I guess," she said, not mentioning the priceless power stone dangling just beneath her clothing.

Since meeting Visla Palmarian, she'd taken to keeping the Magus stone concealed at all times. You never knew when a power user might be looking, and she did not want to draw any unwarranted attention to the magical item.

It may have been bound to her family line, but that wouldn't stop a *truly* powerful visla from taking it by force. Given the stone's unexpected reaction so recently, she felt her decision had proven to be a wise one. If it had flared to life in front of the visla's trusted captain, there was a very real chance he would report the occurrence to his employer.

"We've been at this for a long time," Captain Sandah said. "Too long, in fact. As I've mentioned previously, I really must get back to the Palmarian estate. I worry the visla will be put out if my absence continues much longer. I'm sorry we haven't tracked down your friends, or located this system you believe they'll be heading toward, but I'm afraid there's not much more I can do."

"I understand," Leila said, though she was clearly at odds with the captain's decision.

Leila paced a bit as she thought about the situation. If Eddie and Rip were nowhere to be found, then she had hoped to at least get close to the portal. There were hostiles there, but with her comms, if her friends had wound up back there—any of them, for that matter, not just Eddie and Rip—then she'd hoped to perhaps make contact with someone, *anyone* from her home.

But the space outside the windows was empty. Just the quaint planet of Yukanat below their orbit. A place where Sandah had, yet again, proven unable to secure any information they might find of use.

Leila's gaze shifted toward the soothing yellow sun warming the eleven worlds of the system. It wasn't so unlike the one back home. Her new home, that is. The one where the portal had been lowered into the blazing plasma of that system's star.

"Prepare to jump," she heard Captain Sandah say. "We return to Slafara."

The Drooks were ready for the command, having been expecting it to come for some days now.

"Wait! Stop the jump!" Leila blurted.

Captain Sandah gave her a startled look but relayed the command to his Drooks. "Do as she asks. Stop the jump." He turned to his guest, not annoyed, exactly, but not amused by any means. "What is it, Leila? I understand you wish to keep up this ongoing search, but I've told you, while I'm sorry we have to return, in the absence of any progress—"

"That ship," she said, pointing to a distant craft that was rapidly making its approach to the planet from the other side of the sun.

Had she looked just a few minutes earlier, all she'd have seen was the burning orb. But timing was in her favor, and the craft had rounded to a position allowing its dark shape to be better illuminated by the yellow sun.

"What of it?" Sandah asked.

"I can't be sure, but I'm almost certain it's from the fleet that attacked my friends. It's going to the surface. Take us back to Yukanat. We finally have a lead."

Sandah squinted out the window at the ship. "I don't know,

Leila. Pursuing what appear to be regular vessels, in the visla's personal craft, no less––"

"Then do it slowly and from a distance if you must. Sandah, this could be the break we need. Please, I implore you!"

Reluctantly, the captain agreed to follow the ship back to the planet, but he would most certainly be doing so from a distance. "We will be acting as we have on all of our previous excursions, I must remind you. Though not on the visla's official business, we must comport ourselves accordingly. That means we are subtle and unassuming. Can you keep Baloo under control?"

"You don't have to worry about him," Leila said. "He's a good boy. At least, until it's time for him not to be."

Sandah's head of security's stoic expression faltered slightly as the faintest hint of a smile curved the corners of her mouth. She'd spent a little time interacting with the beast on her off hours. Heaven help any on his bad side when he chose to not behave.

"Very well," Sandah said, pulling a skree from his hip. "We depart as soon as we land. I'll call ahead and ascertain the whereabouts of their crew."

The smile on Leila's face was radiant. It had been so long since she'd felt this sensation. It was one she'd been sadly lacking since her friends had failed to return for her. It was hope.

CHAPTER TWENTY-TWO

Priority clearance was afforded the visla's ship, and Captain Sandah's crew brought it in for a smooth landing in short order. The captain was busy on his skree, sending multiple messages as his men put together a small team to accompany him and his guest as they investigated the mysterious ship.

If these people had truly attacked her friends as she said, the possibility of hostilities was a very real threat, he had told her. Better to travel with a group of trained men to accompany her than on their own.

"We will need to travel by conveyance," Captain Sandah informed her as they disembarked from his ship. "I've been informed the craft you noted has landed at a more remote port site."

"Can't we just land over there?" Leila inquired.

"Unfortunately not. This is Visla Palmarian's personal vessel. To take it to such a landing site would only draw much unwanted attention, which is something I'm sure you agree we do not wish to bring upon ourselves."

Leila had to agree with the captain's assessment. "I see your point."

"I'm afraid there will be no room aboard the conveyance for your pet, however."

"Oh, don't worry about him. Baloo needs a good run, anyway."

"Again, drawing attention to us," Sandah noted.

"Yes, but given what we're dealing with, where I go, he goes."

The muscle in Sandah's jaw twitched for an instant. This was going to be a delicate situation, and his charge was not making it easier. But he had a job to do, and he would do his best to complete it.

"Very well," he finally said. "But we will be moving at speed, and covering quite a distance."

"Trust me, he can keep up. And with that nose, if we pull ahead, he'll find us straightaway."

"Then let's not delay any further. Load up with the men. I will join you momentarily," he said, once more slipping his skree from his hip.

The ride across the city took almost twenty minutes, but with occasionally thick traffic, Baloo was able to keep pace most of the way, catching up fairly quickly the few times they were separated.

After a long stretch of unobstructed travel, the speeding conveyance was just pulling up to the docking facility when a large shadow passed overhead.

"No! They're lifting off already!" Leila exclaimed, jumping from the stopped conveyance. "What's happening, Sandah? They only just got here!"

"As I feared might happen," the captain replied as he and his men joined her on the vacant landing pad. "It would appear someone tipped them off."

"Someone on your crew? Who would do that?"

"No, my men are loyal to a one. This had to be someone else.

I fear we must have been observed heading for the landing site with some numbers accompanying us."

"But why would they––?" Leila began to say when the guard directly beside her was thrown violently aside by a vicious spell.

"Ambush!" Sandah bellowed, pushing Leila behind a nearby stack of cargo. "Take cover!"

Magic flew fast and thick as nearly twenty hidden attackers burst into view from their hiding places among the assorted ships' stacked supplies and wares waiting to be distributed to the proper craft.

Some of the attacks, however, were coming from thin air.

"Shimmers!" one of Sandah's guards warned. "They've got shimmers!"

This changed things. It was a far more serious engagement than they'd initially thought. And with hidden attackers, the tide of battle could shift at a moment's notice, and likely not for the better.

Sandah's men charged as best they could, bringing the fight to the greater numbers of their opponents. If they could just close the distance enough, magic would become a secondary means of attack rather than primary, as the use of it in such proximity to their own men would risk inflicting harm on their own numbers. And at hand-to-hand combat, Sandah's guards were very skilled. Working for a visla of Palmarian's wealth, fame, and power, they had to be.

Leila, though pushed to the side by the big, strong men, was not some helpless waif, as they might have expected. The stories of how she'd beaten up several Tslavar bullies who had been harassing the visla's daughter had spread through the ranks, but seeing her in action was far different than hearing tales they thought had almost certainly been exaggerated.

They had not.

Leila, after so long cooped up and stressed out, let loose with her fists, elbows, and feet, throwing in some knees for good measure when opportunity presented itself, as Rika had gleefully taught her.

She was pretty efficiently taking down a Tslavar attacker when a shimmer-cloaked assailant bowled her over from the side. It was an opponent she could not see, and that put her at a decided disadvantage. Leila scrambled to her feet, eyes wide as she looked for any sign of her assailant. A little smile creased her lips. She wouldn't *need* to see them. And boy were they in trouble.

Baloo's nose was a thing of wonder, able to sniff out treats and wild game with frightening accuracy. It was that skill that now let him zero in on the otherwise invisible men trying to hurt his mama.

The enormous canine had fallen behind the conveyance for a stretch, but when he rounded the corner and spied Leila in the thick of a fight, he picked up his pace from a fun but casual run, to an all-out charge.

The poor fool in the shimmer didn't stand a chance.

Baloo tore into the invisible man, green blood flying as he was quickly snuffed out by the enraged animal. *This* was why she had wanted him with them. This was Baloo in his element.

He dropped the raggedy corpse, still largely invisible but for the pool of green blood forming beneath it, and charged into the fray, shrugging off glancing magical blows as he bee-lined for the other invisible prey, leaving those lacking shimmers for Leila and her friends.

It was a bloodbath.

Literally, it seemed, as Baloo's method of dispatching his enemy was far more violent than the clean efficiency of a spell or a blade.

The attackers weren't all Tslavars, though. It seemed there were some mercenaries of other races in this squad as well, all of them fighting for the same commander. It was a brutal engagement, but Sandah and his men were slowly driving the enemy back.

Then, just as it seemed the tide was turning, the attacking forces quickly withdrew, turning and fleeing as fast as their legs would take them.

"We did it, Captain!" one of the weary guards said. "They're on the run!"

They turned to gauge their losses and count the wounded and dead, when Sandah noted something very disconcerting. One of their party was missing.

"Where's Leila?" the guard asked, surveying their numbers.

Baloo stopped shaking the screaming man in his teeth at his mama's name, dropping him in a writhing heap. He sniffed the air, his ears suddenly high and alert.

Leila had been captured. His mama was gone.

CHAPTER TWENTY-THREE

Sandah and his men were quick to clean the battle site, paying off the facility staff to dispose of the bodies and ensure not a word was said about Visla Palmarian. Given the amount of coin the captain handed out, there was no doubt the men would gladly keep quiet.

It had been fortunate the ship had landed where it had. The remote location had ensured that the engagement had gone unnoted by all but the few working the facility. It couldn't have been planned better. And from what they'd seen with Leila's abrupt disappearance, it had indeed been a far from random occurrence.

Captain Sandah was gathering his men to discuss their next course of action when Baloo took off at a run.

"Uh, sir?" a guard said.

Sandah let out a little sigh. "So much for planning," he said, jumping on their floating conveyance. "Follow the beast."

Apparently, whoever had taken Leila had been waiting patiently, cloaked by their shimmer while the others drew the fight to them, including her beast, leaving the woman vulnerable. They had then snatched her right out from under their noses. One nose in particular. And he was not amused.

But that nose was now what would get her back. That, or die trying, and likely taking out a great many with him in the process.

Baloo's stride was enormous, and now that he was onto Leila and her kidnappers' scent, he was only moving faster. So fast, in fact, that Sandah found it hard to keep up, as they were subject to obstacles a running canine could simply weave around.

But they kept him in sight, all the way up until he dove headfirst through a warehouse door, the material shattering from the force of the great beast's impact. The screams coming from within alerted the men that Baloo had already engaged, and the hapless men inside had quickly gone from silent hunters, snatching their target, to prey.

"Find the woman," Sandah ordered as they charged into the building.

Normally they'd have taken their time, establishing an orderly stack and breaching the building with precision and professionalism. But with Baloo having thrown the interior defenses into total chaos, that plan pretty much went out the window, much like the fleeing, bloody man missing his arm had just done, hitting the pavement hard, then scrambling to his feet and running away as fast as he was able.

The visla's men swarmed the location, quickly taking down the hapless men inside. Baloo had truly done a number on their carefully ordered defenses, racing through the building at speed in search of his mama, taking down anyone in his way in the process.

A few were killed outright, his powerful jaws crushing the life out of them before moving on to the next room. The others found themselves lucky to only be missing a limb or two and a lot of blood.

One room at the far end was sealed tight, however, and that was where Baloo was, anxiously clawing at the door.

Sandah carefully approached the animal. "Hey, fella. It's okay. We're going to get her back. Just calm down."

Baloo, for his part, was as calm as could be expected. And fortunately for Sandah, he'd become accustomed to the man over the course of their flight. Reluctantly, he stopped his clawing and stepped back, allowing Sandah to get up close to the door.

"Hello, in there," he said. "As I'm sure you know by now, your friends are scattered or dead. We really have no wish to harm you, so why not just give us the girl and save yourself a lot of trouble."

"You have the beast with you?" a shaky voice asked.

"Yes, but he is under my control," Sandah lied. "He will not harm you so long as you come out immediately."

What Baloo would *actually* do was completely unknown to him, but in the moment, it seemed like as good a thing to say as any.

"Okay, I'm opening the door," the man said.

Moments later, the door slid open and Baloo charged inside, rushing straight to Leila where she sat bound to a chair. The lone Tslavar in the room held his hands up high in surrender, just glad the blood-soaked animal was ignoring him in his joy at finding Leila. The other man was a pale orange color, and obviously in charge. Both were immediately restrained and disarmed.

"Unbind her and get her back to the ship," Sandah ordered. "All of you, back to the ship. And take this one and put him with the other prisoners," he said, shoving the cowering Tslavar to his men. "Deposit them with the city's constabulary. We are not here on official visla business. We will let the locals deal with this."

"What about this one, Captain?" his guard asked, gesturing to the pale orange man.

"I'll take him in myself after I've questioned him. Now, get moving. I'll be along shortly," Sandah replied.

"As you wish, Captain," the man said, then quickly joined the others outside as they loaded up their prisoners onto the conveyance and headed out.

Sandah walked to the mercenary team's commander and looked him square in the eye.

"Hello, Naral," he said.

"Sandah," the man replied. "Been a while."

"Indeed," the captain replied. "Quite a long time. How are the kids?"

"Bigger every year," the prisoner replied, looking at the gore and dirt on the captain's uniform. "Looks like you've had a rough day, Sandah."

"You as well, my friend," he replied, his eyes fixing on the golden collar affixed around the man's neck, just barely visible through his open uniform top.

The men stood silently a moment, then Sandah drew his blade from his hip and sliced the prisoner's bindings, resheathing his knife in one smooth motion. "You take care of yourself," Sandah said. "And send my love to Farallah when you see her."

Naral merely nodded, then walked calmly from the building. A minute later, Captain Sandah did the same, taking the long way back to his ship, taking a much-needed respite before getting back to the business at hand.

CHAPTER TWENTY-FOUR

Things are sometimes not as they appear.

And what is not what it seems can be deadly.

This was a key tenet of the Wampeh Ghalian philosophy, and was part of what had made them the most feared killers in the galaxy. And while a pale-skinned Wampeh would always stand out in some places, their mastery of disguise was such that no one could be taken at face value as what they were.

A green-skinned Tslavar or blue-skinned Bantoon could be a Wampeh Ghalian in disguise, a combination of practical makeup and carefully crafted magic altering their appearance so perfectly that none could detect the subterfuge.

But the one thing a Wampeh Ghalian could not do was impersonate an Ootaki. It was the hair that made the task impossible, for a power user could sense the living magic dripping into the hair from the Ootaki growing it. The sensation might be incredibly faint and only detectable up close, but it was there.

A wig would not do, nor would a deceptive spell. For that reason, no Wampeh had ever successfully posed as one of the golden-haired slaves.

But now they wouldn't have to.

Hunze had been accepted as a full-fledged member of the Wampeh Ghalian. The first ever Ootaki of the Order, and the first ever Ootaki to control their own magic. The Masters wondered what such a being might be capable of, given the skills she possessed.

But one thing had not transferred over from her love when he gifted her his knowledge. Namely, the difficult upbringing that had presented him with the moral flexibility to carry out his deadly work. And even then, Bawb was different than most Wampeh Ghalian, in that he actually possessed a rather overdeveloped sense of honor and fair play. Funny from a man who had killed so many for coin in his day.

She had been training with the Wampeh Ghalian since her arrival at their secret facility several days prior, sharing what she knew first-hand of the Geist. To them, he was legend, one of the greatest of the Order to ever pass through its doors, vanished without a trace at the destruction of Tolemac. Hunze filled them in on the rest.

Her revelations about how they had met, and how the man tasked with killing Visla Maktan had instead befriended a human slave and the Zomoki blood-bonded to him, setting them off on a crazed adventure before he finally managed to land a crippling blow on the visla the same day he rescued Hunze from her enslavement.

Then there was his shift in life purpose once he found himself in a new galaxy, no longer bound by his oath, free to use his skills however he saw fit. And apparently, fighting alongside his friends for a noble cause was a life that truly agreed with him.

It was a change of perspective that a few of the Order found difficult to fathom, being so wrapped up in their oaths and lifestyle that they couldn't imagine another way. But others pondered just what it would be like, to be in the legendary Geist's shoes. What would they do?

Whatever the answer each came to individually, Hunze had just expanded their world, and with it came the realization that with what was happening between galaxies, their old ways may soon be coming to an end, forced to evolve for changing times.

The Masters sent word out to their spy network and were awaiting word back on the particulars Hunze and her odd friends had brought to their attention. In the meantime, they would gladly welcome her embodiment of Bawb's skills as they continued to train another generation of Wampeh Ghalian.

Dukaan, though not a master assassin, nor a magical being, was accepted as a temporary pupil given his role in the mission Hunze and the Geist were on. And with four arms at his disposal, as well as a second set of eyes on the back of his head, the Masters of the Order could not help but wonder how deadly a tool they could hone him into in the short time they had.

The Chithiid took to the training quite well, his time in the fight clubs of Earth paying off in spades, allowing him to easily pass many of the beginner level tests. The Masters then decided to include him with the others for a time, and, despite his seemingly tranquil nature, Dukaan found he really had an affinity for the deadly arts.

Hunze imparted what knowledge she could to both the novices as well as the Masters in their daily sessions, the wonders of her grasp of so many fine points of Wampeh Ghalian combat astonishing them every time.

"As I said, it was through a device called a neuro-stim," she informed them. "It is a non-magical piece of technology that can map out a brain, then seek out specific learning centers and implant pre-stored knowledge over a lengthy time by a drip feed."

"Why so slow? It seems it would be more useful to quickly train your forces than slowly," Kort asked.

"That's the issue with the technology," she replied. "It can be deadly if too much information is transferred at once. There are limiters in place that prevent such things from happening."

"Yet you possess the Geist's knowledge. And it is expansive."

"It may seem that way, but Bawb had spent a lot of time trying to slowly feed me these skills. I had the benefit of that slow-feed, but, until I came into my own power, I was unable to use any of it."

"And he just gave you this secret knowledge? Without your having to train? To go through the trials?" Zilara, the tall woman, asked.

Hunze could sense her conflict. On the one hand, Bawb had sworn an oath to keep those secrets safe. A vow that would cost him his life should it be broken. But on the other hand, he was no longer in the same galaxy, and with no hopes that he would ever return. As such, that vow would not apply in his new home.

It was tough for the assassins to accept at first, but, much as they all hated to admit it, his logic was beyond reproach. And more than that, they realized the new technology-magic the Ootaki spoke of could have huge potential.

Wampeh Ghalian were often on the cutting edge of new training methods, and from the sound of it, a neuro-stim was just another such method, albeit from a different galaxy and using this thing called technology rather than magic.

So long as the end result was the same, what did it matter?

"With this device we could harness the knowledge of our greatest masters, sharing it with the pupils we deem worthy of the gift. Those who have passed their trials and proven themselves as full and accepted members of the Order," Kort noted.

"Yes, I would think so," Hunze replied.

"This means the most difficult and arcane of skills need not be lost with the passing of a master," Zilara said, the potential of the neuro-stim truly dawning on her. "Can your craft demonstrate for us? You say this is a tech-magic device. Kip is one, is he not?"

"Allow me to answer that," Dukaan interjected. "Kip, while a very competent AI, only possesses the most basic iteration of the neuro-stim. As a short-range ship, he never needed the more powerful units used for long-range flights and mission data uploading."

"Ah, so it is not possible for the Wampeh Ghalian to archive and share our knowledge this way," Kort said.

"Actually, I believe it is," Dukaan replied. "Only, the tools required are all on the other side of the portal that brought us here. And in order for us to reach them, we'll first have to defeat whoever it is that is threatening our home on the other side."

The Wampeh Masters conferred a moment in hushed tones. From the looks on all of their faces, it was a most serious discussion. Finally, they broke from their impromptu huddle and faced their visitors.

"Can you promise us the use of these neuro-stim devices if we help you achieve your goals?" Zilara asked.

Hunze stepped forward. "I cannot make promises for those in charge of the technology on the other side of the portal, but I will give you my word and bond that I will do all in my power to make it happen should we succeed. In fact, if you can help us defeat whoever it is that threatens both of our galaxies, I think Zed and Cal would *gladly* offer you use of the tech."

Zilara and the others seemed to like her reply.

"Then it shall be," the deadly woman said. "For the first time in over three thousand years, the Wampeh Ghalian will back one side of a conflict."

Hunze and Dukaan felt a modicum of the stress they'd been carrying lighten at those words. They didn't know what exactly the Order's help would entail, but having the Wampeh Ghalian on your side was clearly never a bad thing.

"Thank you," Hunze said. "You will not regret it."

Zilara smiled a pointy-toothed grin. "If what you say is true, I would agree. Now, what of this smaller unit you say is housed aboard your craft?"

CHAPTER TWENTY-FIVE

Setting up the neuro-stim unit aboard Kip was easier than the little AI had initially anticipated. Wampeh were a completely foreign species, and, thus, some incompatibility was to be expected, however, Hunze and Bawb had successfully utilized their custom unit, courtesy of Cal, and residual traces of the patterning map on her mind were visible to the unit as it attempted to calibrate.

Essentially, the unit took a faint fingerprint from prior experience and utilized it to recreate enough of the settings for basic functionality. Or so Kip hoped.

While the quirky AI was doing his best to ensure he didn't accidentally lobotomize one of the deadliest people in the galaxy, Hunze was given a little treat. A bit of backstory about her love she hadn't heard before. While she had been filling in the Order about Bawb's life since his disappearance, they, now, were telling her about his past.

One thing in particular seemed of great importance. Vital, even. Bawb, it seemed, was one of the Three—a trio of the most senior Wampeh Ghalian, each entrusted with knowledge, only passed to the next member upon the death of one of the three.

As the Wampeh Ghalian almost always worked alone, there was no way a single event could snatch all of them at the same time, and the system had worked for thousands of years.

What this knowledge was had been kept secret from all but the highest ranking of the high. A secret even within the secret society, known to but a select few. Hunze just so happened to be in the presence of six of them.

"So it was some sort of vault he knew the location of?" she asked, mulling over what she'd been informed.

"We cannot say for certain," Zilara said. "Truth be told, it could be anything. All we have are stories, passed down for hundreds of years. It was a repository of the vast Wampeh Ghalian wealth, accumulated over millennia. And not just wealth in the sense of coin, but also magical relics and devices of devastating power."

"Slaaps, I assume," Hunze said.

"At the least. We believe there were enchanted weapons as well, such as your and my vespus blades. It is said there are even a few claithes there, though few possess the power to wield one. But now, all of that is lost to the ages."

"Wait, you said there were three of them. When Bawb vanished all those centuries ago, the other two would have selected a replacement, right?"

"Normally, yes," Zilara said. "But the event at Tolemac was singular in its damage to our order. While the Geist was in the skies above, thrown through time and space as you've informed us, another of the Three was completing a job on the surface of that very planet. The odds of them both being in the same place at the same time for such a cataclysmic event stagger the mind, but sometimes even those odds play out."

"So you lost two of the three at the same time," Hunze realized. "But what of the last one? Surely they would have been contacted immediately."

Kort looked at Zilara and sighed. "That," he said, "should

have been the case. But Quinlantz, the final survivor of the Three, was away, operating an infiltration under deep cover. It was a difficult assignment. One that only the most powerful of our Order would even dream of attempting. But the price was exceptional, and the one making the contract's coin was good for it, so he accepted the challenge."

"It was a many months-long engagement, so his absence was not particularly noted until he had been gone six months. But even then, sometimes we are pulled away for excessive lengths of time beyond our control. However, when he had not been heard of for a year, the worst was expected," Zilara said.

"Since then, the knowledge has been lost to history," Kort said. "But with the Geist alive and well, and back in our galaxy, no less, we have the opportunity to finally regain this arsenal of powerful tools once more."

"And from the sound of it, we will need them all for the fight to come," Zilara added. "I hope this neuro-stim device is worth it."

At that moment, Kip signaled he had the unit as ready as it was going to be. All they needed to do was come out and have someone give it a try. Kort volunteered, as he was the one who'd brought them to the Order in the first place.

Seated in one of the memory foam seats, Kort seemed rather at ease, despite the strange metal band resting around his head. It was a somewhat clunkier unit than the most modern ones, but that was because Kip wasn't expected to use it for anything more than the most basic of skills updates for whoever was crewing with him.

Navs upgrades, comms coding changes, things of that nature. But for the Wampeh Ghalian seated inside him, he selected something he knew far better than any of that.

"It's just going to be a really basic test this first time," the AI informed his Wampeh guest. "I'll take it really slow until we have the parameters better locked in, so just sit back, relax, and I'll see what we can do."

"I am ready," Kort replied, utterly calm in the face of the unknown.

It was a confidence and control of emotion that Hunze was familiar with, having witnessed Bawb do the same thing on many occasions. She was missing him terribly, but somehow, being with these distant brothers and sisters of his order, she felt the sting a little less sharp in her heart. There was something comfortingly familiar about them, she supposed, and that would do. For now, at least.

Kip engaged the neuro-stim and began the transfer. It was agreed he would run the system for an hour, utilizing the lowest settings for safety, while transmitting the most basic of data. Kort was a test subject. A guinea pig of the most deadly variety, and Kip very much did not want to damage him.

An hour later the Wampeh opened his eyes, blinking rapidly a moment before settling back into his customary calm.

"Toast," he said. "I now know all there is to know about preparation and serving of countless varieties of toast, as well as a multitude of other baked goods."

Dukaan rested his head in his hands. "Why, Kip?" he groaned.

"I have limited neuro-stim files, Dookie. And I wanted to be sure it would work, so I needed to use something I know. And this I *really* know."

"Yes. Fine. But please, this simply will not do. Show him something more substantial," Dukaan requested.

"Oh, fine," Kip replied. "Sorry, Kort. Would you mind lying back for one more round."

"So long as I will not awaken with an entire recipe book in my head," he replied. "It would be a shame to have to dismantle you."

"Hey, a joke," Kip said. "I didn't know Wampeh Ghalian joked."

"We do not," Kort replied, flashing a quick wink to Hunze and Dukaan.

"Uh, well then, here we go," Kip said, starting the neuro-stim once again.

Two hours later, a far more substantial skill set was safely lodged in the assassin's mind.

"I know how to fly this ship," he said, eyes bright with excitement. "This is amazing. The functioning of this technology. It truly is far different from our magic. And it is *wonderful*."

"Yeah, pretty cool, right?" Kip asked.

"It is. And without a magical signature, it is a power none from our realm will sense coming until it is too late," the assassin said with a bloodthirsty smile. "And the weapons this ship possesses. railguns and pulse cannons. So foreign to our kind, yet so deadly. Oh yes, we will be wonderful allies, indeed."

"Oops," Kip said. "I didn't mean to leave that bit in there."

Hunze chuckled at his mistake. "That's all right, Kip," she said. "I think you've just unintentionally provided an even greater selling point for our Wampeh friends."

CHAPTER TWENTY-SIX

The outer layers of spells binding the mysterious and powerful ship trapped on the chunk of shattered moon at the far end of the system had been a tough nut to crack. But with their combined powers casting together, Korbin and his niece had managed to at least release the ship's lesser systems, if not the craft itself.

The ship was still quite securely bound to the stone around it, but they were at least able to access its exterior airlock doors. It was a technology utterly foreign to the magic users from this non-technological galaxy, but Pod was more than happy to help.

Kara had Daisy's personal voice-access code to his systems, after all. That meant the young woman who had spoken it was entitled to whatever she needed of him. Later, Freya and Daisy might rethink that weakness in their system. But neither had anticipated a series of events quite like these.

"The spell is strange," Korbin said. "Can you feel that?"

"I feel *something*," Kara said, reaching out with her senses as her uncle had been teaching her. "But what is it?"

"You *do* sense it, then. Good," Korbin said with a pleased smile. "What that is, is some rather rare, and extremely powerful magic. And it is doing something quite different from its original intent."

"What do you mean?" Vee asked. "I don't sense anything. Of course, I don't have any power, obviously."

Korbin let out a little chuckle. "Yes, Visanya, of course you don't." The way he said it unsettled her slightly, but just for a moment. "The thing about this spell is, it is an unusual one. Almost never seen. A specially modified military application rarely used, and then only by elite casters and a tiny handful of pirates. A slaver's tool. Or a conquering fleet gathering resources."

"But what does it do, Uncle Korbin?"

"It's designed for immobilizing entire crews while in space without damaging their craft, Kara. But the way this was cast, it somehow reacted to this ship's unusual shielding and superstructure itself. I'm sure it wasn't the intended outcome, but that's neither here nor there. The end result is this ship became bonded to the rock of this floating fragment of moon when it crashed here. I would think only its momentum kept it from immediately binding to the surface."

"Can it be freed?" Visanya asked.

"I really don't know. We'll have to get inside and see what shape it's in."

"Pod, can you tell us how to open this inner door?" Kara asked over the open skree to her uncle's ship, where the little pod was sitting.

"My pleasure, Kara," Pod said. "We are in proximity now, but I still cannot reach Freya for some reason."

"I believe the spell restraining your friend has also incapacitated her from speech," Korbin said, his understanding of AI slowly growing with every interaction with the little pod.

"Can you help her?" Pod asked.

"I don't know, Pod. But I'll try."

Pod sent Kara a series of override commands that had to be

manually entered into the small keypad to the side of the inner airlock door. Normally only Daisy would have access to these backdoor codes, and even then, they'd only be used in the most dire of emergencies, when Freya couldn't let her in herself. But this was just that sort of situation. Only, it wasn't Daisy breaking in. It was strangers.

The door hissed open, and the three stepped inside the incredibly advanced ship.

"Oh my gods," Vee gasped. "It's amazing."

The others agreed, taking in the bleeding-edge futuristic interior of the brilliant and deadly stealth ship. It was dark, save the emergency lights providing a faint red glow, but even then it was clear Freya was in a class of her own. In fact, even those from her own galaxy were routinely amazed by her. For tech-ignorant people of this strange galaxy, the effect was only amplified.

Korbin reached out with his power, trying to get a feel for the magic binding the ship. The spell holding her fast to the surface was utterly massive in power, so he decided to leave that be for the moment. The other spells binding her systems, however, seemed within his grasp.

"Kara, could you assist me with this, please? I think we can release the locks placed on the craft's interior functions if we work together. The spell wasn't meant to freeze this type of being, but magic and this technology thing Pod had described to us seem to often have unexpected interactions."

"I can see that," Kara replied. "But how can I help you? I don't know what to do, and my power is weak."

"You know that's not true," Korbin said. "And I will teach you the spell. Just listen and learn. Then we will cast together, okay?"

"I guess," Kara said, unsure.

Korbin had her recite the spell slowly, taking care to do so without intent, not casting, just learning the words. But Kara was always a quick study at magic––at least, the spell-learning part of it. It was the casting where she'd always lacked power, using her little konus most of the time, as her own power was sadly lacking.

In just a few minutes she was ready.

"Now pull from your konus, but also your own power, Kara. You can do this," Korbin said as they began casting together.

Amazingly, Kara felt the bonds of the magical restraints begin to fall, the blind, deaf, and restrained ship suddenly surging back to freedom. At least within her own hull.

Lights flashed on. A split-second later internal defensive cannons sprang from invisible seams in the walls, targeting the invaders within her craft.

"**Who the fuck are you?**" an angry female voice boomed.

The weapons powering up didn't seem like they'd wait for a reply.

CHAPTER TWENTY-SEVEN

"These are friends, Freya!" Pod transmitted the moment he sensed her comms systems unlocking.

The deadly ship's weapons systems froze in place, a hair's breadth from vaporizing the three intruders she suddenly registered within her walls. Freya quickly linked with Pod, sucking the data from his far-lesser AI mind, filling herself in on the events since they'd separated.

Her cannons retracted into their hidden compartments.

"Sorry," Freya said over her internal speakers. "Didn't mean to scare you there. I'm a little on edge."

"Quite understandable," Korbin replied, becoming accustomed to the idea of speaking to a vessel with a mind after a few days with Pod. "I am Korbin, and these are Karasalia and Visanya."

"Just call us Kara and Vee," Kara said. "I'm Kara, she's Vee."

"Pleased to meet you guys," Freya said. "And thanks for taking good care of Pod. He's kinda slow, but a good guy."

"Slow? He seems quite clever for a vessel," Korbin said.

"Thank you, Korbin," Pod said over his renewed comms link with Freya.

"You've obviously not met a lot of AIs," Freya said with a laugh. "Don't worry, you'll see soon enough. And sorry, Pod. No offense."

The ship shuddered, but didn't move.

"What the fuck?" Freya blurted, the ship rumbling more violently.

"You should probably not try to fly," Korbin said. "We were able to release your internal bindings, but your craft is still firmly tied to this moonlet."

"Moonlet?"

"Yes. You are attached to a piece of a shattered moon. We're trying to find a way to get you free, but until then, and unless you are powerful enough to pull a moon, I'm afraid you're stuck here."

"Well, shit," Freya grumbled. "That's just great."

"A sarcastic vessel," Korbin chuckled. "This is a most unusual day, indeed."

Kara looked in wonder at the magnificent craft's interior. It was unlike anything she'd ever seen, and it was amazing. Yet somehow, this powerful being had become trapped, separated from her friends.

"Freya?"

"Yeah, Kara?"

"What exactly happened to you? I mean, we have ideas, but how did you wind up stuck here?"

"Oh yeah. *That*. Craziest damn thing, that was, and believe me, I've seen some *crazy* things."

Korbin chuckled. Given this ship's demeanor, and her startlingly free use of sarcasm, he had a feeling she most certainly had.

"So there we were, minding our own business, when we got sucked through some strange swirly thing that looked like an Einstein-Rosen bridge. This was a few months ago I see, now that I can sync with Pod, though I don't know how I lost that time."

"I believe your mind was locked in an unusual form of stasis spell," Korbin said. "But please, continue."

"It all happened so fast. We were just minding our own business––we'd literally just warped back to Earth after our latest survey mission––we were searching for inhabited systems. Anyway, we'd just warped back, when all of a sudden, this *thing* grabbed us, and we found ourselves yanked into another system, and with my warp system totally on the fritz. I have to wonder if it was still active from our warp the moment we hit the damn thing."

Little did Freya know that the same flash of powerful magic that had sent Charlie and his friends forward in time into her home galaxy, had also snared her and her pilot, who just happened to be in the wrong place at the wrong time. The unusual magic had sucked them in all right, but not to another system, but another galaxy entirely.

"So you wound up here?" Korbin asked. "But why was a ship after you? And why was this Daisy person trying to kill the visla?"

"Hang on. She was doing *what*? Oh hell, what did she get herself into?"

"Attempted assassination, apparently. But what we do not understand is why."

"She's pretty damn kick-ass, don't get me wrong, but that's not her style. Pod, you know what she was trying to do? I didn't see anything in your files."

"I'm sorry, but I was not provided with that information," the little pod replied.

"Didn't think so, but it was worth asking. I'm just going to have to ask her when we meet back up. I wonder if it was the ships attacking us that made her try something that crazy."

"Wait, did you say ships were attacking you?" Korbin asked, his interest piqued.

"Yeah. When we arrived here, there was a massive fleet of strange ships just sitting there. We tried to hail them, naturally. I mean, this was first contact. Not exactly how we'd intended it, but there they were. But instead of responding, they opened fire on us with some weird stuff I couldn't even read on my scans."

"Magical attacks. Yes," Korbin said. "Pod has difficulty reading magic as well."

"Magic? You're kidding, right? When I saw that in Pod's logs, I thought that was just a bug in his recorder."

"No, I am quite serious. But please, continue."

"Right. So we were getting dog-piled by these ships and getting our asses handed to us––my weapons couldn't seem to pierce their shields––and there were *hundreds*. A full-on fight would have been a total mess, so we warped away and came up with a plan to try again to open comms with them."

"You would still attempt to have discourse with these vessels, even after they attacked you?" Korbin asked.

"Hey, we're on a mission to contact new races. Sometimes things get off to a rocky start. But I also fired up *all* of my weapons systems, just in case. Talk if you can, kick ass if you need to, right? Anyway, we were ready to give it a try, but when we warped back, we wound up in a totally different system. And every subsequent warp did the same thing. We were warping all over the damn place, but never where we wanted to go."

"This 'warp' sounds like a jump," Korbin noted. "Likely a translator spell error."

"Tomato, tomahto," Freya said. "Anyway, we'd made, like, a dozen quick warps when we wound up in this system. We were about to warp again when I picked up a ship like we'd seen when we first arrived on my scans. I'm a stealth ship, but that didn't seem to stop the bastards from reading me on their scans when we first popped into this mess, and I wasn't sure if my adaptive camouflage was glitching, so we decided to just follow them for a little bit, keeping our distance. But then a smaller ship launched from the big one."

"Likely a transport to the surface of one of the worlds," Korbin posited.

"Probably," Freya said. "Kind of a similar design to the one I see parked outside, actually. But we needed answers, and *both* ships were potential sources of intel, so Daisy decided to fire up Pod and pilot him to track the smaller ship, even though he wasn't really ready to be activated. I would track the big one, then swing back around and pick them up to compare notes."

"Only that didn't work out, did it?" Vee asked.

"Not at all. After we split up, the ship I was tailing noticed me. And let me tell you, I'm the stealthiest freakin' ship in the galaxy, so that's really saying something. But when they opened fire with that invisible stuff again, *this time* I shot back. Nothing too massive, just a little punch on the nose to get them to back off, right?"

"You managed to damage them?" Korbin asked. "But I thought you were unable to defend yourself against their shielding."

"Initially. But then I fabricated some new railgun sabots on the fly. I took the data from my scans and incorporated that into a coating of some rather nasty nanites. The first shot was to hit, then spread out and pierce the shielding. The subsequent ones then went through that little hole and made my point quite clear. And let me tell you, I'm a *very* good shot."

Korbin couldn't help but grin. He liked this intelligence and her cocky self-confidence.

"But you know what happened then?" Freya said. "They called in friends. Not cool. So suddenly I was facing *three* of 'em, all unloading everything they had at me. And I couldn't warp. Not without stranding Daisy. So run it was."

"They called for backup," Korbin said. "Interesting. That

means they were within long-distance skree range, and while far, that's not *terribly* far."

"Skree?"

"A form of communication, usually used for short distances, but a few very powerful users possess skrees that can reach across a few systems."

"Interesting," Freya noted, storing that little tidbit away in her massive brain. "But more importantly, where's Daisy, exactly? I need to reconnect with her ASAP, and Pod's records only go as far as his landing on some floating garden thing."

"Captured and imprisoned in my father's tower, I'm afraid," Kara said.

The ship rumbled as Freya tried to break free from her rocky prison.

"We have to get her!" Freya said, straining against the magic binding her. Oddly enough, a few tiny parts of her actually moved before being pulled back to the rock.

"That's strange," Korbin said, noting the unexpected movement. "Perhaps you are not as firmly bound as I originally thought."

"Just my nanites learning how to counteract this force field," Freya said. "Though they're going to need a while to really dial in this strange energy signature."

"It's magic," Korbin said. "Magic is what is restraining you."

"Fuck. Magic. Figures. I mean, who could have anticipated that, right? Just our luck," Freya griped.

"You accept it, just like that?" Kara asked. "Pod still doesn't believe us."

"Logic says that's what's up. And from what I can see in my scans, crazy as it sounds, the explanation makes sense. Besides, magic is just a name for science we don't understand yet. Pod, however, is a limited AI, so he doesn't have much beyond the basics needed to fly at the moment. Daisy and I hadn't figured out a way to upgrade him yet. Sorry, Pod."

"That's okay," Pod replied.

Korbin reached out with his magic, feeling for Freya's "nanites," whatever they were. Strangely enough, indeed, this craft was somehow affecting the magic binding it. Only on a minuscule level, but nevertheless, she was doing it.

"Your nanite things are able to cast," he said, shocked. "That should be impossible."

"If what you call magic is this power holding me here, then all I'm doing is just breaking it down into its base energy components and reworking their fields in a way that lets me manipulate it enough to loosen the element binding me here. I mean, magic or tech, a force field is a force field, no matter what you call it."

"You are a most amazing intellect, Freya," Korbin said.

"Thank you."

Kara reached out with her konus, trying to do what her uncle had done, sensing the magic being slowly tugged at by Freya's unusual tech.

"What are you doing, Kara?" Freya asked. "I feel some sort of energy from that thing on your wrist pulling at my link with the force field."

"I'm just trying to get a feel for those nanite things," she replied.

"And what's on your wrist? It's too small to be a power whip."

"A what?"

"Ra'az tech. Stuff we commandeered in the war. Daisy has one. But that's different."

"It's a device that stores magic for those who don't have any of their own."

"You *do* have magic of your own, Karasalia," Korbin said.

"But it's weak," she replied.

Korbin didn't say anything, but his face showed he didn't believe those words.

"Can I get a closer look at it?" Freya asked.

"It's a really underpowered one, but sure," Kara said. "Uh, do I just wave my arm in the air?"

Freya laughed. "Sorry, I should have been clearer. I have a spectral analyzer. Put it in there, and I'll be able to get readings of this power stored in it."

A small device slid forward from a formerly seamless panel in the wall. There was a round dish that was clearly where you put whatever was being analyzed. Kara slid the konus from her wrist and placed it on the machine, which then slid back into the wall, the nanites sealing the panel once more.

"Freya, I'm afraid I cannot free you without help," Korbin said, again pulling from his substantial power, but still unable to break the spell holding her. "This magic is incredibly strong, and it misfired into a strange form that I can't seem to break. I'm going to need to retrieve some supplies from back home. Some tools that might help me negate it."

"You're going to leave me here? Great."

"I promise you, we'll be back as soon as we can."

"Well, I'll be here," Freya grumbled. "I don't have anywhere else to go, apparently."

"We'll be quick. I'm sorry, but it's the only way. Come on, girls. We really need to go. But, Freya, we *will* be back."

"Do you need this konus back?" Freya asked.

"You can hang on to it," Kara said. "I can't really cast with or without it anyway."

The trio stepped out of the trapped stealth ship and boarded Korbin's craft, then quickly lifted off. Destination, Slafara.

Before they'd even taken off, Freya's incredible mind had already finished her external scan of the konus in her analyzer.

"Hmm. Why not?" she mused, setting her nanites to work on the slender band.

Within seconds, the microscopic nanites had already begun disassembling and logging every detail of the konus, building her understanding of both the device's power, as well as its composition down to a molecular level.

Freya had a new toy. And things were looking to get interesting.

CHAPTER TWENTY-EIGHT

Ara had arrived in the system containing the planet Rupsaval without incident, but rather than flying directly to the planet their ill-fated captors had blurted the name of––before being rather unceremoniously chewed up and digested by the mighty Zomoki––they stayed well clear. Scouting. Watching. Waiting.

The thought was, given what they'd dealt with so recently, there seemed to be a decent chance someone knew they were poking around. And if that was the case, there could very well be another welcoming party waiting for them. And that they did not want.

They were hopeful that Rika and Marban had successfully made it through when they were scheduled to make their attempt the other day, and that Rika was resetting the portal's timing at this very moment, as Ara had discussed with her.

But until they had actual confirmation from their friends that it was a success, they had to operate under the assumption that the portal clock was still ticking down.

"Better safe than stranded," Charlie had said.

And if the worst had in fact come to pass, that meant they

only had two more cycles before the portal lowered itself into the sun permanently. And *that* would be bad.

If the final days ticked down and they hadn't heard word from Rika by then, the three of them had agreed that *they* would fly back to the portal, cross over if they could, and reset it themselves, though in so doing they'd likely lose any leads they'd gathered as to the true nature of their mysterious enemy.

Visla Dominus was a made-up name. That they were sure of. The only question was, who was he, *really*?

"You see it?" Bawb asked over their suit comms.

"Yeah, I see it," Charlie replied. "That big freakin' ship is still out there."

Ara angled her flight back away from the craft, tucking herself small and drifting like debris so they could get a better look at it. This system lacked any convenient asteroid fields or moons behind which to hide, so hiding in plain sight was the order of the day.

"It's been out here for days now, sending its landing craft to Rupsaval but staying well clear itself," Ara said. "And it is definitely from the fleet we encountered upon exiting the portal. I can smell it."

"Me too. You think they've abandoned the portal?" Charlie asked, though he knew the probable answer.

"I think not," Ara replied. "More likely, they have split off to resupply, leaving the others waiting as before."

"And if they're using smaller ships to restock, then that means they don't want to draw attention to themselves. At least, not to their big, bad warship. You think we can track one of their smaller ones to the surface? It'll be pretty hard to miss its crew once we know which part of which city they've landed in. This might be our best chance to get some actual first-hand intel from the enemy fleet itself."

"I can do that, Charlie. But after our last run-in with unfriendly Tslavars, I suggest Bawb employ a different disguise this time. I fear our friend Binsala the trader may have been compromised for use among this enemy."

"I agree with your counsel, Wise One," Bawb said. "Fortunately, I have many others to choose from."

An idea began to blossom in Charlie's mind. "Hey, Bob. You know what? I've got a really interesting idea."

Walking the streets of the city surrounding the spaceport landing area as the sun began to lower in the sky, Bawb moved like a predator. An openly aggressive and very scary predator at that. He was most certainly *not* blending in.

His normally immaculate hair was a mess, his skin colored to a reddish brown. And his clothing bore the marks of many scuffles, and what very well might be blood from any number of species. The master assassin's posture and gait had also changed, shifting from Binsala's drunken swagger to a brute's stalking stride.

He hadn't actually grown any larger, but everything about his carefully constructed persona gave that impression. He was a big, scary man, and where Binsala floated through the crowd as only a drunk can, *this* iteration didn't have to do so, namely because the crowd parted before him.

Even ruffians seemed to want no part of him, instinctively recognizing an apex predator far more deadly than they could ever hope to be.

Charlie, in the meantime, used the distraction to enter the establishment they'd seen a group of Tslavar crew disappear into well before his menacing partner drew close.

The Tslavars were sitting to one side of the long central bar, a small cluster of men at a table, drinking away the day's aches and pains. Charlie walked right by them, not paying the slightest attention, his eyes fixed on the assets of the buxom waitress coming to take his order.

His leering gaze was precisely what any watching would expect in that sort of establishment, and thus, he went unnoted, just another patron on an otherwise normal day.

A few minutes later a hulking menace of a man shoved his way inside and took a seat at the bar on the opposite side of the Tslavar crew. Despite having greater numbers and a proclivity for violence, the Tslavars sensed the raw danger wafting off the man. It was so powerful, in fact, that they subconsciously turned their bodies, angling away from him as they continued their conversations.

This was exactly as Charlie and Bawb had intended. A squeeze play of sorts, with Bawb forcing their targets to speak directly in the direction of Charlie, who was sitting with his back largely to the men, pretending to watch the women dancing across the room as he took mental note of every word the Tslavars said.

It seemed they were indeed on a resupply run, but having been stuck in space for so long, they decided to take a little extra break for drinks before heading back up to their ship to unload their cargo.

"Yeah, it's a resupply crew," Charlie informed his friend via their silent connection.

"As Ara suspected. Have they said anything else?" Bawb asked, while loudly demanding another drink with his outside voice.

"I'm listening, but they're just talking about—hang on a minute," Charlie said.

The conversation had shifted, and one of the men––somewhat more inebriated than the others––let slip that he heard Visla Dominus was going to have them stop at a nearby system to collect all of the power at their disposal.

Charlie was about to see if Bawb had any idea why the visla would do such a thing when the blabbermouth loosened his lips once more, saving him the trouble of hypothesizing.

"One of my buddies who works with the Drooks said it looks

like they figured out the portal's schedule. It's not based on that system's solar day, but one of the casters just happened to take note of the first seven cycles, and when it switched to the longer ones, he did some math and figured out when it'll pop up next."

"Really?" one of the other men asked.

"Yeah. Rumor is, the visla's going to use all of that extra power and make a run for the portal when it opens."

"Shit. Bob, we've got a real problem here."

"What is it, Charlie?" the Wampeh asked, his posture shifting ever so slightly as he readied himself for combat if need be.

"They've figured out the portal's timing without needing a chrono. Damn, we should have randomized it at least a little," Charlie lamented. *"Shouldn't have been so predictable."*

"To be fair, we had no idea we would find ourselves in this situation," Bawb noted.

"I know, it's just, this means the visla's team is observant. Like, really observant. And they're going to be going to a nearby system so the visla can collect some sort of power thingy. They didn't say what, exactly, but I think it's how they're going to crash the gates and get through to the other side."

"This would be bad," Bawb said. *"We've seen the power this visla possesses. And if they're gathering more on top of that? It could be disastrous."*

"Agreed. So you know what this means," Charlie said. *"This means we need to find out where the power source is located and get to it first. We need to head off the visla at all costs."*

CHAPTER TWENTY-NINE

The Tslavar who had let slip the enlightening bit of information in the bar was a slight man. Not a fighter. A logistics type, obviously down on the surface to ensure their wares were loaded properly and all was accounted for.

His associates, on the other hand, were made of hardier stuff. They also seemed likely to fall for one of Bawb's oldest and simplest diversions.

Charlie, being unnoted, no more than just another regular patron in the establishment, had promptly stepped out into the city upon hearing the man's comments about their visla's intentions. He had silently communicated with his scary Wampeh friend, and a plan was rapidly devised. All Charlie had to do was put it into action, and quickly.

No more than twenty minutes later, a group of laughing women entered in a boisterous cluster and made their way to the bar, more than one of them appreciatively eyeing the Tslavar crew seated at the table at the far end. The men took note, and the apparent group alpha quickly rose and made his way to the bar, offering to buy the ladies a round of drinks if they came and joined him and his friends at their table.

Pockets already lined with plenty of freshly acquired coin, the women readily accepted, and there just so happened to be precisely the same number of them as there were Tslavar mercenaries. The unassuming, smaller man, however, was left awkwardly at the fringe of the new merriment. Precisely as Charlie had intended.

Conversation turned from a group interaction toward the one-on-one variety in short order, leaving the runt of the litter sitting quietly with his drink, watching his cohorts enjoy themselves from a distance, yet so close.

"I should get back," he finally said, rising from their table. "I'll see you all back at the transport."

"Don't wait up," one of his associates replied, the woman on his lap giggling with laughter that seemed very much the real thing to the unassuming man.

Charlie had said his friends were weary from a long time in space, and had paid the ladies each handsomely to entertain the men––but only to a point. If they decided to segue to something beyond merely providing company in the bar, that was a far different transaction, and entirely up to them.

The Tslavar bean counter stepped out into the early night air and began walking back to their ship to wait for his gregarious comrades to finish their festivities. Charlie and Bawb knew where their craft was waiting, and had plotted out the most likely routes back to it.

Fortunately, and playing into their plan, the Tslavars were overconfident from years being the big dogs in whichever system they visited. As such, the lone man walked back through the narrow side street that was a more direct route to their ship without paying the absence of his large entourage a second thought.

Though no one knew who they worked for, everyone knew not to mess with the Tslavar crews that had been frequenting the world of late. That is, all but the large, menacing man who now stood blocking the path.

"Your coin," Bawb said, his eyes conveying a lust for violence that would be just as happy taking the man's possessions by force as not.

"I'm sorry? Are you talking to me?" the Tslavar asked, stunned anyone would dare talk to him like that.

"I said, give me your coin," the intimidating man growled.

"You don't want to do this," the Tslavar said. "You have no idea who I am. Who I work for."

"Don't know. Don't care," Bawb replied. "Now, stand and deliver. Your money or your life."

Charlie heard Bawb utter the command from where he had been waiting, tucked in the shadows just around the corner. He was quite amused that his friend remembered the ancient Earth expression, mentioned to him during their time in the UK of old. And now Bawb had appropriated it for this persona, and, amazingly, it really worked. It was also likely the first time any in this galaxy had ever heard it.

"I wonder if it might catch on?" Charlie mused.

"Look, you really don't want to do this," the green man said, trying to display the confidence and bluster of his far more violent friends, but sadly failing.

Bawb grabbed him roughly and threw him up against the wall. Hard, but not so hard as to cause any real damage.

"What are you doing?" the man cried out.

"Your coin!" Bawb commanded, then began beating him with solid blows.

"You think that's a bit much?" Charlie silently asked his friend.

"He'll live," Bawb replied over their non-verbal link.

Charlie let his friend have his fun for a few moments longer, then stepped into the light when the poor Tslavar's back was to him.

"Hey! What are you doing? Leave that man alone!" he shouted, racing down the narrow street.

"Stay out of this, pissant. This is not your affair," Bawb growled in his most threatening tone.

"Not happening," Charlie shot back.

Bawb didn't hesitate, punching the Tslavar hard in the stomach, dropping him to the ground, gasping for air, before launching his attack on Charlie. It was part of the plan, of course. They couldn't very well have the man run away while they carried out their little charade.

Bawb and Charlie had been training together a long time, and while Bawb was a far better fighter, by virtue of his being one of the deadliest assassins to ever live, Charlie was no slouch, having trained under the famous Ser Baruud in the gladiatorial arts for years before he and Bawb had even met.

The result of both their familiarity with one another's techniques, as well as their silent connection, meant they could ramp up their fight to levels that seemed far more violent and deadly than reality.

The two spun and whirled through the street, throwing one another against the walls, landing what *appeared* to be violent punches, kicks, and elbows as they fought over the downed Tslavar. They were careful, however, not to step on the man. They didn't want him to *actually* be harmed. Just shaken up.

"You think that's enough?"

"I believe so," Bawb replied. *"Let us finish this act and get on with it."*

Charlie unleashed a furious series of blows, driving his opponent to his knees, then delivered what looked like a devastating knee to the ruffian's head, dropping him to the ground, unconscious. Or at least, seeming to be.

"Are you okay?" he asked, rushing to the fallen Tslavar, helping the man to his feet.

Bawb had delivered the gut punch expertly, the fallen man's ability to breathe returning just as the fight ended.

"Thank you," the man said. "That was incredible. I've never seen anyone fight like that."

"It was nothing," Charlie said modestly. "I couldn't stand by and let some thug rob an innocent man like that. Are you sure you're okay?"

"I think so, though my ribs might be broken."

"I did not break his ribs," Bawb silently noted.

Charlie struggled a moment not to laugh. "I'm just glad you're all right."

"I'll live," the man said, trying to sound tougher than he was. "But please, how can I repay you for your help?"

"You don't need to––"

"Please, I insist," the man said, reaching for coin in his pocket.

"Well, I suppose a drink or two would be nice," Charlie said, stopping the man from merely rewarding him with currency.

"I really should be getting back, but you can buy yourself several drinks with––"

"You know," Charlie interrupted, "I actually left a couple of lovely ladies not so long ago at a bar just around the corner. If we're lucky, perhaps they'll still be there. What do you say?"

"*Two* of them?" the Tslavar asked, his curiosity suddenly piqued.

Charlie noted he had stopped digging in his pocket.

"Yes, my friend. One for each of us. As it should be!" he said with a jolly laugh. "Come, let us go and see if they're still there," Charlie said, starting to walk without waiting for the Tslavar to reply.

It wasn't a risky move. They'd set him up perfectly, setting the stage, making him feel left out by his friends. Bawb was a master of psychological manipulation, and this man was an easy mark for this one of his talents.

"Okay, then," the man said. "Hang on. Just one thing," he said, turning and kicking Bawb's seemingly unconscious form in the side. "Okay, let's go."

"You okay?" Charlie sent to his friend.

"He kicks like a child," Bawb silently replied, amused. *"Go, gather information."*

"I'm on it."

With that, the rescued Tslavar and his new friend made their way to the establishment for a drink or two, and surprise of surprises, the two women were still there. Charlie hoped they would be, since he'd paid them enough for several nights of their services. And tonight? They'd been hired for just their company, no less.

The four of them drank and laughed for a few hours, the men enjoying the presence of their surreptitiously hired company.

"Yes, I've seen more systems in the past few months than all of my years crewing ships prior to this," the Tslavar said. "It's been an amazing experience."

"Oh? Is something interesting going on?" Charlie asked.

"I really can't talk about it," he replied. "Suffice to say, it's been a great experience."

"I can imagine. All of that travel. I envy you that. Any idea where you're off to next? How long are you staying here, anyway?" Charlie asked as casually as possible.

"We've got to finish loading supplies here for a little bit longer, but then we'll be off to our next destination."

"And where's that?"

"I really can't say," he replied.

"No worries," Charlie said, keeping his disappointment to himself.

"Looks like we need Plan B," he silently informed his friend after several more attempts failed over the next half hour.

"Very well," Bawb replied.

They chatted a while longer, Charlie gathering what little additional intel he could from the man, before he finally signaled the ladies to excuse themselves. Minus the warm company of the women, the Tslavar's interest began to wane, and it *was* getting a bit late.

"I really should get back," the man said.

"Of course," Charlie said, rising to his feet. "It's been fun."

"Yes, it has. A surprisingly good result of an unpleasant encounter," the Tslavar said.

The two men exited and walked back the way they'd come, the Tslavar heading back to his ship, and his new friend happily joining him for the stroll. They rounded a corner and came face-to-face with the man they'd left unconscious so long ago. And he was smiling.

"Hey," Charlie said.

"Hello," Bawb replied.

"Wait, what's going on?" the Tslavar asked, confused.

"Oh, my poor friend. If only you'd just been a little more free with your information," Charlie said. "Oh well. Nothing more to do for it. Shall we?"

"Yes," Bawb said, then stunned the man with a quick spell, the two of them putting his arms over their shoulders, supporting him as they walked, making him appear to be merely drunk.

Twenty minutes later, their interrogation complete, the Tslavar logistics expert was frozen with a powerful stasis spell, courtesy of Bawb, hidden from sight but perfectly safe in a crate in a little-used warehouse. Bawb said it was a waste of magic, but Charlie didn't want to kill the man.

He'd had many bad experiences with Tslavars in the past, but this man, despite who he was and what he was part of, didn't seem like such a bad person. For a brief moment, Charlie even found himself reflecting back on all of the Tslavars he'd killed so recently and feeling uncomfortable about it.

But he caught himself and forced those thoughts from his mind. There could be no mercy. This was war, and the very survival of his home world was at stake.

"So," he said, looking at his Wampeh friend, "we finally got the name out of him."

"Indeed," Bawb replied, satisfied with his impromptu interrogation. "And it looks like we're going back to Slafara."

CHAPTER THIRTY

While the corporal known as Hicks was mapping out the lay of the unusual ship, Sergeant George Franklin, hero of the Great War, was helping Jo and Marban fix the hurt his little gunship had suffered upon entering the hostile galaxy.

The exterior damage was surprisingly minimal, given the ferocity of the barrage it had been subjected to. Thanks to Eddie and Ripley's intel––carried back to the fleet when they crossed over––the magical adjustments made to its shielding had been possible.

The warp drive, however, was another story.

Whatever spell had made it past the craft's defenses had done a number on it, throwing the carefully reconfigured device into disarray. Had the small, yet potent craft actually been able to engage the systems during its confrontation with the enemy forces, there was a very good possibility the warp would have overloaded, blowing George and Hicks to bits rather than merely inconveniently spitting them out at some random part of the galaxy.

But things were coming together rather nicely, all things considered.

"You see this?" Jo asked, pointing to what appeared to be some sort of coupling unit dangling from the warp core. "The polarity got reversed on it by whatever those bastards did. I'm gonna have to talk to Rika about this."

"Is that bad?" Marban asked. "I mean, obviously it's bad, but I still don't quite understand all of this tech stuff you are working on. Not yet, anyway."

"Hey, don't knock yourself, man. You've already been a big help fixing up the mech, and I'd wager you know more about Earth tech than anyone in this galaxy at this point," Jo noted.

"Yeah, you move around this equipment like you're one of us," George added with a warm smile.

Marban had taken an immediate liking to the square-jawed soldier. His calm under pressure and jovial demeanor despite difficult circumstances reminded him of someone he liked. Namely, himself. Fortunately, the feeling was mutual.

"You've really got a knack for warp tech, Jo," George commended the mechanic/co-pilot/gunner.

"Well, that's kinda how Rika and I joined up," she replied. "She'd been flying a ramshackle little ship called the *Icarus* during the big fight with the Tslavars when they tried to mess with Earth, and Cal wanted to do some upgrades for her."

"Yeah, we heard all about that attack when we got back from our survey mission," George said with a scowl. "I just wish we'd been there to help. I would have loved to kick those bastards' asses all the way back to their own galaxy."

"With your reputation, I don't doubt you could have," Jo said with a laugh. "Anyway, Cal and the gang souped up the *Fujin* all nice and spiffy-like. New guns, cutting-edge shielding tech, and, of course, a new warp drive. But it still needed a bit of a break-in period and some fine-tuning, so they sent me to help get her up and running properly."

"And then shit went sideways, huh?" George said with a laugh.

"Yep," Jo replied.

"Murphy. He just loves paying a visit, doesn't he?"

"You said it."

"Ah, Murphy." Marban said. "Charlie mentioned him before, but I haven't met him."

"You were buried alive for a few hundred years just when things seemed to be going your way, right?" George asked.

"Yeah," Marban grumbled.

"Then trust me, you've already made his acquaintance."

"What Sergeant Franklin is saying is, Murphy's a nickname for things going horribly wrong when you least expect it."

"Ah, I see," Marban said. "Sounds like what my old chief said a long time ago."

"Chief? You were in the service?" George asked.

Marban shifted uncomfortably. It had been a long time since he'd told anyone of his life before piracy. He didn't wish to bring any shame or dishonor upon the house that employed him. But they were all long dead. Everyone he ever knew from that life was gone.

"I did a fair amount of time, yes," he finally replied. "Mostly small unit combat and hostage rescue. We were a fairly specialized group."

"Sounds like special forces," George said, clapping the man on the shoulder. "We're cut from the same cloth, brother," he said with a grin.

"Perhaps at one time, but after my service ended, I was privately employed by a powerful family, tasked with protecting their son and heir. Unfortunately, we were fallen upon in transit. I failed."

"Shit, I'm sorry," George said. "Never an easy thing, losing a man."

"No, it is not, and I swore I'd get revenge."

"Did you ever find them?" Jo asked.

A grim look flashed across Marban's face. "That's a story for another day, I think," he replied.

George knew that look. He'd seen it plenty in men who had been through a bit too much at one point or another. "So, the *Fujin?*" he said, changing the subject. "I like your choice in names, Jo. The old Japanese god of the winds, if I'm not mistaken."

"You're mistaken," Jo said.

"Wait, really? I'm sure that––"

"No, not about the ship's name. About who named it. That was all Rika, before I even joined the party."

"She has good taste," George mused. "A fitting name."

"Yeah, she's got quite a bit of fire in her belly, that's for sure," Jo said. "Hardly surprising, though."

"Oh?"

"Yeah. She was taken prisoner along with Charlie. I'm sure you know the story, Marban."

"Yes, Charlie shared it with me a long time ago."

She turned to George. "Rika was tortured," she began. "Tortured and then had her mind burned. A lot of her memories were wiped as they made her a docile slave."

"That's horrible," George said, suddenly ready to do harm to whoever had done such a thing.

"Well, she later wound up being acquired by a real nasty piece of work named Malalia. That's the daughter of the man who bought Charlie."

"I heard the basics of that from Cal," George said. "They ran and wound up back on Earth."

"Yes, but there's more to it, but that's her story to tell. The end result of that whole thing was Rika wound up back on Earth with Charlie, healed from her injuries––at least as best she could be. And Malalia was killed, thrown into the void of space through her backfired spell."

"Holy shit, you guys get up to all sorts of crazy, don't you?" George said with a chuckle.

"I'm almost glad I slept through it," Marban said. "Almost."

The pirate brushed off his hands and stepped back from the little gunship. "Looking better," he said. "I think it's time for some chow, though. You guys game?"

Long accustomed to the bonding that took place over a meal, Jo and George readily agreed, though the food would do nothing for them.

"You know," Marban said as they walked, "I'm thinking we'll need to stop and get some *real* food. These Tslavars didn't have anything with *spice* on this ship."

"Oh, you want spicy? I can get you spicy," Jo said with a laugh.

"Really?"

"Ever heard of Nasturian?" Jo asked.

"No? Is it hot?"

"Meet me in the galley in ten minutes," was her reply.

"What did you do, Jo?" Rika asked when she walked into the galley a short while later.

Marban was seated at one of the long tables, face bright red, sweat dripping from head to toe as he downed cup after cup of icy water. George was seated beside him, an amused smile on his face.

"I didn't do anything," Jo protested. "He wanted to try it. It wasn't my idea."

"Well, it kind of *was* your idea, to be fair," George said.

"Who's side are you on, George?" Jo shot back with a crooked grin.

"The winner's side, of course."

Rika shook her head. "You're ridiculous. *All* of you are. Now, finish up here, and let's get back to work. We've got George's ship nearly ready to fly, but its warp system is still relatively vulnerable to magical attacks. We'll have to find a way to make it more robust."

"What about your magic?" Jo asked. "I mean, it was strong enough to break through their defenses back in the Balamar Wasteland battle."

Rika's grin faltered. "Yeah, about that. It's sort of fading."

"What is? Your magic?" Jo asked.

"Yeah. Just the part from here, though. The pigments in my skin are strong as ever, but I guess I used more of this place's magic than I realized."

"Wait, you also have magic from this galaxy?" George asked. "How is that even possible?"

"She absorbed it when we were in a rare black sun system. It kind of supercharged her powers," Jo replied.

"You know, I have to wonder. Can you just go and refill it when it runs low?" Marban wondered, eyeing Rika's swirling tattoos.

"I'm not sure. I suppose I could," Rika said. "What do you think, Jo?"

"We could really use some more star maps now that we've got a ship that can actually follow them. And if we got a couple of strong enough konuses to weld into George's ship and the *Fujin*, I bet we could boost their magical shielding several fold."

"You have a resource for these things?" Marban asked, taking another swig of ice water.

"Oh, yeah. I know just the place we can acquire them while Rika's out doing a little sunbathing in the dark."

"I *do* have a much better handle on the magic now, so it shouldn't be dangerous like last time," Rika said.

"Yeah, that was close," Jo noted.

"Close? How so?" Marban inquired.

"Don't worry about it, Marban. We've got it all under control. And George, I think you're going to get a kick out of this."

Rika and Jo shared a somewhat scary smile that both men found more than a little unsettling. Whatever their plan, it was going to be an interesting one.

CHAPTER THIRTY-ONE

Rika and Jo had never actually gotten the name of the dark world with the black sun. Their visit had been an impromptu one, and their departure rather hasty, after their run-in with Jorall, the unsavory Wampeh restauranteur and mob boss.

He had thought to rig a test of fortitude, betting the much-needed star maps the newcomers sought against their own bodies if they failed. The contest seemed straightforward enough. Eat an entire plate of his chef's special Nasturian-spiced dish and the prize was theirs. There was just one catch. Nasturian was the spiciest thing within twenty systems.

On top of the plant's naturally occurring heat, it also possessed a magical enhancement that made it feel as if your mouth was being consumed by lava bathed in acid. Jorall could count on one hand the number of hardy men who had successfully bested the challenge over the years, and he'd amassed quite a fortune in the process.

Rika and Jo, however, presented an unusual opportunity. He found the pinkish women enticing, and had unsavory plans for them when they lost the wager. Only, he hadn't counted on one thing.

Jo was the one who had accepted his challenge. And unbeknownst to him, she was a cyborg.

The ability to turn off all pain sensors in any part of the flesh body covering her metal endoskeleton was a skill the poor man had no idea she possessed. And with a stomach made of a metal far hardier than mere cast iron, she demolished his rigged game with ease.

The mobster hadn't wanted to let the women go, unaccustomed to losing in such an unexpected and humiliating fashion. Jo had made it look easy, and he'd lost face in front of his men. That meant he'd take his prize from them in a more forceful way.

Except he hadn't counted on one thing. Rika. The magical pigments inked into her skin were absorbing the powerful ambient energy given off by that world's most unusual sun. Its light was invisible, past ultraviolet, but the magical effects were undeniable.

Her other-galaxy magic was absorbing the power like a sponge, and when Rika got upset, she discovered her ink started to glow. Not white, as before, but purple, alive with the new magic bonded to hers. This in itself wasn't the big problem.

That she could seemingly cast without realizing it was.

The new amalgam of power tapped into her will, allowing her to cast silently, not voicing the words of her spells, just as Charlie and Ara could.

As a result, she'd very nearly killed them all before Jorall and his men wisely fled. Rika and Jo had done likewise, abandoning the planet at once, while the pilot from Earth tried to learn to control this new and unpredictable power. It was a dangerous place for her to be. Dangerous for herself, as well as others.

And now they were going back.

Marban's Drook navigators were of exceptional skill, but even they required several attempts to narrow down the location of the unnamed world that was their new destination. Jorall possessed star maps in abundance, and while Marban knew of other planets where they could source them, that knowledge was a few hundred years out of date.

So, back to the dark system it would be.

On the fourth jump the Drooks steered them to a system that just barely lined up with the periphery of the piecemeal star map Jo had cobbled together with the *Fujin's* navs systems.

"They've got a fix on our position. Once the Drooks have rested, the next jump should take us to our destination," Marban informed Jo when he saw her in the corridor on the way to the cargo bay. "Your star mapping was a big help to the Drooks. I don't know how much longer it would have taken them to pinpoint this precise solar system without them. Rare as they are for inhabited systems, there are a surprisingly large number of this kind of sun throughout the galaxy."

"Glad to have been of some use," Jo said. "I tell ya, for a while we were pretty much up shit creek without a paddle."

"I've heard Charlie use that one before," Marban said with a laugh. "Some things the translation spells don't quite get, but we had the fortune of spending a fair bit of time together in the past. The *distant* past, that is."

"Yeah. Mind fuck, waking up hundreds of years in your future, eh?" the cyborg said with a chuckle.

"You can say that again."

"Mind fuck, waking up hundreds of years––"

"It's a figure of speech," Marban said.

"I know," she replied with a wry grin.

He liked the woman. She was a spitfire, and one hell of a wrench, quite capable on tech and magical craft alike.

"Jo?"

"Yeah?"

"I was wondering. I mean, I had a––uh, you and Rika, you've been together a while, right?"

"Not that long in the grand scheme of things."

"But you're close."

"Obviously. She's a kickass pilot, and has become a really good friend."

"Just a friend?" he asked, trying his best to seem nonchalant. He failed.

Jo burst out laughing. "Oh, man. You thought we were an item?"

"Well, there'd be nothing wrong with that. You're both exceptional women, and if you and Rika––"

"I'm gonna cut you off there, bud. Rika and me? We're just friends. And besides, I'm a cyborg. I mean, how would that even work?"

"A what?"

"A cyborg. You seriously don't know about us?"

"I've been frozen a few hundred years beneath a desolate wasteland. Forgive me if I'm not entirely up to speed," Marban said with a confused smile.

"I'm like Sergeant Franklin and Corporal Hicks. Meat on the outside, but metal on the inside."

"Like George? And Hicks too, you say?"

"Wow, you really *are* out of the loop. Okay, so you know what an AI is, right?"

"A what?"

"Artificial intelligence. I don't really know how to explain it in a way that'll make sense to a magic guy."

"I'm not a magic guy. I don't have any power of my own, though I can use a konus and a slaap pretty damn good."

"Well, you're a magic guy to me, okay?" Jo said with a chuckle. "So, basically, me and the other cyborgs are built rather than born. And our minds, while alive, are made of technology instead of meat. That's really the best I can sum it up without diagrams and charts."

"And you're metal inside your body? Amazing."

"Hang on, I've got a portable scanner on me. I was using it to trace some power lines in George's ship. I'll just tweak the settings a bit and––"

She adjusted the little machine then held it over her hand, wiggling her fingers as she did. The small display screen showed the faint outline of her flesh body, but clear as day was the metal hand wiggling its fingers inside it.

"Amazing! I'd never have guessed."

"Well, that was kind of the point, originally at least. Metal people make meat people uncomfortable, but if we look like everyone else––"

"Then no one would be the wiser. You know, this would be a marvelous infiltration tool."

"How so?"

"You could look like anyone. Within the constraints of your physical size, that is."

"Huh, I never thought of that," Jo said. "You're a clever dude, Marban."

"Thank you. And you're a fascinating woman, Jo. I must admit, I am quite curious what other wonders there are on your world."

"Plenty. But it's the same for us on your home turf. I mean, we don't have magic where we're from. Or so we thought, anyway. It seems our home system just hasn't evolved to use it yet."

"Really?"

"Yeah. But we'll get there. Someday. Evolution always wins."

One of Marban's crew called out over his skree. "Captain, the Drooks will be ready to jump within the hour."

"Excellent news," he replied. "Well, my friend. It seems we'll be arriving at our destination a little sooner than I thought."

"I'll tell Rika and the others," Jo said. "Buckle up, Marban. This is going to be interesting."

CHAPTER THIRTY-TWO

Slafara was a surprisingly pleasant world, Charlie noted, as Ara completed her last jump from Rupsaval. It was the planet where the mysterious Visla Dominus was to gather his cached power—whatever that was—in preparation for a full-scale attempt to breach the portal and invade Earth and the other planets in that galaxy.

It was going to be a difficult process, narrowing down a location, as a strange mix of so many magic varieties lingered in the atmosphere, a side effect of such a magicall charged world. Many very powerful casters visited, worked, or resided on Slafara, and their powers were wreaking havoc with Ara's sense of smell.

Add to that, there was still that odd magic masking it all. Obfuscating a great many of the spells and power signatures, until the mighty Zomoki was left unable to discern origin or source. That was going to make things difficult.

Their Tslavar victim hadn't known *what* the magical power source or sources the visla was going to procure were, nor their size, or even which city they'd be located in. Just the planet. And there were several regions of exceptional wealth and power on Slafara to choose from.

Ara thought it best to start with one with a small magical presence, the logic being that it would give both her and Charlie an opportunity to fine-tune their senses, and hopefully work out a way to dial down the interference.

The search went both well and poorly. Well in that they were better able to smell the different magic types coloring the air. Poorly in that there was absolutely no trace of any type of magic that would be a game-changing power source for the visla. But stored power was far harder to detect than the live, flowing kind.

One thing they did learn that they'd not known on their prior visit to the world, was that there was an incredibly powerful visla on the planet. So powerful, in fact, the capital city was named for him. And from what they'd heard, he had just returned home to discover his daughter had gone missing. Surprisingly, the visla had not gone out and torn the city to pieces, but had rather become reclusive, grief-stricken and avoiding the outside world.

"I'd be upset too," Charlie said. "And they'd already kidnapped her just a few days before? That's more than a coincidence."

"I agree," Ara said. "Does anyone have an idea what happened?"

"Maybe Visla Dominus kidnapped her," Bawb posited. "A means to control this Palmarian, perhaps."

"The thing is, no one really knows," Charlie replied. "They said there was no sign of how they got her. No sign of a break-in, no ransom note. Nothing. And after what everyone was whispering happened to the last kidnappers, I'm surprised anyone would even have the balls to try it again."

"What happened to them?" Ara asked.

"Dispatched," Bawb replied. "And most violently."

Charlie shared a look with his assassin friend. "You thinking what I'm thinking?"

"That this Visla Palmarian is not someone on whose bad side you wish to find yourself?" Bawb asked.

"That, and that maybe it would be best if we put off searching *his* city for a while. Maybe until things have quieted down there a little."

"Agreed. While we've got stealth on our side, there's nothing quite like a riled-up visla to throw a plan into disarray. Let's try another one of the most likely cities on our list and go from there," Charlie said.

The two men took their places atop the Zomoki's back, settling in for the trip. Ara took off fast and made a steep climb to the edge of the atmosphere, then dove quickly, shortening their flight time from hours to minutes. She swooped down toward the green spot below that signaled their next target. A city called Zimofa.

She leveled out just above the surface, carrying her friends low and fast, avoiding prying eyes as best she could by sticking to skimming tree-lines, where any who happened to glance up would only see a strange blur, not a Zomoki.

The giant dragon landed in a little patch of thinner trees, where she could hide her mass between them easily enough. It was far too close to the city for her liking, but they were faced with a bit of a time crunch, and there was simply no time for her passengers to trek hours upon hours in order to catch a ride to town.

Fortunately, the odds of being stumbled upon in the woods, even this close to the city, were slim, for Slafara was a modern planet. A civilized one. And traipsing through the woods was something more often done by youths and laborers.

Charlie and Bawb made quick time into town, not using Binsala, or any of Bawb's usual disguises, but, rather, improvising entirely new ones, tailored to the specific needs of their intelligence-seeking mission.

Having spent a good amount of time working with one another, the pair made a rather efficient team, leading conversations in the direction they wanted them to go, while gathering what information they could from the loose-lipped local populace. And, fortunately for them, most they met on this stable and conflict-free world lived with their guard down. All the better to pry information from them.

In their discussions, they heard much of what they'd already found out on their prior visit repeated, but with minor bits changed, though nothing consequential. The core story was the same. The visla had returned and found his daughter missing, but there was a new wrinkle they hadn't heard before.

Apparently, there were also massive surges of magic seen flashing from high up in his towering estate when he came home to discover the unfortunate news. His was a power that, despite his position and rank, was not always entirely contained within him. That made him even more dangerous.

But since that night, the magical flares had ceased, the visla himself remaining in seclusion. Word was, he had become overwhelmed with grief and had not even left his chambers since that first night.

There was something else, though. More than one person had reported seeing a strange, almost shimmer-like object fly from the visla's tower right about the time his daughter went missing.

"You know what that means, right, Bob?"

"I'm afraid I do."

"Yep. It looks like we're going to the city of Palmar sooner than we'd planned."

CHAPTER THIRTY-THREE

Flying closer to Visla Palmarian's city, Ara and Charlie were now picking up that same disconcerting jumble of magic with far greater strength. It was undeniable. Something was in the air. Something was up. And whatever it was, it was far stronger than the last time they'd been on the planet.

"You smell that?" Charlie asked, as he focused his powers on the strange magic traces.

"Yes," Ara replied. "And it is different. Stronger. *Recent*."

"Yeah, I noticed that," Charlie said. "Whatever's going on, this is new. And some *really* strong magic is masking whatever it is."

"This is disconcerting," Bawb interjected. "I can only sense a slight trace of this novel power you both feel, but even my Ootaki hair is reacting to it without my conscious effort. I fear Visla Dominus may have already arrived."

The very thought sent a chill down Charlie's spine. Yes, they were powerful magic users in their own right, and with their powers combined they were an almost unstoppable force at times, but from everything they'd learned so far, it was sounding like they very well might not be a match for this Visla Dominus, even working together.

"But we had to have gotten here first. There wasn't any word on the street of unusual ships arriving," Charlie noted, hoping they would not have to face off against this deadly foe just yet.

"True," Bawb replied. "But *something* is different. And I can assure you, the Tslavar who provided us this information was telling the truth."

Charlie had witnessed his friend's interrogation, and while it was not a violent or painful one, the skill with which he had magically twisted the man's mind, prying closely guarded secrets from him no matter how hard he fought it, was a bit disconcerting. Once again, Charlie found himself quite glad that Bawb was on his side.

"Whatever the case may be, we need to ascertain the whereabouts of this power cache the visla intends to utilize. From what our little Tslavar friend told us, it is rumored that they've been very patient about using this secret supply for quite some time. For this Visla Dominus to now gather their stockpile with plans to finally use it bodes very poorly for us."

"So we go into the city center and see what we can find," Charlie said. "We go in fast, quiet, and as unassuming as possible. If Visla Palmarian throws another tantrum, we sure as hell don't want anyone of his power to know we're nosing around in his domain."

"Agreed. Though, it would be most interesting if Palmarian were to encounter Visla Dominus. The conflict could be most devastating."

"Now *that*'s a fight I'd pay to see," Charlie said with a forced laugh. "All right, then. Let's get started. Ara's gonna have to land far away from the city if we're going to stay unnoticed."

It was true, with not just the local population of the bustling metropolis, but also the mere presence of so powerful a visla to contend with, Charlie and Bawb were going to be in for a rather long trek into civilization. The outskirts of Palmar were rather vast and wooded, and their Zomoki friend would have to make her landing well beyond even those.

Fortunately, there was ample traffic flowing into and out of the city, so, despite the long trek the two men would be forced to make to reach the nearest transitway, at least they would have little issue procuring a ride.

Charlie and Bawb headed to town at first light. They each brought a small pack with nicer attire to change into once they'd reached civilization, and tucked in with Charlie's was the Balamar water orb, the map to which Ara had retrieved from the very same system's sun so recently.

They had been so close, the key to finding the item capable of defeating Dominus hidden in the same system. It was quite a coincidence, Charlie mused. Or, more likely, it wasn't a coincidence at all.

In any case, should they encounter Visla Dominus, he'd have one shot at taking him down with the magical waters. If he actually was a Wampeh, that is. But if he possessed anywhere near the skills of disguise that Bawb did, his true nature might not be readily noted.

The mood in Palmar was a bit tense, they noted as they flew into town on a small cargo conveyance. Apparently, not only word of the visla's daughter's disappearance had gotten out, but also the violent nature of his reaction to the news when he'd returned home.

But people spoke well of Visla Palmar. For all intents and purposes, he seemed like a perfectly normal leader. The only difference was, he possessed incredible amounts of power, and, on occasion, in times of high emotion, he'd been known to lose control of it.

And having his daughter go missing again certainly fell into that category.

Charlie could barely stand the strange magic buzzing in his

head as he and Bawb did their reconnaissance of the city. Whatever it was, the sensation was maddening. But through all of the mixed magical signals, Charlie could tell one thing. There didn't seem to be any trace of stored magic anywhere near the quantity Visla Dominus was coming to retrieve.

That was the thing about storing magic. For smaller things, like a konus or slaap, you'd have to be right up on the thing to feel any of it. But for massive power vaults the likes of which Visla Dominus was to collect, there was always a trace of the enormous energy stores. And in this city, despite all the magic floating about, there was no such signature anywhere near.

"It's weird, Bob," Charlie said. "You'd think it would be here. Especially with all the interference."

"Perhaps," Bawb replied. "However, it is also quite possible this Visla Dominus wants no part of Visla Palmarian's wrath should he learn what is happening on his soil."

"Turf war?" Charlie asked.

"Essentially," Bawb replied. "But if that is the case, then we must depart this city at once. Time is running out, and we must find this item before Visla Dominus does."

"But how? There's so much magical disruption going on around here, I haven't the foggiest idea how to begin."

Bawb walked in silence a moment as he pondered the situation. "I was thinking. If this item contains stored power, wouldn't its general signature, its *smell*, as you and Ara call it, then be different from other magic?"

"Well, it would be, sure, but it might be tough to discern from the ambient magic," Charlie noted.

"And if you could focus only on non-active magic? On *stored* magic?"

Charlie saw where he was going with that idea. "With you there to keep an eye out for regular magical disruptions, Ara and I could cast spells to filter it all out. Or most of it, at least. And that would *possibly* allow us to pick up a hit if something particularly powerful was out there. Holy crap, Bob, that might actually work!"

"I hope so. For if not, finding this repository of power may prove incredibly difficult, and our time is little."

"We need to get back to Ara. Night's coming, so we should have cover to get started immediately."

Charlie and Bawb hurried out of town, crossing the outskirts of the city until they reached the spot they'd hidden their trekking clothes. They quickly changed and began the run back to their Zomoki friend.

It felt good to run. Their bodies reveled in the exercise, though soon enough they'd be back in their space suits, aloft and searching.

They'd been seated atop Ara's back far too long for any of their liking at this point. Things hadn't gone as expected, and this was all dragging on much longer than anticipated. But soon, hopefully, if they could beat Visla Dominus to their hidden power cache, they'd have the upper hand, and maybe be able to end this conflict and go home.

Rejoining their friend, they relayed the plan, cast the appropriate spells, and took off into Slafara's skies as night fell, off to survey the planet in the safety of darkness, their senses reaching out for whatever powered artifact they might find trace of.

CHAPTER THIRTY-FOUR

Ara flew a cautious circuit around the great city of Palmar as she and Charlie dampened their blood-bonded senses to as much *active* magic as possible. Bawb sat astride Ara's back as well, alert, reaching out with all of his abilities, but not filtering one bit. He was the lookout for his hampered friends. If anything was going to come their way, he'd be the one to see it first.

But nothing came at them. In fact, they seemed to avoid being detected entirely. That was a pleasant outcome to a situation they'd been quite nervous about. To be discovered in Visla Palmarian's realm while he was in such a state of distress could have played out very poorly for the trio.

Something else happened as well. Something they hadn't expected. Despite the churning magic of the city––and, more importantly, the mysterious layers of powerful spells obfuscating the nature of some of it––once all of that was tuned out, there was simply no sign of a magic storage device remotely as powerful as they'd had described to them.

"It's not here?" Charlie wondered, confused.

"You searched as I did," Ara replied in his head. *"I'm afraid whatever that magic is stored in, we are not going to find it here."*

"*We need to expand our search immediately,*" Bawb noted. "*There are still many areas we can reach while protected by the cover of night. It would behoove us to begin surveying them at once.*"

"*Agreed,*" Ara said, banking away from Palmar and heading off into the dark.

"*And away we go. Sleep is for wimps, anyway,*" Charlie said, trying to lighten the mood.

But a shadow hung over the search party. This was not going to be easy. Not one bit.

Not long after the mighty dragon flew from the skies of Palmar, a far different shape drifted through the night air. A vessel containing far more power than it let on. One that also carried the visla's missing daughter and her friend.

Korbin and his niece had briefly returned home to Slafara to gather still more magical tools to help free the unusual ship they'd found trapped on a piece of moon. But then Korbin got word that Visla Palmarian had come home and was beyond furious to find his daughter was missing. Plans quickly changed.

If Korbin had been on the fence, it was at that moment he knew the girls had been away from home for too long. His decision had been made in no small part because of Kara's father's temper tantrum magical flare-up.

Korbin's network of ever-watching eyes and ears had dutifully described the incident, and with that bit of information, he decided then and there that the situation had simply become too dangerous *not* to bring Kara back home.

Fortunately, no matter how upset he might be with her, Korbin knew that Kara's father would never harm her. He loved her more than anything in the world and would sooner meet his end than let something happen to her, despite his occasional appearance otherwise.

Korbin's ship dropped down to the landing field nearest

Visanya's home first, discharging his niece's best friend before taking her home.

"Now, Visanya, remember what we discussed. There can be *no* talking about what you may or may not know is going on with Kara's father. You're home, but there could still be danger, so make sure to be alert. And for goodness sake, you really must dye your roots, lest someone realize what you *really* are."

Vee paled at his words, her eyes going deer-in-the-headlights wide.

"Yes, Visanya. I know you are an Ootaki," Korbin said with a warm, non-threatening smile. "And don't worry, I won't tell anyone. But you need to be more careful. Did you really think one of your potential would go unnoticed forever? I just happen to be more observant than most."

"I, um——"

"Your parents did a noble thing, taking you at such a young age and hiding your true nature. It afforded you a normal life, something very few Ootaki ever get to have. So be a good girl and protect yourself. And if your parents need any help, just have them reach out to me. Your mother and I are old friends."

Vee felt her panic dissipate as she realized she was, indeed, still safe. "Thank you, sir."

"Of course. Now, go on. I'm sure your parents will be thrilled to see you."

Vee lurched joyfully forward and gave the man a big hug and a kiss on the cheek. Korbin, for once, was caught off guard, a slight blush coming to his face.

"You be careful," Vee said, turning to Kara, holding her hands tight in her own. "You still don't know what your father's up to."

"I'll be as careful as I can, Vee. Don't worry about me, I'll be fine."

"And *both* of you need to remember you cannot speak a word about Freya or Pod. It is imperative they remain secret, at least until I figure out some way to free her from that chunk of moon."

"We know, Uncle Korbin. Don't worry, we won't say a thing," Kara said.

"Okay, then. Good night, Visanya. You've done well these past few days."

Vee smiled brightly, then exited the ship, making sure to heed Kara's uncle's advice and stick to the brightest, most well-traveled streets.

"And as for you, it's time to get you home as well."

He powered up his Drookonus and made the quick hop over to Visla Palmarian's grounds, landing in the expansive space out front of the tower.

"What about Daisy? She's not what Father thought she was. I don't think so, at least."

"Perhaps not, but this is your father's estate, and we dare not interfere with his dealings until we know full well what's really going on. But it's late, Kara, so you go on in and get some sleep. Don't worry about having left the tower. Just tell your father I had invited you to come visit me if you were able to. Blame your absence on me, and he'll let it slide."

"You're not coming in?"

"No, it's an unseemly hour for guests. But don't worry, I'm only going home to see what I might have that could be powerful enough to help us free Freya from her bondage. I'll be back in the morning to have a proper visit with your father and get a better feel for what he might be hiding. Then, perhaps we can broach the subject of his prisoner. We'll play it by ear, and we can then plan our next steps from there."

CHAPTER THIRTY-FIVE

The security staff at the front doors went wild when they saw Karasalia walking up to the entrance. To say they had feared for their lives when her father discovered she had gone missing was not hyperbole.

He wouldn't harm his staff. Not normally, at least. But when his daughter was believed kidnapped again, and right out from under their noses—inside his own residence, no less? *That* was something that might push him over the edge. And that would not be good. Not at all.

"Hey, Shozzy. Hey, guys," Kara greeted the familiar faces as she strolled in the doors.

A massive throng of guards was already swarming the entryway, forming a protective wall behind her, blocking any pursuers who might be chasing her from the outside.

"Guys? What are you doing?"

"Get inside, Denna Palmarian! We will protect you!" Shozzy said, his eyes rapidly scanning the grounds outside.

"Protect me? From what?"

"Your kidnappers. How did you manage to escape?"

"I wasn't kidnapped. I was just visiting my uncle. Didn't anyone get my note?"

The men looked at one another with panic in their eyes. If there'd been a note that would have explained the whole situation and they had somehow missed it, there would be hell to pay.

Of course, there was no such note, but Kara had concocted that twist to her story on the fly. She didn't want the security detail to suffer for it, though, so she was going to quickly write one up and crumple it into her belongings, then act surprised and embarrassed that she had forgotten to leave it for them. It would likely draw some anger her way, but it was the right thing to do.

"Is my father in his offices?" she asked, walking to the lift disc.

"You do not know?"

"Know what?" she asked, concern growing, and quickly.

"Your father is in his chambers. I'm sorry to be the bearer of bad news, but the visla has taken ill after the shock of your supposed kidnapping."

Kara felt her adrenaline spike. Had she caused this? Without another word she activated the disc and flew to the top of the tower, rushing straight to his chambers.

"Father!" she exclaimed, seeing him lying in his bed, eyes closed and his skin much paler than usual.

He did not wake, nor did he even stir. Her heart rate spiked, a crackle of power flickering from her chest to her fingertips as the surge of panic took hold.

That was new, she realized, shocked at her own magical growth.

"Father, can you hear me?"

"Kara! You're home! And safe!" Mareh gushed, rushing into the room. "The guards told me you were back. Oh, darling, where have you been? Your father was worried sick!"

"What happened, Mareh? Why is he not waking up?"

"I don't know what it is, dear. He was beside himself when he returned home and found you missing. It was all I could do to keep him from tearing the city to pieces, he was so enraged."

"But he's so weak."

"I know. It's the weakest I've ever seen him, and I haven't a clue what to do about it. With powerful men as strong as he is, the reactions they have can be utterly perplexing to the rest of us."

"But have you called the healers?"

"Yes, but this is far beyond their scope. I'm flying out personally in the morning to retrieve one of the healers from my friends' distant estate. They've got a practitioner of exceptional skill, and I'm sure they'll let her leave with me for an urgent matter such as this." Mareh looked at her stepdaughter's concerned face and gently grasped her shoulder. "I'm sorry, I'm making you more concerned. We're doing all we can, Kara, know that. But you've been gone, quite impossibly I might add. Come, let's get you some food, and you can tell me where you've been."

Despite her reeling emotions, Kara also had ideas rushing through her mind. Things she could possibly do that might help her uncle free the strange ship far out in the system.

"I'll join you in the dining hall in a few minutes," Kara said. "I just want to change into something more comfortable."

"Of course. I'll meet you there," Mareh replied.

Kara walked with her to the lift disc and gave her a warm hug. "I'll be down in a minute," she said, watching her descend.

Kara then rushed off, but not for her chambers. Not yet, at least.

She came into the dining hall ten minutes later, clothed in a comfortable, loose tunic and flowing harem pants, both items complementing her pale violet skin.

"Everything all right? That took a while," Mareh asked.

"Yeah, everything's fine. Sorry, I was just being indecisive," Kara replied, taking in the spread her stepmother had arranged for her return.

In just those few short minutes, Mareh had already had Tulagda whip up a few of Karasalia's favorite dishes, each laid out on the long table, steaming hot. The chef was quite skilled, and quite magical at that, and at moments like this, those talents truly shined.

"Wow, that's a lot of food," Kara said, appreciatively eyeing the selection.

"I didn't know what you'd want, so I thought it made sense to simply have Tulagda make a few options."

"It all looks amazing," Kara said, sitting down and tucking in to the assorted dishes.

"Now, tell me, dear. Where have you been all this time?"

Kara swallowed her mouthful of food and wiped her mouth before replying. Her magic may have been lacking, but her manners were always those expected of a visla's daughter.

"I was just visiting Uncle Korbin. He sent a message that I hadn't been to his estate in ages and I was welcome to come for a visit. He invited Vee too," she added, knowing the story would check out if anyone bothered to contact her friend's parents.

"But the tower was locked down, Kara. And I'm sorry for that. Your father was quite upset after you were kidnapped, you know. But given my way, I would have avoided such excessive measures."

"I know you would have, Mareh, and I appreciate it."

"But you haven't told me how you managed to leave the grounds."

"I was bad. I used my bloodline ties to father to get around one of his wards. You know how sharing common blood can make some spells misfire? Well, I used that to effect a workaround spell."

Mareh's eyes widened slightly. "Oh? Well, your power must

be growing more than expected," she said, piling up a plate of food for herself. "But now, tell me all about your visit with your uncle. We haven't seen him in quite a while."

"Oh, you'll see him tomorrow."

"What?"

"Yeah, he's coming by in the morning."

"What fantastic news. I'm sure your father will be thrilled to see him. I just hope I'm still here when he arrives. Acquiring the healer for your father is urgent business, and I'm afraid that takes priority over being a good host."

CHAPTER THIRTY-SIX

What Mareh hadn't known when she sat down to dine with her recently returned stepdaughter was the *real* reason for Kara's delay in joining her in the dining hall. Kara actually *had* gone and changed into a more comfortable outfit, but only after doing what she really wanted to do.

With Mareh in the dining hall, Kara had quickly rushed off to her father's offices. With him being home in the building, she only hoped he had left them in their usual state, rather than warded with additional spells. There simply wasn't time to take the roundabout path through the floating gardens otherwise.

Fortune smiled on her when she reached the entrance. There was no magic barring her entry whatsoever, so Kara proceeded with her plan as rapidly as she was able. Fortunately, she'd worked out the details in her head well before reaching the room, the spell she needed already on her lips.

The secret door to his vault slid open for her as she uttered the requisite spell.

"Still there," she noted with a relieved sigh. "Father won't notice it missing. Not in his condition."

She grabbed the braided rope of Ootaki hair the visla had

stashed there and tucked it into her shirt, winding it around her waist in a hasty wrap. It was funny, in a way. Her best friend was a disguised Ootaki, with more than enough magically charged hair to make the attempt to free the trapped ship. But the very thought of Vee being used as a thing, not a person, was utterly abhorrent to Kara. Fortunately, her father's cache provided an alternative.

Kara was about to close the compartment and reseal it, but hesitated, looking at the image discs showing what had been of such great concern to her.

The Ootaki hair he possessed had been stashed mostly out of sight within the compartment, beneath some notes, an odd bracelet, and several other pieces of jewelry. But the image discs were just sitting in plain view. Taking all of them would have simply been too obvious.

"Nobody will miss just one," she told herself, pocketing a disc at random to show her uncle when they returned to try and use the Ootaki hair to free Freya. She sincerely hoped her idea would work. If her father found out, furious would be an understatement for his reaction.

Karasalia then shut the compartment, placing the magical lock back in place, and rushed off to change clothes for dinner with her stepmother. The meal went quite smoothly, and she followed the story she, Visanya, and Uncle Korbin had rehearsed.

The girls had come to visit him, on his invitation, Uncle Korbin not being aware Kara was essentially grounded and confined in the tower. Kara once again lied about the note she had thought she left for them, only to find it deep in her belongings upon her return. She even handed the crumpled page to Mareh to bolster the story.

But Kara needn't have worried. Mareh had always been so kind to her, and on this occasion, she was no different.

"Darling, I know you didn't mean to worry us, but you see how this impacted your father's health," Mareh said.

"I know. And I'm really, really sorry," Kara replied.

Mareh flashed her trademark loving smile and accepted her apology, and the two chatted comfortably for the rest of their meal. Afterward, Mareh even offered to braid her stepdaughter's hair before she went to bed. It was something of a bonding tradition they'd had ever since Kara was a little girl when Mareh married her father, and Kara always slept most soundly afterward.

The following morning, Korbin arrived at the tower bright and early, striding up to the front entrance as if he hadn't a care in the world. The reality was quite different, however, as his mind was running through lines of questions he might ask his dearest friend to find out what was really going on. The two never had secrets from one another, but something was up.

He was also working out how best to release the magic binding the strange craft that called itself an "AI" from the far edge of the solar system. *That* was going to be a difficult task, though he didn't want to worry Kara or Freya with that tidbit. The magic that had bound the ship there was not only twisted from its original intent, it had also been cast by an extremely powerful user, though the feel of the magic led him to believe it was possibly stored magic rather than live-cast.

The implications were enormous. For someone to be capable of giving that kind of power from themselves and placing it into a repository without weakening excessively was unheard of. Strange things were most definitely in play. He just had to figure out what, exactly, they were.

For the moment, at least, he had to focus.

"Gentlemen!" Korbin said as he strolled into the building. "Good morning to you all."

"Visla," the men replied respectfully.

He hated when people did that. He tried so hard to cultivate a life where he was valued for his friendship and knowledge rather than his natural-born powers. But for today, he would have to play the part.

"I have come to see Nikora," he said, knowing using the men's employer's first name so casually would only enhance the image he was expected to present.

"I'm sorry, Visla, but I'm afraid Visla Palmarian is ill. I was told not to admit any guests."

"Ill? Is he all right? I must see him at once!" Korbin said, legitimately alarmed. His friend was many things, but frail was not one of them.

"I'm sorry, Visla, but my orders are to not——"

Power crackled angrily from Korbin's fingertips. The guards looked at one another, then wisely stepped back. The enraged visla stormed past them, right onto the lift disc, then disappeared upward.

Only he wasn't enraged. Concerned? Yes. Enraged? Not at all. But knowing how Nikora could sometimes bleed off power when he was angry, Korbin thought a little display for show would be the fastest way to overcome any objections. He felt bad for it. The poor men were only doing their jobs. But if his friend was ill, there was no way he would not visit him.

"Uncle Korbin!" Kara said, giving him a big hug when she saw him coming down the hall.

"Kara? What's happened?" he asked, his concern growing. "Are you okay?"

"I'm fine. Just worried about father," the teen said.

But he wasn't so sure about that. The bags under her eyes had returned, but it felt like something more. She was weaker. It was a tangible change from the spry, chipper girl he'd just spent the past few days with.

"What's happened, Kara?"

"It's all my fault. Mareh said he was so upset when I wasn't here. He thought I was kidnapped again. Oh, I'm so stupid. I should have left a note."

"But you didn't know you'd be flying off in an invisible tech ship, did you?"

"Well... no."

"So you couldn't have known to write that note ahead of time, could you?"

"I guess not."

"Then don't feel bad for it, Karasalia. These things happen, though I am quite concerned that your father would have this strong a reaction and fall ill rather than go on a bit of a rampage. He's never been a weak man. Not in all the years I've known him."

"I know. It's scaring me. Mareh too. She was so worried about him."

"And where is your stepmother?" Korbin asked, scanning the halls.

"She left at first light. She's jumping a whole bunch of systems away to see if one of her society friends will be willing to part with their best healer for a few days to come and see Father. Another friend of hers came earlier to help, but father is still quite weak."

"Healers. For a visla of his power. It's ridiculous." Korbin saw the look in Kara's eyes. "Ridiculous, but it might actually help this time. But come, let me go see him myself. Perhaps I can be of some assistance."

CHAPTER THIRTY-SEVEN

Korbin and Kara walked the halls to her father's chambers. Staff were nowhere to be seen. Mareh had been very careful to ensure no one would catch sight of the visla in his weakened state.

"Father, look who's here to see you," Kara said, catching the man's attention.

Visla Nikora Palmarian, quite possibly the most powerful man in all the systems, looked utterly drained as he lay reclining on his bed. His skin was ashy, and his eyes hung deep in their sockets.

He turned his muted gaze to his visitors, taking several seconds to register their faces. "Oh, Karasalia, you're here," he said weakly. "I was so worried about you."

"Hello, Nikora," Korbin said.

The visla turned his gaze to his lifelong friend, but didn't seem to register who he was for a moment. Then, with a slight surge of power, he seemed to come to his senses.

"Korbin? What are you doing here?"

"Visiting you and Karasalia, of course," he replied with the best grin his concerned mind could manage.

Korbin summoned up a very minor force spell, far less than he normally would. Since their youth, he and his friend had always made a magical game of knocking each other over when they weren't expecting it. Today, however his target was already lying down. But this was not a friendly bit of messing with his pal. This was a test.

He gently cast the spell, worried how the visla might react. Surprisingly, the spell was dispelled with ease.

"Still have your strength, I see," Korbin said with a laugh.

"You'll have to try harder than that, Korbin," Nikora replied.

Korbin smiled at his friend, but his sharp eyes noted the thick, powerful konuses the visla wore on each arm beneath his bedclothes. Visla Palmarian was cheating. Cheating because the only way he could maintain the impression of possessing his power was by using his strongest konuses. All to keep up appearances.

Korbin's smile faltered a split second. Something was seriously wrong for his friend to be in this state.

"I was going to ask Karasalia if I might raid your kitchen for a snack. I'm famished. Can we get you something, my friend?"

"No, I'm fine," the visla replied. "I'm just going to rest my eyes a moment."

"You do that, Nikora. I'll be back later."

Korbin and Kara stepped from the room, leaving her father to rest, albeit fitfully, then quickly made their way to the empty dining hall.

"What happened to him, Karasalia?" Korbin asked. "This is not normal. Your father is far too powerful for this. Even sleeping he possesses more power than others could ever hope to wield. But now? He's using konuses to cast. It doesn't make sense."

"I know," Kara said. "Whatever he's involved with, it's taking its toll on him."

She reached into her pocket and removed the image disc she'd stolen from her father's secret cache. "Maybe this will help," she said, offering it to her uncle.

"What is it, Kara?"

"One of the discs I told you about. From Father's vault."

Korbin took the disc and studied it a long moment, then cast the spell to activate it.

Images of a massive fleet sprang to life, floating in the air before them. Kara couldn't be sure, but it seemed as if her uncle even recognized some of the vessels.

"Does your father know you've seen this?"

"No, Uncle Korbin."

Karasalia's uncle fell silent a moment, staring intently at the images flashing before him. He looked at his niece, her pale, violet skin and slightly sunken eyes. She had the spirit, but something was wrong. This was not the same girl he'd dropped off only the night before. Something had happened. He just didn't know what.

"Kara, I want you to come with me. There's someone I want you to meet."

"I really don't know if I can leave, Uncle Korbin. Father already fell ill, and Mareh said—"

"This isn't a request," Korbin said, tender but firm. "I'll have you back before your father misses you. By the look of him, he'll be resting most of the day."

"Well—"

"This way," Korbin said, taking her by the hand and leading her to the lift disc.

They descended to the lobby in a stomach-churning drop, Korbin putting an arm around his niece to help her keep to her feet in her weakened state. It took her a few steps once they exited the lift to regain her balance, but she recovered fairly quickly.

The two crossed toward the exit when a thick-necked, gray-skinned man with heavy konuses on his wrists came hurrying across the foyer to intercept them. He placed his considerable bulk in front of the two, blocking their exit.

"Denna Palmarian is not to leave the building," the man said.

"And who are you to give orders in this household?" Korbin asked, sizing the man up.

"I am Emmik Trepenan, come to look after the family as a favor to Mareh Palmarian. The youngster is not to leave."

"Are you telling me that *you*, a stranger, mean to prevent my niece from leaving with *her uncle* to procure goods to help bolster her father's spirits and health?"

"That is precisely what I'm saying," the man said, crossing his rippling arms and puffing his chest.

Trepenan could see that Korbin was clearly outmatched, not so much as a simple konus on either wrist. Against a well-armed emmik like himself? The poor man didn't stand a chance.

Or so he thought.

Korbin moved to walk around the man, but Trepenan was not having it. He quickly cast a powerful force wall spell, blocking the path with a nearly impassable spell. To most, anyway.

Korbin paused, studying the magic in his path. Trepenan smiled with cocky delight. Korbin sighed, casually raised the hand not helping support his niece, and reduced the spell to shreds with barely a whisper.

The gray man went several shades paler at the sudden realization that the big fish in the pond was actually just a tiny one in a far larger ocean. And he was in the presence of an apex predator.

"Are we quite done here?" Korbin asked lazily, a flicker of violent power shining in his eyes.

Trepenan, wisely, kept his mouth shut and simply nodded.

"Good," Korbin said. "If it makes you feel any better, we will be back relatively shortly."

He then led his niece from the building and to his waiting ship. A minute later they were safely in the sky, destination a few systems away. Korbin was taking Kara to a safe place. A specialist. A friend.

CHAPTER THIRTY-EIGHT

In the cozy warmth of a dimly lit restaurant out in a far off solar system warmed by a black sun, a pirate with a long scar running from the crown of his head to his collarbone and his square-jawed, human-appearing friend sat at a low table.

A small, but quite respectable, pile of pillaged goods from the Tslavar ship taken in battle sat before them in a small pile. The normal din of the establishment was notably absent, and most, if not all, eyes were upon the newcomers.

It wasn't for their rough good looks, by any means. Nor was it because they cut a particularly dashing figure against the backdrop of pale-hued locals. No, it was for another reason entirely. These two were going to be the evening's entertainment.

Jorall, the Wampeh proprietor, returned to the table where he'd left the men sitting with a small package under his arm.

"That all of it?" Marban asked.

"As agreed upon," Jorall said with a grin, opening the container and removing a pair of particularly large konuses, far too large for either of the men, but perfect to weld to the frames of George's little gunship and the *Fujin*. And in addition to those, there were a handful of rare star charts that included many systems devoid of residents but still inhabitable. "Top of the line, every bit of it. And worth far more than mere coin can buy. And you?"

The duo's pilfered goods on the table were enough to buy most items one might require, if they had time to shop, that is. But they didn't have much time, and some things, as Jorall had said, mere money couldn't buy. For that, something special was needed. Something unusual.

Sergeant Franklin opened the box in front of him and placed its contents on the table. It was a simple tech's diagnostics tablet. The device had a strap allowing it to be worn on the forearm, if desired, or simply held in one's hands. George tapped the power key, and the device immediately flashed to life.

Gasps from the crowd told him the item had the impact he'd desired. Rika and Jo had already filled him in on the value of novel items in this galaxy. And this was definitely something none of them had ever seen.

George then turned on the 3D hologram projector that allowed for better diagnostics of complex componentry. He'd loaded the device with all sorts of images, from ships to complex parts, broken down to their individual details.

It was information he'd never leave with the man, obviously. But he had no intention of losing this bet.

"Here it is," George said, placing the device alongside the star maps and konuses. "As you said, something mere coin cannot buy."

Jorall smiled greedily as he eyed the glowing device. It was unlike anything anyone had ever seen, and its magic was undetectable. The value was incalculable.

"Yes, yes. This will do just fine," he said, already thinking how he might best sell the strange thing and set himself up even better than he already was.

Or he might just keep it, using the novel item as a status

builder any time a cocky trader or self-important emmik or visla dropped in––which, admittedly, was quite rare. In any case, he would have plenty of time to think about that once he'd won this little wager.

"So, this natrian stuff I keep hearing about. Just *how* hot is it, exactly?" George asked.

Jorall grinned warmly, though his intentions were anything but. "Oh, it is quite spicy, I assure you. I wouldn't make this wager otherwise. And it's pronounced 'Nasturian,' by the way."

"Ah, my bad," George said. "But I'm glad to hear it's hot. I've developed something of a resistance over the years. Have to keep searching out new spices to give my food any flavor."

"Believe me, this will definitely fill that need," Jorall said with a confident chuckle. "But first we will each have one of our men sample the dish to ensure it is a good batch."

"Don't trust your own cook?" George asked, flashing his opponent a wink.

Jorall's smile faltered for just a moment, quickly glued back into position on his face. "I'm just ensuring the challenge is a fair one for all involved," he said, turning to his rippling-muscled assistant. "Tell Froozal we are ready."

The man nodded and strode off toward the kitchen, returning a minute later with a sizable plate of a steaming stew-looking dish.

"Smells great," George said.

"But first," Jorall replied, nodding to one of his servants.

The man stepped forward, then reluctantly dipped a small piece of bread in the sauce and popped it in his mouth. Marban, observing the proceedings, then did the same. All that remained was to wait.

They didn't have to wait long. Within ten seconds both men were sweating profusely, their faces remaining quite flushed even as they drank several cups of water apiece.

"Oh, hell. That's hot," Marban managed to say.

Jorall's man didn't seem to have the capacity to speak at the moment, only able to nod his agreement between swigs of ice water.

Sergeant George Franklin grinned with anticipation. "Okay, then. Let's do this," he said, digging in to the blisteringly spicy dish with a lack of hesitation that, for just a moment, made Jorall's confidence falter.

That reaction soon proved prescient, as George powered through the meal with gusto.

"Hey, do you guys have any more of that Nasturian stuff?" he asked through a full mouth. "It's still a little mild for my taste."

Marban, his face still beaded with sweat, nearly burst out in laughter. Only the pain on his tongue prevented it. Jorall, on the other hand, reacted in a far different manner, pushing his men aside and swiping a taste from the utterly unfazed man's plate.

The Wampeh's eyes grew wide, and sweat immediately began to bead on his forehead as the heat kicked in. Farzool, it seemed, had not skimped one bit on the Nasturian for this dish.

George watched as the man struggled to keep a calm face, showing no sign of the burning pain in his mouth, enjoying this little charade immensely. He then took another slice of bread and mopped up every last drop on his plate, downed it, then burped with gusto, thanks to a small addition he'd had installed several years ago to better bond with the soldiers he was embedded with.

Farts and burps, it had been proven, were the universal humor language of men everywhere, requiring no special translation protocols whatsoever.

"Oh, man. That was *good!*" George said, gathering up their prize and tucking it into his pack while Marban stowed their part of the wager back into his gear bag. "Well, fellas. I'd love to stay and have some dessert, but we really must be going."

The cyborg and his pirate friend strode out into the darkness of the black sun's orbiting world, knowing it was midday, though it looked like night.

"That went well," Marban said as they walked.

"I agree. Not bad at all," George replied.

As he'd done with Rika and Jo not so long ago, Jorall had rushed ahead and was lying in wait in the shadows, only this time he had far more goons with him. Fifteen, to be precise. And this time, all of them were armed.

"I think you cheated," Jorall said, stepping in front of the men. "Nobody abides cheaters around here."

"Cheat? How could I cheat?" George asked, his AI mind clocking the location, weaponry, and weaknesses of every single man present in the dark roadway. Sometimes, being a cyborg really did have advantages.

"I don't know how you did it, but there's no way you ate all that Nasturian without even breaking a sweat," the Wampeh said. "Now, give me those bags."

"You really don't want to do this," George replied, making no move to hand over anything. "Two of our friends will be along shortly."

Jorall laughed. "There are fifteen of us. What could a couple of people possibly do?"

It was a question that fate decided should be answered immediately.

A purple glow began to illuminate them from above, causing all of the men to turn and look at the sky, watching the glowing woman descending toward them as she flew with no apparent assistance.

As the glowing woman flew, another approached from up the road. And this one you didn't have to squint to recognize.

"Oh, hi, fellas," Jo said merrily as she walked up to the gathered goons just as Rika touched down from her rather impressive entrance. "Funny seeing you all again."

The fifteen men of violence didn't say a word, but just briefly glanced at one another, then turned and ran, Jorall at the front of the fleeing throng.

"You good?" Jo asked her glowing friend.

"Yeah. Better than good, actually. I feel freakin' amazing."

"And you're flying," Marban added.

"Yeah, that too," she agreed with a stupidly happy grin.

"So, ya seem to have gotten control over this particular strain of magic since last time we were here. You remember, right? When you nearly killed everyone, including *us*."

"Jeez, Jo. It was an *accident*," Rika said, rolling her eyes.

"Doesn't make it any better," her friend replied with a laugh.

Rika sighed exaggeratedly. "Ugh. Fine. Come on. Let's go," she said, then began glowing again as she lifted off into the air.

"Impressive woman," Marban said appreciatively as he watched her fly ahead.

"You've got some interesting taste, man," George said with a chuckle as they headed for their ship. "I think we're going to be good friends, you and I."

CHAPTER THIRTY-NINE

The woman with the golden hair hadn't always been this way. Fierce when need be. Strong. Dangerous. Prior to her union with the deadliest man in more than thirty systems, in fact, she'd been a timid and compliant slave.

Then Bawb happened, saving her life, though that hadn't been anywhere in his thoughts of battle outcomes for that day. But when he saw Hunze, trapped in her ruined ship, all the other Ootaki slaves around her dead or dying, something in him had twinged.

The man who had killed so many ignored his training and listened to that tiny little tug in his chest.

The resulting union had blossomed into a fulfilling love neither could imagine being without, and the sharing of his knowledge and skills with his dearest only strengthened that bond. It also made Hunze into one of the most dangerous women in the galaxy, for she was an Ootaki in control of her own power. And more than just that, she was now a Wampeh Ghalian––though as an Ootaki, it was by skill and name, if not species.

But despite possessing Bawb's talents, she had no intention

of ever assassinating anyone, and her loving nature still guided her daily interactions, even with the Master Assassins of the Order she was now part of.

It was with those six Wampeh Ghalian that she was now planning their next move to stop whoever was threatening not one but two galaxies she called home. Intel was minimal, and options were few. But if anyone might find a way to make this work, the collective experience and skills of those brilliant minds could.

Filling those eager brains with information, Kip's modified neuro-stim had been able to transfer quite a bit of useful, if only basic, knowledge about things the quirky ship had solid data on. One such aspect was small ship piloting.

"We understand the basic functionality of your galaxy's vessels," Wagyah, the youngest of the Wampeh masters said. "This may prove quite useful in later stages of this conflict. However, in order to disrupt a fleet of this size, we would have ideally embedded our agents weeks, if not months, before they even began their operations."

"I know, Wagyah," Hunze said. "And I understand the reluctance to engage."

"It is not a reluctance to engage," Farmatta, the old, and deadly, woman interjected. "It is that any plan, especially one of this magnitude, requires intelligence. Information that we simply do not possess."

"Farmatta is correct," Kort added. "This is going to be a major undertaking, and we cannot be underprepared. We will need to place some of our people aboard these craft, even if they are already in position in this distant system."

"But they'll be ready," Dunaak said. "They kicked our asses when we first crossed over. What's to make them sit still while your guys secretly board their ships?"

Kort pondered the situation a moment. "We will need a decoy, obviously," he replied. "And we will need to acquire weaponry not traditionally utilized by the Wampeh Ghalian. Something more military in nature. More overt. And that sort of thing can be rather difficult to source on short notice."

Hunze felt a smile grow on her face. "Don't worry," she said. "I know a guy."

It was with a renewed confidence in her stride that Hunze, hood pulled low over her head, walked the streets of the now-familiar world where she hoped to acquire both the connections and the services of a particular smuggler.

Where last time she was on this planet she was on the defensive, worried about fending off potential attackers as she kept her identity secret, this time, while still being cautious not to be observed, she had not only her four-armed friend at her side, but also several Wampeh Ghalian shadowing their every step.

Of course, to look for them, one would not see anything out of the ordinary on the streets. But that was the nature of the master assassins. Blending in and being invisible, even when in plain sight. Often, that was under the guise of a character that couldn't help but draw attention, and thus became free of suspicion, for who in their right mind would hope to conceal themselves in such a manner?

Master assassins. That's who.

And those assassins were her brothers and sisters now. And they were going to war. For that, they needed equipment, weapons, and vessels. An expedited process was required, and Hunze felt she had just the man for the job.

"Yeah?" a voice called through the sealed door to a rather nice home in a good part of town.

"Olosnah, it's Hunze," she said, knowing the smuggler would be more than pleased for the opportunity to trade with her again, especially if another strand of her powerful hair was in the cards.

But for some reason, he was reluctant. "This really isn't a good time," he said through the closed door.

"Olosnah, this is Dukaan. Please, we have a very lucrative engagement we wish to discuss with you."

Still, the door remained shut.

"Can you come back in an hour? I just––Hey!" he abruptly blurted.

A moment later the door opened from the inside. Pimbrak, the dapper master assassin, was casually holding the blue-skinned smuggler in a somewhat painful armlock with one hand, while ushering out a partially nude woman with the other. He flashed an amused smile at Hunze and Dukaan, then bade them enter.

Hunze politely averted her eyes. "Put some clothes on, Olosnah. You're naked."

"Ya think? Of course I'm naked. This crazy bastard just appeared out of nowhere and grabbed me. Neat trick, by the way. All of my doors are sealed with high-end magical wards. You'll have to show me how you did that," he said, his annoyance matched by his appreciation of the skill required to break into his place and curiosity about the technique.

"We need your help," she said as he quickly donned a robe lying on the floor where it had been hastily discarded.

"*We*? Who's 'we'? I have a feeling you're talking about more than just yourself and your buddy Dukaan, here."

"You are correct," the dapper Wampeh said with a pointy-toothed grin.

At that moment, despite all of his bravado and bluster, Olosnah felt his bowels slightly loosen as a burst of adrenaline flushed through his system.

"You... you're a––"

"Yes," Pimbrak replied with a little bow.

The assassin was enjoying this unusual game. Normally those he snuck up on didn't live to appreciate his handiwork. This was a fun change of pace.

"We are with the Wampeh Ghalian now," Hunze said, catching the smuggler's attention once more. "I think you can appreciate the severity of the situation if they have become involved."

"You hired a Wampeh Ghalian? You really are crazy, you know that?"

"We did not *hire* anyone, Olo. We are working together toward a common goal," Hunze said, not mentioning that she, too, was a member of the Order. "My friend here will tell you what we need. I know you'll be happy to help us, won't you?"

"Of course," Olo replied with an audible gulp.

He wasn't going to help out of fear. That wasn't his style. But being on the good side of the Wampeh Ghalian? *That* was worth nearly as much as the strand of Hunze's hair he still carried safely coiled in a charm he now wore around his neck at all times.

"We are in need of supplies," Pimbrak said. "Ships. Weapons. Not your run-of-the-mill stuff either. We require a more *robust* nature of equipment."

"I can get you whatever you need," Olo said. "Ships? No problem. How big? How fast? How many Drooks do you need? I can source it all. And if you want combat-grade slaaps––"

"Those we possess, as well as claithes,"

"You have *claithes*?" Olo said, impressed.

"We are the Wampeh Ghalian," Pimbrak replied. "Of course we do. But we shall be engaging large vessels, and overtly at that. We shall require modified ship's konuses to focus attacks."

"I can get those."

"Good. And pilots. We will need pilots."

"Hmm, I think I can source a few I trust. But this ain't my fight. No way I'm flying into battle. I'm just a smuggler."

"Of course," Pimbrak replied. "I understand that facing a force of skilled pilots could be disconcerting."

"I'm the best pilot in fifty systems," Olo said.

"Of course you are," the Wampeh said with just the right hint of a smirk.

Just enough to plant the seed he hoped would sprout and grow into full-fledged assistance. Regardless, there was more this man could do for them than merely fly.

"Another thing," Pimbrak said. "I was thinking, we could really use a distraction. You wouldn't have any Zomoki lying around, would you?"

"Hell no. And why would you even want any of those deadly beasts?"

"Oh, no reason," the assassin replied.

Hunze had watched the exchange quietly, but at this, she felt an interjection was warranted. "You want Zomoki? Don't worry, I know a guy."

CHAPTER FORTY

Korbin's craft had exited the Slafaran atmosphere at speed. He didn't have to fly so fast, per se, but nevertheless, when he'd taken his niece from her father's estate, he hurried her aboard his ship and off the planet.

The girl was weak, and her father weaker. Whether there was some sort of illness in their house, or something more sinister, he simply wasn't sure. But he'd been around long enough to know this was not normal. To know to be concerned. And this type of problem was beyond his considerable skills. For this, he needed a specialist.

It was two quick jumps to the quaint planet on which his longtime friend lived, but Korbin jumped a half dozen times instead, backtracking and overlapping, just in case they were somehow being observed despite having scanned his ship for tracking spells.

Amazara was doing him a favor, and he would not allow anything bad to befall her if he could help it. This had to be a quiet visit. Not covert, per se, but certainly as low-key as he could make it.

Fortunately, Amazara lived atop a hill outside the quaint town at which she resided. The location provided rather convenient cover for Korbin's ship as it made a casual approach, then landed behind the hillside. It was an unnotable arrival of just another ship to the area. He wanted to make sure it stayed that way.

"Come with me, Karasalia. We are going to take my conveyance," he said, unloading a small, sturdy craft from its storage compartment.

It was not designed for more than two people, and it was ruggedized. While the vast majority of the magically flying craft used for transport on all of the inhabited worlds could easily cover relatively smooth surfaces, this particular unit had been specially adapted with Korbin's own powerful magic. As a result, even small boulders were not a problem for it, though actual flight was beyond its capabilities.

For scaling logs and rocks on the long climb to Amazara's charming lodge, it was perfect. And, much as he enjoyed that walk, given Kara's weakened state, it was essential.

Korbin helped his niece onto the conveyance and ensured she was well seated, then loaded a few small bags of her favorite delicacies one wouldn't ordinarily find in this system. Amazara would balk at any offer of coin, but he wouldn't dream of coming to her empty-handed.

The ride up to the top of the hill was lengthy, yet relaxing, mostly shaded but with just enough clear sky to allow the gentle sunlight to warm your bones. The entire point was to slow visitors enough to require them to face a period of introspection as they approached, hopefully arriving at their destination in a calm and open mental and physical state.

Kara, however, was so weak that no such tricks were necessary in order to bring her to that mental state, and she was more than ready for Amazara.

Pulling up to the lodge, Kara saw a lithe woman, roughly her uncle's age, standing on the wrap-around porch, watching as the conveyance crested the hill. She was tall, her pale blue hair setting off her silver eyes, the corners of which were graced by fine lines from years of joyful laughter.

They could have easily been removed by a simple spell, but Amazara seemed not to mind them one bit. In fact, she embraced them. This woman was confident. Utterly comfortable in her own skin. Kara liked her at first sight.

"Amazara, thank you for seeing us on such short notice," Korbin said, embracing his friend warmly.

"You know I'm always glad to help," she replied, her eyes flashing a warmth that Kara thought seemed to convey more than mere friendship.

Interestingly, she'd never known the man to have a partner of any kind. It was something Kara never really thought about, its absence just a part of life. But now the void was suddenly illuminated by the unexpected contrast. Kara was curious. She'd have to ask her uncle about that later. But for now, other plans were the order of the day.

"Karasalia Palmarian, this is Amazara Faloral," Korbin said by way of introduction.

"A pleasure to meet you, Karasalia," Amazara said, taking Kara's hand in her own warm grip.

"Please, just call me Kara. And it's nice to meet you as well."

"You've had a bit of a journey, Kara. Would you like to come inside for some tea before we begin?"

"Sure. But what exactly are you going to do to me?"

Amazara turned to the girl's uncle. "Korbin, did you not tell Kara what we were going to be doing today?"

"I know how you work, Amazara," Korbin said with a cheerful laugh. "And that means I had no idea *what* you had planned."

"Oh, you," she chuckled, the amusement spreading easily to her happy eyes.

Yes, Kara thought. There was definitely something between those two. Good thing she had taken an immediate liking to the woman. "Okay," she said.

"Okay, what?" Amazara asked.

"I'll take that cup of tea, if you don't mind."

"Wonderful. Please, follow me. The kitchen is just this way."

The three spent a nice hour chatting, drinking tea, and snacking on small pastries and a dish of fruits that Amazara had picked from her own garden. The kitchen was a cozy place, with comfortable chairs around its small table. It was an intimate, cheerful setting, and Kara felt utterly relaxed and at home.

Of course, that was the point. And while they'd been partaking of comestibles and conversation, Amazara had been doing what she was so good at. Namely, reading people.

While she was indeed a rather skilled healer, Amazara's true gift was in assessing people and zeroing in on what ailed them. The less guarded they were, the easier it was to do. And what better place and way to achieve that end than in the kitchen over a friendly cup of tea?

"Amazara, are you a healer?" Kara asked.

"Of sorts," she replied.

"So does this mean you're going to come help my father?"

"Oh, dear. I'm afraid not."

"Then why are we here?" Kara asked, turning to her uncle. "We need to help him, Uncle Korbin. We're drinking tea while Father is ill."

The calm that had settled over the teen was beginning to crack, and the stress from her life on Slafara was creeping back in.

Amazara rose and fetched a small box from a shelf.

"Would you like to try a Yokam fruit?" she asked, offering the box to Kara. "I only get a few per season, and they're unusually delicious when dried like this."

"I couldn't. You only have a few, and––"

"Please, it would make me happy to share with such a charming young woman."

Manners kicked in, and Kara was loath to offend a host. She took one of the small, dried fruit and popped it in her mouth. The flavor was unlike any she'd ever had before, and amazingly, she felt her stress flee her body as she chewed.

"Why don't you head out to the porch?" Amazara said. "Korbin and I will meet you in just a minute."

"Okay," Kara replied, docilely, then headed outside.

"Spiked fruit?" Korbin said. "You surprise me, Zara."

"She was getting worked up, and I thought she could use it, Korb. You know I prefer to do this without employing outside implements or spells."

He nodded his affirmation. It was true, she almost never used anything but her own natural gifts. But sometimes a situation required it.

"So? What did you find?" Korbin asked.

The silver-eyed woman sipped her tea, thinking. Weighing the meaning of what she'd found. It was disconcerting, to say the least.

"She's an incredibly powerful girl," Amazara said.

"She has some skills, but she seems to be lacking in the magic department," Korbin replied.

"No, Korbin. You're not hearing me. This girl has *power*. It's almost nothing at the moment, just a mere specter of its true self. But I can feel the traces of what it was. What it should be."

"What are you saying, Zara?"

"That the girl is *diminished*. But she is young. Given her age, resilience, and the pure power within her, her gift will start to return. Likely in only a few days."

"You're saying this is not an illness that caused her to weaken, then?"

"Definitely not," Amazara said. "Something caused her to lose her powers, yes, but it was *not* natural."

CHAPTER FORTY-ONE

As evening fell, Amazara took Korbin and Karasalia for a stroll, showing them her gardens as they helped pick the ingredients for the evening's meal. Korbin enjoyed cooking for himself, but Kara had grown up in a household where there was always someone to do that for her. Participating in a field-to-table meal like this was an eye-opening experience, and one she found herself rather enjoying.

The smell of the land was also drastically different from the floating gardens atop her father's estate. There was simply something healthier and more natural in the air itself out in the wilderness like they were. And she was pretty sure it was more than just being on another planet.

This open space, this other world, t just felt right. And with every minute there her stress from back home faded. Her concern for her father's health was still present, but the panic-attack level of fear that had taken hold of her previously was no more.

The three of them took their bounty back to the cozy little kitchen at Amazara's home and stood side by side as they cleaned, sliced, and prepared their dinner. It was a family dynamic, though one neither Korbin nor Kara had experienced growing up. But it felt nice and casual, yet also comforting.

They chatted casually as Amazara blended ingredients and finished the last touches on their evening meal. Once it was all ready, she ushered her guests to a comfortable old wooden table situated in the warm air, where they would dine as they watched the setting sun.

It wasn't until they were well into their dessert, a mélange of berries and homemade frozen fruit slurry, that the subject of Kara's malaise was broached.

"So, I was wondering, when exactly are you going to try to figure out what's wrong with me?" Kara asked. "I mean, I feel better already, so maybe it wasn't anything to be concerned about to begin with."

"A portion of that might have to do with getting you away from Slafara and into nature," Amazara replied.

"We have tons of nature on Slafara. It's a beautiful planet."

"I'm not saying it isn't, Karasalia. What I meant was, perhaps a *change of scenery* after the stresses you've been dealing with has proven helpful in restoring your equilibrium."

The teen noted the pause in the healer's words, and the look she flashed at Korbin. She may have been under the weather, but she was a very intuitive girl, regardless of her current depleted condition.

"What aren't you telling me?" she asked.

Amazara and Korbin shared another look. Korbin sighed and gave a slight nod.

"You're quite perceptive, you know," Amazara said. "Yes, I suspect there is something more, though I cannot be certain of it."

"What?"

"It appears that whatever has caused you to be under the weather may have been done intentionally. I am unfamiliar with the strange traces of magic I've been sensing, but so far as I can tell, someone targeted you, Karasalia. I just don't know how."

"And I don't know why," Korbin added. "But I am damn sure going to find out."

"But how, Uncle Korbin? And why would someone care about me? I'm no one important, and my magic is weak."

"You say that, but you're a visla's daughter," Korbin replied. "And, much as you may not believe it, you possess far more power than you are aware." He turned his attention to the silver-eyed woman. "Zara, will you look after my niece for a little bit while I look into something?"

"Of course, Korbin. She's a charming girl. It'd be my pleasure."

"Thank you," he replied, their eyes locking an extra beat.

"What are you going to do, Uncle Korbin? Where are you going?"

He turned to Kara. "I'm going to investigate what you found. The images captured on that disc. Something is up, and I believe it somehow ties back in to your father."

"But you don't even know where that is."

Korbin grinned. "No, I don't. But I have an old friend who might."

The three of them finished their dessert and cleaned their dishes, but a slight tension hung in the air. Someone was meddling with Kara's health. And now her uncle was going to put himself in harm's way on her behalf. She didn't quite know how to feel about that.

On the one hand, it was a relief having someone care for her so much as to want to do so. On the other hand, if anything happened to him, she'd never forgive herself. But it was clear this had to be done, there was simply no avoiding that fact. And so, Korbin left his niece in the healer's care and flew off into the night.

. . .

"I believe there are some festivities in town this evening, if you'd like to take a look," Amazara said as she and Kara finished putting away the last of the dishes.

"Will there be music?" the teen asked.

"I would think so. After all, what's a party without music?"

"Exactly!" Kara said, her spirits rising at the prospect.

"Then come with me," Amazara said, leading her out of the house to the barn-like structure set a ways back from her home. A gentle whinnying sounded from within as they grew nearer.

"Are those Malooki?" Kara asked, her eyes widening.

"You know your animals," Amazara replied with a warm smile. "Have you ridden before?"

"Me? No. We have gardens at home, but they're floating and don't really lend themselves to that sort of thing. Plus, living in the city, you know."

"I do, but that seems rather a loss of wonderful life experience. Would you like to learn? It's quite easy."

"Really?" Kara replied, her spirits rising at the unexpected offer. "Now? But why not take a conveyance?"

"I much prefer them to a magical transport. I like to be in touch with nature," Amazara replied.

"But magic *is* natural."

"Yes, but in a different way. You'll see," the healer said as she opened the doors to the barn.

"Isn't it too late, though?"

"Late isn't a concern, so long as there is light. And the orbital path of this planet at this time of year lends itself to plenty of illumination from our moons."

"Well..."

"You don't strike me as a timid type, Karasalia."

"Just call me Kara. Only my dad and uncle call me that."

"Okay, Kara. So what do you say? Are you feeling brave enough to try something new?"

Amazara knew which buttons to push to help guide her

young friend, and fifteen minutes later they were riding atop the firm backs of the beautiful Malooki. The animals were similar to Earth's horses in shape and size, but possessed longer, wiry hair that had its own slight bioluminescence in the dim light.

It was a faint, inherent magic within the creatures that tapped their inner power and expressed it outwardly in their coats. In times of joy or stress, the brightness and color could change, though that really depended on each individual animal. Tonight, they were glowing with warmth, happy for the outing as much as their riders.

Kara and Amazara rode the winding trail through the trees, slowly descending from her hilltop to the town below. And as the minutes passed, Kara realized Amazara had been right. It was a different kind of magic, bonding with nature.

"Amazara?"

"Yes?"

"Can I ask you something kind of personal?"

"Of course."

"Were you and my uncle ever a thing?"

Amazara's blush was hidden by the dim light, but Kara noted a slight shift in her posture atop her Malooki.

"Why would you think that?" the woman asked.

"It's just that I've never seen him with anyone as long as I can remember. And it seems like he likes you," Kara replied.

Amazara's blush deepened in the dim light. "We've been friends a very long time. That's all," she said.

Kara heard the hitch in her reply, though, and wasn't buying it. "Really? Because you seem to like him too."

The healer took a deep breath and counted to five, then slowly let it out. "Your uncle is an important man. A busy man. He has far more things to be concerned with than affairs of the heart," she said.

"Hmm," was all Kara said.

Amazara wasn't the only one who could read people, but the

teen decided not to push the subject. They had only just met, after all, and to do so would be rude. And a visla's daughter is never rude.

She pushed the welling thoughts of her father from her mind as best she could. They were going to town, and it would be a pleasant evening. Dwelling on the troubles at home wouldn't make them any better, and Amazara was right, new experiences were a part of growing up.

And tonight, Karasalia Palmarian decided she would heed that call and broaden her horizons, even if only by a little.

CHAPTER FORTY-TWO

The gas and debris rings surrounding the planet Goom were a beautiful sight to behold, even with the knowledge that much of the colorful stripes of the multi-hued bands were formed by the planet's gravitational field having pulled in waste and debris jettisoned by myriad craft over the centuries.

The rings acted as a natural buffer, keeping it from entering––and burning up in––the atmosphere. And as Captain Sandah piloted Visla Palmarian's vessel around the rings, Leila couldn't help but marvel at the sight, even after being briefed as to their true nature.

Captain Sandah had been planning to finally return to the visla's estate on Slafara, but Leila had convinced him to make one last stop before giving up their search for her friends and the strange fleet that might point her in the direction of the portal.

If her friends had already come back for her, the odds were good Eddie and Ripley would spend at least a few days searching for her, so no harm would come from spending one more day of searching. At least, she hoped not.

The planet also happened to be within long-range skree

reach of Slafara, so Sandah utilized their stop as an opportunity to finally contact the visla's estate while they were coming in for a landing. They'd been gone too long without contact, he noted.

The surface of Goom was somewhat oppressive for taller, leaner species, as its gravity was double that of most other inhabited planets. But Leila had no intention of staying on board, despite her most recent capture and subsequent rescue.

"If you insist on joining me on this excursion, then at least send Baloo out first," Sandah said. "He has a keen sense of smell, and if there are any Tslavars lying in wait, he will sniff them out long before we catch sight of them."

"Okay. That's actually a good idea," Leila said, conceding that, though she had no intention of staying aboard, perhaps a little additional caution *was* warranted. "All right, Baloo, go see what's out there," she said as the door opened, letting in a warm, humid breeze.

Baloo, being a good boy, stepped right out to the surface, though the strange pressure he felt weighing on him made him want to take a nap. It was similar to how he sometimes felt after a really, really good hunt, when his entire body was tired from the exertion. But there had been no hunt, and Baloo was a little perplexed by the sensation.

But his mama was heading out, and nothing would keep him from protecting her, his senses on high alert. Bad men had tried to hurt her recently, and he was not going to have any of that. Not again.

He sniffed the air, scanning the streets surrounding the little landing port to see if any of those green people he didn't like were around. Fortunately for any Tslavars who might be simple residents, minding their own business, they weren't in the area at that moment, and the planet was not very populated with that particular species.

Baloo looked over his shoulder, his expression one of, "Come out and play!" rather than, "Danger!"

"Baloo doesn't sense anything," Leila said, stepping out of the ship.

Free of the magically stabilized gravity, Leila's lithe frame felt abruptly yanked downward the moment she set foot on the hard-pack.

"Whoa," she exclaimed, despite being ready for it, forcing her muscles to fire up and cope with the increased load. "Okay, that's a bit of a shock."

"My apologies, Leila. I regret your having to deal with the increased gravity. But Goom was the nearest world within the likely path of your friends, and there is a trading hub here as well, which might provide an opportunity to gather the information you were seeking."

"Don't worry about me, I'm fine. It was just a surprise, is all."

"Very well. I have had the men remove a conveyance from the cargo hold for us. I think, given the physical demands of this place, we would be better off saving our energy for more important things than walking."

Leila felt a swell of relief in her body. "Thank you, Sandah. That's a great idea. Any ideas where to start?"

"Not a one. But we should head into the city center and see what we can discover. I haven't seen any sign of the ship you described, but perhaps someone else has spotted them at some point."

They loaded onto the floating conveyance and made the ten-minute hop into the bustling commerce hub of the region when Leila spotted something.

"Stop!" she called out.

Captain Sandah's crew had become accustomed to following the whims of his privileged cargo, and thus did as she asked, the driver pulling aside and setting the little craft in a low hover.

"What is it, Leila? What have you seen?" Sandah asked.

"There!" she said, excited. "They can help us!" The olive-skinned woman jumped from her seat and trotted over to the establishment that had caught her eye, Baloo glued to her hip.

Captain Sandah looked at the sign hanging above the door and shook his head with a resigned sigh. "A seer," he said with clear annoyance. "I hate seers."

"Shall we fetch her, Captain?"

"No. If this is where our guest wishes to go, then so be it. We head home straightaway, and perhaps this visit will help put her mind at ease. Anyway, she has already gone inside, and as you've all seen, she's a stubborn one, so there's nothing for it at this point. Come, let's join her and see what this charlatan has to say."

The thing about seers was the vast majority of them possessed no actual power at all. It was akin to the cheap parlor tricks of Earth's sham psychics, only once in a long while, one would stumble upon an actual power user. Those were not always perfectly accurate, but frequently accurate enough.

But those were few and far between. And as was often the case with prophesies, you wouldn't know they'd been telling the truth until events unfolded long after you'd left their presence.

This particular seer wasn't an old hag in mystical robes, but rather, a well-dressed young man. *Very* young. No more than a teenager, in fact. He turned when Sandah entered, assessing him with tranquil eyes that were both youthful, yet many years older than their owner.

"Nothing," he said.

"I'm sorry?"

"Nothing for you," the youth said. "I see nothing."

He turned his attentions back to Leila, where she was seated before him, a curious intensity flashing in his gaze. For Leila he most certainly saw *something*.

"Not all are as they seem," he said after a long pause.

"What does that mean?" Leila asked, hanging on his words.

"It means he is saying what all seers say. The obvious, for no one is as they seem. This prophesy applies to all people."

The young man smiled knowingly and fixed his gaze on the captain. "The loyal servant, faithful since his youth. A chance for a normal life given up for promise of what? More service? I wonder, how will your sacrifice ultimately be repaid?"

"I'm a captain of Visla Palmarian. Anyone who saw my vessel land would know as much. And my personal history is well-known as well. You speak plain facts, and nothing more."

"Believe as you wish," the teen said with that damnable calm smile that drove the captain mad. "But," he turned back to Leila, "beware the false friendship and niceties of serpents. They shall try to bite you, in the end."

"Enough of this. We are leaving. Come, Leila. We must get back to Slafara."

Leila was reluctant to depart, wanting more information. Some clarity. But as was the case with seers, she would leave bearing more questions than she'd arrived with.

CHAPTER FORTY-THREE

"Look out!" Rika shouted.

"I see it, woman! My gods, you're worse than my father when he first taught me to fly his conveyance," Marban replied with a chuckle and exaggerated sigh as he swerved around the small asteroid in their path, then leveled out the *Fujin*.

Jo snickered from her seat behind the pair. "Nice flyin', Marban," she said.

"Shut it, Toaster," Rika said, flashing her a halfhearted glare.

"Hey, that's Kip's thing," Jo replied. "Me, I'm much more about flying and shooting things, as you well know. And our boy Marban here seems to have the touch."

It was true. Marban was an alien, and from a magic-using universe no less. Technology was simply never part of his life until very, very recently, yet here he was, in a rather advanced ship, soaking up the fine points of space flight like a sponge.

Part of that was due to his prior military training from long before he was ever a pirate. But that was a part of his life he didn't really ever talk about. The pirating, however, was a different story, and he had many tales of action and adventure ready to go at a moment's notice.

In any case, both of his careers led to a flexible mind that was ready to adapt and overcome whatever situations the universe might throw at him, be they magical or technological in nature.

"When can I shoot the cannoons?" he asked.

"*Cannons,*" Rika corrected. "They're pronounced 'cannons.' Let's get the flying thing dialed in a bit before we start blasting things, okay?"

"Copy that," Marban said with a merry grin.

"Where'd you learn that? You guys don't use comms," Rika noted.

"Charlie was in the habit when we first met. I just kind of picked it up. Rolls off the tongue nicely, wouldn't you agree?"

Jo had watched the two sniping and bantering back and forth for the better part of an hour, and judging by the little glances she kept seeing him throw Rika's way, she was pretty sure there were other things Marban would like to do with his mouth than talking.

But she was a cyborg of great tact. That, or she just didn't want to provoke too much of a response from her friend now that she was supercharged with black sun magic. At least, not while they were floating in the confines of the *Fujin.*

She'd save her teasing for open spaces.

"Now, we're not going to play with the warp system just yet, even with that new konus welded into my baby's frame. We need to do some testing first, to make sure we understand exactly how it'll all work once we fire it up," Rika said. "But you should know where those systems are."

"Excellent! I'm looking forward to––"

"No, were you listening? I said *not* to use them, but to make sure you don't accidentally activate them in some ham-fisted 'Arrrr, Kill!' pirate shenanigans."

"What kind of pirate would I be if I shouted 'Arrr'?" Marban asked. "That's ridiculous. Who would be afraid of any pirate who said that?"

"Obviously one more difference between our galaxies," Rika replied with a little grin.

Jo kept her mouth shut, but the exchange, she thought, was getting interesting. Oh yes, she'd have to grill Rika about it later. She was even considering giving her a little carefully placed prodding when their proximity alarms suddenly flashed to life.

"What is it, Jo?" Rika asked.

"A ship just jumped into the area. It's heading toward the *Coratta*. I don't think they've seen us yet."

"Shit, are they hostiles?"

"It's a Tslavar ship, so the odds are good it is," Jo replied.

"Same markings as the ones we commandeered," Marban noted. "They're hostile, all right."

"Captain, we're being hailed," Marban's second-in-command called out over his personal skree. "What would you have us do?"

"Stall them. Do the garbled transmission spell trick and buy us some time," the pirate replied. He turned to Rika. "Can you block them from jumping with your magic?"

"Do what?"

"Block them. Your magic interferes with theirs."

"I... I really don't know. I can try."

"Well, get trying, then, because if that ship realizes the *Coratta* isn't crewed by their friends anymore and jumps away, it'll bring their whole damn fleet down on our heads."

"How did they even find us? We're in the middle of nowhere," Jo wondered.

"No idea. Maybe there's a beacon or something we missed. We just need to stop them," Rika said, as she focused on her combined powers, the purple glow of her tattoos growing by the second.

"Just don't blow up our ship, now. Okay?"

"Shut up, Jo. I'm concentrating."

The Tslavar scout ship was still moving toward the *Coratta*, but had slowed its approach.

"They sense something is wrong," Marban said, watching the events unfold on the ship's displays as they magnified the craft ahead of them. "If you're going to do something, you'd best do it soon." Marban then gunned the throttle, the ship bolting ahead, rapidly closing the distance to the Tslavar ship. "Jo? I think this is a good time to show me how to use the cannons, wouldn't you agree?"

"I'm already on it," the cyborg said, activating their weapons systems from her wireless link.

She much preferred interacting with the *Fujin* hands-on, but Rika was occupying her usual seat, and she was preoccupied with casting a spell to save all of their asses, so she'd make an exception this once.

The cannons swung into place and tried to lock onto the Tslavar ship, but it was still too far out. A blast of purple light flooded the cockpit, the strange magic then focusing into a ball and flying right through the hull as if it weren't there, zipping through space, and into the enemy craft.

The magic-powered scout ship was rocked by the impact. Damaged, but not destroyed. It shimmered for a moment as it jumped––and reappeared a few kilometers away.

"You broke their jump navs," Marban exclaimed. "They can't escape."

The ship jumped again, again reappearing in the same general area.

"Looks like it's going to be a goddamn game of whack-a-mole," Rika grumbled, wrapping her hands on the controls. "I think I'd better drive," she said, then set off in a spiraling weave as they engaged the enemy craft.

The two vessels were both fast and both deadly, though one relied on magical weapons, while the other used Earthborn ones. Neither could land a hit on the other, though, despite their best efforts.

"Their jumps are getting longer," Jo noted. "I think your spell is wearing off. How long does it last?"

"How the hell should I know? I've never cast that before. I was just making it up as I went. And the way they're moving, I won't be able to land another one."

"This is not good, Rika. We need to get them before they jump away."

"I know, I know. Marban, get your guys on the horn. See if they can target this bastard before he——"

The Tslavar ship abruptly burst into pieces, ripped apart by a violent barrage of plasma bursts.

"What the hell?" Rika blurted, scanning the space around them for the source of the attack. "That wasn't magic. That was Earth tech."

"George's ship isn't space-worthy yet. We still haven't finished the last repairs," Jo replied. "I have no idea what——"

Her words trailed off as a familiar shape grew closer.

"Is that my mech?" Rika asked. "How the hell——"

"Hey, guys," Sergeant Franklin called out over comms. "Saw you were having a little trouble out here, so I borrowed your ride. Hope you don't mind."

"George? How did you get it operational?" Rika asked. "It needs my magic to power it."

"Oh, does it? Sorry, my bad. But you know what they say, 'The impossible is accomplished by people that didn't know it can't be done.'"

"But how——"

"Hicks and I just pulled the backup power cells from our gunship and kind of jury-rigged them into this bad boy. Things have gotten a lot smaller since it was built, so they seem to be able to power it quite well, though I do worry they might rattle around a bit, seeing as the old socket for the power supply was made for tech from a few hundred years ago. I should probably fix that when I land."

"Hang on. The cockpit wasn't exactly air-tight last time we tested it. I still need to tighten the hinge seal. Unless you fixed that too, while you were at it."

"No, that'll need looking at," he replied. "But it's an easy fix. And me, well, I'm a cyborg, so I don't technically need to breathe. I've got enough oxygen stored inside my endoskeleton to keep my flesh well supplied for at least a few hours."

"You don't need to breathe?" Marban asked. "That's amazing, George. One more thing to learn about your kind," he said with astounded appreciation.

"Without actual muscles and organs, we really don't use that much oxygen, Marban," the soldier replied with a chuckle. "We're fine without it, so long as temperatures stay reasonable. And even if they don't, our bodies are genetically engineered to be particularly durable. And in a worst-case scenario, we can redirect some of the heat running through our internal heat dampers outward to keep it from freezing over. I mean, in a *true* worst case, I suppose I could just get another meat suit, but I've grown fond of this one, and really don't want to go through the process again if I can avoid it, ya know?"

"Did you seriously just call it a meat suit?" Rika asked.

"A rose is a rose," George replied. "Shakespeare," he added.

"Yes, I know some of the classics," Rika replied with a laugh. "You're just full of surprises, aren't you, George?"

"I aim to keep things interesting, when I can," he said with a chuckle.

"And you got my mech's boosters working. You're pretty good with that thing, you know."

"To be fair, it's a giant metal man, and me? Well, I'm a smaller metal man inside the bigger one, so..."

Marban's deep laugh resonated in the *Fujin's* cockpit. "Oh, you are a most amusing one, my brother. And a very talented pilot of that metal man."

"Well, you know this style of mech went out of fashion not long after the *Asbrú* vanished. It isn't the most efficient of human-operated platforms. They found keeping it balanced on two legs required a level of skill most pilots simply lacked, so they shifted for wheels and treads instead. They weren't as cool-looking, but they had far fewer accidents with them."

"You should see Rika drive it," Jo interjected. "She puts all y'all to shame."

"It's not a contest, Jo. And I do have magic on my side, which is kind of an unfair advantage. But thanks for the support," Rika said.

"Any time."

Marban pivoted in his seat and cast a thinly veiled appreciative look at the talented woman beside him in the cockpit. "From what Charlie told me, you were quite the pilot even before you possessed magic."

Rika's tattoos flushed the slightest bit red before returning to their nearly invisible white. "Thanks, Marban," she said.

Jo found that particularly interesting. She'd never seen her ink turn that color, and couldn't help but wonder if the pirate's interest might be in some way reciprocated. But that was a good-natured grilling for a later time. For now, they had to get on with their flight prep, making themselves ready for their jump to the portal.

"All right. Let's get these birds back on the *Coratta*," Rika said. "We've still got a lot to do."

While George had unintentionally thrown a wrench in their prior attempt, with the captured Tslavar ship, they hoped they would be able to jump in relatively close, then slide through the other ships and not be noticed. Just another part of the massive fleet, quietly moving into position. And when the portal opened? They'd fly right through, their chrono giving them a head start on the other craft and allowing them to pass to the other side first.

Once there, the plan was for Rika to do as she and Ara had discussed and reset the portal––minus George's interference this time. And then, finally, they'd be in complete control of the gateway between galaxies. And from there, a proper response to the alien menace could be formulated.

CHAPTER FORTY-FOUR

"It'll fly just fine without 'em, Sarge," Corporal Hicks said as he tightened the last several bolts to the little gunship's reserve power compartment.

"That's all I needed to hear," Sergeant Franklin replied with a grin. "I think the upgrades to the mech take a bit of priority at the moment, so the sacrifice of a few power cells is well worth it. That means one more piece of kit we now have in our arsenal. Technically, it already was, but now any of us can operate it, not just the lone magic user among us."

"It's still kind of hard to get used to. People using magic," Hicks said. "I mean, we've heard stories and fairy tales, but to see actual magic being done in front of our eyes, it's pretty amazing."

"Agreed. But you know what the scientists say. 'Magic is just science we haven't figured out an explanation for yet.'"

The two men had been busy since pretty much the moment the mech and the *Fujin* had returned to the ship. Being mechanical men meant they didn't need to stop their work to eat or sleep or use the head. And with an actual project to complete, the duo had put their cybernetic noses to the proverbial grindstone.

Not that a stone could do much to their ceramisteel endoskeletons.

The little gunship was all patched up and ready to fly, a powerful konus now welded to its internal framework and charged with as much magic as they were able to spare. That device was then tied into the *Coratta*'s magic, allowing its warp system to use the stolen ship as a tether of sorts, guiding it through space when they jumped and warped in tandem.

The mech was also pretty much ready to go, though they had ultimately needed Jo's particular bit of expertise. The cyborg was almost done getting the troublesome final seal to seat properly in place, her swearing as she struggled to lock in the last piece muffled by the thick impact glass.

"How's your ship?" Rika asked as she and Marban joined the pair of cyborgs in the cargo bay. "Did you guys sleep at all?"

"All patched up and ready to rock," Hicks said with a huge grin. "And sleep? We don't need it!"

"Pardon his enthusiasm," Sergeant Franklin said with a chuckle. "He gets carried away sometimes."

"Yeah, Sarge. So says the man who went charging off into space in an antique, jury-rigged mech," Hicks replied with a laugh.

"Hey, it was combat," the sergeant joked. "Anyway, we're all good here, and with Jo's help, we managed to get that final seal fixed on your baby. Should be air-tight now. We also locked in the power cell upgrades so they won't go rattling around in there."

"Wait, you kept all of them in the mech? But you need them in your ship."

"Eh, they're just redundancies."

"For a reason," Rika shot back. "And besides, I can power the mech just fine without 'em."

"And if you're not in the mech? You know, it does help to

have it rigged so someone else might be able to use it in time of need."

"Someone like you, perhaps?"

He shrugged, noncommittal. "Just saying."

Jo popped out of the mech's cockpit and climbed down to join the others. "Done. Finally got that little bastard locked in."

Rika smiled wide. "Sweet. Thanks, Jo."

"You got it, Skipper. My pleasure."

"Anyway," George continued. "Marban, did you and your fellas have any luck with your search?"

"Yeah," Marban replied. "We had the Drooks help out. It was hard to find, seeing how small it was, but they tracked down the signal. It wasn't really a beacon, per se. More of a marker spell with no real reach over any distance."

"So, more of an ident code, then? Like one of our transponders back on Earth?"

"Precisely," Rika said. "Just a little something to let the ships around it know it's one of theirs. We weren't broadcasting anything the fleet would follow. In fact, if that scout ship hadn't jumped into this system they would never have noticed us. A true fluke, that was."

"So the other ships you guys have staged and waiting? They're still safe?"

"Looks that way, George. They should be fine unless the baddies happen to jump into the system where they've grouped. And that's not an inhabited one, so the odds of those assholes picking that one system my guys are in to make a stopover is slim to none."

"Don't go tempting Murphy," Hicks called out from inside the little ship.

"Yeah, he's right. You know how he loves to pay surprise visits to the overconfident," Sergeant Franklin agreed.

"Ah, Charlie's infamous Murphy," Marban said with a laugh.

"But even if another scout did manage to find them, there are over a dozen of them. I think they could likely take one down before it figured out something was wrong and jumped away."

"But weren't those ships off gathering crews? You mentioned being a little shorthanded, pirate-wise."

"They were. But trust me, George, my men are very experienced. If they were being followed, they'd notice. Pirate life is all about watching your back and disappearing when need be."

Marban's attention shifted to the little work bench near the ship. A jar of Nasturian was sitting there, full to the top. But their supply of the spicy herb had been smaller just the other day, and that was safely tucked away in another compartment.

"Hey, where'd you get that?" the pirate asked.

George and Jo shared a look and burst out laughing.

"You don't want to know," Rika chimed in. "Trust me."

"This Nasturian, it's not so bad, really. I mean, it's hot, sure. But once you get past the searing pain, it's actually got a really nice flavor. I'm thinking maybe I'll eventually even build up a tolerance to it."

"You're going to keep eating that stuff *willingly*?" Rika asked, shaking her head.

"Just in teeny, tiny amounts. Like I said, it's got a nice flavor."

"So, you like spice, eh? Well, I'll introduce you to a whole variety of peppers once we make it to Earth," Rika said. "I think you'll approve."

"I'd like that," the pirate replied.

"I bet you would. But first we have to make it to the portal. And then we have to actually get through it in one piece without being torn to pieces by the Tslavar fleet. *Then* we can think about filling your belly. But for now, we prep for a fight."

"Music to my ears," Marban said.

"Mine too, brother," George chimed in. "I love a good fight."

Rika looked at the two men, ridiculous, yet competent in their machismo.

"Be careful what you wish for, fellas. You just might get it."

CHAPTER FORTY-FIVE

It had been a relentless series of jumps, Korbin using the stored power of his Drookonus to power his craft through the back-to-back expenditures of magic far faster than any Drooks could possibly recover. He was pushing the device hard, and it would cost a pretty penny to recharge it once again, but given the circumstances, it was well worth it, and necessary.

He touched down in one of the less frequented landing facilities on his destination world, quickly exiting the craft and blending in with the teeming crowd. He hadn't been to this place in quite some time, but he knew its streets well, and he walked them with confidence.

The grungy clothes he was wearing allowed him to blend in, adopting the persona of a commoner. A worker. Someone like everyone else, and not worth taking note of. Much like a Wampeh Ghalian, he became someone else when required, and the thoroughness of the transformation would have shocked those who only knew him as laid-back Korbin.

He took the side streets and back alleys, making his way to his destination, a dingy cantina with a rough clientele.

"Been a long time," he murmured with a nostalgic sigh, then put on his game face and stepped through the doors.

The music wasn't particularly loud. Either that, or his memory of the place had embellished his previous encounters there. He still bore a small scar from one of them. But that was a long time ago, and he'd learned a lot since then. In any case, this was going to require some finesse.

An ochre-skinned man with horned protrusions sprouting from the back of his head bumped into him and flashed an angry glare. Despite his grungy disguise, the fellow seemed to take interest in the newcomer.

"I don't know you," he said, turning to face Korbin fully.

"No, we haven't met," Korbin replied.

"Give me your coin," the man growled.

Korbin was amazed. The idiot was actually attempting to rob him *inside* the establishment. And in plain sight, no less. He didn't know whether to react or just laugh about the absurdity of the situation.

One of the drunks seated nearby was watching with amusement. "You sure you want to do that, Azok? You already got banned the last time you––"

"Shut up," he shot back. "Now give me your coin."

Korbin couldn't use his magic. Not here. Not if he wanted to remain anonymous among these people. That meant tact.

"Friend, of course. Let me buy you a drink. What are you having?"

"I'm having *all* of your coin, fool," Azok said, roughly grabbing Korbin by the arm.

The disguised man sighed. "Bad move, friend."

Korbin may have possessed a deep well of powerful magic to draw from, but he had spent many, many cycles studying with the best teachers he could find in the darkest corners of the galaxy. Often with men who seemed like nothing at a glance.

Men no one thought twice about. Men he spent a long time seeking out. Some of the most dangerous men alive.

Azok's arm was made of sturdy stuff, and likely wouldn't break upon impact, but that didn't stop Korbin from violently twisting it and pummeling his joints with his fists, dislocating them before kicking the man square in the chest, sending him flying backward into the crowd.

Ah, there you are, Korbin noted, as he saw his target through the crowd. A crowd that had just erupted into a full-fledged bar brawl. And the man he wanted to see was on the other side of the room, feet up on the table, watching the crowd erupt with calm, amused eyes.

Korbin dove into the fray, employing the more subtle of the techniques in his arsenal to move the men and women swinging wildly around him out of his path without causing damage. Or not *much* damage, if that was the only option. Azok deserved what came to him, but these others were mere fodder. Bystanders of no importance in a far more serious game.

He kept his magic tightly under wraps, though a surprise punch that caught him on the ear almost elicited an instinctive defensive reply. But Korbin had spent a long time learning to control himself, and he'd not slip up and blow his cover. Not that easily.

A dozen punched, thrown, and knocked-out people later, he finally emerged from the brawling crowd on the other side of the room. The man was still sitting where he'd first spotted him. Blue-skinned with a devil-may-care attitude, he couldn't help but like the fellow.

"Korbin," the man said. "Been a long time."

"Too long, old friend. It's good to see you, Olosnah. You look well. Have you put on some weight?"

"Oh, fuck you," Olo said with a laugh. "Come on, let's get out of here, and go somewhere we can actually talk. You've started quite a melee."

"That idiot started it. I just finished it."

"Ah, Azok. He's kind of obnoxious like that. Come on, we'll leave through the changing room exit in the rear," Olo said, rising to his feet.

His hands, Korbin noted, while empty of weapons, were ready to deploy the magical charge in the konuses on each wrist at a moment's notice if the fight had interrupted his leisurely evening.

A drunken brawler came flying his way, but rather than engage and get dragged into the fray, Olo simply sidestepped, expertly giving the man a little shove as he passed, directing him right into a rather solid wall.

"Same old Olo," Korbin chuckled. "I've missed your ways."

Rather than trek all the way to the good neighborhood in which Olosnah lived, they opted instead for a neighboring bar with far less colorful patrons. A quiet place they could catch up without a riot breaking out.

Olo ordered a round of top-shelf drinks for them and took a seat at one of the more secluded tables.

"Your treat. I had to leave a perfectly good beverage back there. That's alcohol abuse, you know."

"Of course," Korbin replied as he paid the bartender.

Comfortably seated, each of them having a clear line of sight of the establishment in each direction, the two men finally could get down to business, both of their backs covered.

"So, Korbin. I assume this isn't just a pleasure visit," Olo stated rather than asked.

"You hurt me, Olo. Maybe I just wanted to see my old friend."

"The only time you seek me out here is if something is up. So? What is it this time? A run-in with some Varsuvian traders again? Or maybe some trouble with an emmik's wife—"

"That was just *one* time," Korbin objected.

Olo smiled wide. He'd missed busting his friend's balls.

"Go on, then. Fill me in."

"I need information. I was wondering, do you still run with Torbin?"

"Does a Rodvan shit in the woods? Of course I do. He's one of my most reliable and trusted associates. After you, of course."

"Oh, so is that what I am now? An associate, not a friend?" Korbin said with a laugh.

"If only it were so easy. But what kind of information are you looking for? If I recall correctly, you had a pretty robust spy network last time we worked together."

"I do, but they've been coming up dry. Hence my wondering if Torbin or one of your other associates might be able to procure me this knowledge. I'll pay handsomely."

Olo leaned back in his chair with a merry grin. "Back in the game, eh?"

"Never left it, my friend."

Olosnah raised his glass in a little toast. "Just quiet about it. Like old times," he said with a nod and a wink. "So, what is it you're looking for?"

Korbin then told him what was afoot and went so far as to describe the images on the disc his niece had secreted from her father's vault, keeping its provenance to himself, of course. He trusted Olo with his life, but that didn't mean he wouldn't eventually speak if captured and tortured. Hopefully, that wouldn't be the case.

Olosnah gave him a funny look when he finished explaining the situation.

"What?" Korbin said.

"Nothing."

"That wasn't a 'nothing' look, Olo."

"So perceptive," the smuggler said with a chuckle. "No, the thing is, you don't need Torbin's services. Or anyone else, for that matter. I already have the information you're seeking myself. And you should know, you're not the only one inquiring."

CHAPTER FORTY-SIX

Korbin had once again flown hard and fast, jumping in rapid succession to get back to his niece as quickly as he was able. It was a long flight regardless, and that time in the vast silence of space afforded him the opportunity to ponder the news Olo had given him.

He now knew the location of the strange, massive fleet of craft, as well as the presence of what appeared to be a portal of some sort, though that was spewing forth the burning fire of a sun.

Likely, whoever had cast it had miscalculated, dropping the other end mistakenly into a star in whichever system they'd been attempting to reach. It was incredibly rare magic, and to keep a portal open more than a few seconds would require massive quantities of power. And this had been open far, far longer.

The very existence of such a thing should have been impossible. *No one* had that kind of power. But Olo relayed what he'd heard, and the man's intel was infallible. Korbin would be able to verify the specifics soon enough, though, for he felt it was quite likely he'd now have no choice but to fly there himself. And soon, by the look of it.

And there was another twist. There was an Ootaki in play. A *free* Ootaki. It was such an incredible rarity, if the news had come from anyone else, he'd have laughed them off the planet.

But Olo had shown him the two halves of incredibly powerful hair he'd received from her in payment. It was no ordinary Ootaki hair. This was magnitudes stronger than the most powerful he'd ever been fortunate enough to wield. And the owner of that hair had not been alone. She traveled with a four-armed giant of some sort, but that wasn't what caught Korbin's attention.

The golden-haired woman was apparently accompanied by a most curious man. A Wampeh. And a Wampeh Ghalian, by the sound of it. Now *that* was a very interesting wrinkle in the current events. He was now facing the deadliest of the deadly. Korbin would have to stop off at home to retrieve his most valuable possession as soon as he was able. But he had one more pressing duty.

Kara would need to be returned to her estate first, naturally. The girl had to be kept safe, and there was nowhere safer on Slafara than her father's tower. Even ill, Visla Palmarian was far too terrifying for any to dare make a move on the girl. So home she would go, as soon as possible. But after that, Korbin would be free to get the potent item from his home.

It wasn't big. No bigger than a small ball, really. And yet, it had cost him a small fortune, as its contents were not supposed to exist anymore. But small amounts did still turn up from time to time––one of the rarest and most valuable of substances in the galaxy.

It wasn't for its value that he had acquired it––and he'd spent an unfathomable sum in that regard. There were plenty of other assets with which to store one's wealth. But what the little ball actually contained might very well save his life, for he had procured the impossible. Korbin had sourced a container of Balamar waters. And now, with Wampeh Ghalian in play, should the infamous assassins come for him, it could prove to have been a price well worth paying.

The sun had just crested the horizon when Korbin landed at the foot of the hill beneath Amazara's home. By the time he reached the top, the silver-eyed woman was already waiting for him, fresh griddle cakes steaming on a platter and a cup of a strange, dark brew placed before him in a thick-walled mug.

An assortment of homemade preserves and local nut cheese rounded out the spread. Korbin couldn't help but feel a warmth that had nothing to do with the rising sun.

"I'm glad to see you made it back so quickly," Amazara said. "We were wondering how long you might take."

"Things went faster than anticipated. It seems the information I was seeking was already at hand."

"Oh?" Amazara asked, surprise in her eyes. "This isn't good, Korb. You're digging into things. You remember what happened last time."

"It's not like that, Zara. And this involves more than just Kara and her father. Something bigger is at play." He hesitated.

"What is it?"

"There was a Wampeh Ghalian involved."

Amazara paled at the words. If the deadliest of the deadly were truly a part of this, then all bets were off. And for one of them to be *overtly* seen and the witness left alive to tell the tale? She could only guess what that might mean. In any case, it did not bode well for her friend's safety.

"You need to keep her safe, Korb. And yourself."

"Don't worry about me. I've got a few tricks up my sleeve, yet. And if I can just get Kara back safe in her home, no one will be able to touch her there. Weakened as he might be, her father is still the most powerful visla we've seen in ages. Only a fool would make a move on either of them there."

"But if they know he's weakened, they might try."

"But they don't know. No one does. And he was using his konuses, putting on a good show of it too. Anyone that didn't know him as well as I do would be fooled by it and think he was in full command of his powers. Only his closest friends and family would be able to see the deception."

"And if someone makes an attempt regardless?"

"He should be stronger by now. A man like that doesn't stay down long. And he won't be happy with me when I show up with his daughter at my side."

"You did right. I tell you, the girl has been specifically targeted. I don't know how, but someone managed to weaken her without her even realizing it," Amazara said.

A curious look crept onto her face.

"What is it, Zara?"

"I'll be right back," she replied, hurrying out of the room.

A few minutes later she returned, carrying a small, ornate charm on a sturdy chain. She reached out and handed it to him. "Take it," she said.

"What is it?"

"A charm. It warms against your skin in the presence of a Wampeh. The power-sucking Wampeh."

"Not any old Wampeh, then?"

"No, that would be bad, seeing as only a fraction of a percent of them possess that power," she replied.

"So how do you know it works?"

"Because I trust the woman I acquired it from," Amazara replied. "I want you to wear it."

Korbin took the pendant and held it in the palm of his hand. It wasn't much to look at, but things of power often weren't. The most nondescript item could be a repository of great magic, and some enchanted weapons even developed a near-sentient state of power.

This, however, was no such item. It was a simple charm that happened to react when in the vicinity of a particular type of power, nothing more.

"Thank you, Zara," Korbin said, slipping the chain over his head.

"Hey, what's that?" Kara asked, the sleepy-headed teen padding into the kitchen.

"Just something for Korbin," Amazara replied. "A little gift."

Kara smiled and gave her a wink. No matter the woman's protests, the girl was sure she had a thing for her uncle, and this only confirmed it.

"Are you hungry, Kara?" Amazara asked.

"Famished, actually."

"A good sign," the healer said. "It looks like your strength is already returning."

In short order she placed a pile of griddle cakes and bowl of fresh fruit in front of her guest, who didn't wait on formalities, digging in with gusto.

"Hey, what's that you're drinking?" Kara asked, noting Korbin's mug.

"I'm not really sure," he replied. "Zara? What exactly is this stuff you made?"

"It's something I heard about from a trader a few years ago. Kind of a local secret on the world his family came from. They called it, 'Kawfee.' It's made from Tsokin berries."

"Eww, those are bland," Kara said.

"Yes, eaten raw they are. But if you peel the fruit off and roast the seed inside, then grind it and mix it with hot water, you get a rather surprisingly tasty drink, and one that can even boost your magic a little, though that doesn't work for everyone."

"Ooh, can I try?"

"I don't see why not," Korbin said, sliding her the cup.

Kara took a tentative sip, followed by a far larger swig. "This is good!"

"Then we'll get you your own cup," Amazara said, pouring her a tall one of her own.

Kara downed half of it quickly, enjoying the caffeine buzz from the hot beverage. A gleam of sunlight coming in through the window hit her eye just right, making her sneeze. When she did so, however, the bowl of fruit at the end of the counter slid off and crashed to the floor.

"Was that me?" Kara asked, embarrassed.

"I think it was," Amazara said.

"I'm so sorry——"

"Nothing to be sorry about," the woman replied. "But it is interesting to see that apparently you're sensitive to Tsokin berries. I grow them out back and roast them myself, you know. I'll give you a small bag of ground ones to make this for yourself at home. Would you like that?"

"Yeah, that would be fantastic," Kara replied. "Thank you, Amazara."

"It's my pleasure. Now, let's get your stuff. I can see your uncle is antsy to get you home. I know your father will worry if you're not back soon."

That wasn't the real reason she suggested their departure, of course. Amazara knew full well that Korbin needed to move, and move quickly at that, if he was to address this mystery threat before it evolved into something beyond his considerable power to handle.

Kara rushed off to gather little the local artisan trinkets Amazara had purchased for her on their outing, while Korbin helped clear the table, affording the pair a moment alone. Amazara stopped cleaning and took him by the hands.

"Promise me you'll be careful."

"You know me, Zara."

"And that's why I'm asking. I know how you can be for those

you care about. Don't do anything foolish. Kara is far better off with her uncle in her life."

"Just Kara?"

Amazara blushed but didn't say anything more. A minute later the teen rejoined them, and she and her uncle departed on their conveyance. Soon after, Amazara watched as their ship lifted off and disappeared into the sky, hoping she'd see them again. One in particular.

CHAPTER FORTY-SEVEN

The rotund man who ruled his realm with violence and intimidation was standing at the open window to his offices on the top level of his arena in the center of town.

The sounds of the milling throngs in the courtyard below wafted up to his ears in a pleasant din. All of those voices meant more bodies inside his arena for the day's entertainment, and he'd had quite an enjoyable and profitable afternoon thus far.

The gladiatorial bouts had pulled in a very acceptable amount of coin for a non-headliner tournament. The locals wanted entertainment, and Emmik Hunstra was glad to provide it. A good fight meant profit, and Hunstra loved profit above all else.

On top of the success of the day's bouts, the new slaves he'd acquired from a passing Tslavar ship had been purchased from their owner for a fair amount below their true value, in exchange for a few hours with some of his finest brothel workers.

The whores were his slaves anyway, so that little transaction had saved him much coin at the meager cost of a little wear and tear on his property. But it was early enough in the day that business would have been slow, and the women and men servicing his customers would have been sitting idle. And if the Tslavar got a little rough? They'd heal soon enough.

Emmik Hunstra had proven to be nothing if not practical, and any way to squeeze a little more profit out of a situation was the right course of action in his greedy mind. But he had a far different, and far more profitable, transaction about to come to a close. One that had him more excited than even his favorite concubine could make him.

He had received word from a particular party he'd recently employed to retrieve something for him. An Ootaki woman who'd bested his men and humiliated him in front of the locals. That simply could not stand.

It had cost much to procure the services of his deadly freelancer, but he had lost face and had to regain it. And the Ootaki was more than just a nuisance. She was a priceless repository of magic. Once he had her in his grasp, he'd be the wealthiest man in the system by far. Wealthiest, and most powerful.

It was early afternoon when he got word that the strange craft the Ootaki and her four-armed accomplice had fled in had just touched down at the nearby landing field. His men reported that both had been seen exiting the vessel, followed by a Wampeh.

"Excellent," Emmik Hunstra said, rubbing his hands together with anticipation. He grabbed his skree and called down to the ground floor, where his security staff resided. "Durkhoz, prepare a cell for our new gladiator trainee," he said, referring to Dukaan, whom he intended to train briefly, then throw into the arena. "They should be with us shortly."

No one had ever seen a four-armed gladiator before. The draw to see the freak fight would be good, and Hunstra would make a nice profit, so long as his new toy managed to keep all of his limbs. And even if one were to be sliced off in combat, he'd still have novelty value with three arms.

If he was reduced to just two arms like everyone else, however, well, that would be boring. If that was the case, he'd wind up being used as food for the beasts within the arena walls. Hunstra was not one to waste perfectly good flesh, after all.

The emmik went to his window once more, scanning the throng below for the arrival of his new prize. It took him a while to single out the woman and her captor. The Wampeh was good, making their approach appear as normal as three people simply out for a walk.

But soon the Ootaki would be his. And who knew what might happen then? He would shear her, naturally, but after that? He didn't really have a taste for close-shorn women, but for sheer novelty value if nothing else, he thought perhaps he'd have to check that one off his list.

"Emmik, you have visitors," a control-collared young woman notified him, averting her eyes as she did so.

She was one of his newer acquisitions, and a favorite plaything, though he felt she needed more training.

"Excellent. Send them to my conference chamber," he commanded.

The young woman hurried off to carry out the emmik's orders. Hunstra walked to his bar and made himself a drink. It was not every day a man could make a Wampeh Ghalian wait for him, and, though he knew better than to test the man, he felt a little rush in his minor act of faux bravery.

Finally, Emmik Hunstra strode into the adjacent room, where his deadly bounty hunter and his prize were waiting for him. The Ootaki and her multi-limbed associate were both standing. The Wampeh, however, was seated comfortably, his feet propped up on the emmik's desk.

And he was sitting in Hunstra's chair.

The emmik felt a surge of anger flush his system. He was an *emmik*, and his power was considerable, even if he was not of a visla's caliber. But that was the thing about Wampeh Ghalian. One simply could not know if he was already carrying a load of someone else's stolen power.

Or if he might simply take your own.

Hunstra wisely swallowed his pride and put on a relaxed smile as he strode leisurely into the room, acting as if he didn't care one bit about things so petty as someone sitting in his seat. He was an emmik, after all. A man of considerable power and clout.

"A pleasure," he said, nodding to the Wampeh, knowing the man would not offer his name even if he asked. "And a job well done."

He then turned his attention to the Ootaki woman and her freak-show friend. The four-armed creature stood nearly seven feet tall, and the eyes on the back of his head added to his strangeness far more than his additional limbs could.

The Ootaki, he could now see, had already been partially shorn, the sides and back of her head close-cropped. But the mass of priceless hair atop her head was still incredibly long. In fact, even braided and wrapped around her body as it was, he thought it might be possible that it had never been cut. And if that was the case, its power would be even greater.

It was interesting, the slave woman held his gaze, not lowering her eyes by so much as a fraction. The defiance in the air around her was almost palpable, and—much to his amazement—she actually looked angry, and was making no effort to hide it.

Emmik Hunstra smiled menacingly as he lecherously ran his eyes over her body. She was a fine specimen, and he'd definitely enjoy breaking her in once he'd shorn her. His enthusiasm abruptly ceased when his gaze fell upon her neck. He'd missed it at first. He hadn't even considered it a possibility that she'd not be collared. But that was the truth of it.

The Ootaki was not wearing a control collar.

Such a valuable prize left unrestrained? He knew the Wampeh was skilled, but this was far too important a slave to leave in such a state. Quickly, he cast a minor stun spell, intending to disable the woman until he could properly affix a collar on her.

Nothing happened.

Disconcerted, he cast again. This time stronger. Again, the spell failed. The Ootaki woman's angry scowl transformed to an amused grin. Something was *very* wrong.

Emmik Hunstra wasn't going to waste any more time playing around. Instead, he cast the most powerful disabling spell in his entire arsenal, blasting it out at the woman. In a flash of golden power, the spell was batted aside. *She* had batted it aside. The Ootaki was in control of her own power. And she was so much stronger than he was.

The realization was almost as terrifying as the look she was giving him. The powerful man was no longer the toughest guy in the room. Not by a long shot. He tried to turn and flee, but a mighty spell froze him in place. His feet could not move, no matter how much he exerted himself.

Hunstra's bowels gave way as panic washed over him, the fear reeking off of him almost as much as the shit that now filled his trousers. The woman slowly walked closer, her gaze not wavering, her eyes unblinking. It was a trick she'd inherited from Bawb, and it was certainly doing its job of unsettling its intended target.

"You are not a good man," Hunze said coolly.

"I don't know what you––"

"You'd be wise not to speak," Kort said. "I've seen what this one can do when she's angry. You wouldn't like her when she's angry."

"Little secret," Dukaan interjected. "She's *always* angry."

Hunze laughed on the inside, amused at the charade, but keeping her exterior façade locked in place. Her? Angry? She was one of the most loving and good-natured people in the galaxy. But Hunstra didn't know that.

"You've lived a foul life," she said. "But you have the opportunity to do right. To start to redeem your miserable self, just a little."

At that moment, his young, new addition stepped into the room, intending to pass a message to the emmik. She sensed something was wrong, but the sight of the golden-haired woman froze her in place.

"Are you an *Ootaki*?" she gasped.

"Yes," Hunze said, her eyes locking on the thin collar around the young woman's neck. It was incredibly weak, but enough to control her just the same.

"Come here a moment, would you, please?" she asked.

The slave hesitated, glancing at her owner. Hunstra, wisely, nodded his approval, the load in his trousers slowly sliding down his legs, reminding him who was *really* in charge.

The young woman stepped over to Hunze, as requested. The Ootaki woman wrapped her fingers around the slender collar on the young woman's neck. "Don't worry, this won't hurt a bit."

The collar flashed and glowed for a second, then fell away in a ruined pile of melted and bent metal. It was then that Emmik Hunstra realized how powerful this woman truly was.

His now-former slave stared at the discarded band as she touched her neck in disbelief. She was free. Free of the horrors the emmik had done to her. Rage in her eyes, she turned her gaze to the rotund man. If looks could kill, he'd have died in an instant. As it was, there was suddenly a very real possibility he wouldn't live to see the end of the day if the freed slave had her way.

Hunze snapped her fingers, snatching Hunstra's attention.

"You are going to do something for me," she said. "You have something I want. And if you give it to me without a fuss, I may just let you live."

"What is it? What do you want?" he whimpered.

The shrill cries of the Zomoki in their pens pierced the air. Hunze looked at him and smiled. And the smile wasn't a friendly one.

CHAPTER FORTY-EIGHT

Korbin wasted no time on his flight back to Slafara. If Wampeh Ghalian were at play in this mess, he hadn't a moment to spare. He'd never faced off against one of the deadly assassins. But then, none who did ever spoke of it, for obvious reasons.

He did not intend to become another silent statistic while helping Kara piece together what was going on. Not if he could help it. The pendant from Zara would help, he hoped, but more than anything, he wanted to retrieve the one weapon that would actually work against the assassins. The one he had miraculously sourced all of those years ago against all odds.

"Are you sure about this, Uncle Korbin?" Kara asked as they exited their jump into orbit just above Slafara.

"Your father is involved in something, you were right. But he loves you more than anything, and even weakened, his reputation will keep attackers away from your home. It's the safest place for you to be right now, and I have things I must do."

"But can't I just come with?"

"I wish you could, but it will be more dangerous if you're with me. Dangerous for *both* of us. I can't watch both of our backs and do what needs to be done."

Kara wasn't thrilled with his reasoning, but she couldn't argue against his logic. Her uncle had always looked out for her best interests, and she was one hundred percent certain this occasion was no different.

"Okay," she relented. "But hurry back, okay?"

"Your father will protect you, Karasalia. You will be safe in your home. Now come, let's get you back and indoors. Once you're secure, I have a few things I must do before Nikora and I can have a proper conversation about what he's really up to."

"You're going to confront Father?"

"Not confront, exactly. But you were right. Something is going on, and he and I have known one another far too long for it to be kept secret."

"You won't tell him I stole the disc, will you?"

"No, of course not. In fact, I want you to put it back where you found it," he said, handing the device back to Kara.

"But don't you need it? For proof, or something?"

"I do, but I've already made a copy of it."

"You can do that?"

"*I* can. Most do not possess the knowledge, skills, coin, and power to do so. It's a tricky bit of magic working with these discs, but fortunately, I have some prior experience with them."

Kara pocketed the disc with a new curiosity. Not about her father, though. About her increasingly surprising uncle. He'd always seemed the laid-back, relaxed bachelor living out on his own. But more and more, he was revealing that there was quite a lot more to him than met the eye.

Korbin turned up the hover spell to protect the grounds, then dropped down right in front of Visla Palmarian's estate. There would be no parking at the nearby landing field today. Kara was in jeopardy, and he'd be damned if he'd give any Wampeh or other hired thugs the opportunity to reach her. Not on his watch.

He cast a special spell, seeking out hidden shimmers in their immediate proximity. All clear. Korbin then quickly ushered her from his craft into the building, much to the relief of the security detail, who had obviously been torn between the girl's uncle and her stepmother's emmik friend he'd bullied out of the way upon their departure.

"Hi, Shozzy," Kara said as she strode into the building.

The security chief nodded once to Korbin in greeting, then ushered Kara to the lift disc to take her up to her chambers. Mareh's friend, Trepenan, came rushing into the foyer moments later, just in time to see her ascend to the top floors with her security escort.

He locked eyes with Korbin, but knew better than to tangle with the man who was far more powerful than he let on. Korbin, for his part, merely smiled politely, then turned to leave, keeping a defensive spell in full effect behind him as he did. They may have been in his dear friend's house, but he didn't trust Mareh's troublesome associate to not attack him in the back.

But he exited the building unscathed. Once he was safely on his ship, Korbin lifted off, first casting a probe spell to ensure no Wampeh Ghalian had snuck aboard his craft in his absence. It should have been impossible with the wards he'd cast, but the assassins weren't legendary for no reason, and the extra caution was well worth a few moment's delay.

The flight home was a quick one, his Drookonus pushing the craft far harder than usual, though not so much as to make it stand out excessively to casual observation. He was in a hurry, yes. But he did not wish to lose the element of surprise. If he still had it, that was.

From the air he could see that the wards and traps he'd carefully layered all around his property, leading up to the increasingly deadly ones at his house itself, were all intact and untampered with. His home was secure.

Korbin landed and rushed inside, hurrying to the hidden, secure vault mounted in his floor. With his secret passphrase, the tiles beneath his feet slid apart, revealing a staircase down to the little room containing his wealth of coin and weaponry.

He gathered up the most powerful of his items, filling two packs with everything he could possibly want in a lengthy battle against an unknown and powerful enemy. He then grabbed his go-bag of coin and magical items for trade and barter. Lastly, he slid his enchanted body armor into its floating carrying case and cast the spell that had it follow him wherever he walked, floating on its invisible cushion of magic as he exited the chamber.

As soon as he was clear of the stairs, the floor tiles slid back into place, once again sealing off the vault, hiding it from detection by all but the most skilled of observers.

But that was the thing about hidden rooms. Someone always had the ability to find it, no matter how careful you were. And there would always be someone able to force the wards and open it as well, given enough time.

It was for that reason he kept his most prized of all of his magical possessions hidden somewhere else. Somewhere even the most skilled of thieves would be unlikely to find the undetectable item. It gave off no magical signature, despite the incredible power of its contents. Just one of the many unusual traits of the Balamar waters contained within.

He'd tested them, of course, applying a single drop to his skin before completing the purchase. The sensation of the water's healing power flushing through him from just that one drop had proven that he was indeed dealing with the real item. He'd paid dearly for it. A fortune several times over. But now it would all be worth it. He possessed the greatest defense against the silent assassins.

And it was sitting on his shelf with a dozen other random items, completely unguarded and unnoted. Just a plain-looking decorative orb among the other knickknacks adorning his home.

Thieves wouldn't bother taking the ordinary-appearing item,

and magic users wouldn't sense its power. And anyone actively seeking it, or any of his other valuable possessions would undoubtedly search high and low for the most secure vaults and hiding spots in his home.

Meanwhile, the priceless orb casually sitting on his shelf would not be paid a second thought.

Korbin held the Balamar orb in his hand a moment, a slight rush of adrenaline flooding his system. This might actually be it, he realized. He might be in for the fight of his life. Not a training bout, and not combat with mere thugs or mercenaries, but a foe worthy of every bit of his training.

Despite the unusual sensation of concern in the back of his mind, he couldn't help but smile. Things would be interesting, whatever happened. He sincerely hoped he came out on top.

Korbin slid the orb into his pocket and headed out, on a mission to gather the last thing he thought he might require from his sources on Slafara. A team of Drooks, powerful enough to do what he needed of them without relying on his rapidly depleting Drookonus. Then, and only then, he would confront his lifelong friend.

It was promising to be an interesting day.

CHAPTER FORTY-NINE

Two nights aloft on the back of a Zomoki, using cover of darkness to scan the globe for signs of the magic they sought.

Two days of searching on foot, pursuing leads during the hours their friend couldn't fly for fear of being spotted.

And still they hadn't managed to uncover so much as a trace of the elusive power source Visla Dominus was going to collect any day now. Time was running out, and they were at a loss.

The inquiries Charlie and Bawb had made fell upon not deaf, but rather, ignorant ears. The men and women who controlled the networks of information peddlers, dwelling just beneath the gleaming veneer of culture and class that covered the planet's civilized cities, weren't being coy, or holding out for more coin or a better trade. They simply didn't know.

For Bawb, a man accustomed to procuring all manner of information far beyond the abilities of your average investigator, or even spy, it was more than a little disconcerting. For all intents and purposes, it really did seem that there was simply nothing that fit the description of what they were seeking anywhere on the planet. At least, not that *anyone* had heard of.

It wasn't impossible. If someone as powerful as Visla

Dominus wanted a thing kept hidden, it was well within his considerable means to do so. But there was *always* a weak link in the chain. Some lower-level henchman or servant *always* knew something. And the tiniest of hints of a detail could quickly snowball into actionable intelligence.

But not this time.

And it was not for lack of effort. Charlie and Bawb had been tireless in their on-foot pursuit of the desired information, trekking from bar to bar, seedy trading hub to underground marketplace, interacting with the most unsavory of types more often than not. They always brought ample coin, and, yet, even that was not enough to get what they sought.

A few attempted to make up something to satisfy the curious duo, but Charlie and Bawb could spot the ruse a mile away. They paid for tidbits from a few of those who did have solid networks in place, though. Not because they believed the intel, but to lay the groundwork for potential dealings in the future, should they need to call upon those people at some later date.

It was a habit Bawb had adopted many, many years ago, and it had served him very well in his life as an assassin. Of course, his old network was all long dead now, but the principle was the same regardless of century, and he thought it wise to begin cultivating those ties again. Information was a very valuable commodity, after all.

But for now, they were striking out.

And that wasn't only during the day as they spoke with information brokers. Even the mighty Zomoki was having no luck.

That night, while Charlie and Bawb finally allowed themselves a bit of rest from their many hours awake, Ara soared above the landscape alone, stretching her senses to their limit as she tried to find any trace of this mysterious, hidden power cache. By the time morning came around, she was exhausted from the effort, gladly landing and handing off the baton once more and curling up to nap and replenish her energy for another night's searching as her friends took up the task yet again.

After much searching, though, they were all getting nowhere, and fast.

"A big, fat nothing," Charlie griped. "This is getting ridiculous. I'm beginning to think that maybe this thing doesn't even exist."

"It is a big world, Charlie. We have searched a sizable area, but this is a *planet*, not just a city or two. It takes time."

"Which we don't have," he noted.

"We have *some*. We simply do not know how much," Ara replied.

"Okay, it's a big world, I agree," Charlie said. "But we should have sensed *something* by now, right? I mean, between the three of us, using all of our powers, as well as reaching out to the whisper network everywhere we go? There should have been some trace, but we haven't had a single hit. I don't know. Maybe it's not actually here."

"The Tslavar we questioned was not lying," Bawb said. "Of this I am quite certain."

"I'm not doubting your interrogation techniques, Bob. And he may have been telling what he thought was the truth and been wrong. I'm just saying, it seems like we might be shit out of luck, here."

"It is perplexing, no doubt. But Ara is correct. The planet is a large one, and if this cache of power is being shielded and hidden from our sensing spells, then we could be relatively close to it and simply not able to detect it unless we're right on top of it."

"In which case we'll never find it," Charlie grumbled.

The three pondered their plight a long moment, the uncomfortable silence thick enough to cut with an enchanted blade.

"I hate to admit it, but Charlie is right," Bawb finally said. "We may need a backup plan."

"Such as?" Ara asked. "We are somewhat limited with our options."

"While I'm not exactly thrilled to suggest it, if it comes right down to it, we can follow this Dominus person when he lands and let him lead us right to it," Charlie said.

"That would entail combat with a caster of frighteningly impressive power," Ara noted. "Even working together, I fear we may not prevail."

"I wasn't thinking of trying to win, but rather, using a quick fight as a diversion. Two of us fight him, while the third snatches up their power repository while he's distracted. Once we know where and what it is, of course."

"That plan is madness, Charlie," Bawb said.

"I know. But it just might work," he replied. "And unless we can somehow track that thing down before he gets here, do you have any better ideas?"

"Sadly, I do not," Bawb admitted.

"Nor do I," Ara added. "But let us consider this to be a plan of last resort."

"I agree with the Wise One on that point," Bawb said. "A head-on confrontation, even as a diversion, would be an extremely dangerous prospect."

"I know, Bob."

"I hope we can find it before they arrive. I know I speak for us all when I say I have no desire to face off with this visla in an overt fight. But if that's what it takes to keep him from retrieving this vessel and drawing out its power, then so be it."

A perplexed look flashed across Charlie's face. "Guys? I just had a crazy thought."

"And how is this unlike your other thoughts?" Bawb asked.

"Ha-ha. Seriously, though. What if we're not getting any hits not because we're looking in the wrong place, but because we're looking for the wrong thing? I mean, what if this cache isn't what we think it is? What if it's some other sort of power vessel? Then our spells would turn up nothing, even if we were right on top of it."

"I don't see how that's possible," Bawb said. "The Tslavar definitely said Visla Dominus was coming to Slafara to retrieve his cached power. It seems quite cut and dried."

"Maybe, Bob. But I fear we may need to exercise *all* of our options at the rate we're going."

CHAPTER FIFTY

Captain Sandah seemed rather distracted as he piloted his craft through the series of jumps that would return his craft to Visla Palmarian's estate. He wasn't doing a poor job as he carried out his duties, and nothing was slipping through the cracks, but it was clear that things other than the immediate job of flying the ship were on his mind.

Leila didn't concern herself with it, though. They'd return, and she would just have to figure out another way to find her friends. Fortunately, being in Visla Palmarian's good graces meant she could likely find other means to send out word. If Ripley and Eddie weren't around, maybe she could find the others.

A skree, while expensive over long distances, could be used to put word out to search for Charlie and Ara, as a last resort. But she didn't want to put the Zomoki on *anyone*'s radar unnecessarily. She should remain a secret, if at all possible.

They were close, though. Slafara was only one more jump away. They were resting stationary in space, though, at least for a little bit longer. The Drooks had been pushed hard and needed rest before the final burst of their magical powers took them the rest of the way home.

"Captain, there's a private skree coming in for you," his second-in-command informed him.

"I'll answer it in my quarters," he replied, then hurried off to take his call.

Five minutes later he returned to the command center, his face doing only a mediocre job of hiding his concern. Something was bothering him, but the tight-lipped captain wasn't about to say a word.

"Prepare the Drooks. We make the final jump in ten minutes," he ordered.

"Sir? The Drooks still have another twenty minutes in their rest——"

"I said ten. Make it so," he replied, his tone a bit sharper than his usual relaxed vibe.

Something was definitely perturbing him, but what would remain an unanswered question, it seemed.

The Drooks were powerful, and their rest periods were typically falling in line with a common trick they used to make it seem like they were outperforming when called upon in times of need. Really, they were perfectly ready to jump in half the time they were allotted, but it was moments like this that reinforced why they didn't ever mention that.

If someone wants something done in half the time they think it can be and you perform, it makes you look good. And for a team of collared Drooks, looking good was one of the few things they could do to show worth beyond simply driving the ship.

The visla's craft entered the atmosphere without incident and dropped smoothly toward the approach path leading in from the outskirts. Then they took a little detour.

"We need to land for a moment," Sandah said. "Put us down just over there, the other side of those woods."

"Sir?"

"Just do it."

The crew did as they were told and adjusted their course accordingly, coming to rest in a clearing eighty miles outside of Palmar City. A thick patch of woods stretched toward the city itself, eventually giving way to the outer residential neighborhoods and industrial hubs.

"Why are we landing?" Leila asked. "Is something wrong with the ship?"

"No, nothing like that. We had word that there was a small craft in distress and are going to investigate. Perhaps you could be of assistance."

"Me? How?"

"If you could task Baloo to sniff out the injured, we could reach and assist them far faster. We only have a general approximation of their location."

"Oh, of course," Leila said, glad to help.

"Thank you. Your assistance is greatly appreciated," Sandah said, then directed his crew where to take the ship in to land.

There hadn't been any signs of wreckage that Leila could see as they arrived, but Captain Sandah had said it was a very small recreational vessel that had sent the distress call. With all of those tall trees, it was only natural they might not see overt traces of it.

"You ready, Baloo?" she asked her furry critter as the doors opened.

Baloo looked up at his mama and let out a little whuff of affirmation.

"Okay. Go find them," Leila said.

Baloo jumped out of the ship, his nose furiously taking in all of the exciting new scents in the air. They'd already been in nearby Palmar City, and he was now quite familiar with all of the interesting smells of that place, some of which he could even smell faint traces of all the way out in the wilderness. But there were other things out here too. New things. Animals to hunt. Places to explore. And something else. Something familiar.

"Leila? Would you take a look at this?" Sandah asked.

"What? Oh, sure," she replied, stepping back inside the ship.

The door slammed shut, sealing them inside.

"What are you doing?" she blurted. "Baloo!"

But the beast was trapped outside, and all sound was sealed off when the spell was cast. He did, however, notice the ship suddenly lifting off into the sky, Leila still on board, leaving him all alone in the wilderness.

"What the hell are you doing? We have to go back and get Baloo!" Leila blurted, the Magus stone hidden within her clothes warming briefly with her distress.

"Please escort our guest to her quarters. She will remain there the rest of this journey."

"Journey? We're back. Where are we going? Why are you doing this?"

Captain Sandah raised a hand and gestured for his guards to pause a moment. "We have one more stop. A final item to bring back home. And I am sorry for having to do this, but orders are orders."

He nodded to his men, and Leila was hauled off without another word.

"That went better than expected," he said quietly. He'd been loath to hurt Baloo, and was glad his orders had been to "get rid of the beast." A command that left plenty of leeway in the interpretation of those words.

Stranding Baloo had worked out well, and it was a good thing, because even with his men at his side, he wasn't sure he could kill him. Nor did he want to.

Captain Sandah then made his way to the command center to complete the final part of his orders. One last item to retrieve before finally coming home.

CHAPTER FIFTY-ONE

Charlie and Bawb were out on yet another survey of yet another city, searching for any trace of the hidden power cache they were seeking when the human stopped dead in his tracks.

"What is it?" Bawb asked, a pair of blades somehow appearing in his hands, though Charlie didn't even see where he'd drawn them from.

"I'm not sure, dude," Charlie replied. "But we've gotta get back to Ara. Something's up."

Bawb had complete trust in his friend, and given the bond of magic they shared through the unexpected linking of Hunze's hair, he also knew the human had more than a little power flowing through him. Quite a bit more.

"We'll head to rejoin the Wise One immediately," Bawb said. "She's not too far out. I think we can connect from here."

"I'm trying. She's at the periphery of our reach, but we can still use the comms."

The odd magical interference on the planet was making their silent conversations increasingly difficult. The power linking them still allowed it, but conditions had to be optimal and distances relatively short. Fortunately, no one on Slafara used Earth tech, and the comms were another thing altogether.

"Ara, you read me?" Charlie quietly asked over his comms unit as he and Bawb made for the edge of the city.

"I do, and I was wondering when you would be calling."

She sensed it too, then. *Something* had changed. It was brief, but it was definitely there, and it seemed that both Charlie and Ara's heightened senses had flared momentarily.

"Ara, did you smell that?"

"Yes, Charlie. Something has happened. A flash of power. It's almost as if whatever has been obstructing us all from properly searching just had a small hiccup in its casting, providing an instant of partial clarity."

Bawb strained with his Ootaki hair-strengthened senses. "I do not feel this power. Only the faintest residual traces," he mused.

"It's already gone, Bob. Came and went in a flash, before you could power up to really sense it."

"A very short-lived surge of power, then? Most interesting. And disconcerting."

"You can say that again," Charlie replied. "Ara, did you notice anything unusual about it?"

"I did, in fact. I assume you did as well."

"Yep. I don't know what it was, exactly, but that power felt strangely familiar. And did you notice where it seemed to be coming from?"

"I did, indeed, though the residual trace is fading quickly."

"I know. It's dangerous, but I think we need to get closer to Palmar to scan the area again immediately. That's where the block was the strongest, that's where it felt like this was coming from, and I'm willing to bet that's where we'll have the best chance of finding out what that was."

"But it is daytime," Bawb noted. "People will undoubtedly observe our flight."

"Yeah, but if we can stay low and fly fast, the majority won't know exactly what it was they saw. And even if a few do, realistically, our time on this world is limited regardless. Either we find the cache of stored magic and bail out of here, or the visla gets here and recovers it before we do. Regardless, I think we have days, if not less, before this thing comes to a head."

"I agree with Charlie," Ara said over their comms. "And I have already taken to the air. I will land as close to the city as I can to shorten the time it will take for you to reach me. If we hurry, I am hopeful we will reach Palmar before all traces are gone."

Charlie and Bawb took off at a quick run, ignoring the stares of the locals.

"We're going to have to give Ara some cover," Charlie silently sent to his friend as they ran. Fortunately, that method of communication did not require breathing, and his words sounded normal in the Wampeh's head, not at all like a runner's speech.

"Yes, I was thinking the same thing," Bawb agreed. *"We shall cast every diversionary spell at our disposal as she flies. With any luck, few, if any, will take note of her."*

"You know someone will."

"Yes. But if we're truly fortunate, it won't be anyone of note. No one takes the ramblings of rustic people terribly seriously. Even on a highly developed world such as this."

"I hope you're right," Charlie said, pushing the pace even harder.

The two reached Ara in surprisingly good time and scrambled up onto her back. The enormous dragon lurched into the air the moment they were secure, flapping hard as she made for the city of Palmar, skimming the treetops while her friends cast every diversion they could think of.

Ara locked her senses onto the faint trace of the scent still lingering in the atmosphere. It wasn't a lot, and a younger

Zomoki would have lost it in the mix of magic and smells of the vast world. But Ara was old. Old, wise, and powerful. And with her senses pushed to their limits, she managed to follow the link all the way to the gleaming city of Palmar.

She dove low over the sprawling forests outside the city, swooping up the back of a craggy hill just at the outskirts, dropping down quickly beside the broken rocks at the summit. She wasn't really camouflaged, and shimmer spells didn't work on Zomoki, but Ara picked up a few other tricks in her long life.

She hurried over to the largest pile of rocks and nestled down among them. The coloring was off, but if she held still, she would be hard to see from a distance. It was motion that drew the eye more than anomalous color, and she was *very* good at staying still when need be.

"Something's up," Charlie said, watching the ships in the transit lanes flying overhead. "There's a lot more air traffic than last time we were here."

"Yes, I see that," Ara said.

Bawb squinted, watching one of the ships in particular. "I cannot tell for certain, but it looks as though at least one of the vessels may very well have come from Visla Dominus's fleet."

"Shit, which one?"

"To the right of that tall tower, a fair distance out."

Charlie was always amazed at his friend's visual acuity. "Ah. See it. Yeah, I think you're right. It could be one, though there's no way to know for sure."

"If I may make a suggestion," Ara interjected. "Given this wrinkle in our plan, I think it would be prudent to pause and watch for a bit. What we sensed might very well be a trap, and it would behoove us to not rush in."

Charlie didn't like sitting and doing nothing but watch, but Ara was right. Stealth and caution were in order. As the saying went, 'only fools rush in.'

"Well, that's just great. It looks like we've got a bit of a wait in store for us," he grumbled.

CHAPTER FIFTY-TWO

Morning came, and with it the Zomoki and her companions greeted the welcome warmth of the rising sun. They'd taken shifts sleeping and watching, and while each had managed to slumber, it had not exactly been what any of them would call restful.

The ship traffic in the area had thinned overnight, but several suspect craft had been observed entering and leaving the city's airspace. But not knowing exactly what to be on the lookout for, the trio had stayed in place until daybreak. At that time, Bawb embarked on a quick reconnaissance run into the city as its residents began their days and the rumor mills would start their whispers.

Charlie would have liked to accompany his friend, but for this they would need the pure speed, stealth, and skills of the Wampeh Ghalian. Bawb was simply far more proficient, and with his shimmer cloak aiding his approach, he could move with an ease his human friend would be unable to match.

Charlie had a shimmer cloak of his own as well now, captured from the Tslavar forces that had invaded Earth, but it was tucked away in his home back on Earth. He'd been practicing with it, but controlling it as he attempted multiple other tasks was more work than he'd realized. It *seemed* a simple thing, and it was—if you were standing still. But to achieve anything near Bawb's proficiency would require months, if not years of training.

Additionally, the shimmer brought with it a bit of baggage, but only on the rarest of occasions. While Visla Maktan had been strong, he was not near the potential of the man they were seeking. A visla as powerful as Dominus, though, would likely be able to sense a shimmer with the right spells, much like Rika's new gift allowed her to see through them, courtesy of her inked magic.

Ultimately, Charlie and Bawb had agreed it was simply safer and more efficient for just one of them to make the run, while the other remained with Ara, looking out for signs of trouble.

The Wampeh had only been gone an hour when that trouble reared its ugly head. But it wasn't what any of them had expected.

High in Visla Palmarian's tower that morning, Karasalia Palmarian was beside herself with worry. Not for any punishment she might have faced for rushing off with her uncle so unexpectedly, but because upon her return, she found her father had departed with Mareh to seek out a healer to bolster his health.

The house staff had been told his daughter was to be kept home when she returned, no matter who said otherwise, even her uncle. The edict seemed a bit strange, but they all knew better than to speak ill of the visla. But Kara was loved among them, and one of the chamber maids did let slip a few additional details of what had transpired in her absence.

"Oh, your stepmother returned just after you left with your uncle," the maid informed her. "She said she hadn't been able to bring a healer from her friend's estate, but she could bring your father to them instead. The visla was still angry with you and didn't want to leave, but your stepmother convinced him it was urgent, and they departed that very day."

So, her father was away. And angry. And apparently, he was still under the weather enough to seek a healer. It was odd, though. The chamber maid said he *seemed* in fine health, so far as she could tell, and Kara wasn't sure that using his konuses could have that sort of effect on him.

In any case, it seemed she was grounded once again, bound under house arrest until her father came home. So, Kara did what any teen would do after coming back from an impromptu adventure to a distant planet with no one to talk to about it. She skreed her best friend.

"Come over, Vee," she urged.

"I don't know, Kara. Even after your uncle talked to them, my parents are still pretty pissed we took off without saying anything like that."

"You'll be in my father's tower, not off-planet. Come on, Vee, I have so much to tell you about Amazara. And my uncle? I think he has a thing for her, though he won't admit it."

Visanya wavered a minute, but the opportunity for some good gossip with her best friend was simply too tempting.

"Let me ask my parents. If they're okay with it, I'll let you know."

A half hour later, Visanya arrived at the visla's towering estate.

"Hey, Shozzy," the teen said, waving to the increased guard detail, likely caused by her and her friend's impromptu escape, as she entered the building.

The head guard nodded his greeting. "Nice to see you this morning."

"Kara's expecting me."

"I assumed as much. Shall I notify Denna Palmarian of your arrival?"

"No, that's okay. I skreed her when I got here."

A lift disc descended to the ground floor a moment later and Kara stepped into the lobby space. Her father had apparently forbidden her from going anywhere near the doors now, so her appearance was something of a surprise to the men on duty.

"Hey, Vee," she said, running over and giving her friend a big hug. "Cute outfit."

"Thanks. You wanna go up and grab a bite?"

"You read my mind," Kara said, just as a blast of magic whizzed past her, knocking one of the guards to the ground.

The girls froze in place like terrified animals. An attempt made on the visla's daughter *inside* his estate? It simply couldn't be happening. Only it was.

"Get down!" Shozzy yelled as he pushed the girls aside, casting a powerful defensive spell just in time to deflect the incoming barrage of stun magic.

Half of the guards in the lobby were unsure what to do. The attack was coming from inside, but that wasn't possible. The other half of the guards took full advantage of that delay and fired spell after spell into their midst.

Quickly enough, the guards realized they had traitors in their midst, and, having identified the culprits, they did the most unexpected of things. One of the few things they hadn't prepared for.

They engaged their own comrades.

Only, they weren't their comrades. Not really. They'd been paid off, or were loyal to someone else. Whatever the truth of the situation was didn't make a difference at the moment. Protecting the visla's daughter was all that mattered.

The opposing forces closed on one another, shedding magical attacks for brutal hand-to-hand combat in a clashing battle of identically garbed men. To anyone observing from outside the fray, it would have been impossible to determine who was on which side of the conflict.

Kara grabbed her skree and made a frantic call. "Uncle Korbin! There's fighting in the tower! The guards are fighting each other!"

Her call was abruptly disconnected when a force spell bowled her and Vee over despite Shozzy's defenses. The guard growled and pulled deep from his konus, reinforcing the spells even more as the girls scrambled back to their feet.

Shozzy's own skree was blaring a stream of updates over the din of the fighting, and what it said was not good. Apparently, things had gotten worse. Considerably worse, in fact. Whoever had triggered the attack had also notified their other colleagues throughout the structure. The fighting was now taking place on most of the lower floors.

Whatever was happening, whoever had done this, one thing was clear: Visla Palmarian's estate had fallen.

CHAPTER FIFTY-THREE

"Get to the lift!" Shozzy commanded, shielding the girls as they pushed through the fighting toward the lift disc.

"We need to get out of here!" Vee shrieked.

"The exit is blocked, and my men are reporting fighting throughout the lower levels. We need to get you two somewhere safe. Somewhere defensible where only specially cleared personnel are allowed."

"The top floors," Kara realized.

"Exactly," Shozzy replied, holding his skree close to his mouth, ensuring his message would be heard. "Grundsch, there's an attack on the visla's daughter in the lobby. The lower levels have fallen. We're taking the express lift to the top. Meet us there. And bring the beast."

He didn't wait for a reply, spinning to avoid a pair of blade-wielding attackers who were more than willing to skewer him if that was what it took to reach the visla's heir. Shozzy moved with speed and grace, and for that moment, Kara realized why her father had made the unassuming man head of security. He was pretty damn good.

Parrying the blades hissing through the air around him,

Shozzy carefully drove his own knife between the weaker seams of the nearest man's uniform. He knew the soft spots well. Hell, he'd been trying to devise a way to reinforce them without sacrificing mobility for some time. Today, however, he was glad he hadn't yet succeeded.

The man into whom he'd plunged his blade screamed with pain and tried to pull away, but Shozzy yanked him closer, twisting the blade until it cut the vital bits he was aiming for. The man let out a pained gasp, then died in his arms.

Shozzy couldn't pause to reflect on the fact that he'd just killed a man he'd shared many drinks with in their off hours. There was still another adversary, and he was far more cautious in his attacks than his deceased counterpart had been.

"Just stop, Horth. You don't have to do this," Shozzy pleaded.

The guard ignored him, casting an unexpected tripping spell that knocked Shozzy off his feet. The man lunged, and it seemed the downed man was done for, when Horth suddenly flew a few feet up in the air, landing in a heap beside the security man.

Shozzy didn't hesitate, plunging his knife into the downed man's neck, which erupted in a short-lived gush of blood. Kara looked at her own hands in shock. Had she actually done that?

"Go, go, go!" he hissed as he regained his feet and hurried the girls into the lift. "Squeeze your legs and stomachs," he said as he prepared to activate the express lift. "This is going to move really fast."

The girls did as they were told, having ridden the lift disc for fun in the past. They knew the force would push the blood from their heads and could make them black out if they didn't do as he suggested.

Up the platform flew, whipping through the air in its rocketing ascent. Shozzy stood in front of the teens, muscles tensed, ready to fight the moment they stopped if need be. Given the forces exerted on his body during the short ride, he certainly hoped that wouldn't be required.

The massive Ra'az standing with his fierce beast at the lift when they arrived was a sight for sore eyes.

"Grundsch!" Kara exclaimed, rushing out and wrapping the huge alien in a hug, much to his surprise. "They're fighting! Everyone is fighting!"

"So Shozzy informed me."

"But why?"

"Not important. Keeping you safe is."

"They wouldn't dare have tried this with my father at home. How could they have known he wasn't here? Or that he wouldn't be back at any time? Only the top-level staff even knew he had left."

"Grundsch is right, that doesn't matter right now," Shozzy said. "Though it does mean someone up here is a turncoat. Grundsch, your beast doesn't wear a control collar. Have him take the lead as we make for the visla's conference chambers. They're heavily reinforced to protect his guests and should be a safe place to regroup."

"What does Bahnjoh's not having a collar have to do with anything?" Visanya asked. "I mean, you're huge, Grundsch."

"My size does not matter in this fight," the alien replied.

"He cannot in any way attack a member of the Palmarian family or their staff," Shozzy added. "It was a precautionary layer placed on his collar, given his violent tendencies."

"I've never seen Grundsch be violent," Kara said.

"Which means the collar worked. Without it, he'd just as soon tear us all to shreds," the security man said. "But Bahnjoh is not constrained in that manner. *He* can do things his master cannot. Now, come quickly. I hear a commotion ahead and fear they may have already breached these levels."

They all hurried down the corridors, passing Kara's room in the rush to her father's conference chambers. Deadly magic flew at them as they rounded a corner, and Shozzy took the brunt of it, despite the shielding spell he'd been continuously casting.

Grundsch pulled him back, while Bahnjoh raced off into the fray, holding back their would-be assailants.

"Let me see," the Ra'az said.

"It's fine," Shozzy lied.

Grundsch ignored his protests and pulled his uniform open. The burn on his chest was severe, and that was after the spell had already dissipated through his shield.

"Can you still cast?"

"Yes. I'll be fine. We have to get the girls to safety."

"The way seems to be blocked."

"And why is Bahnjoh so quiet?" Shozzy asked.

"Magic," was the alien's grim reply.

Kara peeked her head around the corner and saw what Grundsch was talking about. Bahnjoh was frozen, immobilized by a holding spell. He was a fast creature, and likely very nearly avoided the spell. But nearly wasn't good enough, and he was now bound fast where he stopped mid-stride.

"Can you get her to the conference room?" Shozzy asked, then fired off a series of spells at their attackers.

"No. I am unable to engage the visla's staff," Grundsch replied.

It was looking grim. They were unable to advance, and all that was behind them were a few recreational rooms and sleeping chambers.

Kara's eyes lit up. "I'll be right back!" she said, then turned and bolted down the hallway.

"Wait!" Shozzy called after her, but she was already gone. "Grundsch, go after her! I'll hold them back!"

The Ra'az nodded once and took off down the hallway, surprisingly fast for a creature of his size, with Vee following close behind. Up ahead, they saw Kara race into her room. They hoped she was alone in there.

CHAPTER FIFTY-FOUR

"This is not a safe place," Grundsch said as he entered Kara's room, on guard but unable to do much, given his restraints.

"What are you doing, Kara?" Vee asked as her friend dug in her belongings.

"I have an idea. It's something I read about once."

She turned to her friend. Visanya's whole life had been about concealing her identity as an Ootaki. Her adoptive parents went to great lengths in keeping her a free child, not some slave to be used for her magical hair.

"Don't freak out, Vee, okay? I found this in my father's vault," she said, pulling the braid of Ootaki hair from its hiding spot.

To her credit, Vee didn't react. Not on the outside, at least. But inside was anyone's guess. "What are you going to do with that?" she asked.

"Help Grundsch," she replied. "Come here," she said to the enormous man.

Her enslaved bodyguard did as he was asked.

"Bend down. You're too tall."

He bent.

Kara took the Ootaki hair and carefully wrapped it around

the golden control collar on his thick neck. Suddenly, the power whip bracer worn on his wrist sprang to life, surprising them both.

"There. That should hopefully have freed you. At least for the time being."

Grundsch had been a slave for so long, he'd forgotten how it felt to be totally in control of himself. Unrestrained. Free. Kara wasn't there when he had first demonstrated why he needed this particular type of control collar, and her father had kept that secret from her. Knowing her personal bodyguard was a brutal, horribly violent creature of enormous wrath would not have put her at ease one bit.

But now he was free, and *anyone* in these walls was fair game. Grundsch felt the warm rage flow in him once again, a familiar friend rejoining him for battle. He spun and eyed the puny girls, and for a split second, he considered crushing them like the weak beings they were. But then something strange happened. Something highly unusual for a Ra'az.

He felt a warm rush of affection.

The thing of it was, he'd known Kara since she was a little child, and despite being forced into his duty at her side, he had, quite in spite of himself, grown rather fond of the girl. And with the rest of his race likely wiped from existence, the connection was something he had come to value.

"Stay behind me," he said with a wicked grin, then stepped into the hallway.

Shozzy was wearing out, the strain of single-handedly holding back what had grown to a dozen or more attackers had taken its toll. His eyes went wide when he saw the golden hair wrapped around the brutal man's collar.

"What have you done?" he gasped, just as Grundsch roughly shoved him aside, sending him flying.

The giant didn't so much dislike Shozzy as much as he was reveling in the ability to do as he wished to whomever he wished. He stepped from behind the corner, but the men standing ready for battle didn't seem terribly worried. The beast was hobbled by a control collar and couldn't lay a finger on–

They saw the Ootaki hair. Grundsch was free.

"Stop him!" one of the turncoats managed to yell before Grundsch's power whip beam blasted forward and wrapped around him, crushing him as he swung him into his comrades.

Vicious spells landed on the Ra'az, but he shook them off, injured but not feeling the pain as he reveled in the carnage.

"Come!" he called out, urging the girls to follow him as he cleared a path.

Kara and Vee stepped from cover and ran toward him, but someone had been waiting for just such a blunder. Grundsch saw the movement from the corner of his eye and spun. There was no way the girls could get out of the way in time, and despite her konus creating the illusion of power, Karasalia was nowhere near as strong as her father made her appear. The attack could very well kill her.

Without a moment's thought, her lifelong protector hurled himself in the path of the devastating magical attack, designed to incapacitate a mighty spell caster, not an entirely unpowered being from another galaxy.

Grundsch took the hit full-on, the blast sending the large alien flying across the room, where he smashed into the wall and fell into a heap. His power whip fizzled and died, the impact cracking the housing on his beefy arm.

The attacker was startled, but regained his composure quickly, again targeting the visla's daughter. This time he would not be so rudely––

The man exploded into a red mist.

The other attackers found themselves shattered before they could even react, the result of them all being flung violently into the walls at once.

Slowly, a man Kara had only ever known as a kind and

gentle soul stepped fully into the chamber from the stairway to the gardens above. And his eyes burned with a protective rage.

"Uncle Korbin!" the girl nearly shrieked, rushing into his waiting arms.

"I've got you. It's okay," he said, pulling her in tight. "Are you two okay?" he asked.

Kara nodded, her face buried against his chest.

Vee stared, wide-eyed. "I...I think I'm good," the stunned teen replied.

She knew her friend's uncle was far more powerful than he let on, but she had never expected *this*. This was true visla power, and not just any low-level caster, but a strength that could possibly even rival most in the known systems. And here he just played the bumpkin on his farm, never once letting on to his true capabilities.

"I got your skree, but it cut out."

"We got hit by a spell. It broke the connection," Kara replied.

She then noticed that her uncle, despite all of his vast power, was incredibly on edge, his eyes darting around the room as if he expected to be attacked at any moment despite the carnage he'd just wrought.

"Uncle Korbin?" she asked.

He saw the look of concern in her eyes and relaxed his posturing, but only a little. "I sensed something in one of my trap spells I left around the city when I dropped you off."

"I didn't see you cast them."

"You wouldn't have. That's the whole point. To leave thin lines of power keyed up to warn me if any of a particularly deadly enemy were to show up here."

"And they did, obviously," Vee noted, looking at the bodies strewn about.

"Yes, but these are mere foot soldiers. What I sensed was a shimmer-cloaked Wampeh Ghalian, and in this very city."

"What does that mean?" Kara asked.

"It means that now that I have a bead on their shimmer, I will be able to detect it, hopefully before it's too late. They can always switch to one of their many disguises, perhaps posing as another species altogether, as they are wont to do, but at least I'll have a chance to see them coming."

It had been a rather obscure bit of magic he'd employed in setting his detection snares, and Korbin didn't know if it would truly work. He'd never needed to actually use it before, but nevertheless kept amassing arcane tools that might one day prove useful. Today, this one had. He'd caught wind of a cloaked Wampeh, and he was ready.

But his niece was in jeopardy, and he was a magnet drawing even more danger her way. Korbin strode to the lift shafts and cast powerful blocking spells, disabling them entirely. No one would come up, and no one would go down. He then cast once more, placing a series of obstructing spells in all stairwells leading up from the levels below.

On top of those, he also added a few demolition tripwires as well. If, by some feat of magic, someone were to pass the blockades, the stairwells would collapse in on themselves, preventing any further ingress.

"You'll be safe up here. I've made sure no one can reach the top floors."

"But you're staying with us, right?"

"I cannot. I am being hunted, and you are more at risk the longer I am here. I will get help and send them to protect you, but for now, I have to get clear of this place, lest I bring more danger to your door."

Grundsch groaned and pushed himself up. "Leave me a weapon. I will protect the child."

Korbin assessed the alien's injuries. Magically inflicted, he noted, and quite severe. Without treatment by someone more skilled in the healing arts than he was, Grundsch wouldn't survive the day. He had seen the violent creature at work, and also seen him sacrifice himself for his niece. Maybe, just maybe, that act of selflessness earned him a second chance.

Korbin cast a levitation spell and lifted the enormous man into the air.

"What are you doing?"

"Taking him with me. I've cast what I can to help his injuries, but the damage is beyond my skill. If I can save him, I will, Karasalia. But for now, you must stay here, where it's safe."

"What if someone comes? What if they get in somehow?" Kara asked.

Korbin paused, then cast a release spell, freeing Bahnjoh from his invisible bonds. "He'll guard you and keep you safe. Now, come with me. I have things to tell you before I depart."

CHAPTER FIFTY-FIVE

Bawb had shed his shimmer cloak once he'd made his way to the source of the magical disturbance he was clearly feeling. It was time to act like a local and walk the area, taking in the sights, while casually evaluating whatever it was that seemed to be going down at this very moment.

It was something substantial, that was for sure. Even without Hunze's hair, he'd definitely have noticed it.

The walk had been circuitous by necessity, the key to not being observed by the searching eyes cities like these always had on the lookout. But he had finally made his way to the epicenter of the event. A tall estate surrounded by floating gardens. Obviously, a person of great power and great wealth.

"There appears to be some sort of conflict taking place in one of the larger towers in the center of town," he silently informed his friends in their vantage point above the city. *"I fear this is the residence of the visla we heard about."*

"Palmarian? Shit, that's not good. Any idea what's going on, or who else might be involved?" Charlie asked.

"Not yet, though I can tell someone of great power resides in this

place. And, Charlie, the blocking magic is stronger here. I think this may be the source of it."

That revelation gave Charlie pause. If the visla was actively the source of the blocking magic, then it was entirely possible he was secretly Visla Dominus, using his position on this world to hide his true intentions.

Their situation just went from bad to worse.

Korbin led the way onto the floating gardens of Visla Palmarian's estate, the incapacitated form of Grundsch floating in front of him, Kara and Vee following close behind. It was a practical formation, though he didn't tell the girls as much. No need to scare them any more than they already were.

He didn't want to use the fallen alien as an impromptu shield, but if somehow someone had managed to get past the visla's defensive spells, his life and that of his niece took priority. It was a sacrifice he was prepared to make.

But as he reached out and touched the invisible magical strings of the wards and protections, he found they were all in place, and no attack befell them. Fortune, it seemed had smiled upon them––for a moment, at least.

Korbin's ship was hovering just above the surface of the nearest of the gardens. He'd crushed a bit of the landscaping in his hasty arrival, but given the urgency of Kara's skree call, a little damage was the least of his worries.

He quietly uttered his personal opening command, deactivating the additional protections he'd placed on the craft that he, and he alone, knew existed, then led the girls inside.

"He's badly hurt, but I think we can save him," he said as he strapped Grundsch onto a makeshift gurney fashioned from an oversize work table he had in the cargo bay.

It wouldn't be the most comfortable of places to lay, but it would hold the man's considerable weight and keep him from being thrown about in the event they needed to perform any sudden aerial maneuvers.

"Wait a minute," Vee said, looking around the empty space. "Where's Pod?"

"Ah, yes. That's what I wanted to talk to you two about."

"Is he okay?" Kara asked, concern for the little AI clear in her voice.

"He's fine. He just requested that he fly here under his own power. I was reluctant, given his odd camouflage and how it appears from the ground, but given the urgency of your call, I decided we had much larger things to be concerned with."

"But, where is he?"

"He's here by now, I assume. He said he was going to wait for you where you'd previously discovered him hiding. Oh, and he gave me this for you," he added, handing Kara a comms unit. "He said it is a portable communications device, though I can't sense any magic in it. In any case, you should be able to speak with him through it, much like a skree."

"Hello!" Pod said in a chipper voice. "I'm standing by if you should need me."

"Uh, thank you, Pod," Kara said into the strange metal device.

"My pleasure, Kara," the pod replied.

"Now, listen. I want you to stay indoors," Korbin said. "It's safer there. Out of sight. Protected. Only use Pod as a last resort. Only if something goes terribly wrong, okay?"

"Okay," the girls replied in unison.

"Good," he said, walking the girls back to the tower's entrance at the edge of the garden. As before, none of his invisible tripwire alarms had been touched.

"Uncle Korbin? What if someone else arrives up here and tries to come in through the gardens?"

"Your father has a lot of spells in place to prevent that.

Fortunately, I'm family, so I know them all and have free access. And I've added a few of my own on top of them."

"Yeah, but what if?"

He looked at the massive beast standing obediently at the girl's side. While he served Grundsch in his duties, the animal had an obvious bond with the girl.

"Have Bahnjoh guard the door. He'll know if someone is attempting to breach by that avenue. If he's positioned just inside, the likelihood of anyone hitting him with an immobilizing spell or worse is greatly reduced."

"They already got him once."

"Yes, and it's time you learn a valuable lesson, Karasalia. Much as you may find it distasteful, as a visla's daughter, you are a valuable prize for some who would seek to influence your father. While I do not believe one person's life has more value than another's on a general level, it is a sad fact of life that there are some exceptions. And you, Karasalia, are one of them. If a person, or even an animal such as Bahnjoh, might fall protecting you, that might be the key to your survival. You must come to terms with that possible eventuality. I know it's unpleasant, but it's the truth."

Kara was not naive, and much as she'd have liked to believe her uncle was mistaken, she knew from years under her father's wing that he was correct in his statement. Not that she herself might be more valuable, but that her father might be manipulated because of her. And *he* was powerful.

Korbin walked the girls back inside and reinforced his protections blocking them from the lower levels.

"Shozzy, how are you holding up?" he asked the guard stoically trying to act as if he was not in pain.

"It's okay, Visla," he replied, using Korbin's rank with a tone of actual respect for the first time since he'd known the man he'd always assumed to be just a minor visla. He wasn't, though.

He was a caster of extraordinary power. After his demonstration of power today, Shozzy would never forget it.

"Let me take a look at that," Korbin said, carefully opening the injured man's uniform. "Ah, yes. A nasty burn, and it must hurt like hell. But I do not sense any internal damage. At least, not from the magical attack."

"Yeah, Grundsch kind of shoved me a bit hard," he said with a pained grin. "Must be his being released from his control collar."

Korbin pondered it a moment. "Yes and no, I think. If he wanted to truly harm you, he could easily have done so. More likely, he exerted more strength than intended, as he is so used to the collar restricting him."

"That doesn't exactly make me feel better," Shozzy said with a chuckle.

"No, I'd think not. But this will," Korbin replied, then cast a healing spell he'd learned from Amazara when he'd needed it himself many years ago.

The guard's flesh didn't mend to a fully healed state, but the burn was greatly lessened, and the pain was entirely gone.

"You'll still need to see a proper healer to get that finished, but this should do for now."

"Thank you, Visla."

"You're welcome. Now, protect my niece. The longer I stay here, the more risk I bring upon this household. But I will send reinforcements shortly."

Korbin hugged Kara goodbye, then took off out the door to the gardens, quickly boarding his ship and departing in a flash.

Charlie, watching it all from a distance and alerted to the battle by his Wampeh on the ground, leapt atop Ara's back. "That's gotta be the visla," he said. "We've got one chance to stop him."

"But he's too powerful," Ara replied. "And the Geist is still in the city."

"Then we down that ship, and you leave me to distract him while you get Bob. It's not ideal, but if we don't at least try, he'll have all of that saved up power in his hands, and then we really won't be able to stop him. At least there's a little chance if we move fast."

Ara had to agree with his logic, even if she disliked what it meant. "Very well. Hold tight."

Charlie did, and they lurched into the air, the Zomoki flashing through the sky in plain view. That didn't matter now, though. What mattered was stopping that ship. Running his hands over the orb of Balamar water in his pocket, Charlie just hoped it wouldn't be the last thing he did.

CHAPTER FIFTY-SIX

Korbin's craft was on its way out of Palmar, flying over the woods nearest to the outskirts of the city, its team of Drooks doing their finest to make it appear like any other vessel when Ara finally caught up with it.

"*Can we take it down?*" Charlie asked.

"*Yes. I believe he has not noticed me yet. Most who are on alert for potential threats in the air tend to look for magical conveyances, but I am making this approach using only my wings for power. But at this speed, I will not be able to keep it up much longer.*"

"*Then pull close and blast him with whatever you've got. I'll pile everything I have on top of that. Maybe we'll get lucky and end this thing before our dear Visla Dominus gets a chance to fight back.*"

"*And if we are unable to destroy the craft?*"

"*Disable it, if we can. Then drop me near where it goes down.*"

"*If it goes down. I smell powerful Drooks on board.*"

"*I feel bad about it, but we can't afford to play this nice. And if they're with Dominus, it's an unfortunate cost of war. Because that's what this is at this point. It's not a skirmish, it's not a mere invasion. This is a full-fledged war.*"

"I know," Ara replied. *"Prepare yourself. When I pull up behind them we attack. I will cast my strongest immobilizing spell in my flames. Hopefully, if they penetrate their shielding enough, we will be able to knock the Drooks from the equation."*

"And the ship will fall. Ending this."

"Precisely."

The Zomoki and her human friend pulled into position behind the heavily shielded vessel, unaware that the visla inside had layered many additional spells to protect himself for fear of a Wampeh Ghalian on his tail. If not for the extra magic, Ara and Charlie might actually have succeeded.

"Now!" Ara said, spewing forth a blistering stream of fire.

Charlie cast alongside her, adding to the power as their combined energy managed to pull the magical shielding open, but only just. The ship was far better protected than they'd expected. But they still managed, and the stunning magic found its targets inside, knocking the Drooks unconscious, sending the ship into a dangerous plummet from the sky.

"We got it!" Charlie exclaimed.

Korbin's ship plunged toward the ground, devoid of power as it fell like a stone. Only its owner's last-minute activation of his Drookonus stopped it from smashing into the dirt and exploding into a million tiny pieces, but the ship still hit hard, taking out several trees as it did.

"Drop me in that little clearing. I'll make it to the ship on foot."

"Consider it done, Charlie. I will circle back and retrieve Bawb at once. Remember, only delay the visla until we both get back. You aren't strong enough to take him on yourself."

"I know. Believe me, the last thing I want to do is go toe-to-toe with this guy, so hurry back."

Ara tucked her wings and dove into the small gap in the trees one could perhaps call a clearing. It was all she could do to not get hung up in the branches at that speed. Her magic cushioned her landing, though, and Charlie leapt from her back, ready to do battle, but hoping he wouldn't have to.

"Hurry back," he said as his friend took to the air, racing to Palmar City to retrieve Bawb and rejoin the fray.

Charlie took off at a run toward the downed ship, but his progress was hampered by the sheer quantity of verdant growth all around him. Eventually, however, he spotted the crashed vessel.

The forest in this area was quite dense, and the fact that the downed ship had somehow survived impact with those trees spoke as a testament to the visla's powerful magical shielding the craft had in place. Any lesser caster would have perished. Visla Dominus was obviously a substantial wielder of magic.

Charlie moved toward the ship, senses on high, ready to engage if need be. He'd taken a pulse rifle from their cache of weapons in Ara's storage bin as well. They'd been trying to go unnoticed. To fit in. But for *this* encounter he wasn't leaving anything to chance.

A bloody man abruptly lurched from an opening that hadn't been in the ship's hull moments before. A secret egress, it appeared to be.

Charlie shouldered the rifle and fired off a pair of shots, the plasma bursting into the trees the man just happened to stumble behind.

"Shit!" Charlie exclaimed as he tried to line up another shot, to no avail.

Korbin had been dazed when he jumped free of his ship, but the instantaneous attack on him with some unknown form of sorcery quickly snapped him back to his senses. This energy was not normal magic, and judging by what he could sense of it, his typical shield spells would do no good against it.

Fortunately for him, Korbin had trained long and hard with the best masters he could find over the years, and one thing they'd all instilled in him time and again was the instinct to adapt to changing threats without thought or hesitation.

He dove aside, realizing this novel attack could still harm him by showering him with shrapnel from the blasted trees. A gap would be required. Korbin quickly fell back, putting a row of trees between himself and where his attack had come from. He then reached out and did what he could to sense the strange power that had been launched at him.

It was like no magic he'd ever felt, but that could be pondered later. For now, survival was key, and that meant adjusting his shield spells to neutralize the flaming pulses of energy flying past him.

Charlie was peppering the area with pulse fire, hoping to keep the visla pinned down long enough for his friends to make it back. With three of them creating a crossfire, perhaps they'd be successful. Head-on, odds were slimmer.

A flurry of spells flew his way, smashing into the dirt around him, kicking up a whirlwind of dust and plant matter that obstructed his view. Charlie quickly switched tactics, opting for his magic to dispel the blinding attack. No sooner had he done so, however, than he saw a terrifying sight.

The bloody man was charging right for him. Charlie quickly did the same, rushing head on into close battle.

It was something his teacher, Ser Baruud, had taught him in gladiator training. When your enemy expects you to retreat, attack. It seemed his opponent had learned the same lesson.

Charlie instinctively batted aside the stun spells coming his way, well aware they were merely a ruse. He could feel their power, and it was limited. The visla wasn't wasting energy on his diversion, just trying to distract his enemy. But Charlie wasn't falling for it. Instead, he stood ready, waiting for the *real* attack he knew was coming.

This was Visla Dominus. A master spell caster. Whatever he was about to do would be massive. Charlie quickly pulled all of his substantial power, readying for a one-shot attempt to stop the deadly man.

Korbin, likewise, realized the deadly assassin sent to kill him was toying with him. He could sense the huge power the man possessed as he closed in. He must have fed recently, using his Wampeh Ghalian powers to absorb another's magic. He was damn well not going to let that happen to him.

Both men cast with all their might simultaneously, a release of magic that exploded in a violent impact as their spells collided. The power tore out from the two-man epicenter, blasting a perfect circle of shattered trees that fanned out over a mile in all directions.

It was an exhausting exchange, but there was no time to waste catching one's breath. Both men were back on their feet in a flash, drawing their blades as they rushed one another, casting spells with both their own power as well as that of their konuses. Korbin was impressed with the assassin's unusual tactics. Charlie was just amazed Visla Dominus hadn't actually killed him yet.

The fight shifted to hand-to-hand combat as the men clashed, their weapons ringing off each other, sending sparks flying. As there were no others near them to be concerned with, both men were casting as they fought. There'd be no taking out of bystanders in this battle.

Charlie switched his style, opting for an Earth technique, landing a flurry of Wing-Chun-style blows to Korbin's chest, driving him back a step.

Korbin noted the unusual tactic and met it with one of his own. A flowing kicking style he'd picked up training in the jungles of Rapsadar. He spun and whirled, his feet flashing in a blur until a windmill of kicks rocked Charlie's ribs and the arm attempting to protect them.

The men were well matched, both physically and magically, and it seemed the battle might rage for longer than anticipated.

Charlie reached into his pocket.

Korbin did the same.

Shoving one another away, they each threw the contents of their pockets with all their might at one another. The resulting splash was rather unimpressive.

Both men paused. This was not what either expected.

This was something completely different.

CHAPTER FIFTY-SEVEN

"Did you just throw *water* on me?" Korbin asked, baffled by his opponent's unorthodox maneuver.

"Did you just throw water on *me?*" Charlie replied. "And why aren't you burning up?"

"Why aren't *you* burning up?" Korbin replied, just as he felt the liquid absorb into his skin. "My gods, is this Balamar water?"

A sinking feeling hit Charlie's gut. He'd not only failed to kill his opponent when he splashed him with the water, both healing to some while deadly to others, he'd accidentally made him stronger. Then he, too, felt the rush of the same waters soaking into *his* skin. He'd been doused in the same thing.

"Hang on. Time out. Something's not right here," Charlie said.

"I'd have to agree with you on that," Korbin replied, though remaining on guard. "I thought all Wampeh of your sort combusted on contact with this stuff."

"Well, *they* do. But I'm not a Wampeh. They don't even look like me."

"Wampeh Ghalian are masters of disguise. They can look like anyone."

"Okay, fair point. But I'm not a Wampeh Ghalian. But what about you? We were told that the mighty Visla Dominus was susceptible to these waters, ergo, a Wampeh."

Korbin's posture relaxed, and a low chuckle began forming in his chest. "You think *I* am Visla Dominus? Oh my. Yes, I do believe this *has* been one rather massive misunderstanding."

"So you're not him?"

"No, I'm not him. And you're obviously not a Wampeh Ghalian, though I sensed one nearby, and my detection spells are quite infallible."

"Oh, that'd be my friend, Bob."

Korbin immediately raised his defenses.

"No, no, it's okay. He's cool, don't worry."

"A Wampeh Ghalian is in play, and they are deadly adversaries."

"Well, not Bob. I mean, he *is* deadly, and when we thought you were Dominus, sure, he wanted to kill you. But it's cool now. He'll leave you alone."

"So, you're saying we're fighting for no reason?"

"Seems that way," Charlie said. "No hard feelings?"

The visla stared at him a long moment, judging the strange man's countenance. Oddly, he sensed no deception.

"I suppose not," Korbin finally replied.

"Great, 'cause you're a seriously powerful guy, and we could really use someone like you on our side. What do you say I buy you a drink and we talk about it?"

"I guess that's as good an idea as any at the moment," Korbin said, surveying the destruction the two had wrought in their combat. "You're exceptionally powerful as well, uh..."

"Charlie," he replied.

"Like the rebel of old? Nice. I'm Korbin."

"Nice to meet you, in a weird, knock-down-the-forest-and-nearly-kill-each-other sort of way."

Korbin laughed. "I suppose that's one way to put it," he said, realizing he felt *fantastic*, despite using so much of his power. "Shame, we both wasted our Balamar waters on a case of mistaken identity. A silly error, and a priceless one."

"Oh, don't worry about that. I'll get you a refill," Charlie said.

"What?" Korbin replied with a shocked expression.

"Oh, yeah. We've kinda got plenty of the stuff. Getting ready to fight a Wampeh, after all."

"But where did you ever come across it in any quantity? It has been gone from the worlds for many, many centuries."

"Trade secret," Charlie said, tapping his nose. "Anyway, Ara's carrying it. We'll get you some when she gets here with Bob."

"Ara?"

"You'll see," Charlie said with a grin. "Let me ask you something. If, say, this entire galaxy was in danger, as well as another, might I be able to persuade you to come with us to see if we could save it?"

"Another galaxy?"

"Yeah. Where I'm from. There's a portal that's going to open to it very soon, and a massive fleet of—"

"Yes."

"I didn't finish."

"I know this fleet you're speaking of and have been trying to discern who is really behind it. Visla Dominus is not a real name, as I'm sure you know by now."

"Obviously."

"Then, yes. I'll join you. But if this portal is opening soon, we should depart at once. I have already acquired the coordinates from one of my people. Come, we'll take my ship once I rouse my Drooks and make repairs from your rather unconventional attack."

"I've got my own ride," Charlie said with a laugh, looking forward to seeing Korbin's face when she landed. "Here she is now, in fact."

The visla's reaction did not disappoint, his face running the gamut from shock and fear to joy and amazement in a flash. Korbin was not easily surprised. *This*, however, was very surprising.

Then the Zomoki spoke.

"This is the one we pursued?" Ara asked.

"She speaks?"

"Yes, she speaks," Ara replied. "You may call me Ara, Korbin."

"She knows my name?"

"She's pretty awesome like that. Super powerful," Charlie replied, not bothering to tell him he'd silently communicated the situation to his friends while he and Korbin had been speaking.

"And this must be your Wampeh friend. A pleasure to meet one of your order not out to kill me," Korbin said.

"And I am pleased not to have to," Bawb replied, surveying the destruction wrought by his power. "You shall prove a most valued ally."

"Yeah, for real," Charlie said. "But we don't have much time, and we need a plan. We're about to jump into the midst of an unknown enemy force, and we don't even know how many there are, where they're positioned, or anything remotely tactical like that."

Korbin grinned and reached into his pocket, pulling out his copy of Kara's pilfered image disc. "I think I can help with that."

CHAPTER FIFTY-EIGHT

"We need to find out what's really going on. I think we should ask Daisy what she knows," Kara said.

"But she *did* try to kill your father, right?"

"I'm starting to wonder. From what Pod and Freya have told us, it doesn't sound like the sort of thing she'd do. Not without a good reason, at least."

"But how can we talk to her? She's bound by your father's spell."

Kara reached into her pocket and removed a thin braid of Ootaki hair. "I held this piece back, in case we needed something in an emergency. Sorry to use it again."

"You're not the one who took it," Vee said. "And I know you wouldn't. And someone already gave it up. It would be a waste of their sacrifice to not use it."

"Thanks, Vee. I just know it's hard to see people use Ootaki hair around you."

"What needs to be done, needs to be done. Let's just get it over with."

Kara nodded, then she and Vee made for the stairs, as the lift discs were inoperable, courtesy of her uncle Korbin.

"Where are you going?" Shozzy asked, rising to his feet as the girls passed him.

"Stay here with Bahnjoh. Guard the door," Kara replied. "We've got to talk to Daisy."

"Who?"

"The heretic assassin."

"Denna Palmarian, is that such a good idea? She did try to kill your father, after all."

"I know what we've all been told, but I have reason to believe there may be more to that story. And she might even be able to help us get out of this mess."

Her father's security chief was visibly torn. He had a duty to protect Kara at all costs, but he also knew the most likely route of attack would be either the gardens or the lift discs if someone managed to break Korbin's spell. The thing was, the heretic was safely locked in her thick-walled cell, and Kara would probably be even safer up there than with him.

"Very well. Bahnjoh and I will stay here. But be careful, and do not hesitate to call if you need me."

"Will do," Kara said, already running up the stairs with Vee in tow.

They raced to Daisy's cell and pounded on the heavy door.

"Daisy! We want to talk to you!" Kara shouted into the slot.

A fast rustling told her the woman had obviously heard her name and quickly gotten to her feet.

"Okay, give me a second. I think I can break the spell keeping you from speaking. Hang on."

Kara wrapped the Ootaki braid around her hand. "Never done this before, so I don't really know how it works. You have any idea, Vee?"

"Not a clue."

"Most. Useless. Ootaki. Ever."

"Yeah, yeah. Just try casting and see what happens. You were getting stronger when we were training with Korbin, I don't see why you shouldn't be able to make it work."

Kara could feel the power in the hair wanting to be used. "Well, here goes nothing."

There was no flash of magic, no zapping power. Just a girl standing in a corridor with a braid of golden hair wrapped around her hand.

"Uh, did it work?" Kara wondered.

"Goddammit, get me the hell out of here!" Daisy shouted through the slot.

"That answers that question," Vee said with a chuckle.

Kara leaned in to the door's small opening. "I can't open the door. Father sealed it. But you can still help us. We have many questions for you."

"Yeah, like why did you try to kill Kara's father?" Vee added.

"Kill someone? Who thought I was trying to kill someone? All I was trying to do was get some goddamn answers. I followed a ship all the way to this tower, but when I tried to sneak inside, someone zapped me with a stunner."

"Stun spell, you mean."

"Semantics."

"But you broke into our home carrying a weapon."

"People have a really bad habit of trying to kill me," Daisy snarked. "Of course I was armed. Speaking of which, where's Stabby?"

"Stabby?"

"My sword."

"You named your sword Stabby?"

"Stabby McStabberton. Yeah. Where is he? Oh, man, he's gotta be hungry."

"It's stuck in the wall where you left it. And, I'm sorry, did you say hungry?"

"Long story. Now get me out of here. I need to get Stabby and find Freya."

"We found her, thanks to your cryptic help, but she's stuck, kind of like you are."

Daisy started pacing in her cell. The girls could hear her muttering to herself, having one side of a heated discussion.

"Okay, okay. Yeah. That should work," she finally said.

"Uh, who are you talking to?" Kara asked.

"Never mind. Tell you later. But what I need you to do is to get me my power whip."

"Your *what*?"

"It's a wristlet device I was wearing when I was captured. Metal, kind of clunky, though I did bling it out a bit when I modified it."

"A whip bracelet? Huh, sounds kind of like what Grundsch wears."

"What's a Grundsch?"

"Our servant. But I don't think I've seen anything like that in the––" Kara suddenly realized she had. "Wait. In my father's vault. I think I might have seen the thing you're talking about."

"Excellent! Bring it to me, and I'll get myself out of here."

"I don't see how it can––"

"Just get it!"

"*Fine*. But then you'll answer my questions. Deal?"

"Sure, kid. But first the power whip."

"Okay, I'll get it. Back in a minute. Come on, Vee."

Kara took off at a run, Vee following close behind. They took the stairs three at a time as they bounded down to her father's offices. Fortunately, being a blood relative of the visla, the ward on the door allowed her in when she pushed with aid of the Ootaki hair. It was a funny quirk of magic and family. Sometimes, blood was thicker than magic.

In this case, a visla's daughter was able to override his wards, albeit with the help of some powerful Ootaki hair. In other instances, certain spells simply would not work against family members. It was somewhat hit-or-miss how it would play out for each bloodline, but it was a well-documented phenomenon.

Kara went straight for the hidden compartment in the wall and uttered the little spell that opened it. Silently, the wall slid open.

"It's that easy?" Vee asked, startled. "How are you so powerful, Kara?"

"It's not a power thing at all. It's just an old spell I heard my father use to keep me from wandering when I was little. He was sloppy, is all. It's funny, really. He always stressed changing your pass-spells, but this one he left in place all that time."

Kara rifled through the contents of the compartment. There was no use trying to be subtle about it now. Not with the entire estate in disarray and a slew of dead traitors strewn about the place.

She found the unassuming wrist gauntlet where she'd noticed it before. It *did* look a little like what Grundsch wore on his wrist, but this was far sleeker and tasteful in appearance. But she could think about that later. She tucked it in her pocket. She paused a moment, then started grabbing all of the image discs.

"Help me carry these," she said, handing several to Vee.

The teens stuffed their pockets, then Kara sealed her father's vault once more and took off back up the stairs to the cells above.

"I've got it," Kara said, barely squeezing it through the slot in the door.

It was funny. The cells were designed to be impregnable, but they all shared the same vulnerability. The slot in the door. It was too small to fit anything of use through, and the magical wards would not allow any konus or slaap or other magical tool to pass through the opening. But Daisy's device didn't operate on magic. At least, not any type any caster in this galaxy had ever encountered. And for that reason, it passed through the opening without triggering a single safety.

Daisy grabbed the device and slapped it on her wrist, feeling the stolen Ra'az tech link with her on a visceral level. The whip would do as she wished with no more effort than lifting a finger.

Lookee what I've got, Sis, she silently said to her sister's neural clone ride-along.

"I see it," Sarah replied in her head. *"And it's about damn time. Now get us the hell out of here, will ya?"*

"Don't have to tell me twice."

"What did you say?" Kara asked.

"Nothing," Daisy replied, realizing she'd used her outside voice to talk to her dead-not-dead sister riding shotgun in her heavily modified mind. Explaining how the copy had been loaded into her head when Sarah had died would just complicate things, and they didn't have time for that right now.

"You might want to stand back," Daisy warned.

"What are you going to do?"

"Get out, of course," she said, then made the power whip thrust out a beam of energy the strength of which should have smashed through the door easily. But the magic holding it stymied her.

"Damn. That thing's on there tight," Sarah said.

Surprisingly so. But this isn't a Chithiid whip. It's a Ra'az one.

"Heavily modified, no less."

Yeah. It'll work. I mean, they use these things to help freakin' ships dock. I think if they can move thousands of tons of spaceship, they can open one simple door.

"So do it, then."

So demanding, Daisy chuckled as the whip lashed out, this time snaking through the small slot opening and flaring out, grabbing onto the door and pulling *inward* with the effortless force of the alien device she'd stolen in the Great War against the Ra'az Hok.

It was a marvel of technology, the power whip. When activated, the energy beam could move huge weights without throwing the user off-balance. A woman such as Daisy could lift a few thousand times her own mass and not feel the weight on her joints.

Or she could pull in a tug-of-war no one could best her at. Least of all a simple door. And it appeared the power holding the door was more focused on preventing someone from forcing the door outward than pulling it in. Daisy felt it start to give and grinned.

The door ripped free, the magic traces around it shredding to bits as it crashed into the cell's back wall.

Kara and Vee stared in awe at the redheaded woman standing before them. The thing they'd brought her was indeed like Grundsch's device, only it seemed to be more powerful somehow. Tuned to the user in a different manner, the coil alternating between flowing and rigid, crackling against the floor as Daisy took in her surroundings.

She was of medium height and appeared to be in her early forties, though she possessed the physique of someone far younger. Judging by the way she moved, it had likely been attained by hard training, and not just the kind done in a gymnasium. This woman's motions radiated functionality.

"Hi, girls," she said with an amused chuckle. "So, how about we get the hell out of here?"

CHAPTER FIFTY-NINE

"Take me there," the somewhat intimidating woman said. "Now."

"You're scaring them, Daze," Sara pointed out.

"So what? Scared is good. Scared keeps you alive."

Kara and Vee looked at one another, more than a little confused as they led the way.

"Uh, Kara? She's talking to herself," Vee said in a hushed voice.

"Yeah, I noticed. Just ignore it. Being locked up must have gotten to her," Kara replied, taking the new member of their group through the expansive top floors of the estate.

"Nice place," Daisy said as they walked. "Looks like you had a bit of a party, though," she added with a chuckle, when they reached the carnage wrought by Korbin and Grundsch.

The odd woman was utterly unfazed by the blood and death, the girls noted. She must have seen some serious shit in her day to react in such a blasé manner.

"It's just out this way," Kara said as she led the way to the outer patio, where Stabby was embedded in the wall.

"Denna Palmarian, what are you doing?" Shozzy exclaimed

when he saw the heretic assassin with her. "She is a dangerous assassin!"

Daisy's power whip leapt to life, crackling with energy. "I don't know about that assassin stuff, but dangerous? You try and zap me with that stun shit again and I'll show you dangerous."

"Shozzy, stand down. She wasn't trying to kill Father. There was a huge misunderstanding."

"A misunderstanding? She was sneaking into the estate––your *home*––armed and looking to do violence."

"Armed? Yes. Looking for a fight? Not if I could avoid it. I just wanted to find out who the hell was trying to blast my ship out of the sky. We tracked what looked like one of the culprits back here. So *you* started it. Not me."

"Very mature, Daze. I'm rubber, you're glue?"

Hey, it was the truth, wasn't it?

"Fair point," Sarah conceded.

"Shozzy, there are things going on. Things with Father's dealings. I don't know what, exactly, but I believe Daisy. Now, please stand down."

Reluctantly, he did as the teen asked. It was a tough position, but she was technically the ranking Palmarian in the estate, and as such, her orders had weight.

"Good. Now, come along. We're heading to the terrace to get her sword."

Without further discussion, she continued on her way, the anxious visitor close behind.

"There it is," Kara said when they reached the terrace where Daisy had been stunned and captured, but not before driving her sword into the wall. "No one's been able to get it out. Not even the strongest of Father's men could budge it."

Daisy chuckled and walked over to the yellowing handle of the weapon, running her fingers over it with a happy smile. "Hi, buddy. Good to see you," she said, wrapping her hand around the grip and easily pulling her sword free from the wall.

"How did you do that? You didn't even strain at all?" Kara wondered, gazing at the white blade. "Is that sword made of *bone*?"

"Very observant. Yeah, Stabby was grown from a sample they took from me a long time ago. Molecular bonding, he only recognizes me. And look at the poor thing," she said, noting his discoloration and fine cracks marring his surface.

"You, there! Halt!"

All four of them spun at the command, which was rather odd as they weren't actually going anywhere at the moment. It was Trepenan, Kara's stepmother's friend, only he was not seeming terribly friendly at the moment. At least, not to Daisy.

"You are to come with me, child," he commanded.

"No, I think not," Kara replied.

"It is for your own protection. Your mother tasked me with guarding your safety."

"So where were you when all the fighting went down? I didn't see you up here. Only now that my uncle is gone are you showing your face."

Trepenan's smile faltered a second, and that was all Shozzy needed to decide the best course of action. Kara was to be protected at all costs, and this newcomer, even though an emmik and friend of her stepmother, was nevertheless not to be trusted.

"I'm afraid I cannot allow that," he said, stepping between the girl and the emmik.

Trepenan's smile fell entirely. "And you have this authority, how, exactly? You are a mere servant."

"Perhaps. But Denna Palmarian is the ranking member of the household, and if she does not wish to accompany you, she will not."

"And *you* will stop me?"

"If I must," he said, moving a step closer.

Trepenan didn't say a word but merely cast violently,

sending the poor man into the wall. He landed on the floor in a heap.

"Shozzy!" Kara shrieked.

"Okay, that's just not gonna fly," Daisy said, lazily swinging Stabby in a series of casual arcs. Casual, but clearly masterful. This woman knew what she was doing.

Trepenan laughed at her, utterly unafraid. "You think to harm me with that? Fool, I cast protective spells about my person every single day. Many have tried and many have failed over the years, but no enchanted blade can touch me."

Shozzy slowly tried to regain his feet, but judging by his movements, he had at least a few broken ribs, and possibly one of his arms. But he also had a konus and was ready to use it.

The emmik turned and blasted him again, this time shocking him with a particularly painful spell, making him cry out in agony. This wasn't simply stopping a threat, this was torturing a man to death. And judging by the look on Trepenan's face, the sick bastard was enjoying it.

He didn't even flinch when Daisy rushed at him, Stabby aimed right at his torso. His wall of defensive magic against enchanted weapons would easily deflect the foolish attack. Or so he thought, until the yellowing blade plunged into his chest. The look of utter shock and confusion on his face brought a grin to Daisy's.

"Stabby's not an enchanted blade, dumbass."

While that was true, the bone sword was, however, alive. And it had not been fed in a very, very long time. Stabby was hungry.

The wound should have been easily healed. Daisy hadn't been going for a killing blow, but merely something substantial enough to take this bastard out of action for a good long while. Stabby, on the other hand, had a different idea.

A ravenous slurping sound filled the air as the genetically engineered sword quickly drained the emmik dry of every last drop of blood, healing its own damage, while leaving nothing but a dried husk of Trepenan behind.

Daisy pulled the blade free, the last traces of the powerful caster's blood absorbing into it and vanishing without a trace.

"Shit. I didn't mean to do that."

Daisy could feel her sword's glee with the kill and subsequent feast. She'd always had a visceral link with the weapon, but now it had absorbed something new. The blood of a power user. And Stabby felt *good*.

The sword began to happily vibrate like a purring cat in Daisy's hand.

"Well, this is different," Sarah said.

Yeah. And do you feel that? What is that?

"Some kind of power, I guess. Seems your pet absorbed more than just blood."

The sword's yellowed exterior began flaking away, sloughing off and revealing a gleaming freshness, made better than new by the powered blood.

Karasalia, a visla's daughter, could sense the change. "Your sword. It has power now," she said, taking a step back. "It's taken it and made it a part of itself, like a Wampeh," she gasped.

"A vampire?" Daisy asked.

"A what?"

"What you said."

"I said Wampeh."

"Whatever that is. Sounded like you said vampire. But that doesn't matter. What does is finding my girl. You said you know where Freya is. I need you to take me to her."

"She's trapped way at the edge of the system. My uncle was working on freeing her, but then all of this happened."

"Pod is here, though," Vee noted.

"Pod's still hiding up here? Excellent! He can get me there. Take me to him!"

"Shozzy first," Kara said, crouching over her injured guardian.

The way she said it, Daisy could tell there was no talking her out of the delay. "Okay, we'll patch him up as best we can," she replied.

He would live, though it would take the skills of a good healer to get him walking properly again. But that would come later.

"Rest here. My uncle is sending help," Kara said when they'd done what they could, then turned to her dangerous new friend. "Okay. You want to see Pod? Let's go see Pod."

CHAPTER SIXTY

Stabby in hand, Daisy followed the teens back through the upper floors on the way to the floating garden. Shozzy was propped up in as comfortable a position as they could manage, given the injuries he'd sustained. Injuries that, while not life-threatening, simply made it impractical to move him any farther than they already had.

Kara had been reluctant to leave him behind, but he had agreed with the woman who had unexpectedly saved his life. They needed to get Karasalia out of there, and if she had a plan, he had no choice but to support it.

They were racing to go find Pod where he was camouflaged on one of the floating gardens when Daisy came to a screeching stop, her sword held aloft as she prepared to kill the evil beast waiting to pounce on them.

"Stop! What are you doing?" Kara said, placing herself between Daisy and her four-legged friend.

"It'll kill you! Look out!"

"He will not kill me," Kara said, walking to her pet and scratching the coarse-furred hide behind the ears.

"You have a freaking Graizenhund as a pet?"

"A *what*?"

"That thing."

"He's not a *thing*. He's Bahnjoh, and he's a good boy."

"Banjo? You named a ferocious Ra'az killing-machine Banjo?" Daisy shook her head. "This place just gets weirder and weirder."

"Well, you'd better accept it, because he's with me," Kara said, the Ootaki hair she was still carrying giving off a dangerous magical pulse.

"Easy, Kara," Vee said.

Kara realized what was happening and immediately released the power she'd latched on to. *That* was a new sensation, and for just a moment, it felt like it wasn't entirely fueled by the Ootaki hair she possessed.

"Okay. Fine. Banjo's your buddy," Daisy said. "But if he acts up, he loses a limb."

Kara rolled her eyes at the threat.

Did she just roll her eyes at me?

"I believe she did," Sarah replied with a chuckle. *"I'm liking this girl more and more."*

Of course you like her. She reminds you of Ripley, I'm sure.

It was true, she did have a certain snark that was rather similar to a certain human teenager they knew. Daisy had a feeling the two would hit it off famously. If they survived this ordeal, that is.

"Come on, kid. Take me to Pod," Daisy urged.

"On it. Follow me," Kara said, then took off out the door onto the gardens at a run, Bahnjoh at her side.

Kara and Vee had played on the gardens for years and were familiar with their occasionally unusual terrain. It could make for an interesting run, but despite a lengthy captivity in a cell, Daisy had no trouble keeping up with the teens as they raced across the floating gardens. They leapt from one to the other with ease as they moved closer to her little pod's hiding spot.

"He's just up ahead on the next garden," Kara said over her shoulder as she ran. "We have to go around to the left, though. It's longer but the other way is too hard to pass."

"I'll take your word for it," Daisy said.

A deep, rumbling growl reverberated in Bahnjoh's throat. Daisy felt the power whip on her wrist charge, ready to strike if need be, but the deadly animal wasn't looking at her. He was looking *past* her at the three hostile ships that had just landed on the adjacent garden.

"You know these guys?" Daisy asked.

"Nope. And if they're landing here, they've gotta be backed by some pretty serious magic. Come on!"

It would be a really tight fit, but if they could make it to Pod, maybe, just maybe, they could all squeeze inside and let his active camouflage hide them from the invading force.

They ran as fast as they were able, lining up to jump to the next and final garden, when two of the hostile ships swooped around and dropped down in front of them, cutting off their path.

"Shit, they're on to us," Daisy growled as twenty Tslavar mercenaries spilled out of the ships onto the gardens, ready to engage. "Is there another way out of here?" she asked, very much wishing she had a pulse rifle right about now.

"No. The garden was put out here to quarantine it. There was some sort of blight. But that means we're at the very edge."

"So nowhere to run."

"I'm afraid not."

Daisy powered up her whip and tightened her grip on Stabby. "Well, then. I guess we get to go down in style."

It was looking like they might very well do just that when a sleek, black ship suddenly rose from below the gardens, weapons hot. Seconds later the Tslavars and the two ships were reduced to little pieces, though the mercenaries' remains were of a squishier variety than those of their craft.

"Freya!" Daisy shouted with unrestrained joy. "Where've you been? I was worried about you!"

"Sorry, Daisy. I was kinda stuck. But I'm free now!" the stealth ship replied over her external comms system.

"The kid said you were trapped somewhere way out on the edge of the system. How'd you find me?"

"Pod keyed me in to your coordinates."

"Good boy, Pod! Speaking of, where are you?"

The little pod deactivated his camouflage and flashed into view. "I'm over here, Daisy," he replied.

"Hi, Pod!" the girls called out.

"Hello, Vee. Hello, Kara. You may find it of interest that Korbin seems to have been pursued when he departed the tower. I believe he was likely under attack shortly thereafter. I thought you'd want to know."

Kara's alarm went off the charts. "Which way, Pod?"

"Toward the wooded region," he replied.

"We have to help him!"

"Hang on, kid. We have to help *who*?"

"My uncle."

"I don't know——"

"I agree with Kara," Freya said. "Korbin tried to free me. He released my mind from the weird magic that was holding me out there."

"Did you say magic? Are you buying into this hocus-pocus crap now too?"

"It's not crap, Daisy. It's power of some sort, and I don't know all the details, but this stuff's real. Trust me."

"How did you even get free?" Kara asked. "We couldn't get you out, and Uncle Korbin is a really powerful visla."

"I disassembled the magic thing you left with me."

"My konus?"

"Yeah, that. I figured if I could learn how it worked, maybe I could replicate its effects. It took a while, but I had my nanites break it down to a molecular level, then replicate the power structure and integrate it into every aspect of my hull. From there it was just a matter of determining the proper use of that energy to negate that which was holding me in place. Pretty simple, once you get the hang of it, actually."

"You're saying you made yourself into a magic ship?" Daisy asked.

"Figures your kid would do something like that, Daze," Sarah said with a laugh.

I thought she'd outgrown these surprises. I guess not, Daisy agreed.

Freya spun. A quick burst of railgun fire tore the third Tslavar ship to shreds as it tried to circle around them. Its stealth maneuver was quite unsuccessful.

"Good eye, Freya," Daisy complimented her ship.

"Oh, I've been watching them for a while, waiting to see if they'd try anything stupid. I thought maybe we could capture them, but then they tried that little trick, so fuck 'em, right?"

"I'd have to agree."

Daisy looked at the two teens and the huge beast that was acting surprisingly like a house pet and not a special-bred killing machine. They reminded her of more than a few people she knew, and those ones she cared about greatly.

"Oh, fine," she relented. "Freya, come on down here. We're gonna go find this Korbin guy."

Freya dropped down to land right in front of them, her doors opening as soon as she touched down.

"Come on, you two. Load up," Daisy said. "But if your critter poops in my ship, you're cleaning it up."

CHAPTER SIXTY-ONE

"What in the ever-loving hell happened here?" Daisy wondered as they flew over the area Pod had said Korbin had passed as he departed the tower.

"Daisy, I've run a thermal, radiologic, biohazard, and incendiary residue scans, but I think it was something else that did this."

"Look at that blast zone, Freya. Sis, what do you think?"

"I think something blew the hell out of that forest, that's what I think."

"Who do you keep talking to?" Visanya asked.

"Vee, don't be rude," Kara hissed.

"What? It's a legit question when the lady piloting the ship you're on is having full-on conversations with herself."

"Technically, *I'm* piloting the ship," Freya interjected. "Mainly because I *am* the ship. But Daisy's a pretty good pilot too."

"Gee, thanks, kiddo," Daisy said with a chuckle. "And to answer your question, I'm not talking to myself. It'll be a bit much for you guys to understand the technical details, but, basically, I've got a neural clone of my sister living in my head."

"A neural what?"

"Clone. It's a copy of my sister, Sarah's, mind. It's a long story and we're in a bit of a hairy spot, so I'll explain later. Suffice to say, some people hear voices they make up. Mine happens to have a mind of her own."

Freya banked hard and came to an abrupt stop. "Heat signature moving in fast from the tree-line."

"What is it?"

"Looks like a canine. But holy shit, it's a big one."

"Put it on screen."

Freya did as she was asked, the image of the beast flashing to life.

"Baloo!" Kara blurted.

"You know this thing too? Jesus, kid, are all of your pets scary beasts?"

"He's not mine. He belongs to our friend Leila. But what's he doing out here all by himself? He should be with her. And she should be with Captain Sandah––oh," Kara said, falling silent.

"What?"

"What if Sandah is with the people who attacked me at home?"

"Oh, shit," Vee blurted. "That would explain why Baloo is out there. He probably kicked him off his ship. Baloo likes you, so he wouldn't want anyone loyal to you on board."

"But what about Leila?"

"I don't know, Kara."

Down below, the huge canine slowed his run near a trampled area amidst the destruction. An area at the epicenter. The place that still smelled like his friend. Charlie had been there, and recently. Baloo sniffed the wind and looked all around, but all he could sense was destruction. With a low whine, he sat down, unsure what to do next.

"We have to get him," Kara said.

"That thing's like a dire wolf on steroids, Daze. You sure you want that on board too?"

"Well, the kid vouches for him, so I don't see why not," she said aloud. "Freya, take us down."

The sleek ship silently dropped to the surface, landing a good twenty meters from the perplexed animal. Baloo, for his part, did not run, nor did he show any fear. Rather, he cocked his head to the side with a curious tilt.

"I swear, I'm becoming a freaking petting zoo," Freya grumbled as she opened her airlock doors. "Okay, go get your buddy."

Kara jumped to the ground and ran to the exhausted animal. "Baloo! Oh, look at you! How long have you been out here? You poor boy."

The tired beast's tail thumped happily, increasing its fervor when his buddy came out to say hello. Bahnjoh kept his enthusiasm in check for once, seeing his friend was wiped out from his miles and miles of running. Instead, he licked his face and sat protectively beside him, like a big brother might look after his sibling.

"Come on, you two. Let's get you inside and get you something to eat. And maybe Freya has something we can clean you up with," Kara said, leading the two animals back aboard the climate-controlled comfort of the mighty ship.

"Hey, Freya?"

"Yes, Kara?"

"Do you have anything I could use to clean up Baloo? Like a towel and some water or something? He's kinda funky."

"I can do better. I've got a full bathing compartment. I put it in for Daisy––she really loves her showers, especially if Vince is on board."

"Hey!" Daisy blurted. "Not cool, Freya!"

"Sorry. Anyway, if you'll get your friend inside, I'll make sure he's nice and clean."

"Thanks," Kara said, then followed Freya's directions to the bathing compartment, her furry friend in tow.

"Daisy?"

"What is it, Freya?"

"I had my nanites run a scan for any unusual energy signatures, like the type that I had them incorporate into their own structures. Well, it looks like they got a hit. It's here in this site, but they tracked residual traces of it to a little speck in the sky, moving away with speed."

"Wait a second. On screen."

Freya popped up the image, enhanced and enlarged with her impressive optics array.

"That's Kara's uncle's ship!" Vee said. "He's alive!"

"Can you lock in on that, Freya?"

"Already done."

"Of course you did. Okay, so run with me on this. If you've integrated elements of this freaky power source with your nanites, can you actually use the power like they do?" Daisy asked.

"I don't see why not. I've already used it to break free from that stupid chunk of moon. How hard could it be?"

"Wait a minute," Vee said. "You can *cast*?"

"What, you mean like spells and stuff? I don't know about that. But I was able to devise a power algorithm when I used my modified nanites to invert that force field––or magic, if you prefer to call it that. So, I suppose I could learn other uses for it as well. Like right now, for example. I can actually sense that ship's energy signature and follow it. Pretty cool, right?" Freya said, launching up into the sky in pursuit.

"A 'magic' leash?" Daisy asked.

"Kinda, I suppose."

"Kickass. Go get it, Freya."

Visanya was a bit confused by the technological jargon, but

the basic idea was more or less clear. "You can follow it? Even if it jumps?"

"If you mean that thing I've seen some of the ships doing when they pop into orbit that looks like some sorta weird version of a warp, then yeah, I think so," Freya said. "Oh, shit."

"What is it, kiddo?"

"Looks like we get to test that theory, because they just jumped. Actually, I got *two* jump signatures, though there was only one ship up there. Not what I expected, but hey, learning curve, right?"

"Right on," Daisy replied as she slipped on her slender neuro band, allowing neuro-clone Sarah to communicate with Freya directly as well. "Can you maintain this gap between us and them when we come out of warp?"

"Don't see why not."

"You guys thinking what I'm thinking?"

"I think we are, Sarah," Freya replied.

"All right, then," Daisy said. "Fire it up and follow that ship. Let's see where they're going."

CHAPTER SIXTY-TWO

Freya made the warp to the general region of the ship this Korbin fellow was piloting, expecting to arrive in the calm black of space, where her nanite construction allowed her to blend in even better than the active camouflage her nanites employed.

She was in for a bit of a surprise.

The high-tech stealth ship popped out of warp with a faint, blue crackle, her now magically altered nanites allowing her to tie her warp drive in with the unusual powers of this place and fly, more or less, on course, unlike her initial arrival and subsequent flight. That, however, wasn't the problem. The raging space battle she'd warped into was.

"What the hell?" Daisy blurted as Freya immediately took evasive maneuvers, dodging the magical attacks of a cluster of smaller Tslavar attack ships. "Freya, are we back where we first got dragged into this mess?"

"Gee, ya think?"

"Don't sass me."

"Just stating the obvious. You want to hop on one of the cannons and help? I'm trying to not get us killed, here."

Freya's newly configured nanites read the incoming magical

attack and adapted their shielding output, canceling the odd energy, and even managing to absorb some of the power hurled at them.

But there were other attacks as well. Projectiles magically launched with great speed. *Those* required an entirely different phasing of her shields, and even with her amazing AI brain processing millions of calculations a second, it was still a challenge. There was just so much to keep track of.

"What's going on?" Kara said, stumbling from the corridor, a soggy, but clean, Baloo padding alongside her.

"Strap in tight, kids. We've got problems," Daisy said. "Lots of them."

Kara quickly dropped into a seat beside Vee and pulled the strange harness straps into place. It was quite different than the soft, magical force restraints used in her world, but the basic design was easy enough to figure out.

"Baloo, go in there," she said, pointing to the space under a stowage rack where Bahnjoh had already squeezed himself, using the bulkhead to hold himself in place. "Where's Uncle Korbin?"

"He's out there," Daisy said, as she fired off the cannon again and again, its pulse blasts shaking but not disabling the enemy ships. "And he seems to be fighting alongside a—holy shit, is that what I think it is?"

"It's a dragon, Daisy," Freya noted.

"What's a dragon?" Kara asked.

"On screen, Freya."

The ship flashed the image for all to see. A giant red dragon with what appeared to be a harness and two men in spacesuits on its back.

"What in the actual hell is going on, Freya?"

"It's a Zomoki!" Kara and Vee both gasped in unison. "And a *big* one!"

"A what?"

343

"That. It's a Zomoki. Fierce animals that sometimes possess powerful magic. They can fly in space, and they can even jump on their own. I learned about them from Father," Kara said. "They're quite dangerous."

"Great, now we're fighting space dragons," Daisy groaned.

"They seem to be fighting on our side," Sarah noted. *"Maybe we have an unexpected ally."*

"Maybe," Daisy admitted as she loosed another flurry of pulse cannon fire, but the swarming ships were only mildly affected by it. "Freya, this isn't stopping them!"

"I know! Gimme a second. I'm gonna have to adjust the power output and mix in some of this new magic power to see if it'll be able to overpower their shielding. I just need more time."

"We don't have more time."

"Again, thanks for stating the obvious," the ship snarked.

"Freya, don't you get——"

"Let it go, Daze. She's under a lot of pressure," Sarah said.

Freya spun a quick barrel roll, dodging a crossfire attack. "Thanks, Sarah."

"No worries, hon. Just keep on keeping us all alive."

"Two on one. Not fair," Daisy griped, then let off another volley from the cannons. "Hey, whatever you did seemed to work a little. That shot made it partway through that one's shields. Just scorched it, but it's a start."

Freya took note, working to adjust the other weapons to the somewhat effective configuration, while trying to keep them from being blasted from the sky.

Meanwhile, Korbin and his new friends found themselves in a likewise difficult situation as the enemy ships swarmed them in wave after wave of attacks.

"We have to hold them back," Korbin sent over skree, already so used to his Wampeh-detecting pendant heating against his chest from Bawb's presence that he didn't even notice it anymore. Not much good if one of the people it warns against happens to be your ally, it seemed. "If we join our magic, maybe, just maybe, we can block them. But the portal will need to stop spewing flames first for us to get into position."

"Agreed, but we can cast together against them to slow their progress in the meantime. Stay in one piece while we figure out a plan," Charlie said, then switched to his silent bond. *"When the hell does the portal open?"* Charlie grunted as he cast his strongest defensive spells, keeping Ara free to use her magical fire to try to clear a path through the Tslavar barrage.

"The chrono said it was to open within minutes. But we were following Korbin's lead, and he took us right into the heart of the fleet, not the outskirts, as agreed."

"I believe he jumped exactly where we agreed upon, actually, but the enemy had adjusted their position," Ara said, torching one of the enemy in a blast of her flames.

The plan had been to arrive a few minutes prior to the portal's scheduled opening, then place themselves in position the instant the sun's flames began to recede, to prevent Visla Dominus from crossing over by any means necessary.

The plan, obviously, was a bust.

Whether their enemy had somehow managed to recover the cache of power without their realizing was unknown. What was certain, however, was, no matter the cost, they could not allow the visla to make it to the other galaxy. To Earth.

"What's that over there?" Charlie said as a series of violent plasma blasts ripped through the enemy ships. "Is that one of ours? I don't know that ship, but it's obviously Earth tech. Look at those cannons. How did it get here?"

"I do not know," Bawb said. "But they are fighting our enemy, and making a good show of it, despite the numbers against them."

It was true, Freya was beginning to kick ass as her nanites gradually tuned in her armaments to the particular type of magic being used to defend against them. But for all the progress she was making, there were simply too many ships for one, or even two craft to successfully hold off, even with a fire-breathing dragon on their side.

"Korbin's holding his own, but we're all screwed. Can we jump out of here?"

"They've blocked our way," Ara said. "We're absorbing power from the Earth's sun at this range, but despite that, the spells are too many and too strong to break free. We are stuck here."

"Shit. I'm going to hail the other ship on comms. If it's from Earth, maybe they'll hear us, and we can try to join forces."

"We are in a difficult spot, regardless," Bawb noted.

"But every little bit helps," Charlie replied, switching to all channels open. "Unidentified ship. If you're from Earth, please respond."

Nearby, the nanotech stealth ship heard the unexpected transmission.

"Incoming comms, Daisy."

"Put it through, Freya."

"Unidentified ship. If you're from Earth, please respond. Do you guys think they hear me?" the voice asked, comms still open.

"We hear you. Who is this?" Daisy replied.

"Charlie Gault, here. Are you the black ship out there tearing into the Tslavars?"

"I don't know what a Tslavar is, but if you mean these fuckers trying to blow us out of the sky, then yeah, that's us."

Despite the deadliness of their situation, Charlie couldn't help but laugh at the woman's salty language. "Yep, that answers my next question. You're obviously from Earth."

"And you too," Daisy said. "Wait a minute. Charlie Gault? Like the guy who helped build that ship that got sucked through a wormhole forever ago? The colossal fuck-up?"

"Yeah, thanks for reminding me. It's a long story."

"If we survive, you can tell it to me. Is that you riding on that dragon? I thought I saw one of our EVA suits. Newer model too."

"Courtesy of Cal. Do you know him?"

"Know him? Oh yeah, we have a lot to discuss. Freya, get us over there. We need to link up with those guys."

"On it, Daisy."

"Daisy? Ripley's aunt?"

"You know Rip?"

"We *do* have a lot to discuss," Charlie agreed.

Freya spun into a tight corkscrew around a dozen swarming ships, their attacks bouncing off her modified shielding as she made her way to the unlikely Earthman and his dragon ride.

"Charlie, can you warp out of here? This is a shit-show," Daisy said.

"No, we're blocked by their spells. They call it Jumping here, by the way. But what about you? Can you warp?"

"What do you think, Freya?" Daisy asked.

"Warp? Yes. Use the power everyone is calling magic to do so? I don't think so. They've blocked us somehow."

"What about the other one. Korbin's ship? He with you?" Daisy asked.

"Yeah. We're trying to stop the visla from crossing the portal to Earth."

Daisy glanced at the blazing eye of plasma in the darkness. "So that's what that is."

The enemy cut their conversation short, having regrouped and redeployed as soon as they saw the Zomoki, the unusually powerful vessel that had jumped with it, and this newcomer all joining forces.

The battle was raging, neither side expecting to be locked in a fight, but both reacting quickly and efficiently as soon as the engagement began. It was a whirlwind of chaos and casting, and the sheer number of resources at Visla Dominus's disposal were far too great to overcome.

If something didn't shift in their favor, and fast, Charlie worried they'd all fall on this day.

Aboard the command ship, Visla Dominus grew irritated with this distraction. It was nearly time for the great plan to finally unfold. The visla called up a great surge of magic and flung it forth at the troublesome intruders.

Ara and Charlie sensed it immediately, just moments before Korbin did. Even Bawb felt the spell surge.

"Everyone, cast an *invario pokta*!" Charlie shouted over comms, skree, and his psychic link with Ara and Bawb.

They had just one chance to stop the tidal wave of magic, and only if they joined their magic in the exact same spell. All four of them cast together, a visla, a Zomoki, an Ootaki-powered Wampeh with his highly charged wand, and an unusually powered human.

The spell wasn't an elegant one, but they didn't have time for that. Just a sheer pulse of power to deflect the incoming attack.

Visla Dominus watched in shock as the small group's magic smashed into the offensive spell. It was like a magical tsunami encountering a massive breakwater––one that barely dissipated its force.

But it had worked, the power bursting and fading against the quartet's combined efforts. In single combat none would have stood a chance, but in unison, they were actually cause for concern. The visla would have to shift tactics to speed this to an end. There simply wasn't enough time to leisurely separate and then pick apart their enemy. Something else was called for.

CHAPTER SIXTY-THREE

What had started out as a mere skirmish in the eyes of the powerful leader of the deadly fleet had evolved into something more, it seemed. Judging by the nature of the magic being wielded on the battlefield, there were several powerful casters present among the intruders. *Very* powerful. And one of them was a Zomoki.

More than that, there was a new element in play. A strange craft that wielded an unusual type of weapon that was gradually finding its way through their formidable defenses. There was only one answer for this new wrinkle in their plan. They had to send in more ships to deal with them, for according to their calculations, the portal should be opening any minute, and with it, their triumphant invasion would finally begin.

Not wishing to waste time, ninety more ships were sent into the battle, the idea being to so greatly overwhelm the troublesome pests that the conflict would end in mere minutes. Shock and awe, as it were. A show of Visla Dominus's great fleet's true power.

"Uh, guys? You see this?" Daisy asked as she noted the many, many new signatures on her monitors.

"Oh, fuck," Charlie managed to blurt. "We are so screwed."

The people aboard the stealth ship nearby were also in shock at the ridiculous odds they now faced.

"Freya, you don't happen to have the Big Gun on board, do you?" Daisy asked.

"No, I never carry it. You know that."

"I know. I was just hoping."

"Sorry. It's locked down in its storage vault back in my Dark Side base hangar," was Freya's reply.

"Hey, that's okay, kiddo. I know it was a long shot. Just be ready to tie in all weapons systems for a death blossom discharge if we have to, okay?"

"You sure you want to do that, Daze? That's a last-resort tactic, and it'll take out our new friends in the process."

"I know, and I'm not going to use it unless it looks like there's absolutely no hope. But look at all those ships. We're massively outnumbered. We simply can't win this one without a miracle."

Murphy must have been sleeping, or Lady Luck had simply told him today was her turn to intervene, because no sooner had she spoken than a massive freight vessel jumped into their midst, destroying several of the smaller craft on arrival, causing the others to scatter.

"There's a window. We can jump," Korbin skreed. "This craft has disrupted their casting, but it will only last a moment."

"We can't," Charlie replied. "This is our fight. Go if you have to, but we have to protect our galaxy."

"Then we do it together," Korbin said. "We've seen our powers can at least halt the visla's attacks. And should we fall, oh, it will be a glorious end."

A small craft mounted atop the gigantic freighter detached and pulled clear. The huge vessel had been powered by the last gasp of a very powerful Drookonus provided by his new Wampeh Ghalian friends, so Olosnah felt no guilt at sacrificing the ship he'd guided for them to the cause. Besides, he'd been paid *very* well.

He surveyed the scene, then focused his konus, casting the one spell needed. The cargo doors of the huge vessel began to open.

"And with that, I am outta here," Olo said with his trademark grin, then quickly jumped away, unnoticed, while the fleet was in disarray, preoccupied by the massive disturbance in their midst.

"What's going on?" Daisy asked. "Freya, what can you see?"

"Heat signatures, Daisy. *Lots* of heat signatures."

"But that ship's opening its doors to space. How is that possible?"

Ara's senses were aflame with a surge of something she hadn't felt in ages. She turned her golden eyes to the mystery craft and smiled.

"Oh, now *this* is most unexpected," she said.

"What, the huge ship?" Charlie asked.

"You'll see."

Charlie, Bawb, Korbin, and Daisy watched in shock as the first few Zomoki emerged from the opening cargo hold. They took to space, hungry and angry, immediately attacking the Tslavar ships. Soon, dozens and dozens more followed them. In fact, every last one of the Zomoki formerly held in Emmik Hunstra's clutches were now free.

And they were angry.

These were not higher-intellect animals like Ara. These were younger, more primal Zomoki, as most of them tended to be. Only once in a long while did a mind such as Ara's emerge. But this swarm of raging beasts had been readied for their release, the scent of Tslavar-tinged magic forced on them as they were loaded into the craft. As soon as they'd been freed, it was that smell that drove them into a frenzy at the sheer volume of Tslavars around them.

The space dragons tore into the fleet, wreaking havoc as they followed no organized pattern of attack, but rather, an utterly chaotic whirlwind of talons, teeth, and flames.

And they did not limit themselves to the ships actively engaging Charlie and his new friends. The Zomoki quickly swarmed into the entire fleet, sending the ships held back in reserve into a frenzy as they were forced to deal with this new threat.

In all of the confusion, a handful of small shimmer craft that had been quietly observing from the periphery slipped unobserved into the body of the fleet, latching onto the largest, most key of the enemy ships.

Their Wampeh Ghalian infiltrators quickly sliced through the hulls, entering and re-sealing the breach without a trace in under a minute. With their payloads delivered and safely embedded within the enemy fleet, the shimmer ships peeled off, this part of their mission complete, though they were quite surprised to find a battle already underway even before their Zomoki diversion had been delivered.

Kip had warped along with their Wampeh Ghalian friends, quickly tucking in behind a piece of old debris to observe and provide additional real-time intel to the assassins making their runs.

"I feel him," Hunze gasped as she watched the distant battle among all of those ships. "Bawb is here."

"You sure about that?" Kip asked.

"Positive. I can feel my power and his merging, the bond strengthening by the rays of the sun flowing through the portal."

Bawb, for his part, also noticed the shift, though he was far too busy casting spells to properly comment on it beyond the briefest of notes. "Hunze is near," he said, then directed a series of spells at the disorganized ships.

They were fortunate, being atop an elder Zomoki. While the younger beasts were aggressive, tearing into any ship they could get their claws on, Ara's mere presence was enough for them to stay well clear of her particular piece of space. It was instinctive. Something they possessed down to their DNA. An apex Zomoki was here, and they'd all be very wise to avoid her if they knew what was good for them.

"Where's Hunze, Bob?" Charlie asked as he watched the Zomoki all around them miraculously stay clear.

"She is near. I cannot say where, exactly. But I sense her. And my power is greatly increased for it."

"Then we need to meet up with her. Ara, what's going on with the other Zomoki? It's like we're in a bubble they can't penetrate."

"They sense an Alpha's presence and know better than to come near."

"Then we need to get our friends *inside* this little protective zone. Otherwise they're gonna be fair game as well," Charlie said.

"They're too far away," Bawb said. "We can notify them, but we also risk the enemy catching on and losing our advantage."

"They'll notice soon enough, I think," Charlie replied, then flipped the comms to open broadcast. "Anyone who can hear me, there's a safe zone from the Zomoki in proximity to Ara. If you can make it to us, regroup. If not, stay safe and we'll try to get to you."

"Don't know if we can," Daisy replied. "Do what you have to. We're going to try and use these things as a flying shield of sorts, while we work on getting through these bastards' defenses."

"Good luck, Daisy."

"You too, Charlie."

Not so far away, Hunze opened the skree and contacted her Wampeh Ghalian counterparts. "Things have changed, my friends. Take your ships outside the skirmish lines where the magic is clear and jump away. We will regroup as soon as we are able at the designated rally point."

"But we cannot leave you alone," Zilara said from her invisible ship.

"You must. I will be fine."

"I shall stay with her," Kort said.

"Very well. We look forward to seeing you again very soon, sister," Zilara said. Then she and the other Wampeh Ghalian ships silently wove their way through the jumble of craft and Zomoki to the free space outside the skirmish and jumped away as invisibly as they'd arrived. All but Kort.

"You're up to something, Hunze, aren't you?" Kort asked.

"Bawb is here. I can sense him."

"Well, then. If you are to battle alongside the Geist, I shall join you. It would be my greatest honor."

"We are not going to battle," Hunze said. "I am going to pull him from here, so that we may reclaim the Wampeh Ghalian's greatest treasures––and most powerful weapons. *Then* we will truly engage this enemy."

He had to admit, it was a logical plan. But much as Hunze was prone to putting others' interests first, Kort was a master assassin, and there was no way he was going to sit back while one of their own was in peril.

Fortunately, his ship being invisible lent an advantage. He could pull back and silently engage in key moments, all while appearing to not be there at all.

"Let us prepare ourselves," Kort said. "This is not going to be easy."

CHAPTER SIXTY-FOUR

The Tslavar ships were rapidly adapting to the sheer chaos the Zomoki wrought upon their numbers. And while the animals could inflict damage, their main concern was one Zomoki in particular. The one with passengers and an entourage of surprisingly troublesome craft.

One of those ships was clearly powered by a visla, and a very, very strong one at that. The fact that they'd been able to not only defend against their attacks, but also effectively counter them, and even go so far as to disable more than a few of the smaller craft, spoke to the pilot's prowess.

Then there was the strange, new craft. Sleek, black, and utilizing something other than magic. At least, not traditional magic. It was some form of energy that they had been able to shield against effortlessly at first, but somehow, the energy had shifted its power on the fly so as to pierce their defenses. And there was more. It was also spewing forth a barrage of strange metal projectiles, the likes of which had also been increasingly effective at breaching their defenses.

It seemed this odd craft was far more dangerous than it initially appeared, and therefore, the attack fleet's priority shifted. While Ara was still a great concern, so too was Freya now, and the sheer number of ships engaged against her was steadily mounting.

She was good. *Really* good. And with Daisy helping man the cannons with Sarah's extra eyes tracking everything in the sky, they were a tag-team force to be reckoned with. But at this rate, even they would eventually be overwhelmed.

Zomoki were being killed, taken out of the equation, allowing more of the ships they'd been fighting to rejoin the fray. The tide had turned once, but it seemed to be turning back in favor of Visla Dominus's dark fleet.

"How long until we can warp out of here?" Daisy asked over comms. "We're getting our asses kicked, Charlie."

"We have to protect the portal. We can't leave."

"It's a freakin' ball of fire. I think it's fine without us," she replied.

"It is now, but it should open in just over one minute. When that happens, all that matters is we prevent this fleet from passing through. No matter what the cost."

The tone of the Earthman's voice conveyed more than his words. He was willing to die to protect the portal if necessary. Daisy made a decision based more on her gut than the limited and rather confusing facts in hand.

"Okay, Charlie. We're with you," she said. "But I don't think this is going to end well for us."

And it really didn't look like it would. The enemy ships were slowly chipping away at the diversionary Zomoki attack and refocusing their attacks. The tiny defending force was outnumbered, and there was nothing they could do about it.

"Thirty seconds, until it opens," Charlie called out, glancing at the chrono. "Everyone get ready. They're going to make a big push for it if they can get through the Zomoki."

"Ready," Daisy replied.

"Prepared and standing by," Korbin said over his skree.

"All right. Keep them from the––"

A new ship flashed into the fray, right on top of them and heading toward the portal at speed. A Tslavar ship, and a big one at that.

"Stop that ship!" Korbin bellowed, directing his magic at the new foe.

"Hold your fire!" came over both comms and skree simultaneously, just as they saw the *Fujin* frantically detach from the ship and swing into the fight.

Jo was quickly blasting everything in sight with her magically charged railguns while Rika showed off her piloting prowess as her magic spiked, the purple glow of her ink surrounding her ship despite its metal hull.

It seemed she was now supercharged beyond belief. And she was already an impressive pilot, even without the magic.

Marban's pirate crew was already doing what they did best. Namely engaging the enemy in all directions with no fear, and more than a little glee at the joy of battle. They might die this day, but what a way to go.

"Marban? Rika? What the hell are you two doing here?" Charlie asked over skree and comms.

"So much for this ship blending in," Marban griped. "We weren't expecting a full-on battle."

"You were supposed to have crossed over. You were going to reprogram the portal."

"There was a problem last time," Rika informed him. "And you should know, Leila did *not* make it back across with Rip and Eddie."

"Leila?" Kara said, looking at Vee when she heard the name over open comms.

"Wait, she didn't?" Charlie asked.

"No, she's still out here, somewhere," Rika confirmed.

"Shit! What the hell happened?"

"Long story, Charlie. Suffice to say, last time we tried to cross over was a clusterfuck. This cyborg named George stepped in our plan and messed the whole thing up."

"Hey, it was an accident," George interjected. "And I already apologized."

Daisy's voice crackled over the comms. "George? What the hell are you doing here?"

"Daisy? Wait, are you with Freya?"

"Hi, George," the mighty ship replied.

"Hey, Freya. But what are *you* doing here? How did you wind up in this galaxy? We didn't see you cross over."

"Wait, did you say *galaxy*? What are you talking about?"

"Oh, shit. You really don't know where you are, do you?" George said.

"Guys, stop the chatter. You can catch up later. We're getting our asses kicked here," Charlie interrupted. "Rika, can you still reprogram the portal?"

"I've got a shit-ton of power now, Charlie. It'll be no problem."

"Then you need to get through and do it. And randomize the schedule. They've figured out the timing."

"Shit. Okay. I'll have Jo send you the timing in a comms burst. Should be totally secure from the magic users. Standby." Rika turned to her gunner. "Hey, Jo, you heard——"

"Already on it. Aaaaand, done."

"That was quick."

"AI brain, as you so often forget. Transmitted to the others. Everyone has the new timing."

The *Fujin* spun sideways, rocked by a magical blast while Rika was distracted.

"Oh, you did *not* just do that," she growled, targeting the Tslavar ship nearest and lighting it up with her magically charged weapons. The strange magic easily pierced their defenses, leaving only fragments of the craft floating in space.

"Rika, can you cast that outward? Maybe knock out their shields?" Charlie asked.

"Yeah, I think so. Hang on."

Rika was powering up her magic to try to disable the defensive spells of all of the fleet's ships near enough to be susceptible. Given the amount of power she'd taken on, it seemed highly likely she'd be able to affect them all. If only she and Charlie were in closer proximity they might even be able to join their casting again. But as it stood, taking their shielding out would level the playing field a lot. The Tslavars might have numbers, but they wouldn't be so hard to hit.

"It's starting!" Freya said as the portal started to slide open.

Now the show was *really* going to begin. And it wasn't what any of them expected.

CHAPTER SIXTY-FIVE

On cue, the moment the portal began to slide open, the enemy fleet began moving forward, pressing their numbers toward the gateway as it cleared of the deadly flames. But something unexpected came through from the other side. Something big and black.

"Joshua!" Freya called out.

"Hello, dearest," the ship replied. "Are you okay? You seem to have a bit of an infestation."

"I'm all right. But yeah, we've got a bit of a numbers problem here. I see you're using the prototype. Would you mind lending a hand? I'm really wishing I'd brought the Big Gun, but it's back on Dark Side base."

"My pleasure," Joshua replied, the greatest strategic supercomputer AI mind Earth had ever known turning his attentions on the numbers and positions of all the forces on the battlefield.

"Big Gun? What's the Big Gun?" an excited teenage voice asked.

"Yeah, you never said anything about a Big Gun," another added.

"Arlo? Marty? Why did you bring them here, Joshua?" Freya asked.

"I figured it was as good a time as any for the boys to get a taste of action," he replied. "Don't worry, I've got them covered."

The massive ship then did something totally unexpected. It burst into hundreds of pieces.

Only it didn't. Not exactly.

Each of the individual fragments fired up its engines and weapons and took off at speed toward the enemy fleet, leaving the core, much smaller, heavily-armored ship behind.

Joshua's command vessel was bristling with weapons, but he wouldn't need them. Not if his swarm worked as planned. They all fired up their weapons, unleashing a blistering barrage of pulse and railgun fire, much of it actually landing blows on the enemy fleet, thanks to Rika's magic weakening their shielding.

"Nothing quite like real-world testing, eh Freya?" he said with a satisfied tone.

"Oh, you," she chuckled. "By the way, one of those enemy ships is ours."

"Already logged it. The big one fighting on our side."

"Would someone like to tell me what the hell is going on?" Charlie interrupted. "Who the hell are you?"

"Joshua's the name. I'd love to give you the full story, but suffice to say, the cavalry has arrived, so get your asses through the––"

A massive blast of magic pulsed through the swarm of ships, knocking a large chunk of them out of commission.

"Visla Dominus," Bawb exclaimed. "Rika must clear the portal immediately!"

"But you need me here," she protested.

"Not if it means Dominus might get through. It'll stay open too long otherwise. Besides, I've gotta find Leila, and Bawb needs to connect with Hunze. There's no time to quibble. Get your ass to the other side and seal it. We'll hold them back," Charlie replied.

Rika did the math and knew he was right. Time was short, and there were limited options.

"Don't you go dying, Charlie," she said, turning the *Fujin* toward the portal.

"No intention of it. We'll try to reconnect on one of the next openings. Now, get moving!"

Rika didn't hesitate. He was right. They needed full control of the portal, and she was their best option to do so.

"Jo, up ahead! Blast 'em!" she said as she powered toward the portal.

Several of the smaller ships in the enemy fleet had already passed her and were making an attempt for the opening while others continued to attack her, trying to hinder her progress. Even taking down their shielding, the numbers were too great, and Ara was simply too far to provide support. Marban and Korbin, however, were close.

"I've got you," Marban called out, driving the *Coratta* into the thick of the enemy ships, his men blasting away in all directions, trying to provide her a clear path.

Korbin would have much preferred heading into clear space to regroup, but he was cut off from the others. It was a choice between death or a new galaxy. Reluctantly, he opted for the latter option, tucking in behind the commandeered Tslavar ship as it passed through the portal.

"Freya, let's go!" Joshua transmitted.

"But we can still help here."

"I know. But tactically, you know we need to regroup. And you've got a treasure trove of data to help us do just that," he replied.

The comms speaker had been open the whole time inside the ship. Daisy turned to the two teenagers.

"Sorry, girls, but it looks like you're going to be taking a detour before we can get you home."

Kara and Vee had been sitting silently, almost frozen from the immensity and violence of what they were seeing. Sure, they'd understood this sort of thing happened, but that was on a different level than actually being caught up in the middle of it. And now they were going through a portal? To another *galaxy*?

"Wait. Tell your friend we know a woman named Leila who arrived with an Eddie and Rip. She's with Captain Sandah, from the Palmarian ships," Kara blurted.

"What was that?" Charlie asked, barely hearing the girl's voice over the din of battle.

But before she could repeat herself, Freya had already turned and crossed the portal. Joshua recalled as many of his still-functioning swarm ships as he could and followed her, covering Arlo and Marty as he did.

"She said Leila is with Captain Sandah from a Palmarian ship," Joshua relayed to Charlie. "I hope that means something to you. Sorry to leave you here. But know this: we *will* be back for you."

"Thank you. Just take care of Earth. A few of their ships made it through," Charlie replied.

"On it. We'll be seeing you soon," Joshua said, then flew through the portal.

A dozen Tslavar ships raced for the opening, but flames were quickly beginning to spew from it. The wild Zomoki turned and fled deeper into the fleet, running from the burning plasma, while also attacking anything in their path.

Ara, however, was immune to the sun. Supercharged by it. She directed all of that additional power to protecting her friends as she flew behind the fleeing ships as they raced from a fiery death.

"They need us," Hunze said, her power flaring from the sun's renewed rays flowing through the portal. "This is the moment. My friends are down in numbers, but the enemy is in disarray."

"You heard her," Dukaan said. "Get us in there, Kip."

"On it."

The little ship pulled free from his hiding place and made a quick run through the fleeing ships toward their friends. Kort, still shimmer-cloaked, followed close beside them, taking out enemy craft silently as he did.

"It's Kip!" Charlie exclaimed as the little craft zoomed toward them. "Are we glad to see you!"

"And we you," Dukaan replied.

"Is Hunze with you?" Bawb asked.

"She is. We're fine. Now, I suggest we—"

"I sense a shimmer ship," Bawb interrupted, his magic flaring strong in readiness.

"He is with us, dearest," Hunze said over the comms. "He is one of your brothers."

Only the heat of battle kept Bawb from fully enjoying the warm flush he felt in his chest at the sound of her voice. Her presence, powered by the sun, only made the sensation more acute.

Kip pulled alongside Ara as soon as she was a safe distance from the sun's heat blasting from the portal. Kort, he knew, was close by, not dropping his camouflage while the enemy was still so near and so many.

"They're in disarray for the moment, but any minute now they'll have us completely blocked in," Ara said. "Already, they've closed off most routes of escape."

"I suspect that now that the portal is closed once more, the only reason we have not faced the full might of the visla's power is he has too many of his own craft in the line of fire. Once they are clear, we are done for," Bawb said. "Wise One, is there a way out?"

Ara searched with all of her considerable talent and power.

The enemy had woven a tight net of magic, blocking her jumps and the Earth ship's warp. But then, there was something. Something small. Something organic. She changed course abruptly and sent out a Zomoki hunting growl across the void.

No ears could hear it, but the lesser Zomoki certainly could, and in the absence of other prey, that meant that they were quite likely on the menu for the Alpha hunter. In a panic, they broke from their various battles and fled as one, racing through a thin area of ships.

The ploy worked. The chaotic destruction wrought by the fleeing beasts disrupted just enough of the enemy's vessels to create a break in their net. Ara didn't hesitate. She wrapped her power around Kip's little konus, once again linking them together, and jumped. She felt confident the shimmer ship traveling with them would sense the fine thread she left for it and latch on.

Bawb would have done so, and thus Kort would as well. She expected no less from another of his ilk.

Tslavar ships swarmed the area, ready to engage the depleted intruders, but the Zomoki and her friends were already gone.

CHAPTER SIXTY-SIX

Marban and Korbin both spun into defensive maneuvers as soon as they crossed the portal back into Earth's solar system, and it was a good thing. The massive fleet had every weapon in their arsenal pointed at the gateway, waiting to see just who might eventually come through.

"These two are with us!" Jo transmitted the second the *Fujin* crossed over, blasting the data packet out electronically to all ships in the system. Normally she preferred talking like a normal meat person would, but in this instance, milliseconds counted, and thus her AI mind had no time to waste lest their new friends be blown from the sky.

With Marban and Korbin's ships now on the green list of foreign craft, the fleet was free to target the other craft that had managed to slip through the portal. There weren't many, but there were enough to pose a concern.

Five Tslavar ships were torn to shreds within moments of their arrival, the mighty ships of the defensive net not taking any chances. A few slipped through, however, and several of Earth's ships peeled off in pursuit. One ship, spun on its axis and immediately retreated, heading back through the portal at speed.

"Stop that ship!" Zed commanded as one did a quick one-eighty, but it was too late. The vessel was small and fast and had managed to escape back to where it came from just before the portal dropped into the sun. The others weren't so lucky.

Three of the Tslavar craft jumped away almost immediately, but not before being tagged with tracer sabots, refined from previous encounters with the alien jump magic. They'd be a bitch to track, but it could, and *would*, be done. They could run, but they couldn't hide.

One of them, however, evaded destruction and made a mini-jump, taking it to just outside Earth's atmosphere.

Freya had been right on its tail as they crossed back through the portal. "One is heading to Earth. Hang on!" the AI warned, then warped after them, popping in and out of existence in a flash.

She'd timed it just right and was once again on the aliens' tail as the craft dove through the atmosphere, heading straight for Los Angeles.

"Looks like they know where to hit us," Daisy mused. "How did that happen, I wonder?"

"Doesn't matter. Not at the moment, anyway," Sarah replied. *"We've gotta take them out before they do some serious damage down there."*

I hear ya, Sis, Daisy replied silently. "Freya, I can't get a target lock. They're all over the place. Can you get a shot on them?"

The cannons burped forth a short blast. Most of the barrage missed, but just enough hit to cause the ship to falter and buck. It was just in time, too, as the ship began flickering in and out of visibility, making it impossible for ground defenses to target it.

"Not my best work, but it should hobble them enough to make it impossible for them to do much more than land."

"Unless they go Kamikaze," Daisy grumbled. "Let's just hope that's not in their nature."

"What's a Kamikaze?" Vee asked.

"A really fuc––*messed* up military tactic where they use themselves as living bomb delivery systems."

"But how do they survive?"

"They don't. That's what's so messed up about it."

"Why would anyone do such a thing?" Kara wondered.

"Desperation," was the reply.

The Tslavars were certainly desperate, but was self-sacrifice in their nature? That was something they'd find out very quickly as they plunged toward the surface.

In the area around the sun, the portal had cut off the few ships that had made it through. Only the one had managed to retreat through it before it dropped back into the sun, and of those that jumped away in a panic, only one had made it to Earth.

All in all, it was about as good as they could have asked for, given the circumstances.

Joshua took a moment to pull the surviving numbers of his swarm ships back together to form a larger craft once again, then accelerated toward Earth, ready to help Freya however she needed, though she was quite capable without his aid.

The Tslavar ship made an unsteady approach and a rather rough landing in central Los Angeles, the craft grinding to a halt up against a large residential building. It had crashed, but somehow managed to remain intact, and the surviving crew all scattered out its doors the moment the vessel stopped moving.

"Daisy, that's a residential area," Freya noted. "I'm reading a lot of life signs in there. I can't just blast them."

"Shit. Now it's going to be a whole lot of time wasted hunting down each and every one of these bastards," Daisy grumbled.

"Excuse me," Kara said, quietly.

"What is it, kid?"

"I have an idea that might help."

"Oh? Not even on Earth a minute and already full of ideas," Daisy said with a chuckle. "Okay, let's hear it."

Kara reached down and scratched Baloo's head behind his ears. "All they need is a scent."

Baloo had regained much of his strength since being picked up and cleaned off. The nutrient-dense food Freya had whipped up for him and Bahnjoh from her replicators didn't hurt, either.

"Okay, then. Let's get them a scent," Daisy said as she popped open Freya's airlock doors.

Kara noted that while Daisy had her odd sword in one hand as she scanned the area for hostiles, she was also carrying a strange, elongated device with some sort of curved lever for a finger, it seemed. She'd never seen the likes of it, but judging by the way the woman was aiming it, she wouldn't want to be on the receiving end of whatever it was made for.

They crossed the torn-up roadway where the controlled crash had finally touched down, hurrying along until they reached the downed ship. It seemed to be empty, but they nevertheless carefully approached the open doors.

There was a splash of green blood along the hull where someone had made a painful exit. Apparently not all of the crew had been unharmed after all.

"This good enough?" Daisy asked.

"That'll work," Kara replied. "Baloo, Bahnjoh! Here, boys!"

The two enormous animals padded over to the teen. "Okay, listen. These are bad people. You understand? Bad. Go get 'em!"

Kara hadn't anticipated the manner in which the two animals would feed off of each other's increasing energy, but when they took off in a flash, she wondered if maybe she should have tried to temper their eagerness a little.

But these *were* bad people. Bad people who tried to kill her and her friends. Though she was a teenager, she was a visla's daughter. The realities of the world were not lost on her.

The local populace was incredibly sparse, but even so, the risk of casualties was high in a conventional confrontation. Fortunately, Cal had broadcast an emergency call to all citizens to barricade themselves indoors until further notice. Having survived the Great War, or having parents who had, no one hesitated at the AI's command.

The result was a clear hunting ground for the two beasts.

Baloo and Bahnjoh raced after the fresh Tslavar scent. It smelled like there were only a handful of them. Perhaps ten, if they were lucky. Lucky, because this was a new game for them. The two had each played by themselves, but now they had the opportunity to hunt.

The Tslavar mercenaries were well armed, and the magic cast at Bahnjoh was deadly, but the animal had already experienced their spellcasting, and recently at that. He dodged and wove as he ran at speed, all the while, the nearest Tslavars focused all of their attentions on the enormous beast charging right toward them.

What they failed to notice was his stealthy friend, quickly approaching from the side on silent, padded paws. The first man didn't let out a sound as he fell. It wasn't until the third that they realized something was wrong.

The Tslavars scattered, their carefully planned defensive positions in disarray at the arrival of the terrifying duo. Bahnjoh, seeing an opportunity, lunged into the fray, taking down a pair of Tslavars, one of whom laughably hoped to stop him with his pathetic blade.

Bahnjoh was a Graizenhund, and no ordinary knife would cut his thick hide. An enchanted one? Yes. But this was no enchanted blade. The mercenary had opted to spend the extra coin on women and drinks. It was a regret that would be the man's last thought.

Daisy and the girls held back, letting the animals race through the facility. They possessed the greater skills for tracking down prey, and much as she would have liked to kick some alien ass herself, Daisy realized she'd just be getting in their way. The reality of which was reinforced when the first of their screams rang out from inside.

Maybe I was a bit too quick to judge, Daisy mused.

"Judging by the freakin' bloodcurdling screams, I think you're right," Sarah agreed with a little laugh.

Daisy was enjoying the novel thought of having some quadrupedal killers on the team when a Tslavar burst from the building. This one had apparently slipped the tearing jaws of the terrible duo as his friends were being eaten alive.

He saw Daisy and the girls and smiled a wicked grin as he raised his arm.

"He's got a slaap!" Kara shrieked.

"A *what*?" Daisy asked just as the mercenary unleashed the most lethal spell he could muster.

A violent counter-spell smashed it aside, and Kara hadn't cast it.

Daisy looked at the sword in her hand, feeling its humming energy demanding blood.

"What the hell?" she wondered, then charged the alien attacker. No sense looking a gift spell in the mouth.

The Tslavar drew his short sword and moved to block Daisy's attack. Unfortunately for him, he didn't know that Stabby was a genetically modified bone sword whose edge was honed all the way down to a molecular level, but only when in its owner's hands. And Daisy was indeed the one wielding it.

The seemingly formidable metal of the Tslavar's blade was sliced in two like a hot knife through butter, the bone sword only coming to a stop once it was fully embedded in the man's body. He could have sliced clean through, but Stabby had stopped and was greedily sucking the life force from the man's blood in a flash. He then fell into sated, contented silence.

"Daisy? What the hell just happened?" Sarah asked.

I have absolutely no idea, she replied in shock.

Kara and Vee stared at her with wide eyes.

"You *do* have an enchanted blade." Kara gasped. "You said it wasn't enchanted!"

"It isn't. You wanna tell me what just happened, kid?"

"Your sword. It possesses great power. Far more than I thought it absorbed when you killed Trepenan. But it's more. I mean, it recognized an attack and countered it without you even having to cast. I've only heard legends of weapons so powerful."

"Uh, this is just a sword. I mean, it's alive, sure, but I don't know about any enchantment stuff."

Kara reached out with her magic, sensing the power now contained within the blade, and gasped. "It's Emmik Trepenan's power," she said. "Your sword took all of it when it drained his blood. Just like a Wampeh Ghalian. Just like I said."

"Maybe so, but that doesn't make Stabby enchanted. It doesn't mean he's gonna start talking or anything," Daisy said.

But after what she'd just seen and felt her sword do, she had to wonder what more it might be capable of. And if it drank the blood of another power user, who knew what it might become.

CHAPTER SIXTY-SEVEN

"Cal? What's the update? Any more of these bastards make it through?" Daisy asked the air around them.

Kara and Vee looked at her like she was crazy until the air replied.

"No others, Daisy. And it's good to have you back. We were worried about you. Freya tells me you were pulled into a warp hole a while back. That would explain why no one could find you."

"Yeah, something grabbed us right after we warped back to Earth. But what's this about another galaxy?"

"Exactly as it sounds. We are at war with an enemy from another galaxy, it would seem. And you likely arrived at the wrong place and wrong time, just as Charlie and his friends were thrown through time. You just got caught up in the mix."

"Fan-freaking-tastic," Daisy griped.

"Excuse me," Kara said. "Who is this voice in the sky?"

"Oh, right. Rude of me, sorry. Cal, this is Kara, and that's Vee. They helped free me from wherever the hell I was locked up."

"A pleasure," the city's AI replied.

"Are you a spirit?" Vee asked.

"Hardly. I'm an advanced artificial intelligence. I know the

concept is a bit strange for those from your realm. Just think of me as a mind without a normal body, if that makes it easier."

"Like Freya. Or Pod," Kara said.

"Exactly."

Daisy smiled approvingly. "Smart girl." She then turned her attention back to the conflict in the skies above. "So, where do things stand with all of this, Cal? Are we safe? Or do Freya and I need to go back up there and kick some alien ass?"

"Jo just informed me that, thanks to Rika's new powers, we now fully control the portal. That puts us in the driver's seat. It doesn't open until we want it to. And Joshua managed to secret a little spy satellite on the other side in all the commotion. It's tiny, and hidden. When the portal next opens, we should actually be able to reach it, though barely. That will allow us to leave messages, as the enemy does not utilize our comms technology."

"Clever," Daisy said just as two animals, now covered in green blood, came happily trotting out of the building, unscathed, well-fed, and no worse for wear. Whatever reticence she had toward the beasts, it was gone at that moment. "Oh my! Now who are good boys? You are! Yes, you are!" she cooed, scratching the gore-smeared animals behind their ears.

"You're playing with a Graizenhund, Daze," Sarah said with amazement. *"A blood-soaked Graizenhund."*

I know, right? I guess not everything from Ra'az-land is all bad after all.

"A man named Korbin is asking about medical assistance. I guess Rika's relaying for him. He says he's using something called a 'skree,'" Freya said.

"Direct him to my main medical facility. I'll have staff on hand to meet him as soon as he arrives."

"You got it, Cal," Freya replied.

"Uncle Korbin's here? And he's okay?" Kara blurted with joy.

"Hey, Freya. Prep for a quick hop. We're gonna meet him

there," Daisy said. She turned to the overjoyed girl. "Well, don't just stand there. Mount up."

Kara and Vee raced back to Freya, Baloo and Bahnjoh in tow.

"And clean those two up while you're at it!" Daisy called after her.

The stealth ship had arrived at the landing site well ahead of Korbin's craft, his anxious niece waiting for him with her still-damp, but no longer blood-soaked animals at her side. Also standing by were a team consisting of humans, Chithiid, and medical cyborgs from Cal's state-of-the-art facility.

If one of their people was hurt, they'd do all in their power to save them, as they had for so many who'd come before them. This patient, though, would test their limits.

Korbin's ship swooped to the ground, stopping inches above it and settling into a smooth hover.

"Neat trick," Daisy said.

The door opened, and a man stepped out onto the Earth's surface for the first time. His first time in the galaxy, for that matter.

"Uncle Korbin!" Kara shrieked as she ran to him, wrapping him in a fierce hug.

"Karasalia? Visanya? What are you two doing here?" he asked, shocked. "Oh, my dear. I'm so sorry you've been dragged into this mess. And another galaxy, no less."

"It's okay, Uncle Korbin. Trepenan tried to take me back at the tower, but Daisy stopped him."

"Daisy? You freed the assassin?"

"The *alleged* assassin. It was all a misunderstanding. She's from here. And she was just following one of the bad fleet's ships back to Father's place."

Korbin processed what this could mean. Was his childhood

friend truly so deeply involved in this mess? Unfortunately, he was now in the wrong galaxy to ask him.

"We can discuss all of this later. For the moment, we must get medical attention for Grundsch," he said, summoning the floating gurney on which the enormous being was strapped.

No sooner had the unconscious creature's form passed out into the sunlight than all present reacted. *Violently.* Weapons were drawn by *everyone*, including the medical techs, and all were aimed at the injured being.

"What are you doing? This man needs assistance!" he shouted.

"That's no man. That's a Ra'az Hok," Daisy growled, her sword begging for a drink of the creature's blood.

Bahnjoh raced to his unconscious master's side, teeth bared at the aggressors.

Kara put herself between them and the angry mob. "No! He saved my life!" she cried.

"He's a Ra'az. The only good Ra'az is a dead Ra'az," one of the Chithiid medical attendants said with venom in his words. And as his entire race had been enslaved by them, he was certainly entitled to that opinion.

"He's right. He should be executed," another agreed. "There hasn't been a Ra'az seen anywhere in nearly eighteen years."

"Stand down, everyone. Please," Cal interjected.

Reluctantly, they heeded the call of the city's great AI overseer.

"Kara, you say this Ra'az saved your life?"

"Yes, he did."

"But he wears a collar. I understand they force people to act against their own wishes."

"I wrapped it in Ootaki hair. See?" she said, pointing to the golden strand. "He was free to do as he wanted. The collar had no control over him."

"It's true," Korbin said. "I witnessed it myself. He put himself in harm's way to save my niece. It's the reason he is on death's doorstep."

Cal processed the pros and cons of keeping this particular prisoner alive. On the one hand, it was a Ra'az Hok, and therefore a violent enemy of all non-Ra'az. On the other, this one seemed to have demonstrated utterly foreign behavior for one of their kind.

Much as it would upset a large portion of the populace, a decision was made.

"Bring him inside and mend his injuries. Keep him sedated at all times. Once he has healed and regained consciousness, then we shall properly assess this prisoner and determine his fate."

While the medical team was not thrilled with the decree, they respected Cal's authority absolutely.

"As you wish, Cal," the lead tech said. "Okay, you heard him. Let's get this bastard inside and fix him up."

"Yeah, so the firing squad can do it right, later," the Chithiid grumbled.

Kara watched as Korbin guided the unconscious man into the medical facility, surrounded by people who hated him, but would nevertheless do what they could to save him.

"No dogs allowed inside," a stocky cyborg said as Bahnjoh tried to follow.

The animal let out a low growl.

"It's okay, Bahnjoh. They won't hurt him," Kara said. And she actually believed it. If these people were anything like Daisy, they might not like the prospect, but they were people of honor.

Reluctantly, the huge beast padded back to her side.

"It'll be okay, kid," Daisy comforted her. "And once you taste tonight's homecoming feast, your concerns will melt away. Which reminds me, I'd better call ahead. We're going to have a lot of extra mouths."

She reached out over comms, notifying Ripley's food-obsessed dad that they were going to be having a feast this evening, and he needed to round up the old gang. *All* of them, if he could.

He knew better than to ask what for. When Daisy had *that* tone of voice, you didn't question. Soon enough, they'd all know what was up.

CHAPTER SIXTY-EIGHT

With the *Fujin* flying alongside, guiding the massive craft in, Marban steered the *Coratta* down to a smooth landing at the large field at Schwarzenegger Spaceport, Los Angeles. It was a clear day with blue skies and a glistening ocean. As he made the approach, the space pirate was amazed at this sprawling city of impossible glass and metal construction, stretching from the sea to the mountains.

It was so similar to home, in some ways. Forests, oceans, mountains, and plains. Yet in other ways it was utterly alien. Of course, he was the alien on this world, and all in all, he thought it was beautiful.

"So, this is where you two are from?" Marban said as he greeted the women waiting as he exited his ship.

Jo stood calmly watching the rest of the crew step out onto this world for the first time. Rika, however, was waiting for Marban in particular.

Her tattoos showed none of the purple glow he'd seen when she was in battle, yet they did seem to glow just a little, as if the planet's yellow sun was flowing within her skin. To the weary traveler, it was quite a sight to behold.

"Well, *technically* I'm from here, but several hundred years ago," Rika said with a laugh. "But that's another story entirely."

"Oh yes, that sounds about right. Of course, you're talking to someone who was buried for a few hundred years, so..." he said with a grin. "In any case, it sounds like a tale well worth hearing. Come, let me buy you a drink, and you can regale me with details of your time-traveling adventures."

Rika laughed. "With what money? You're not even from this *galaxy*, remember? Your coin is worthless here."

Marban blushed. "Oh, yes. I forgot."

"Don't sweat it, big guy. This round's on me," she said.

Jo, being a cyborg, had observed every little aspect of the exchange while simultaneously greeting the other crewmembers, as well as her fellow cyborgs, as they disembarked. Sergeant Franklin, with his spec-ops heightened hearing, also heard the conversation, while still making his way out of the ship. He and Jo shared an amused little look.

"Hey, Jo. We're gonna go get a drink. Come on," Rika called out.

"Oh, hey. I wish I could, but George and me, we said we'd show all these guys a good time. Isn't that right, George?"

"Yep. We were just discussing it during the descent, actually," he lied like a seasoned pro. "Probably going to start in Downtown, then maybe drag them off to a little dive I know by the beach. I figured pirates are pirates, right? Even if you guys technically sail in space, the ocean's still got its appeal."

"All right, then. You guys have fun," the inked pilot said.

"With this lot? Trust me, we'll have a *legendary* time," Jo replied with a wicked grin. "Come on, George. Let's get these guys good and drunk."

"Now that's a mission directive I'm confident I can achieve," he said. "Come on, you mutts, this way to booze and festivities!"

The crew of the *Coratta* followed their resident hosts, ready for some much-deserved rest and relaxation after two battles spaced out a few centuries apart, yet also within only a few weeks.

"Looks like it's just you and me," Marban said, having watched the exchange with great interest. Jo, so far as he could tell, liked him and was helping give him an *in*. The rest would be on his shoulders.

Rika sighed. "Well, it'll be a slightly quieter homecoming than I'd anticipated, but we'll make do. I don't think I could handle an entire pirate crew's nonsense after a day like today. Come on, I'll take you to my favorite watering hole. Afterward, maybe we'll even swing by and see if there's any action at the fight club tonight."

"Fight club? I think I may like this city," Marban said with a jolly laugh as he followed Rika to the transit system.

Daisy, upon returning home after such a long and unintentional absence, was all about family. She missed them more than any would expect of someone with such a badass attitude, and Vince and the rest of her clan were priority number one.

Freya was a part of that family and fully understood, so she made a very quick hop to Daisy's home in Malibu, where her dearest loved ones would all be filtering in for the evening's feast at Ripley's place. That her niece lived just a short walk away was anything but unintentional.

The teen's father was a bit of a madman, but he was happy to be called upon to prepare a multi-course extravaganza for the party. When it came to cooking, no one compared in the way of culinary skills. His metal replacement arm on one side with its minor AI booster, and his ceramisteel fingers on the other, just added to the speed with which he could slice and dice. And as everyone knows, chefs love nothing more than chopping small things into even smaller things.

Ripley's mom was humming happily as she set up the long

table in their backyard, her nanite-composite arm easily hefting the heavy wood into position. It had been a while since *everyone* had been over, and it was refreshing to be hosting the old gang again. It would be good to catch up with them all, and she knew Rip and Arlo would be thrilled to hear Aunt Tamara's latest tales of adventure. She and Aunt Shelly were always off galivanting to some distant point on the globe, and she was sure this week was no different.

"We're going to be having a few guests joining us tonight," Daisy informed her friends over a group message. "And they're not from this world. Or this galaxy, for that matter, so play nice. I'm sure this is all gonna be a bit overwhelming for them," she said. "Oh, and they use magic, so, uh, don't let that freak you out," she added.

She needn't have worried. Korbin had decades of practice socializing in unusual environments, and compared to many of those, this was a sheer joy. Kara and Vee, likewise, seemed quite comfortable with the warm and caring reception they'd received.

Ripley had instantly bonded with the two girls, the three of them being roughly the same age. They fell into laughter and gossip almost as soon as they met. Her cousin, Arlo, also took to the girls. One, in particular.

"You see that, Daze?" Sarah said with a chuckle.

Daisy watched Arlo and Kara eyeing one another periodically in a way that she recognized all too well.

Oh, boy. Arlo and a magic-wielding wizard's daughter? This is going to be interesting.

"You can say that again," Sarah replied. *"Oh, Sis, you're in so much trouble now."*

Daisy laughed. *More like Arlo is,* she replied, turning from her observations and back to the conversation around her.

It was a warm outing, and the extended family was back together again. Even the Harkaways made it out, which was a nice treat for the kids, to whom they'd served as de-facto grandparents their whole lives.

Daisy leaned against Vince's warmth and felt the tension of her recent ordeals melt from her body. She was home at last, and surrounded by the ones she loved. Sure, they'd definitely have a very rough road ahead of them, but for this precious moment, all was right in the world.

This world, anyway.

CHAPTER SIXTY-NINE

Charlie and his team had jumped away from the deadly fray at the portal with Kip and Kort tying in to Ara's magical tether as they did. A half dozen jumps later, they finally stopped, having arrived at the secret rendezvous point with Marban's fleet.

Only, on this occasion, Marban would be nowhere to be found. The pirate captain was in another galaxy.

It was a bit of a revelation for the rag-tag group of pirates and new recruits, but these were rough-and-tough individuals, and losing leadership in battle was something they were well accustomed with. Another would rise to fill those shoes, no matter how big, and the fight would go on.

Charlie was sad for the absence of his friend at so crucial a time, especially having only just gotten him back after centuries buried beneath the red sands of the Balamar Wastelands. It sucked, but knowing he was at least safe on the other side of the portal took the sting away.

He wasn't dead, just inconveniently a bazillion miles away in another galaxy. Unfortunately, so were Rika and their new allies, Daisy and Korbin. Though they'd only just met, he knew in his gut that theirs was a substantial loss, given how powerful the latter's magic was, and how deadly the former's ship seemed to be.

But there was *one* new addition to their team, and it seemed to be one that would provide great help moving forward, whatever their plan might be.

Bawb and Hunze rushed to one another upon their reunion on the humid surface of the small planet the pirate fleet was orbiting. The Geist had immediately shed his space helmet as his love bolted from Kip's open door. The two held each other close, foreheads pressed together in silence as they warmed to each other's presence.

A shimmer ship silently uncloaked next to the chatty craft, and Bawb watched a pale man step out. Hunze felt her man instinctively tense ever so slightly.

"It's okay. He is one of us," Hunze said. "His name is Kort. He is a master, like you."

Bawb cast the secret greeting of the highest of his order, met by Kort's reply, cast with but a gesture.

"The Geist," Kort said, reverently with a small, respectful bow. "This is a most auspicious day for the Wampeh Ghalian."

"Kort, is it?" Bawb replied, clasping the man's hand in a firm greeting. "It is good to see one of the Order after such a long time. And you have helped Hunze. For this, I owe you my gratitude."

Kort laughed. "Oh, she is more than capable of helping herself," he replied. "In fact, it would seem this unusual neuro-stim device you utilized on her worked far better than you may have expected."

"Oh?" Bawb said, his interest piqued.

"Indeed. Hunze is now the first, and only, Ootaki accepted into the Order."

Bawb whirled to Hunze. "You've become an assassin?"

"No, no, nothing like that," she said with a warm smile. "I may have learned your skills, but I do not think I am cut out for that aspect of your world."

"What I meant to say is, Hunze faced the Trial of the Six and emerged unscathed. While she may not be one of us in our deadly affairs, she is now our sister nonetheless," Kort clarified.

"You passed the Trial? But how?" Bawb asked.

"Dearest, all of the knowledge we thought was not sticking for whatever reason, was, in fact, compiling in my mind, only I was unable to utilize any of it. But once I took full possession of my power––when you gave me that greatest of gifts––only then did it all seem to begin falling into place. It took time, of course, and the emergence of these abilities was startling, to say the least, but having been pushed to perform by our brothers and sisters, this innate knowledge flowed as easily as breathing."

Bawb looked at her with an astounded, loving gaze, full of pride and warmth. Hunze had become one of the deadliest beings in the galaxy, most likely, and yet she had retained all of what made her who she was.

Hers was a different way, and the dichotomy of deadly skills and deep-rooted love of life made him briefly ponder his own violent existence.

"Wait here a moment," the Ootaki woman said, stepping back inside Kip, then exiting with something long in her hands. "I came across this in a trader's stockpiles. He thought it was nothing more than junk, but with a little love, and a lot of careful honing and polishing, I've restored it," she said, handing the vespus blade to the Geist.

Bawb recognized it before even drawing it from its sheath. "I've not seen one of these in a very, very long time," he said, admiring the blue metal as he pulled the sword free.

Hunze's unmistakable power had coursed through the weapon as she worked on it, and now her overpowered locks cascaded their overflow into the blade as she carried it from the ship. Having been so close to Earth's sun's rays again, she had more than a fair amount of power to spare, and the sword was a welcoming receptacle.

"This is a powerful weapon," Bawb marveled. "And I knew its former owner," he added, a flash of sadness shadowing his countenance for but an instant. "Master Hozark was a powerful Wampeh, and an assassin of great skill."

The way Bawb held the blade, gazing at it with a loving appreciation of not only her hard work restoring it, but also the history it carried with it, Hunze knew in her heart she had done the right thing procuring it.

"And his sword is now yours," she said, a loving gleam in her eyes. "I can think of no one more fitting to carry it."

Bawb didn't argue, for once. This was a gift of incredible meaning, and he would not lessen its importance with half-hearted protests. "Thank you. I will use it well."

"Of that I'm certain," Hunze replied.

"As am I," Kort added. "For it would appear the Wampeh Ghalian are going to war. And led by the great Geist, no less."

"The brothers and sisters have agreed to this?" Bawb asked.

"Given the threat Visla Dominus is, and not just to this galaxy, yes, we have. And thanks to Hunze's clever diversion––with the help of her smuggler friend and a rather unwilling emmik––we have embedded our own aboard what we believe are key vessels in this so-called Dominus's fleet. Soon, intelligence will begin to flow to us, and we will respond accordingly."

Charlie had watched the exchange with quiet fascination. To date, Bawb was the only one of his kind he'd ever met, and now they were joined by not only this newcomer, but also sweet, harmless Hunze was somehow as dangerous as they were.

"Guys, there's something else we need to do. Leila is still out there. Rika said she was taken in one of Visla Palmarian's ships."

"I heard," Bawb said. "And we *shall* retrieve her."

"Visla Palmarian is an extremely powerful man," Kort noted.

"Yes. And does anyone else think it's more than just a coincidence that he also lives on Slafara? I mean, this has to mean something, right?" Charlie said.

"We'll find out soon enough, my friend. But for the moment, we have new allies to liaise with, recruits to enlist, and a pirate fleet to manage," Bawb said. "As you once told me, 'Only fools rush in.' We shall not be fools in this endeavor." He turned to Kort. "Do you have people on Slafara?"

"We did, but all that remain are locals paid off by the Order. Our Ghalian operative there went silent some time ago."

"It will have to do for now." Bawb fixed his friend with an understanding look. "She'll be back with you shortly. And I'm sure she is safe. Remember, she wears a Magus stone, and it seems very protective of her. There is also no reason to assume any would wish harm upon her. She has no enemies in this time and this place. Whatever may be happening there, Leila is almost certainly unscathed."

Charlie wanted to be a fool and rush right in blindly, but Bawb was right. There was no reason to panic. They had the advantage of anonymity. No one knew who they were, so Leila would be safe. Plus, they had several new allies and a growing rebel fleet to see to. They'd find her soon enough, but first, they had a few pressing matters to attend to.

"Yeah," Charlie said. "You're right. Time to organize."

And organize they would. The forces suddenly at their disposal were considerable, and, while they were still shorthanded, Charlie was certain his friends back home would return. And when they did, it would be in numbers, and armed to the teeth. Things were looking up for their rag-tag little group. And soon, they'd put their luck to the test.

Charlie looked out at the setting sun on yet another alien world. He'd seen more planets than anyone in Earth's history, and was now running up that tally. A little smile tickled the corners of his mouth. Soon enough he'd be reunited with his queen, and they would then experience these new places together. It was something he very much looked forward to.

EPILOGUE

Captain Sandah had completed his task, as commanded, and had finally returned to Visla Palmarian's towering estate on Slafara. The journey had been made with great haste, but nevertheless, he was late with his package. He just hoped the repercussions would be minor.

Rather than landing at the nearby field down below, he took the unusual step of dropping into a hover above the floating garden nearest the tower's topmost entrance. In just a few minutes, he would have both packages delivered, much to his relief.

"What are you doing? Where are you taking me?" Leila asked as she was ushered off the ship. It took a moment for her to recognize her surroundings. "We're back in Palmar?"

Sandah said nothing, merely nodding to his men to bring her inside, while a separate team of men led their other package from the craft. Leila only caught a brief glimpse as a team of eight led a heavily chained person into the afternoon sun. It was a man, she could see, and he was well-muscled despite what seemed to be a severe case of malnourishment.

There was a hood secured over his head, but she caught

sight of what appeared to be the outline of a control collar through the fabric. It was his skin that really caught her attention, though. It was pale. Pale like someone she knew quite well.

It seemed as though this other prisoner might very well be a Wampeh.

"Let me go! I'm a friend of Kara's!" she protested.

The guards, however, did not seem moved by her plea one bit. They had jobs to do, and they were going to do them. Automatons merely following orders. At least, that's how they could rationalize the things they sometimes did.

Leila was led to a corridor lined by thick-walled chambers with heavy doors. Each of them had but a single, tiny slot carved in their massive surfaces. One of them, however, appeared to have been ripped from its hinges. What was interesting, though, was it seemed to have been pulled inward, rather than out.

She tried to slow to examine the damaged room, but quickly found herself ushered into the adjacent cell, the heavy door closing behind her, sealing her in and muting all sound. The slot, she noted, was firmly sealed as well.

Confused, worried, and angry, Leila sat down to wait, though for what she had no idea.

Several long hours had passed when she heard the door begin to move, the magic seals holding it fast removed. She rose to her feet, ready to defiantly stare down whoever the hell had the gall to lock her up like this. She was a guest here. A friend of the visla's daughter. Someone was going to be in a world of shit.

The door slid open, and the most powerful visla in centuries stepped into the chamber. Only then did Leila realize *she* was the one in a world of shit, and it was neck-deep.

"*You?*" she said, shocked.

The visla smiled, then cast a violent stun spell, one far greater than necessary for a single person. The magic flashed bright green as the little stone hanging around Leila's neck countered the harmful magic, lessening it to a minor stun. It was still enough to knock her to the ground, but no real damage had been done.

The pendant around her neck fell out of her collar, resting against her chest in plain view. The visla's eyes widened. This was a Magus stone! Such an unexpected windfall from such an unassuming captive.

The visla's magic crackled and sparked as every effort to grab the stone failed. It seemed it was bonded to the unconscious woman, and the attack had set the magical item on edge. It was going to be hard to take, and require great effort, but the visla was patient, and had power to spare.

Unless Leila miraculously broke free––which was near impossible with the additional wards placed on the cells since the heretic's escape––the visla would get that stone.

It was just a matter of time.

BUT WAIT, THERE'S MORE!

Follow Charlie on his continuing adventures in the eighth book
of the Dragon Mage series:
Warp Speed Charlie

ABOUT THE AUTHOR

A native Californian, Scott Baron was born in Hollywood, which he claims may be the reason for his rather off-kilter sense of humor.

Before taking up residence in Venice Beach, Scott first spent a few years abroad in Florence, Italy before returning home to Los Angeles and settling into the film and television industry, where he has worked as an on-set medic for many years.

Aside from mending boo-boos and owies, and penning books and screenplays, Scott is also involved in indie film and theater scene both in the U.S. and abroad.

ALSO BY SCOTT BARON

Standalone Novels

Living the Good Death

The Clockwork Chimera Series

Daisy's Run

Pushing Daisy

Daisy's Gambit

Chasing Daisy

Daisy's War

The Dragon Mage Series

Bad Luck Charlie

Space Pirate Charlie

Dragon King Charlie

Magic Man Charlie

Star Fighter Charlie

Portal Thief Charlie

Rebel Mage Charlie

Warp Speed Charlie

Odd and Unusual Short Stories:

The Best Laid Plans of Mice: An Anthology

Snow White's Walk of Shame

The Tin Foil Hat Club

Lawyers vs. Demons

The Queen of the Nutters

Lost & Found

Made in United States
North Haven, CT
11 November 2024

60111567R00240